MW01687919

To cousin Bryan
Best of Luck
&
Thanks for the review
Ken Kincaid

Game Of The Blues

Night Run

Volume One of the *In A Pig's Eye* Trilogy

Kenn C. Kincaid

A philosophic look at rising crime and violence.

In tribute to officers slain.

ISBN 0-7414-4960-9

Unless otherwise indic6ted, Bible "quotations" are from the *New American Standard Bible: 1995 Update*. LaHabra, CA: The Lockman Foundation, 1995, S.

Published by:

INFINITY
PUBLISHING.COM

1094 New DeHaven Street, Suite 100
West Conshohocken, PA 19428-2713
Info@buybooksontheweb.com
www.buybooksontheweb.com
Toll-free (877) BUY BOOK
Local Phone (610) 941-9999
Fax (610) 941-9959

Printed in the United States of America

Printed on Recycled Paper

Published September 2008

DEDICATION

This book is dedicated to my wife Shirley, who with fortitude, and faithfulness stuck it out through the stress and difficulties of being a police officer's wife. Placed in a position by close association, yet being so removed, she could never comprehend, forever bares the scares of the burdens of trying to understand an undisclosed evil's effect on one she loved so dear.

ACKNOWLEDGMENTS

To God who declined to forsake me, though I embraced the ways of the world so long.

To my parents who brought me up in the way that I should go, and their patient prayers during my rebellious war with God, that I should return to Him in my old age.

To Christians in my life whose faith supported, instructed, and rebuked me to the end that I grew spiritually; specifically Pastors Roy Evans, Michael Diggs, Guy King, and Bob Smith.

A special acknowledgement for the tireless effort of numerous proof readers, and to the suggestions of many. A special thanks to Joseph Thek, author and editor, whose tireless efforts and ingenuous "ferret" were instrumental in turning an idea into a completed work.

Good people do not need laws to tell them to act responsibly, while bad people will find their ways around the laws.

Plato

Ah, me, it's a wicked world, and when a clever man turns his brains to crime, it is the worst of all.

Sir Author Conan Doyle

"It is the nature of criminal violence to escalate. When it reaches the point Police Officers cannot protect themselves, how then will they protect us? If there is a cause there is a cure. If crime can be restrained, it can be reduced. If it can be reduced, why not eliminated?"

Officer Dan Black, *Game of the Blues*

DISCLAIMER

The general nature of police work creates the possibility actual events encountered by real life police officers could resemble an incident or character in this book. However, **no character, event, or place in this book is intended to be depicted or understood as a real life person, encounter or situation. This book is a work of fiction, for the purpose of developing and presenting the author's theme.**

Many of the stories, places, and/or events in this book are based in part in factual experience to give authenticity to the reading. Such has no bearing on the fictitious nature of the events, names, descriptions, actions, outcomes, and characters portrayed. The inclusion of a real place in the book does not change the fictitious nature of the events and characters associated with it. The author has exercised "literary license" to transform any factual foundation to fiction and exaggeration for the benefit of expanding the theme.

Chapter One

The Game of the Blues

"HUSH! If he hears you, he'll loose the hordes of Hades on us."

"Well, it has been. For awhile, anyway," Officer Dan Black replied.

"Curses! You don't say it out loud! It's a jinx."

"To say the streets are quiet? Nonsense! I'll treat. Donuts and coffee at Daily-D?"

"Won't listen, will you? Not believing the Devil's real, doesn't make him less troublesome, Partner," Officer Ben White warned.

"Oh, I believe in a dark force. You and I've seen too much to deny it."

"Then why poke him with a stick when he naps?"

The cruiser neared Daily Donuts, but a hundred feet ahead at the red light a brown Pontiac poised to dispel the quiet. The light changed. The shiny car made an abrupt right turn.

"Follow Him!" Ben said, "Something about that turn."

Dan filled his lungs with a sucking sigh. "Are you nuts!"

"GO!"

Pressing the gas pedal sharply, the cruiser jerked left taking the southbound expressway ramp. Dan glanced at Ben. His attention was locked on the Pontiac. Dan felt the uneasy anticipation in the uncertainty of police work. It was adrenaline stirring. "Don't need donuts anyway."

"Casting aspersions on me?" Ben said rubbing his stomach.

"Asperse you! Never!" Dan replied accelerating the

cruiser. "Such an act could jinx the quiet."

"Jinx! You're chasin' our jinx!"

"Be out of our district in a minute, Ben. We could peel off."

"Shiny new car trying to fade away. Gut feeling." Ben snugged his seat belt. "I finish what I start!"

"Okay, Partner, we'll ride it out."

Traffic was light. The Pontiac maneuvered into the high-speed lane and Dan closed the gap staying in the entrance lane. When close, he read the plate aloud, "Ohio, KJV-316."

Ben checked the hot sheet. "Bingo!"

"Bingo's a dog's name."

"Bingo. On the list..."

"Where? Before you tell me they'll be in Kentucky!"

Ben keyed his radio alerting the dispatcher. "508, 508 following a Brown Pontiac KJV-316 south I-75 approaching Lincoln Park, request theft confirmation."

"I'm not waiting!" Dan said moving behind the vehicle and flipping on the bar lights. The Pontiac sped up.

"Go rabbit go!"

"I warned you. There's your cursed jinx!" Ben shouted over the siren before keying the radio. "508, we're in pursuit of two occupants of a new, dark brown Pontiac Lemans. Occupants believed male, dark shirts. Now passing Lincoln Park exit. Alert Northern Kentucky."

"Appears to be swinging east to Fort Washington Way."

"I'm bettin' Suspension Bridge."

"Why? It's a dead end. He's running scared – lost. And now, we're taking Second Street."

"Whatever he's doin,' he's doin' it in a hurry."

"WATCH HIM!"

The Pontiac swerved off the ramp across the median back onto the parkway. The cruiser's front wheel caught the median. The jolt knocked flashlight and tag books to the floor.

"You tryin' to kill me or just jar my brains?" Ben shouted making the sign of the cross.

"That crossing stuff's from the same empty box as your

jinx," Dan quipped maneuvering around a bread truck. The vehicles continued east. When the suspects took Martin Street ramp, Dan backed off. "He'll crack up for sure at this speed!"

"Whaaaaah!" Ben bellowed as they flew around the high circular ramp. "Hail Mary full of grace! This is fun."

The ramp rose high. Its sharp circle stretched over the parkway. At the posted speed it felt like an airplane on takeoff. At the fleeing vehicle's pace it struck the railings. The impact cradled the vehicle like a pinball in a chute catapulting it through the curve and across the bridge where it came to rest.

"Better'n Coney's Wild Mouse!" Dan commented while breaking.

"We've got him! He's stalled it!" Ben shouted.

"Don't think so! He's moving again." Sparks flew as the concrete retaining wall grinded away at the fenders. The tires spit smoke propelling it forward against the resistance. "Love those fireworks. Hate the smell."

"Taste of rubber ruins it for me," Dan coughed.

"Curses! Pin the fool in!"

Before Dan could maneuver his bumper into the Pontiac it jumped away making a radical left turn and sped down the opposite ramp.

"508, it's a full turn, back on the parkway, west toward downtown, hittin' 70," Ben radioed.

The driver attempted to turn onto Fifth Street ramp at the last moment locking up the breaks. The Pontiac fishtailed and skidded into the hillside.

"508, he's crashed just past Holy Cross Prayer Steps."

Safety necessitated Dan passing the impact site. Quickly backing, Dan watched the occupants flee up the steps. "Those fools goin' to church?"

"'Bout time for confession."

"Too late. Their soul belongs to us, now," Dan said.

Ben keyed the radio, "508, occupants fleeing up the stairs to Holy Cross. One in blue jeans and black T-shirt; other in yellow pants, dark brown shirt."

"103, on Gregory; I'll cut them off at the top," Officer Weldon broadcast.

When Dan stopped at the crash, Ben sprung out of the car giving chase. At the foot of the stairs he paused looking up the twelve-story rise. Seeing the suspects four stories ahead, he stopped and radioed. "508B, they're a third of the way up. Might jump the rail into the wooded hillside. Is there a canine available?"

"K-Four, I'm west on the parkway at Kemper."

Dan caught up with Ben at the bottom of the stairs. "What you waiting on? An elevator!"

"I'm the sprinter. You're the cross country runner."

"You started it!"

"Me! It's your jinx!"

"I'll fetch 'em for you," Dan said taking the stairs two at a time.

"Well, if I didn't have family, I'd have time to work out too!" Ben yelled after him turning to the crash scene to begin the paper work. The new Pontiac's steering column was hot-wired. The car was a total wreck.

"508A," Dan radioed, "I'm on step thirty—figure them –at eighty."

"K-Four, I just turned on Paradom. I'll start down from the top. Put me Signal Thirty-five [on the scene][1], with 103," the radio crackled.

Within a minute, Harry Gordon and his dog, Beacon, appeared on the top step. Dan could hear the dog's ferocious barking.

"K-Four, ask 508A if he wants me to close in?"

"508A, Hold off, unless they jump for the woods."

The chase slowed with each few steps, and although Dan closed the gap, he no longer two-stepped.

"508A," Dan radioed breathing hard, "They're two-thirds…to the top…they gave out… I doubt they've stopped to pray."

---

[1] Glossary of Terms and Professional Acronyms in back of book.

"We give!" one shouted up to Gordon. "Don't sick the dog on us!"

"Then climb up here!" Gordon replied.

"Can't; leg cramps!" the man shouted. "Besides, we're afraid of the dog!"

"Okay I'll give you a couple minutes. But, you jump the rail—dog's coming!"

Dan, having regained some stamina, narrowed the gap. Since the suspects had surrendered, every few steps Dan paused. Five more minutes allowed him to approach within a dozen steps. "You're under arrest!" he shouted. "Hands on your heads!"

They complied.

Gordon kept the dog on standby as Weldon approached from the top. He stopped ten steps away. Dan reached the hundred and twenty-fourth step, and took the suspects into custody.

The subjects were Maurice Hendeson and Keandra Billings, both twenty-four years old, and each having previous theft records. Neither gave the arresting officers any trouble. Dan ascending the remaining steps, then turned and shouted back down to Ben, "One-hundred and fifty!" He then stepped onto the sidewalk.

"First time doing the steps?" Gordon asked.

"Yeah, and I'm swearing off 'til Easter. Rather take the two hours everybody else does."

"508B, tell 508A I'll be processing the scene. He can take his time coming back down."

Dan looked at Gordon, "Always foolin'. Even your dog knows I ain't goin' back down 'em!" Dan keying the radio, "508A, inform my partner I'll be double with 103 processing the prisoners."

"508B copied."

The comments initiated the crackling of "mike clicking" as several officers signaled good naturedly. Ben remained at the wreck for twenty minutes before meeting Dan at the District One Station. After notifying the owner and processing the arrest they started back for their own district.

“You know they don’t count?” Ben kidded.

“What don’t? They’re good arrests.”

“Not the collars, the prayer steps. They don’t count unless you pray on each one.”

“Based on what?”

“It’s a Catholic church. I was raised Catholic. Ought t’ know.”

“Who cares? It’s all a bunch of papal bull anyway! ’Sides, if I’d stopped to pray on each step, I wouldn’t ’ve caught them.”

“I heard they ran out of steam and surrendered.”

“Prayer didn’t make any difference in the carnage in ’Nam, didn’t have any power over Char’s cancer, and I have real doubts about your steps.”

“You’d certainly be the authority, Preacher!” Ben said sarcastically.

The catalyst for the nickname, “Preacher” originated in a rumor Dan left the church pastorate to be a cop. Dan had graduated with an engineering degree and pursued a career for three years. Returning from Vietnam he found it uninspiring and joined the Police Department at age twenty-five. Dan’s father was a preacher, and the reason for Dan’s familiarity with the teaching. However, struggling with his faith from an auto accident which took Dan’s parents as a teenager, his tour in ’Nam, and losing his wife six years later, Dan walked away from the church. He found excitement with the police department, but found no peace. Dan never discusses his past except with Ben. Any who pressed were rebuffed with, “If I had another way of making a living, would I do this?”

“We never got our coffee and donuts. It’s on the way in,” Ben said changing the subject.

“Donuts! I had to fetch your prisoners! Couldn’t make it up one little flight of stairs.”

“Little!”

“Riding shotgun makes ’em your prisoner. You chase.”

“Whipity do! Noticed you slowed down fast enough.”

“Yeah, right.”

Neither spoke for the next three intersections. As Dan approached each traffic signal, he lingered providing time for the light to change. He anticipated someone might come through against the red.

"What's your take on it Ben, really? People gather every Easter by the hundreds to climb a hundred and fifty steps and pray. You really think it does any good?"

"Don't hurt none."

"From my experience, life's a matter of you and me passin' through time and circumstances."

"I think God watches over good people."

"Okay then, we're good folks on rudderless ships. And, God watches."

"Doesn't God stir the winds? Dan, what's itchin' you? Your moods been yo-yoin' last three shifts."

"Oh, I'm pondering something."

"Can't believe you've put your mind to a matter and can't solve it in three months."

"How long we been chasing bad guys, Ben? Over fourteen years? I'm almost forty. What've we accomplished? Haven't stunted crime any."

"It's a job. Sometimes it's even fun, and we're over half way to retirement."

"Then what?"

"We take it easy; enjoy life."

"Then what?"

"I don't know. What's the point?"

"That IS the point, Ben. We die! And then what?"

"I'm not real sure. Church says I pay my dues in purgatory, and then live forever in a blissful heaven."

"My Dad use to say something about 'absence from the body is presence with God'."

"Not much help, is it?"

"Nope, churches skip across the hereafter like flat rocks on a still pond."

"I thought you gave up on God; midlife crisis and all?"

"I did..." Dan gazed out the window, "...could be... He didn't give up on me." Dan checked out two men standing by a parked car as they slowly cruised by. "Ben, I don't know why I'm here! Is that a deep enough pond for your pebbles?"

"A kid runs away from home, doesn't change who his daddy is. You gettin' homesick?"

"Could be—if I knew where home was."

"Who can know? We're here. So, we play out the hand dealt."

"That your take on it? Didn't Plato build his philosophies on the assumption everything has an opposite?"

"I don't know, Dan. I never met him."

"We both agree there's a Devil. Right?"

"Deal with his handiwork every day."

"Based on a reality of opposites; if there's a Devil, there's a God. Even if He isn't involved."

"Still don't see your point, Dan?"

"We keep chasing bad guys and every day there's more an' more to chase."

"It's job security."

"In a pig's eye! Violence keeps escalating, why? If we can't stop it, it'll overtake us. In God versus Devil terms, the Devil's winning! Doesn't that make you itch?"

"I don't know about your itch, but I think that Rambler busted the light."

"Think!" Dan asked turning to pursue.

"Pretty sure, but I was tryin' to scratch your cursed itch."

"Forget the 'mover.' We'll get gas and go on in," Dan said checking his Mickey Mouse watch.

"Pass it up!"

"Well, you aren't sure, plus, it's quitin' time!"

Dan turned toward the city's garage. They gassed their vehicle and arrived in the squad room with ten minutes to spare. Dismissal was routine and Dan went home to Trouble. Dan's garage opened into the kitchen where he made a snack, prepped the coffee maker, and then attended to the needs of his recently acquired pet. Trouble, the ferret, ate a few bites; but realizing he wasn't being let out, curled to sleep.

Hoping to close out his world, Dan went to the main room composed of the dining and living areas. He reclined in an overstuffed chair, set the alarm on a nearby travel clock, and then adjusted a set of headphones. The sax in the instrumental jazz stirred his blue soul. Too many unresolved atrocities kidnapped Dan's peace long ago. The ransom price remained beyond him. Sleep often marked time for Dan, but this was one of the few exceptions. Delayed, it came, and Dan's mind was numb until the buzzing. He ignored it. It grew louder. He reached out swatting, knocking the pipe stand to the floor. The clatter woke him. It was noon.

He went to the coffee pot. *Good, the timer worked.* Still dopey, he filled a cup and drifted into the bedroom to shower and change clothes. *Why'd I ever get involved in this?*

The weather report optimistic, Dan mounted his Harley. The twin cylinders rattled the interior of the garage as he pulled on gloves. *Not enough gas.* He flipped the kill switch and took the Corvette. *The faded paint fit his mood better anyway.*

Ten minutes later he walked into the Sunbright Diner. Taking a stool at the counter, he exchanged nods with the cook. With little delay and no fanfare, his food was before him. Dan looked at the food. It mirrored his mood as two white eyes with yellow pupils staring up from a pea green face wearing a crooked bacon frown. *I know how to make you go away.* He smashed it all together and ate it.

An hour later, Dan stepped out of the elevator into the hospital's cafeteria. The aroma of coffee and fresh bread stirred comforting memories. He paused doting on it while he watched a woman stuffing envelopes across the room. Taking a deep breath he walked toward her. Half way he exhaled in a puff.

"Good afternoon, Dan," the blonde behind the table greeted.

"It's always middle of the night for me."

"Pull your head out of the clouds and see the sunshine."

"I stay in the clouds so I don't feel the rain."

"It's not always raining, Dan."

"What you got me on?"

"You can bag bread or do brochures. Your choice, Sunshine."

I love the aroma, but the old women bakers get on my nerves. "Brochures."

He made his way around the tables arranged in a horse-shoe. Beside the blond woman, another womaen and man were seated at the table. Stacks of brochures surrounded them. One side table stored boxes like children's blocks left behind after play. On the other, cobblestones of brown paper bags contained bread. Blue letters on a cream overhead banner read: *GOOD SAMARITAN CANCER RESEARCH.*

"Grab a seat," the petite woman in her twenties said. "Do you know what we're doing?"

"Yep, stuffin' mailers," he said sitting on a metal folding chair fitted with a thin tie cushion and beginning the routine. "Anybody know if they're making any progress?" Dan asked indifferent.

"There's progress." the man sitting on his left answered. "It's tediously slow, but someday there'll be a cure."

Dan didn't answer immediately. His mind bounced between the competing scents of cinnamon vanilla potpourri, bread, and the disagreeable effluvia from an attendant wiping down tables. "Not to dampen your spirits, but if science was going to save us, it'd done it by now?"

"Can't deny advances. Look back ten years. It'll come for cancer in time."

Cure cancer? Sure? Then they'll find a pill for crime. "Don't count on it. All I see is confusion. Every new discovery reverses some past finding. Medicine's an imperfect science at best."

"Quite the pessimist," the man said before walking off to the coffee pot.

When am I gonna learn. Keep it to myself. He stuffed mailers, taking care to avoid any further personal issues. He didn't really know these people, and didn't want to. In the years he toiled there the people changed, but the futile hopes did not. Two hours later he walked back to his vehicle and drove home. It left his mind listless.

Pulling into his driveway, the bump of the curb jarred his awareness. *Why do I do this?* He went in. Tossing his keys on the drainer he went to the bedroom, set the alarm, and went to bed. *Because it's something I just have to do.* He fluffed his pillow. *Ben'd call it penance*. He slept 'till super time.

At 2230 hours Dan lumbered into the District, prepared his gear, and joined others milling in the squad room. He leaned against the wall and chit-chatted impassively, but his charged subconscious meandered through resident flash-backs. Vexes cloistered there encroached upon him randomly. They were the curse of an anchor car. First on the scene is seldom an accolade. A recent prisoner of his conscience asserted itself, and Dan's mind returned to the past.

He approached the door half off its hinges. Stepping across the threshold, he saw a woman lying on her side, her back to him with no noticeable wounds. The sour odors reminiscent of rotting fruit numbed his sinus. She was fully clothed. His mind told him she would push herself up from the palette shaped mahogany stain on the braided oval rug, but he sensed a stillness his mind ignored: an absence of movement in the silk blouse from gentle breathing. He drew close, his mind denying reality, he took her wrist searching for a pulse noticing her warmth gone. The coo-coo clock crowed midnight. He jumped nudging the woman she rolled on her back. His mind was forced to accept what his eyes viewed. The ragged pieces of the slashed silk blouse draped open, revealing several stab wounds and three long slashes. A bleakness similar to what he had felt carrying fallen comrades from battle visited him.

A nearby recliner cradled a man's remains now sprawled sideways, his face placid as a mannequin frozen in a plea for mercy. Frothy dried blood painted a streak of red scum from the corner of his lip down his jaw line. His chest was half blown away. Blood and tissue splattered over the cream leather of the chair. A sweeping smear, appearing to be made from a large painter's brush, dwarfed the six punch holes in the chair back. It created an angry painting like Dan had seen in the Art Museum. He hated those paintings. Now by the victim's side, smoky eyeballs stared through Dan after a departed spirit. Dan felt uneasy, heavy-hearted.

He secured the scene, made a search, and a cursory evaluation for the responding Homicide 'Dicks'. The raw gruesome scene invaded Dan's subconscious as a conquering army. Memories he wished he could erase, but never would.

"They had nothing to take," a distant voice said, "Wasn't burglary; the place was trashed as a cover up."

"Still no husband," interjected another, "My money's on him as the doer."

"Mark my words. Drug deal gone bad," a third offered.

"What do you think, Dan?" Officer Reynolds pressed. "HEY! DAN! What's your take?"

Dan jerked upright, "Oh—what? I wasn't listening."

"Who killed the Gormans last week?"

"Beats me. We did our job."

"Gotta have an opinion."

"We're street cops, Larry. The Dicks'll figure it out—or not. No purpose chewin' on it like a dog on a dry bone" *An act of anger, passion.* Dan ambled across the room and picked up a hot sheet. *A love triangle; of that, I'm certain. Impossible balancing two love lives; they always implode.*

These were the "Thin Blue Line." Their job was to maintain order in a chaotic society, to prevent crime by creating a false impression of being everywhere. Theirs was an unachievable goal. As first responders they encounter cases which shanghai their peace. First at the murder scenes, first to pull the dead children from the auto crashes, first to aid grandma's broken hip caused by some snatch and run thief. They gallop toward catastrophe and peril, race toward gunfire, dash to dangers. Jeopardy is their banquet.

It's not their job to solve crimes. Theirs is to prevent it; and when they fail, respond and reestablish order. It is their addiction, saddled with the routine and commissioned with the impossible, to serve and protect a sinful city.

"Fall in!" Sergeant O'Toole's voice echoed throughout the station house at 2300 hours. The clattering heels of men formed a semi-rigid line before the man who bellowed the command.

Among the men in blue scrambling to answer the call was B.B. White. At his heels, darted Daniel Black. Twelve year partners, they had met side-by-side in the academy; now unified in experience, action, and thought.

As interesting as Dan and Ben were in their own rights, they were seldom referred to individually. Both veterans of fourteen years, the last twelve assigned to Northside Beat 508, the anchor car for the northern half of the city's Fifth District. The unity, trust, loyalty, and shared fervor for crime fighting earned the team the title of "The Dedicated Duo," often shortened to "Duo."

Tonight there were eleven men in blue toeing the line. At Sergeant Melvin O'Toole's command, "Present Arms," the officers drew their weapons, opened the cylinders, and grasped the revolver around the cylinder and frame ejecting six rounds into the palm of their free hand. Sergeant O'Toole moved down the less than rigid lines with a snappy sidestep. His keen eye checked the cleanliness of the weapons, and verified the bullets were "authorized" loads.

O'Toole was in his mid fifties with eighteen years of service. He conducted briefings with the air of a mean drill sergeant. In spite of his outward appearance, the men knew his true temperament. When out of earshot, he was "Pooh-Bear."

"How come I count five rounds, Reynolds?" O'Toole snapped.

"Beats me, Serge. I unloaded six."

O'Toole's eyes bore into him.

"Honest!"

"Then you best find number six before I finish this line."

Reynolds broke rank searching the floor under tables and chairs.

"Jansen, hair's shaggier 'n a stray dog's tail. Plan to get a haircut sometime in your career?"

"Might consider it, if it don't hurt."

"'DOESN'T' hurt," O'Toole corrected.

"Okay, since it's painless."

"Get your mustache and sideburns trimmed and the hair off the back of your neck by tomorrow." His voice deepened, "Or you'll know what hurt is!"

"Yes, SIR! First thing tomorrow."

"I found it," Reynolds rang out from under a metal table in the corner. Rising, he struck his head producing a "CLANK." His arm stretched out showing his find.

"Oohhh! Bet that felt good," cracked an unidentified voice from the line.

"Well get back in line," O'Toole snapped at Reynolds without missing a side-step, "Rest of you, shut up." He sidestepped confronting Dan, "Your mustache always looks too long."

"No sir," Dan said forcing a big smile drawing his pudgy cheeks up which raised the ends of the mustache to conform.

"You going to walk around with that clown face all night?"

"It's the only one I have, Sir," Dan responded through fixed teeth and a frozen face.

The sergeant ignored the response dutifully bellowing a guttural, "Fall out!"

The line evaporated as the men took seats at two long tables. Metal chairs clanged in the process. O'Toole read the teletype notices while the hot-sheets and wanted posters were passed out.

"First out of the box is a Form 4-7-5 for Officers Black and White. Homicide complimented you two on the way you preserved the scene on the messy murder last week. Cap'n figured, comin' from them, it deserved notation."

"My partner says nobody, then nobody goes by me,"

Ben said.

"You did play football in college, didn't you?" the sergeant asked.

"Play! Cryin' out loud—HE WAS THE LINE," Officer B. C. Castleman chided.

"Glad you gave it up to come play in the streets with us," O'Toole said.

Officer B.B. White, the bronze of this Dedicated Duo, was known to his peers as "Big Ben." A black man of thirty-seven years and six feet three, his solid muscular frame easily carried two hundred thirty-five pounds. His curly black hair sprinkled with gray receded at the temples. The steel grayish haze of his tiger brown eyes appeared ice cold. Most who dared to stare directly into them didn't do so long. He preferred to be called "Ben," but he allowed "Big Ben." His wishes were respected.

"Here's one for you Officer Black," the sergeant said. "for, quote, 'detailed way you processed the scene,' unquote. They didn't have to spend time on preliminaries. Got right into evidence collection and spent extra time on trace; confident of no contamination."

Dan accepted it with a slight nod, "Thanks, Serge."

"Don't let it go to your head."

Daniel Black, stood five feet eleven, and weighed a hundred eighty pounds. Short stubby legs and arms gave a false perception of awkwardness. Quicker than a frog's tongue he was exceptionally agile for his thirty-nine years. Blond highlights streaked his brown hair, a souvenir of Dan's youth.

"Here's the teletype," the sergeant began. "Be on the lookout for a blue Oldsmobile wagon with luggage on top. Driven by male, white, age 48, accompanied by two male teenagers, license Kansas COL 318. If located request driver return to rest stop, I-75 at Lebanon Overlook. Left wife behind."

"He isn't going to do it," Harkins said. "He's just discovered what vacation means."

"Not 'til he drops those teenagers off he hasn't," added

another.

"You might have a chance of catching this villain," O'Toole continued. "Wanted for Bank Robbery is Paul Conroy, male, white, five foot eight, medium build, blond wavy hair with reddish highlights. He visited Harrison Savings and Loan to open an account. Teller noticed red stains on the bills, suspected dye pack markings, requested a driver's license for account information. He complied, but got nervous and left. If you guys can catch up to him in his blue compact car, cite him for no driver's license. He left it at the bank."

"Okay, it ain't that funny," O'Toole demanded. "Write this down! Wanted by Indiana State Trooper for homicide is a white two door foreign car, possibly a Renault, rear bumper damage, right tail light out, rust spots on driver's door, and front fender. Approach with caution! Armed with a sawed off shotgun. Any of you would-be-heroes see it, call in backup. You get your tails shot off and I don't go home on time."

The remaining dispatches were serious. The housekeeping matters few. In all, the briefing lasted eighteen minutes. Sgt. O'Toole stopped reading, as Sergeant Fleischer arrived.

"Anything, Sergeant Fleischer?" O'Toole asked.

He shook his head.

Sergeant Fleischer was the "late" sergeant. He handled the second roll call. The shift was divided in half with a thirty-minute interval. This allowed half the squad to be on the street, while the other half secured. Overlapping squads meant the street was never void of officers. Fleischer was in his early forties, five foot eleven, and weighed 190 pounds. He always cussed in German, his native tongue.

"You men expecting Sergeant Fleischer to sing?" O'Toole bellowed.

"No, SIR."

"Then why you sitting around here? Roll call's over."

Without hesitation the officers headed for the parking lot behind the station to find their assigned vehicles. At the door, Dan and Ben paused at the stern voice.

“Not you two. I want to see you two!”

They turned to see Lieutenant Horace Hess a thirty-eight year old black man. His six foot three inch pencil shaped framed rocked on the balls of his feet. His out of proportion head and round face resembled a slip-on eraser. He cropped his hair so short, it appeared as black felt.An overbite and his constant nipping complaints earned him the nickname “Snaggles.” Lieutenant Hess motioned. They walked over to him.

“Yea Lieut, what you got?” Ben greeted.

“It’s lieutenant, OFFICER White. My name is not – never has been Lieu, Lieut, or Lieuy. Understand?” He peered over small square rimmed glasses hanging on the tip of his long nose accentuating his dark brown eyes, bushy lashes, and high forehead.

“Yes, Sir,” Dan responded. “What can we do for you, LU-tenant?”

“You can start by addressing me respectfully, then go out and write some parkers. You’ve been low for weeks. Pick it up, or I’ll find you some detail time.”

“Lieutenant, this is the Night Run! On the nights the focus is on burglars,” Dan said.

“The focus is what I tell you it is, and that’s what you do. And, tonight you do parkers and door shaking. If you can’t be productive beat men, I’ll find someone else to run the beat.” He demanded peering over his readers.

“Okay, Lieutenant Hess,” Dan said, “But, there aren’t a lot of …

“Have you noticed our burglaries are down almost to nothing?” Ben interjected.

“You two jokers hit the streets. I want parkers and door shaking. Come morning you better have some.”

Without comment, Dan and Ben turned away.

“And, all the doors better be in place!” he yelled after them.

In the parking lot Dan skipped toward his cruiser singing, “Parkers and doors, parkers and doors, got to get us parkers and doors.”

"I wish Snaggles'd get over it," Ben said.

"Affirmative action hangover. Wants to prove worthy," Dan said. "Views everything on how it affects HIS career."

Hess made the effort, put in the time attending study groups, and took a week's vacation to cram. However, exams are highly competitive. When the dust settled he was promoted after skipping past six higher scores.

"Doesn't mean we gotta be his whippin' boys," Ben bellyached.

"Take a pill. He's easy. You make him look good, he likes you."

"Pills I can handle! Suppositories—are a different matter."

They reached their assigned cruiser.

"Too bad he isn't more like Captain Kirk," Ben said.

"That's part of his frustration. He's ours. We'll deal with it. As for now, he's dealt us another hand in the 'Game of the Blues'."

Chapter Two

Two Tragic Thefts

As Dan drove, he speculated how they might play out this hand in the "Game of the Blues."

"He wants parkers, does he? Then we'll GIVE him parkers! If he interviewed victims, maybe he'd get it? Maybe if he hauled the bleeding to the hospital, or explained to widows how they're gonna eat after their purses are snatched! He's skippin' through his own Wonderland." Dan watched a car pass through the intersection. "Parkers!"

"Dan, we can't fight the system. It's numbers to him."

"Parkers don't beat people and rob 'em. Parkers don't kill people. Crime on the rampage and he wants parkers? I'll get him parkers."

"How?"

"I'll come up with them—somehow."

"We'll keep our eye out. Pick up a couple a night. We don't have to let it keep us from the important stuff."

"Be sure on that! But, Hess needs to learn people are getting hurt. I'll figure an angle."

Dan was the brain of the Duo, an ingenuity to conspire and plot with deviousness bordering depravity. His conniving stings were renowned. Even with laws favoring the criminal, once Dan set his sights on a villain, they felt the obsession. In fifteen minutes, Dan had a plan.

"Think I've solved the parkers glitch."

"I'm all ears and more 'n a bit worried, Partner. Can't we just get along with the lieutenant for once?"

"Weren't you just moanin' in my ear about suppositories?"

"Yeah, so I gripe about taking out the garbage. It gets to the curb."

"You're dreamin'. Ben, we don't suffer fools well, let alone ego inflated by-the-book supervisors. You really suggesting we tuck tail?"

"It's co-existence!"

"You've gone 'blooey' on me!"

"Of course not! It's the good guys against the bad guys, and on nights parkers aren't the bad guys. I vote for burglars and thieves."

"Well, we can do that, and maybe, get him off the parkers kick same time."

"And, without shoving it in his face—right?"

"Hear me out."

"Your plans tend to bend rules."

"Ease up, Ben. Hear me out!"

"I'm listening."

"The plan's simple. We strategically choose streets for OTP enforcement."

"OTPs on nights! That law is for clearing abandoned clunkers on days."

"Tell it to your buddy, Snaggles. All I know is 508-12 doesn't stipulate reason. It says they can't remain over fourteen hours. That's the whole point; Day Run versus Night Run. He doesn't get it."

"All you're gonna do is fire citizens up."

"If we're going to get him parkers, it can't be helped. The key is the towing."

"Towing! OH NO! no, no."

"It'll be temporary. We select streets maximizing opportunity for complaints. Tonight, we mark a street. Tomorrow, we mark another, and tag the first street; and the third night, we mark one, tag one, and tow one. Sooner or later we'll hit a nerve."

"'Hit a nerve'? Thought your plan didn't shove it in his face?"

"Maybe a little, but if we follow procedures..."

"Partner, I'm telling you up front, I DON'T LIKE IT!"

"Do it by the book, and his fuming is hot air up a chimney. Snaggles'll have his blasted parkers, and we'll have done everybody a service by educating him."

"Why do all YOUR plans include ME getting MY butt chewed?" Ben asked. "I'm not up for that right now. You think on it. We'll rehash it in an hour."

They made their business checks between routine radio dispatches of domestic disputes, bar fights, and auto accidents. Around 0300 hours the radio traffic quieted.

"You thought on it long enough?" Dan asked.

"What?"

"The OTP Plan."

"Don't misunderstand me," Benn said "The way you play the game amuses, but frightens me. We start laying paper; it's a chain reaction we can't stop. I'm not comfortable pushin' fines on people who don't have a dog in the fight."

"Easy, Partner, I'm figuring warning notices first night. After that, they're not so innocent."

"Reckon that dog'll hunt, but if Hess sees 'em, it'll kill your plan."

"Why you keep putting it on me? Are we partners or not?"

"I don't see gettin' my butt chewed so you can 'one-ups' the lieutenant."

"Okay, it's MY plan, but it's OUR problem. Got a better idea?"

"No, I don't."

"You don't see a problem burnin' time chasin' parkers?

"Of course I do."

"Well then, trust me, Partner. It'll work!"

"OH, CURSES! Partners we are. By your side should I die."

"Then, might as well get started." Dan said pulling to the curb. Will start on Gordon, do Pitts tomorrow. He slid out of the car. He began marking tires at the first vehicle and Ben worked the other side of the street.

Minutes into the chore Dan noticed a shadow moving

fifty yards ahead disappearing near Gundy's Grocery. A cardinal rule of patrol work demands partners maintain full awareness of each other. It is critical when separated. Thus, Dan quickly caught the eye of Ben and signaled what he saw. Ben worked around the backside of the grocery, and they closed on the doorway from opposite directions.

Dan stealthily approached within twenty feet of the figure. Preoccupied it stooped in front of the door. Sidestepping to avoid a bucket, Dan stirred a pebble. The man turned, spotted Dan, and bolted around the corner of the building toward Ben. Extending his nightstick it raked across the man's shins. The suspect lurched forward rolling into the gutter issuing a stream of curses.

"Gosh, mister, seems you tripped," Ben said. "Let me help you up." He twisted each arm of the burglar in turn behind him applying handcuffs. Dan joined his partner.

"What's your name?" Ben asked.

"Tim."

"Put a last name to it, Tim."

"Tim…uhh…Tim Freeman."

A search found a five inch "pegged" knife in his ankle high shoe, seventeen cents, a washer, and a leather bi-fold wallet worn through at the corners. The wallet contained several unimportant notes, a four-month-old pay stub, and a social security and welfare card bearing the name of Fred Morgan.

"If you're Tim Freeman, why do you have Fred Morgan's papers?" Ben asked.

"He's a friend. He's sick, so I cashed it for him."

"You're a lousy liar."

Dan returned to examine the doorway, while Ben called the dispatch on the belt radio relaying the available data on the suspect. Dan's flashlight revealed paint flaking from pry marks on the jamb. Both near the bolt. Within minutes Dan returned carrying a dark brown canvas bag. The bag contained several large screwdrivers, a clawed pry bar, hacksaw, cold chisel, hammer, and flashlight.

"What are you doing with these?" Dan interrogated.

The man did not reply.

"What were you doing in Gundy's doorway?"

"I weren't doin' no door! Twas walkin' home from Stacy's when some dudes got t' chasin' me. Feared f'r m' life, I run, and hid from 'em. Then you comes along and I thought it was 'em, so's I run. And, that's d' honest God's truth officers. Swears it."

"Where you suppose the fresh pry marks came from? And, there's this bag of burglary tools?"

"Them ain't burglar tools! 'Sides ain't ne'r seen 'em before. You ain't got not'in' on me!"

"Wrong mister two names," Dan said. "The lab'll match this pry bar to the door marks."

"Ain't mine. Y'u gots not'in'."

"The cuffs, bag of burglary tools, fresh pries, and an unlawful peg knife are big clues trouble's coming your way," Ben advised escorting the suspect to the cruiser.

"Car 508," the radio called, "you have a Signal Thirty-H [History Record], S-S matches."

"508, copy. We're double, subject in custody. Disregard backup."

They transported Morgan to the district station, and secured him in a holding cell to stew while completing their paperwork. On the way to the desk Dan turned the thermostat controlling the room to eighty. *Uncomfortable solitude increases cooperation.* They went to the front desk.

"Rap sheet in on Morgan yet?" Dan asked the desk officer.

"On the side bar. Get it and get. Snaggles's on the prowl over something."

"Yeah, we know."

The rap-sheet listed a dropped petty theft charge and an active trespass warrant.

Returning, Dan lowered the thermostat to seventy-six. They entered without closing the door hoping to clear the stale air. The prisoner sat at the end of a small aluminum table his head buried in folded arms. He was neither sleeping nor crying, but resigned. Ben raised the long narrow window's sash revealing exterior bars and straddled a gray metal chair backwards. It wobbled from the bent leg causing a "tap-tap-tap." Morgan sat erect. His face carried the expression of a hardboiled egg. Dan leaned back against the brick wall as if weary and spoke softly.

"Fred, it's a busy night. We don't have time to dilly-dally." Then seeing Lieutenant Hess passing Dan raised his voice, "You're a burglar. Tonight's parker night; so we don't have time for burglary work." The Lieutenant continued down the hallway. Dropping the tone Dan reopened, "Simply put, Fred, we have two felony-four charges. Toss in the concealed weapon, and they're first degree felonies. Your facin' three to twenty."

"But, I..."

"But I nothing" Dan interrupted pulling a chair to the table its legs scraping across the concrete floor. He sat ninety degrees from the prisoner leveling clear blue eyes on Morgan. Many a suspect mistook them as compassionate. They were all business. "I'd like to clear this up and get you back with your family, but..."

Ben knew his cue, "BUT, we both know you're guilty as sin! You're going down, and with YOUR RECORD, its bangin' out plates ten to twenty."

"Not necessarily, Ben," Dan said holding his arm out to block Ben's approach. "If he'd level with us, maybe we could cut him some slack." Turning to the prisoner Dan said, "No promises, Fred. We've got you cold. Do the math. Give me somethin' to bargain with."

Fred hesitated. Dan and Ben sat quiet. Ben's chair leg tapped.

"If I'm sent up what'll happen to my wife and kids? How they gonna make it?"

"Should've considered it before goin' night shopping," Ben said harshly.

"Your kids, Fred, they deserve any break you can give 'em," Dan added.

"I can't do time!"

"Can't promise, but we can't do anything for you 'til we

know the score."

Fred rested his face in his open right hand, his elbow supported on the table. The room was quiet with the exception of the whirring exhaust fan.

"Okay. I'll spill it. I needed food. My wife and kids ain't had real food f'r weeks, and one of m' kids' sick. I know'd 'twas wrong, but I ain't had no work. Last worked ne'r three months back for two pennies a brick. Don't salvage bricks like they use to. Anyway, money's gone weeks ago. I'm not trying to make what I done right. Just tellin' what 'twas pushin' me."

"Aren't you on the food stamp program?" Dan asked.

"Sara took sick. Mos' of 'em went f'r potions. She's better now, but m' little one's caught it."

Dan was aware of the custom of selling food stamps off market to provided cash for tobacco, beer, and illicit drugs. Unfortunately, proceeds were less than half value.

"What about a church association?" Dan asked.

"Church! You go to church? They might help your family. I don't know church people. What church goin' to help the likes of us. Did church when I was a kid. Momma made me go, but I don't have much use for religion. Sometimes, Thanksgiving or Christmas church folk drop off a box of food. Guess it makes 'em feel good. It do help us for a few days."

Dan studied the arrest record. "What kind of beer you drink?"

"Can't 'fords no beer, officer. 'Sides, don't much care for it; bitter'n vinegar. I'd much rather do sodee-pop, if'n you're offer'n?"

Dan ignored the hint, "Record shows a petty theft and an open trespass warrant. Care to explain?"

"I took some copper off the site at one of my brick jobs. Foreman told me I could, then went backwards on me. Nobody showed at court, 'cept me. I was let off. The one last year was when I'd sold this feller a radio. Needed cash. He give me ten and promised ten next day. He welshed on me, so's I snuck in his garage to get it. Figured I had right, what you call it? Reprocess it?"

"Repossess."

"Anyways, his fool dog, didn't count on no Doberman, cornered me. He called you guys, and I got jailed."

Dan glanced at Ben to get his impression. Ben nodded implying he bought it. They were in agreement.

"You don't have a phone? Want us to notify anyone you've been arrested?" Dan asked.

"Sara, she's got to know."

"Who's Sara?"

"She's gonna be madder 'n a saint in Hell. It puttin' her on her own an' all."

"Sara your wife?"

"Yes, Sir."

"This address good?"

"No, 2843 Sidney, secon', num'r five. Everythin' else y'u got's honest."

"Be right back," Dan said leaving the room. He returned with a can of Coke and handed it to the prisoner, "Drink up, won't be any where you're going."

Morgan popped the tab and dropped it into the can. He didn't waste time nursing the refreshment. Raising the can he took a long gulp. With a guttural belch, he wiped his mouth on his dirty sleeve. "Thanks, Officer, you ..."

Dan smoothly grabbed the half-empty can, "Good grief man! You gonna kill yourself gulping a pop-tab in my jail! I'll be writing paper for a week!"

"Sorry. Be okay if I sip it?"

"Okay—but, SIP."

"A wagon'll take you downtown in twenty minutes. I think we can write tonight's mess as misdemeanors. You'll see the judge in the morning."

Ben called for a transport while Dan babysat. Bond would not be set until morning, but the charge sheet read "Criminal Trespass, misdemeanor-four." Bound would be less. The amount made little difference, but the charges did.

"Next stop: 2843 Sidney Street," Ben said as he entered the cruiser. Dan pulled away.

"How do we remain sane dealing with tragedy after tragedy?" Dan asked driving away.

"Who says we do?"

"For real, Ben. Take Fred, perfect example, hunger forcing him to steal. I understand it's wrong, but we do our job and it makes matters worse."

"The system is supposed to rehabilitate by teaching him a trade. In which case we've done him a service."

"That appeases your conscience? It doesn't mine. I know better. The bigger offender is the society which forced him to steal."

"What's society got to do with it? It's a dog eat dog world."

"I don't think it's supposed to be, Ben. I keep running into this question."

"What question?"

"What causes crime and why's it on the rise?"

"You and your itches."

"If there's no God, Fred and the rest of us, are the product of chance, and when we die it's back to dust. Nothing else—dust. So logically what does our purpose become?"

"Get as many toys and play with them as much as you can."

"Right, and poor Fred was trying to survive. People everywhere, but hope nowhere. Why? As for society, where's Fred's neighbors?"

"I don't know, but we'll soon find out," Ben answered as the cruiser brought them into a former industrial area. Three story row-houses from the turn of the century lined the streets like teeth in a bad smile. Most converted to flats among intermittent litter strewn lots from raised buildings. Disrepair plagued all. By the time they stepped from the cruiser to the sidewalk another police car approached.

"We miss a run?" Dan asked.

"Didn't hear one. Bet it's Ghost Rider."

They waited for the car to pull to the curb, and an officer of medium frame and height with dirty blond hair emerged. Officer Gary Follert exhibited no clear distinguishing features. A popular tale told of him visiting Kings Island Amusement Park with his kids earned him the handle "Ghost Rider." They persuaded him to have a character sketch made of the foursome. When complete, Gary's face appeared as a plain oval 'smiley face.'

"Sorry if I missed a run. I'm Two-Six," Gary greeted. "What's up?"

"Relax, you don't miss anything on your beat and you know it," Ben said.

Gary looked around as if lost. "This is MY beat?"

"Just an arrest notify," Dan said. "Sorry, should have alerted you."

"What kind of bust? Better I know my people, better I can look after 'em."

"Caught Fred Morgan takin' the door off Gundy's Grocery. Told us he needed food for a wife and sick kid. No phone, notifying his wife he's locked up."

"If he's living in this broken down barracks, like as not, he's being truthful," Gary said. "Let's check it out. Make sure they don't need medical attention."

They found the appropriate entrance, entered the foyer, and ascended to the second floor. Ben raised his night stick to beat on the door frame, but Gary pushed it away tapping on the door with his key ring.

"Who is it?" a female answered.

"Police," Gary announced.

The door opened until caught by the night chain. An eye peered through the opening. "What you want?"

"Are you Sara Morgan," Dan asked.

"What you wan'a know f'r?"

"We have a message for Mrs. Sara Morgan, from Fred."

The door closed, the hall fell silent, and then the door swung open.

"Come in," she said, suspiciously. "I'm Sara."

Gary stepped back allowing the Duo to enter first.

"Sorry to bring bad news, but Fred's in jail," Dan said. "We caught him trying to break into Gundy's Grocery two hours ago."

Mrs. Morgan stared at them several silent minutes. Tears welled in her eyes and ran down her cheeks like large dew drops off a sagging leaf. She was a slim woman not lacking posture or dignity, with short slightly curly auburn hair, and uniform features. In all her plainness she remained statuesque.

While Dan searched for words, Ben stepped in, "His bond will be set in the morning, Court Room Three, at nine."

"Ain't got money for bond. 'Sides, I got a sick child here. Can't be running off to no court," Sara whimpered. A child's crying cut into the conversation and she turned to look toward the only other room.

"I got to fix 'im somethin'," Sara explained turning to a kitchen sink nearby. The kitchen consisted of two base cabinets with single sink top, a small two-burner gas stove, and in one corner the oldest working refrigerator Dan ever saw. She took some bread from one of the two doorless cabinets over the sink. Breaking the stiff slices into water she made mush and carried it into the adjoining room.

Waiting, Dan surveyed the apartment. A dinette set completed the tiny kitchen. A mop handle taped to the broken metal stub substituted for a table leg. Plain brown patches in the patterned imprint of the barren top testified to age. Alongside it were two wobbly chairs, and a wood stool.

Old paint and wallpaper peeled off the walls, two missing window panes were replaced with cardboard, and cracked linoleum partially covered the floor planks. Furniture was scarce. A sagging couch, the missing front leg replaced by a brick served as a bed for a five-year old. Two side chairs with worn ragged upholstery and a fold-a-bed against the wall completed the small apartment's furnishings. Dan noticed an occasional roach, but the apartment exceeded the cleanliness of most he'd seen in this area.

Sara returned to the room. Her tears were dried and her composure regained. She cradled a year-old child to her chest. He fussed as she patted him lovingly. "Is there anything else?"

"How sick's the child?" Gary asked. "Any fever?"

"No, he ain't fevered. He can't keep nothin' I feed 'im down. Mostly hungry. Cries all the time. Why you care?"

"Well now," Gary said ignoring the question. "You bundle those young 'ns and I'll run you to the hospital. Make sure he's okay."

"We don't need no hospital. Been to the clinic. Two days back," she snapped withdrawing.

"Okay, won't make you go. What's the boy's name?"

"Roy."

"I'll be checking back on you and the kids. If Roy takes a turn for the worse, call me?" He handed her a card.

Sara nodded and stood silent.

"We'll be going," Ben said. "We're notifying you for Fred. Good luck."

They started to depart, but half way out the door Gary lingered speaking quietly with Sara. The Duo waited until Gary turned to leave, and they all departed silently not wanting to further upset the woman. At curbside Gary remarked "What are we going to do for them? Can't leave it like this can we?"

"Don't know there's much we can do," Dan answered opening the driver's door of the cruiser. "Some things are beyond our control. It's your beat. Come up with something let me know."

Gary's face showed confusion from Dan's unreceptive response and Ben interjected, "He's got an itch were he can't scratch," and slid into the car.

"Oh, can I help?"

"No, he's lost sight of his purpose in life."

"Can't lose what you never had," Dan shouted through the open window.

Gary grunted as the cruiser pulled away.

"Radio's been quiet, let's head over and work the OTP plan," Dan suggested.

"You're drivin'."

On the way Dan asked, "Well, did you figure out where they were?"

"Who?"

"Fred's neighbors."

"Indeed, his whole family's in a desperate plight, and where are his neighbors?"

"From the looks of things they're consumed in their own survival."

"And, to what end all this striving? It spews out violence, and speeds us toward our end which is nothingness!"

"I gotta find you some salve."

In minutes Dan and Ben were back on their beat working the OTP Plan. The radio remained quiet. They used the opportunity to finish marking the cars, and then focused on preventing burglaries. Methodically, once more, they began checking their businesses.

"I can't believe you're leaving it hang on Ghost Rider," Ben said.

"Letting what hang?"

"Sara's kids, AND you know it! No problem coming up with OTP plans. Numerous ways to mess with Snaggles cascade off your brain like hail from a steep roof. You expect me to believe you can't come up with an angle on the Morgans?"

"Rein your horses in, Ben! I'm chewin' on it! Let Gary have first go. It's his beat, you know."

"Why so testy ? Just asking,"

"Alright already! And, I'm not testy."

"Sound testy to me."

"I didn't STICK nothin' on Gary! He invited himself in. There ought to be some shared responsibility. It's his beat."

"Forget it. Just curious."

"Sure my heart gets yanked around a dozen times a night. Life's a lousy grind and then you die! Nothing more. What can I do?"

"Said forget it. Means nothing to me."

The radio ended the discussion. "Car 515, 515, on Crawford Avenue near the rear cemetery gate, investigate single car accident, no injuries."

"505, my wrecker is pulling away, I'm probably closer 'n 515."

"508," Ben cut in, "We're available. It's our beat."

"515, okay on 508's disregard."

In five minutes they parked behind the accident vehicle and activated their beacon lights. The grill and radiator of an old Impala was wrapped around a metal telephone pole. Not just crushed, but smashed into the motor. The hood resembled a wavy potato chip. Radiator fluid flowed from under the vehicle. The kaleidoscope reflected in its pools contradicted the beat of the blaring rock and roll.

"You're favorite kind of accident," Ben remarked.

"Indeed! No innocent people hurt, and a fool destroyed his own car."

A man squirmed in the driver's seat as if dancing to the thunderous music. Ben was first to realize the driver was working feverishly at the wheel with a large wrench. The driver cursed, shouted, twisted, and banged at the steering wheel.

Ben approached. "Sir, set the wrench down. Step out of the vehicle."

The man looked out through the open door and spoke with heavily slurred diction, "Offishers, I wush jush putshin' sha sherring wheel backsh on."

"Sir, drop the wrench. Step out of the vehicle."

He dropped the wrench.

"Do you realize you hit a telephone pole?"

"Itsh notsh my faulsh. Sheering swheel come offsh!"

Ben and Dan exchanged looks shaking their heads.

"What'd he say?" Ben asked.

Dan stepped in front of the driver to get his attention, "Sir, I want you to think careful before you answer this next question, because it will determine if you are drunk or not."

"Okish."

"Is Mickey Mouse a dog or a cat?"

"Thatsh a tricks quesshun, Offischers. He's 'u famish bashball plaser."

"Right what team was Mickey Mouse on?"

"Wassh it du Yanksh."

Using big words Dan played with the drunk, "Your

immoderate intemperance transcends coherently comprehendible communication, but you know your baseball."

"Huh?" the drunk stared dumbfounded.

"Said you're drunk as a skunk," Ben interpreted. "I think?"

"Nooo Shursss!"

Shaking his head, Ben ended it, "Enough 'shish' talk. We've work to do."

Dan took the hint querying the license plate and investigated the claimed defect while Ben escorted the man to the cruiser. No defect existed. Overlooking one little detail risked embarrassment in court. Neither Dan nor Ben harbored animosity for lawyers. They viewed attorneys as doing their job the best they knew, and the Duo were determined to do theirs better. It made the system effective sometimes. The vehicle was registered to a Benjamin Henderson. There were no wants, but a record of three D.U.I. arrests. Dan joined his partner waiting at the open cruiser door. "Are you Mr. Henderson?"

"Yesh, Shirs, Benshamin Hendershun, jush call me Benshy." he proudly admitted.

Knowing the tedious routine of testing and processing a D.U.I. subject, Ben suggested, "I'll wait for the tow and catch a ride in. You run him."

"Not so fast, Partner. I'll flip you for 'Benshy'. Call it." He thumbed the quarter into the air.

"Sorry Partner," Ben snatched the descending coin. "I did paper on the last one."

"Like you said, I'll process, you tow," Dan smirked. Closing the prisoner's door he slid in and drove off.

Ben cleared the scene in twenty minutes and called 505 for a lift to the station. He found Dan in the briefing room working on reports. "You're done in twenty minutes?"

"Refused to blow."

"That him in the tank screaming slurred profanities?"

"Yep, saved me bunch of work."

"Curses! Next one's mine. It'll probably take two hours."

They transported Henderson to central lock-up. Secured behind the protective screen he remained obnoxious, but harmless. Deputy Ternnka, the jail intake officer, took custody while murmuring in song, "My silence is stolen; robbed of my peace; more scarce 'n hens teeth, Silence is golden, for this I am told. My silence..."

"You can handle it," Dan mused. "Nature of the job."

"Comes with the territory, eh? Easy for you to say. You two are walking out." Then passing the man through the barred gate to another deputy he instructed, "Way in the back. Way wa-a-ay in the back."

The off tune singing faded away as they walked down the hall.

"That'd get on my nerves fast," Dan said. "Aren't you glad you have me for a Partner?"

"Put that way, reckon so. And to show my appreciation, I'll spell you at the wheel?"

"'Bout time you earned your keep."

"Save time taking the interstate and we can spend it on eatin'."

One hundred yards across the district line they came upon a Roadhaul truck on the shoulder with its hazard lights flashing. The driver was working on the hitching mechanisms.

"Rather check it now, than do paper later," Ben said pulling in behind the truck and activating the bar lights. They checked the trailer seals on the way to the driver. He worked at a coupling behind the cab.

"You can't see much. Don't you have a light?" Dan asked.

"Fool thing went dead. I think one of these lines is leaking. Can I borrow yours?"

Dan handed the trucker his flashlight.

"Nice torch." The driver returned to his inspection and found a loose connection. Tightened to his satisfaction, the trucker jumped down from behind the cab.

"Could we get a quick look at your log and paperwork?" Dan asked. *Smart to verify people are who they appear to be. Helps avoid embarrassment.*

"Sure thing Officer," he said retrieving his logbook and handing it down to Dan.

"Your license, please?"

The driver complied. Dan walked the driver to the front of the rig for safety. The paper work matched up and Dan handed it all back.

"Good luck Mr. Manning. Traffic's light, but we'll stay back with our lights. You be careful pulling out."

"Appreciate it Officer," he said climbing into his tractor. Dan and Ben returned to their cruiser. The trucker pulled away without incident, and the officers were on their way with food on their minds again.

"Radio traffic's light. Want to chance the Blue Bird Grille?" Ben asked.

"You're driving."

They ordered the daily special. It was quick and Sharon, their waitress, delivered the orders with her customary, "Bon 'app-e-teet'." Dan took his first bite as the radio interrupted.

"Car 509, and 507, Epworth and North Edgewood, Christos-Drivakis Building, in the candy shop, alarm drop, robbery, shots fired, Rescue 24 responding; 507 copy?"

"507, responding," Officer B.C. Castleman replied on the radio.

"Car 509, copy?" asked the dispatcher.

No response.

"508, 508, cover the run."

Dan tried to get a gulp of coffee to wash down the mouthful of sandwich, as Ben keyed the mike, "508, responding." Both took a longing look at their food, shrugged it off, and headed toward the door. "We'll be back for it," Ben shouted over his shoulder.

Many officers patronized the Blue Bird, and the waitresses were accustomed to sudden departures. She heard the radio, knew the drill, collected the food and sent it back. If they returned, it was ready. If not, it was forgotten.

Ben reached the cruiser first. By the time Dan cleared the sidewalk it was rolling. Several cat-like strides of Dan's stubby legs brought him to the open door. Grabbing it, he appeared to be sucked into the cruiser as the door slammed shut. Halfway to the destination they heard Car 507 announce his arrival.

"508, two minutes away," Dan notified the dispatcher.

They arrived sooner. Spotting BC's cruiser parked at the far corner in front of the Methodist Church, Ben pulled to the curb one plot south of the Drivakis Building. The turn of the century building housed three street level shops. The corner door opened to a confectionary and ice cream parlor, the middle door opened to a grocery store, and the end was a dry-cleaners. A fourth side door led to the third floor Masonic Lodge. The candy store owners lived on the second floor with access to the store's kitchen. Canvas awnings were rolled up revealing blinds lettered with "Closed Please Come Again."

Dan reached for his flashlight as he exited the cruiser. It was not by his side, *BLAST! Let Roadhaul run off with it!* He grabbed a spare from his war bag and caught up to his partner. The officers approached the store from their different vantage points. Distance between Dan and Ben increased with every step positioning Ben centrally, as Dan arrived at the right side, and BC merged from the left keeping the officers out of their own line of fire.

First at the corner entry, BC saw the shattered glass on the floor reflecting golden-yellow twinkles of light from within. "Police! Anyone in there declare yourself!"

"Back here, help us," a woman's weak voice wailed followed by sobbing. "Hurry! My God! Please help. They shot him!"

BC reached through and opened the door with his left hand, his gun ready in his right. Dan joined him while Ben hung back. After the two officers entered, Ben took a position at the door.

Dan's eyes fell upon a man's ashen face clothed in pajamas lying on his back. A woman in her late sixties knelt beside him stroking the balding white hair of the overweight victim. She wore a light terrycloth full-length nightgown. Its white pristine softness smeared with gooey shades of scarlet. The stillness was broken by her sobbing.

They were the owners of this "Mom and Pop" candy store and lived in the upstairs apartment. They addressed patrons by first name, and gave unlimited samples to the children. Year after year they worked to eke out a simple life; his now draining away amid her tears. Her panic wrinkled brow and sunken cheeks bore holes through Dan as she pressed the wadded hem on the man's chest wound. The grapefruit sized bundle of cloth oozed. "Help him please! Do something – please! Oh, why? Why'd they do it?"

The aroma of chocolate in the air and the menthol of peppermint on Dan's tongue collided with the images in his eyes. Dan's mind momentarily went blank. He hesitated.

The woman cried out again, "Help us, please!"

Dan shot like a bullet from a magnum to her side. Blood had left a crimson trail down the victim's side to the floor. Kneeling he checked the victim's wrist for pulse. *Very weak.* Checking the chest wound he saw frothy blood. *Not a good sign!* The sucking sound of the last sip through a straw reached his ear. He grabbed some plastic wrapping from the counter to seal the wound. Placing it over the hole, he reapplied the compress with as much pressure as he dared. Bending his ear over the man's mouth listening for breath, he saw a long nose hair flutter. *He's alive!*

Then came an angelic whisper, "Can you see it? Glorious…never imagined…" The voice faded, the eyes flickered as a candle and went dark.

Dan gently pulled the edge of the compress away. Blood no longer flowed from a now silent wound. He replaced it. "Keep pressing. The paramedics are on the way."

BC looked into Dan's face. It affirmed his suspicion. He knelt at the lady's side, "Did you see who shot him?"

"No," she shook her head. "I was upstairs. I heard shots. Ran down… saw Henry…lying there. A dark car squealed off through there," she looked out the main doorway.

Hearing approaching sirens, her eyes locked there in anticipation.

"What's Henry's last name?" BC asked.

"Tolson and I'm Miriam," she answered between sobs. "I told him not to go. Call the police. He couldn't hurt them. I begged him. Why'd they shoot him? Only forty seven-dollars in the drawer. He did everything they said. He'll be okay—won't he?"

No one answered her.

Dan avoided her pleading eyes. *How can I answer? How do I explain wanton depravity?*

The paramedics arrived. The "WHAP" of their bags dropping mirrored their urgency. Dan greeted them without moving. "Gun shot. No pulse. Sucking chest wound. Sealed it with plastic."

Rick, a paramedic, pulled at Tolson's night-shirt. It tore open with the sound of a hissing snake. He checked under the compress. His partner, Phil, prepared paddles. *Maybe he's got a chance,* Dan dared hope, but noticed Rick raise his thumb inconspicuously in an ever so slight circling motion. He understood the signal, *Circling the drain. Lost cause*. Phil knelt with the paddles.

"Clear!" KAZAP!

Miriam cried out between sobs, "Why! Forty seven-dollars"

"Clear!" KAZAP!

Dan put his arm around Miriam's shoulder nudging her trembling body aside. Both remained fixed on the flurry of action. Serenaded by the sobs of grief the medics worked frantically to resuscitate Henry Tolson.

"They wouldn't be trying so hard if there were no hope," Dan lied to her thinking, *too many times I've encountered violent death at the door; shoving, pushing, unrelenting. Almost never is it repelled!*

After several minutes the medics stopped, silently shook their heads, and rose from the body. Their extraordinary efforts were inadequate to bar the door; powerless to call him from beyond. Dan counted the eyelets in the medic's shoes not wanting to face the eyes around him. His stomach quivered, and he stood emotionally empty. He no longer tasted nectar of peppermint. Taking Miriam's hand a tear slid down his cheek denying his stoic facade.

"I'm sorry."

The sounds of the medics preparing to leave, bounced off the walls of an empty cave. She collapsed sobbing into Dan's chest. Dan first felt the stab of this ice-cold knife when it killed the sweetness in his life. Felt it when his wife informed him, "I'm going to leave you soon. I have cancer. I will not get better." He had suffered it many times, each time it twisted less. *Once more, in a place known for sweet refreshment, death carried in its sour misery.*

A silent awkwardness fell on the normally jovial officers. Their work turned all business.

"Don't stand around," Dan shouted at two other officers who had arrived. "Go out and catch those gristle-gutted mongrels of Hell!"

They did search. Every available car searched for witnesses, door to door, from flat to flat. They stopped suspicious vehicles and identified the occupants, filled out field interrogation reports, and executed endless paper work. When it ended they had nothing, but a description of a ghost in the night. In time, Homicide Squad responded and Dan and Ben were relieved.

"You were right earlier tonight," Ben said. "Tragedies wear on even us. Life shouldn't be like this. It's, as if it's cursed."

"My Dad used to talk about it that way—cursed."

"Preacher, I don't mind tellin' you, these times make me feel it's hopeless. What kind of curse is it?"

"I'm thinking man's curse is the lies he believes. Like the drunk who believes he had two beers?"

"Cursed or not, Dan, we're here, and we must dance the best we can."

"All that door-knocking, and nobody saw anything. I want a name to write on a bullet."

"Whatever the curse, we don't have enough bullets."

"Ben, we keep volunteering to have our guts pulled out through our noses. Muddling around in the dark tripping over ourselves. We need to switch on a light."

"Better be as bright as the sun. I've done too many warehouse searches with my flashlight."

"We agree there's an overbearing force of darkness. So there must be a force of light."

"Let me guess, the light switch is God."

"Possibly."

"And, is it's broke?"

"Possibly."

"Getting to deep for me."

"Well Ben, if we believe there's no God, doesn't all life become equally valueless?"

"You're the one took that road. You tell me?"

"Having only yourself to rely on makes you a bit self centered."

"I hear that."

"Thanks! Anyway, I realized I had nowhere to go, no future. Life's purpose was becoming the present thrill. Ben, I'm coming in for the thrills. And they're dark encounters."

"Umm huh. And that's where you are with the itch thing."

"Started struggling with my principles, I guess. If I stay on that downhill road long enough, I could be Tolson's killer. Scares me!"

"You feel responsible for Henry Tolson? I can't buy it."

"Not him specifically, but our collective choices are the root of our suffering. Everyone chooses the trail he takes, but not what or who he encounters on the trail."

"How you figure, Dan?"

"Simple, what did the killer believe?"

"Don't know, we didn't catch him."

"I think it safe to say the killer believes only his needs matter. And with society's tendency to live without restraint. What can we logically expect?"

"Crime and violence?"

"More important, why did he feel that way?"

"How would I know? But, I know God doesn't want us to be that way."

"Whose god Ben? Society's god is no longer the Creator. It champions evolution and bank vaults of gold."

"Watch your mouth. You'll get a ruler across your knuckles."

"Oh, struck a nerve did I, Sister Mary Ellen Ben?"

"What time is it?"

"You're right. It's getting late. Enough 'phi-los-so-phise-ing.' Let's head in."

The watch ended with little evidence conveyed to the detectives. The Duo headed toward the district in silence.

"Did 509 ever show up?" Dan asked.

"Don't recall seeing him. Keep in mind Martin's off, and Sleep-out's running nine."

Officer "Sleep-out" Lewis was approaching retirement with fourteen months to go. He took the stance it entitled him to be "selective." Dan defined it "slacker." The scuttlebutt at coffee meets complained he routinely napped in the park, tagging him "Sleep-out." Supervision, aware of Lewis' attitude, relieved him of his beat and routinely assigned him duties other than street patrol. Tonight a hole existed.

"Don't care if he has put his time in! He can still take his runs and do his own paper," Dan complained.

"He probably would have taken it, IF he'd heard it."

"Probably asleep in the park, eh?"

"Be my guess."

"Well, let's go roust Sleep-out up. Wouldn't want him to miss dismissal! Swing by the garage first. Let's make it memorable!"

Ben drove to the maintenance barns and Dan borrowed a small hydraulic jack and some bricks. From there they went to Mount Storm Park. With their lights out, they rolled to a stop prior to the parking area. On foot, they located Sleep-out parked between some trees. His head reclined against the headrest.

Carefully slipping up behind the idling vehicle, Dan

jacked the rear axle up as Ben slid bricks under it. With the tires a fraction of an inch off the pavement, Dan and Ben snuck back into cover.

"You figurin' on waitin' for him to wake up?" Ben asked.

"The deadbeat doesn't rate our time!" Dan pulled a hand full of Cherry Bombs from his pocket. "Been savin' these from last July. Perfect occasion."

"They could blow the floor pan out."

"Don't much care. Just came from his beat where Mrs. Tolson had more 'an her floor pan blown out!"

"He's parked on a slight grade. Toss 'em careful," Ben warned. "Snaggles 'd love to kick it back in our faces."

"Be just like Snaggles. Fire me, retire him. Ready?"

"I'll light. You toss."

"If, I blow somthin' up, he can explain it. Time he took heat for something."

Ben fired fuses and Dan tossed them as fast as he could. The firecrackers landed beside Sleep-out's cruiser exploding like giant popcorn echoing off the hillside. Sleep-out erupted flooring the gas pedal. The engine roared, the rear tire whined as it spit loose gravel, but the cruiser did not move. He slammed it into reverse. Metallic noises sounded, faded, and the wheel whirled in the opposite direction. The door flew open and Sleep-out rolled out on the ground with his weapon drawn. He keyed his mike. "Officer needs assistance – under fire!"

The dispatcher having recognized Sleep-out's voice was unrelenting, "Car 509, 509, your location. 509, are you alright. 509, respond!"

The quiet returned. Thick bluish-white smoke lingered. The smell of gunpowder heavy, eyes stinging, and ears ringing, the Duo laughed heartily.

Sleep-out realized he was the recipient of a "Dansting." He snatched the mike from his shoulder, the rubber band holding it to the lapel broke snapping back into his cheek. Dropping the mike, he let go a string of vulgarities.

"Car 509, 509 forty-four location." The dispatcher

persisted, "Attention all cars, no location on 509, last contact was 2143 hours at White Castle."

"509, disregard, all under control!" Lewis finally broadcast.

"It's just a bad dream," Dan added to the broadcast.

Lewis came at the bushes swinging his night stick.

Dan and Ben stepped out and faced him, "Wouldn't do that if I were you," Ben said.

Up against two sizable opponents, he retreated back to his car venting his anger with streaming curses. Running out of strong words, he got back in the car and tried to drive away. Reminded of the problem, he soon found the cause.

"I don't suppose you donkey farts intend to unblock it?"

"After that scathing!" Dan said. "Not in my lifetime! Let it be a lesson."

"I don't need none of your advice!"

"I ain't advising! I'm tellin' you! Take your runs and patrol your beat, or I'll file charges with internal. There's a dead man down there on your beat. A woman's torment and misery you can't change now if you wanted to! Had you been patrolling, maybe she wouldn't be laying in a bed of tears? Think it over! Maybe it'll help keep you awake on patrol."

Dan turned and walked back to his vehicle. Ben followed.

"You think it would've made a difference? If – if he'd been patrolling?" Ben asked Dan.

"Doubt it. Be foolish to think we're all that effective. We're too few to be everywhere. Sometime yes, sometimes no, and that's why we do it."

They went into the station and stowed their gear. Gary intercepted them leaving the lockers.

"Hey Preacher, I've got someone you should meet. You ever go fishing?"

"Some, but mostly see it an excuse to burn time."

"I'm not talking pier fishing for bluegills. I'm talking real fish; Walleye!"

"Never been," Dan said flatly.

"I think you'd like it and I have the deal of deals. The fish are running hot right now! Tonight I thought of you and Ben. What do you say? Checked the line-up. Your three-day weekends are coming up. A professor friend of mine's already in. You guys 'd get along great with him."

"Sorry," Ben declined, "Wife's got me committed to a family picnic, and there's no way out. Wasn't for that, I'd go. Dan you ought to. It's fishin' at its best. When they're runnin'."

"Gary, I don't have any big lake equipment."

"Taken care of. All it'll cost you is for the headboats, hotel, and food. We drive up to Port Clinton Friday. Takes three and half hours. If Erie isn't rough, we rent a skiff for the afternoon. That gives us all day Saturday, and early Sunday, and we drive back late Sunday."

"Fall in," Fleischer bellowed.

"I'll think on it," Dan said heading for the line.

Eleven tired gloomy men formed a sagging line. The sergeant looked the men over and counted heads, "What was all that with 509," he asked looking at Dan. "He on his way in?"

"Think he'll be a bit late."

"He's got car problems, Serge," Ben added.

"I heard the radio. I want to know IS HE OKAY, or need I send someone?"

"We just left him, and far as I know he's okay," Dan answered.

"Blood pressure's up a little bit though," Ben chuckled.

"Don't need to hear anything that's not police business. Do I have to send Day Run to fetch him?"

"The wrecker ought t' handle it," Dan replied. "Guessin' twenty minutes. He's kind of up in the air over that run he missed."

"Wrecker! Is there going to be paper on this?"

"No need when we left."

"Fine! Keys in? Radios charging? Reports and tags? Jansen, hair and mustache. Kirby, clean that weapon. Black and White, did you get Lieutenant Hess his parkers?"

"Not yet Serge, but we're working on it," Dan said.

"It's your butts on the line, not mine. I won't be in the middle. You like your job? I'd hate to see you out driving a bread truck."

"What's to like or not like? It's a life," Dan replied.

"Then consider what it's worth."

Dan's eyes made contact with the sergeant's, "Tonight — 'a life' is worth forty-seven dollars, Serge."

A cold silence, like at the closing of a casket, overcame the room.

"It's a job, men. Don't take it personal. It'll eat your insides out." He paused, "God made tomorrow for the creeps we didn't catch today. And if we never catch 'em, He'll sort 'em out for us." Fleischer paused again then said. "Go home and get some rest. You're dismissed."

Dan glanced at the clock going out the door. *7:06. Route one.* The minutes past the hour determine the route. His mentor taught him as a rookie to create five differing routes home. Picking one at random reduced the chance of some vindictive thug tailing him. He laughed it off until the first time a car followed. Dan's never forgot. Not even on nights he left grieved.

Chapter Three

Benevolence Verses Disdain

"See you tonight," Ben said in the parking lot.

"Give your wife a kiss for me."

"I'll tell Alistia you asked about her, but it's time you get a wife of your own."

"I had one, once."

"Partner, Charlotte's been gone over nine years. I'm not prying, but you need to move past it. Time you had more an' Trouble to go home to."

"Not that it wouldn't be nice, but when Char got snatched away..." Dan looked away watching a raccoon lingering on the wooded hillside. "Don't have that kind of caring in me. It went with her."

"You can't feed me that malarkey! You care. I saw it tonight. I see it with every victim."

"I do my job."

"Fine! Deny it. But, the right woman could chase your demons away. If you'd go half way... AHHH, forget it."

"Women are a dime a dozen. It's a different matter finding a life mate. You found a good one with Alista. After two years of college, she supported your foolhardy idea policing was better than a lawyer."

"Shucks man, she wanted a paycheck and a marriage certificate. Easy bargain."

"Maybe, when I can understand why Charlotte had to go like that."

"Cancer's cancer, it just happens," Ben said. "There's no 'why' to it."

"People die before their time? You say, 'Just happens'!"

"How can we know if it's their time or not? Sakes alive, you know death's not a respecter of age."

"Yeah, guess not. Give Alistia my regards."

Dan turned back to the locker room and found Gary. "I've thought on it enough. Count me in. I need to get away from all this."

"Great!"

"We might want to reconsider a charter. I can afford it."

"I'm for it. Be on our time schedule instead of tied down to a headboat. I'll check with the Professor."

"Good. And while I got you, been thinking on the Sidney caper. You come up with anything?"

"No, but I'm gonna check on them every night."

"I have an idea. You want to hear it?"

"Of course."

"Considering yesterday was payday, I can spare a few bucks. Figured I'd buy 'em some grub at Top's. That's if'n you'll help me deliver it."

"You talkin' right now?"

"They need it now, and there's no time like the present, I'm told."

"Let me call Sharon."

"You gonna wake your wife?"

"She's up. Sets the alarm. Always coffee and kisses waitin'." Gary walked to a nearby desk made the call, "Okay, Dan, take my truck. Your puddle-jumper won't hold us and groceries."

Dan followed Gary to his Dodge pickup. It had more dents than a 'kick-can.' The Ram sported red primer over faded yellow and white paint. The tailgate was a two by twelve. Well maintained, the engine purred on the first nudge of the starter. They arrived at Top's IGA Food Market at 0720. The owner, Roscoe Brogan, was stocking shelves in preparation for the day. He had dealt with the officers on several occasions and respected them. Gary parked in the space nearest the door.

Nice shopping this early, Dan thought, *no lines*. He started to open his door when a car pulled alongside him. He turned and saw Ben.

"What are you doin' here?" Dan asked.

"Same as you. Been partners long enough to know somethin's up."

"I'm just grabbin' bread and milk."

"Sure, you are! And your car wouldn't start so Gary's givin' you a ride?"

"He needs milk too."

"Good enough to share Hess' tongue-lashings, but not this! I'm hurt. Cut to the quick."

Gary shrugged his shoulders at Dan, "Think the jig's up."

"Well, I couldn't leave it hanging on Gary. Could I?"

"You feeling guilty lockin' Fred up?" Ben asked walking along side.

"No! But, being a member of a society which expects the government to fix problems society's own foolishness creates--does perturb me much."

Leaning back against the fender Ben said, "I see you're in a preachin' mode. Go ahead. Get it off your chest."

"I tell you, government's redefining its purpose! All caught up in protecting individual freedoms. Forget morality and principles. It's all about power. All those well t' do politicians, all three branches, quarreling and maneuvering."

"And his point is?" Gary asked Ben.

"You expecting his rattlin's to have a point?"

"The point IS government can't fix anything. It's bogged down in maintaining its own power, bureaucracy, and pursuing an unattainable utopian society."

"What's new there?" Gary asked.

"They've let orderly society fall through the cracks. All the free-to-do-as-they-please self-serving groups are stepping on each other's toes and turning inward for self preservation. That's why the Morgan's can't get help!"

"Amen!" Ben cried in jest.

"Amen and amen!" Gary mimicked.

"Ain't heard a word I said!" Dan barked heading for the storefront.

"Big Ben, did you know there was gonna be a test?" Gary asked.

"No, I'd 've took notes."

"You're both hopeless!" Dan said to the others trailing behind. He stopped abruptly, faced about, and continued, "Politicians are concerned with getting re-elected and lining their pockets. Care about individuals? HA! Only at election time! Politicians care about politics. Takes people to care 'bout people!"

"Ghost Rider, think he's done yet?" Ben asked.

"I'm done!" Dan turned to knock on the door.

The grocer was a tall thin man in his fifties, wearing bib overalls over a yellow T-shirt. He had a grandmother's smile, and the odd shuffling walk of a man with no butt. He welcomed them and went back to stocking. The officers went shopping. Soon the baskets held over two week's supply of food and necessities.

On the way to the register, Dan stopped at the end of the aisle. "You two have families to buy for and I don't. There'll be no argument at the register, now will there?"

"Can't see why, Partner. 'Cause partners are fifty-fifty."

"Fifty-fifty!" Gary interjected. "MY money's no good on MY beat?"

"Okay. I'll catch half, and you two take care of the other half."

"Three ways or no ways," Ben said and Gary nodded.

"OH, all right!"

They reached the checkout and Brogan joined the bargaining, "I know you two. So, at this hour, bickering and all; is this a charity case?"

They took a couple minutes to explain their visit.

"I can't go on-the-house, but I can go cost. How say I ring it up, recalculate it tomorrow, and give you a call. You pay me then."

"Deal."

As Brogan worked the register, the officers boxed. "You fellows are good. Care to work it off stocking. I'm really hurt tryin' t' keep up with it."

"No thanks." they chimed back."

But, it gave Gary an idea, "You really hurting? Seriously need someone?"

"Like a root canal! Can't work school kids this early, and that's when it's best done."

"I've someone in mind, if you're willing to take a chance."

"If you say he's worth it," Brogan said. "I'll have a go, but pay's a buck over minimum."

"This fellow won't be available for a few weeks. Can it wait?"

"No one's lining up."

"Okay," Gary agreed, "I'll check with you in a week."

Although the Duo heard the conversation, they stayed out of it. It was Gary's and they let him run with it. The groceries loaded, they drove to Sidney Street, climbed the steps, and knocked at the Morgan apartment.

"Who's there?"

"Officer Black."

"Done told you. Got no bail. Go away."

"Mrs. Morgan we have good news. Give us a minute," Gary pleaded. "It's worth your time."

A rattle from inside preceded the door opening until the chain caught. Mrs. Morgan peered out, "What's all this?"

"Hallways aren't private. Rather talk inside."

The door closed and then reopened to admit them.

"SO?"

"Good news. Damaged goods. A traffic accident on the expressway last night spilled groceries all over." Gary lied. "Neither the carrier nor the insurance company want it. So, we gathered up a bunch. Thought you folks could use it."

"I don't understand. This some kind a trick? Y'us tryin' to stick m' Fred wit' somethin' more? Y'us locked 'im up. How come y'u bringin' us stuff?"

"Because it's not your, or the kids, fault. Fred made those choices. Whatever the reasons, they're still wrong...."

"Y'u lock 'im up an' bring us charity? Don't need none of y'ur kind o' help."

"I told you I'd be checking back on Roy. No matter what you think of the police, your youngsters need to eat; 'specially Roy."

"Sara, you can take it or leave it," Dan added. "We're going to put it down right here and leave. No strings attached; except one, don't tell anybody we brought it. It'd ruin the police image."

Gary set two brown bags next to the door and left. Ben and Dan followed suit. They made another trip with boxes. This time she greeted them openly, "Put 'em on the table."

They did as directed and turned to leave.

"Thanks. Sorry I talked hateful. We sure 'nough can use it where'er it come from. Ain't ne'r had folk do the likes. Ne'r heard such from no police."

"Neither have I," Ben agreed following Dan into the hallway. "Ain't never seen nor heard!"

"And, nobody better," Dan warned. "You know I'm up to making good on repaying double."

"My lips are sealed forever, Preacher," Ben said.

"Foolish I am, but stupid I am not," vowed Gary departing.

The Duo chatted as Ben drove Dan back to his car. "Since you aren't going to tell me, I'll bite. Why the yellow rose?"

"Why you askin' me?"

"The plastic bud vase on the table. Little silk yellow rose?"

"How would I know?"

"Don't play dumb. It wasn't there when I put my first bag down."

"I didn't leave it. Thought you did. Wasn't gonna mention it, Bein' it none of my business an' all."

"Well, newsflash, it's not my doing, Partner."

"Mine either."

Simultaneously they realized, "Ghost Rider!"

"That soft hearted sneak," Ben chuckled. "Curses! Time for me to retire."

Ben pulled into the station stopping next to Dan's car.

Dan unlatched its top. "Like to see the stars."

"Reckon we've done enough for one night," Ben said as Dan folded the top back. "Time to go home. Right, Partner?"

Dan started the Corvette, "What's left, but to?" He said pulling away. At the street he checked his 'Mickey,' *0840, Might catch Fred Morgan's bond hearing.* Dan turned toward the courthouse. Thanks to Seaborne Worthington, a wealthy businessman the Duo saved from an embarrassing situation, they had no hassle parking for court. Worthington liked fast classic sports cars, which he stored in a warehouse a block from the courthouse. Dan and Ben were entrusted with the combination to the overhead door, along with permission to park there.

Arraignment hearings were on the first floor. Dan entered the courtroom through the officer's entry behind the prosecutor's desk. Court had not convened due to some disturbance in the holding cells giving Dan opportunity to brief the prosecutor.

"Interesting twist," Prosecutor Mendelssohn remarked. "I'll call it as soon as I can."

"Thanks."

"No need. Judge Harding's on the bench. Can't wait to see his reaction."

Dan crossed over taking a seat in the empty jury box with two other waiting officers. He settled in. Five minutes passed and the rear door opened. Another officer entered. The newcomer briefly surveyed the three dozen people in the room then walked to the juror's box. Sitting next to Dan, he whispered, "So this is straight home?"

"Don't recall saying I was going home."

"That's what gave you away. Who's the judge?"

"Harding."

"Hardnails! Unyielding as they come. So, why we here?"

"I'm gonna…"

"All rise," the clerk banged the gavel and called the court in session.

"Docket number one hundred thirty three, State versus

Fred Morgan, charge of Criminal Trespass," the clerk called out.

"All planning to give testimony approach the bench and be sworn," the clerk added.

"Better sit this out. It could ruin your reputation," Dan whispered to Ben.

"You've already ruined it," Ben followed to the bench.

A court officer ushered Fred Morgan through the side door in handcuffs. His head bowed, he shuffled lethargically unaware of the officers. The judge acknowledged the officers with a nod. The prosecutor read the case facts.

"Mr. Morgan, do you have an attorney?" the judge asked.

"No, Sirs, can't 'ford none," he answered in a quiet monotone.

"One will be appointed at no cost, if you request."

"Not much need. I pretty much done what y'u says, y'ur honorship."

"Mr. Morgan, is the court to understand you're entering a guilty plea?" the judge asked.

"Reckon so," he replied shrugging his shoulders.

"What's the prosecution's recommendation on bond?" the judge inquired aware the officer's presence typically meant a high bond request.

"Prosecution has none, however the arresting officer would like to address the issue."

Turning to look at the officers, Judge Harding gestured palm up to the officers. Dan took a step forward. "Your honor, there are extenuating circumstances in this case. The need to obtain food for his wife and sick children motivated the defendant. In the interests of saving the court time, and since the circumstances prompting this crime are temporarily eliminated I'll refrain from all the details. Further, if it should please the court to O.R. the defendant, I have been informed he will have a job upon release."

Recognizing the voice, Fred's visage brightened and his head rose. Turning he exclaimed, "A job!"

A loud murmur went through the large court room. The

judge struck his gavel. The room quieted. He motioned for Dan to approach the bench. Dan stepped into the witness box and leaned toward the judge.

"Your job is to lock them up. Not come here and beg release," he whispered.

"Yes, Sir, I'm aware of that. This case was unusual…"

"Unusual? Understatement," Harding cut in. "Just checking to see how confused you are. 'Cause I'm real confused."

"Sorry, your Honor, the circumstances are…"

"Unusual." Harding waved Dan away.

Dan returned to his place beside the prosecutor's podium.

"You can ASSURE his appearance?" Harding asked Dan.

"If he doesn't appear, I'll personally hunt him down and serve the capias. There won't be a crack small enough to hide him."

The judge leaned back, his authority exemplified in the high back chair. The stenographer poised, her jaws working gum. The prosecutor shuffled papers as if immune to the spell. Finally the judge leaned forward peering at the defendant over Ben Franklin glasses, "If I release you, do I have your word you will appear on the scheduled court date?"

"Yes, Sir!" Fred answered excitedly, "I'll be here. Them officers done me right, I won't do 'em wrong."

With raised eyebrows, the judge looked at the prosecutor to solicit any objection. The prosecutor gave none. Turning back to Fred, the judge spoke.

"I know nothing of you, except you're charged with fourth degree misdemeanors. However, I know, and respect these officers. It's MOST rare," he looked over his glasses at Dan, "for 'A-O's to appear on behalf of the arrested. I trust you will not disappoint this court or their confidence." The judge paused to make notations in a journal. "I will see you in twelve days. Court releases the defendant 'O-R,' custody of the officers."

The bailiff removed Morgan's handcuffs. Morgan turned to the two officers with disbelief. "Thank you, thank you, thank you...,"

They turned to leave for the Clerk's Office as Harding asked the prosecutor. "What's the next curiosity on our docket, Mister Mendelssohn?"

The trio strode down the courtroom aisle to exit. Half-way to the door applause erupted. The judge half-heartedly banged his gavel again, "Order in the court." The courtroom quieted after the doors shut behind the trio.

"What'd Hardnails want with you?" Ben asked.

"Advice on the market. Told him to sell railroads and buy utilities."

"So that's the way it is? Okay, your idea; you walk Fred through the paperwork. I'm out of here."

"Whoa, where you going in such a hurry."

"Sell my railroad stock."

It took twenty minutes to fully process the release. As soon as the clerk sealed the order, Fred turned to Dan expressing glee and thanksgiving. "You done more 'an I could've ask, but I got no way home, an' Sara can't fetch me."

"What do you think I hung around for, Fred. I'll take you home."

Fred didn't speak all the way to Dan's car. Inside the warehouse his eyes widened. "Would y'u looks at all d' fancy wheels? Yours?"

"Only the Corvette over there," Dan said pointing. "The others belong to the warehouse owner."

"One guy owns 'em all? Don't seem right. Can't drive 'em all."

"One for each day or one for every day, you still get there, Fred."

They left the garage and Fred rode along silent for some time. "This 'n rides good."

"Yes it does, thank you. Fred, do you know Officer Follert?"

"Don't think so."

"He's your beat officer; a good man. He went out of his way to get you the job."

"Got me a job! For real? A job!"

"Nothin' fancy. Stocking shelves at Top's, but it'll help get you on your feet."

"A Job! Don't say! When do I start?"

"He'll work the details out soon as your case is settled, and you're time's done."

"I ain't kickin' at no gift-horse, but what'll Sara and the kids do in m' lapse?"

"It's taken care of. What you aren't gonna do is any more thievin'," Dan said sternly. "There's over a two week supplies at your place."

"Where'd it come from?"

"What's it matter? It's legally there."

"Don't say! Food in d' cub'rd an' a job."

Dan pulled to the curb on Sidney, and Fred started to open the door. "Hold on! You be in court Thursday after next. Bring your toothbrush. Expect a short stretch. But, understand, the job's waiting."

"I'll be there."

"Your family's counting on you, Fred. If you need a ride you call me or Follert." Dan wrote on a card and handed it to him. "Here's the numbers and times we're on duty. You need, we'll take you."

"Sure 'nough," he said waving the card. "I will. Thanks f'r standin' up f'r me."

"Well, what you waiting on? Go surprise the family."

"Don't say!" he said darting off for the door. Dan chuckled at his gait: he appeared a stiff legged man trying to skip.

On the drive home the air seemed fresher, the stars brighter, and the drive shorter. The clatter of the garage door didn't even annoy. Stepping into the kitchen, Dan grabbed a cookie and a glass of milk and then went to the "zoo" side of the twin porches.

A porch spanned the front of the original house. When Dan's father acquired it, he split the porch and enclosed half.

Dan preferred the open rear porch, and spent little time here until Trouble arrived. Over a year ago, Dan returned to his cruiser finding a cage and ferret. Animal control wouldn't respond in the midnight hours, and by shift's end Dan had grown accustomed to its shenanigans. He named the ferret Shennana, took her home, and the next day called the S.P.C.A.

"We can take it, but can't recommend adoption without health records," the shelter manager advised.

Dan hung up. "Whatever your crime, I doubt it warrants a death penalty." It was the first time he spoke to the critter as if it could understand and he never stopped. Knowing he would need help considering his work schedule, Dan solicited two neighboring teenage girls to help care for the pet. They immediately fell under its charm. With access to the porch they made the pet their own. A week later they informed Dan, "Shennana is a he," and "Trouble" became his name.

"What's one more trouble in my life, 'till I find a place for you?" he told the ferret.

That place became the enclosed porch. This was Trouble's play ground; plank floors, chicken wire. As time passed, the small cage expanded to a four by six foot complex with tunnels, cubbyholes and numerous ferret toys. Dan accessorized the 'zoo' by hanging an oak swing from the rafters. He paired it with a pine side table, now seriously gnawed, an Adirondack chair, and screwed a brass floor lamp to the floor. A week later he put a small shelf behind the table out of reach of the ferret, and added a small cabinet for storage.

Stepping onto the porch, Dan instinctively opened the windows by the cage. He hardly noticed the musky armpit odor anymore. Emptying his pockets on one end of the swing's cushion, he sat on the other nibbling the cookies and sipping milk. As the sky's curtain opened it brightened, and with the coming light came the rattling in the cage. The rejuvenated ferret scampered from one toy to the next hunching its back to dance at the door. Trouble slept sixteen hours a day, but the other eight he came at you like a freight train at a tunnel.

"Alright, I'll let you out."

Sliding out of the swing, he made his way to the cage on his knees, and opened the door. The ferret ran up his body perching on his shoulder. As soon as Dan reclined in the swing, the critter jumped to the end table sniffing and twitching his head.

"They're all gone. I ate them," he said grabbing the empty milk glass before it hit the floor.

Trouble was the Energizer Bunny with zip. It's the one thing all ferrets have in common; Attention Deficit Disorder. He jumped off the swing, poked his nose inside the crown of a decommissioned police hat. The white saucer tumbled across the floor as if blown by a strong wind. Watching brought memories of carefree childhood days.

How innocent and unthreatening life used to be! Those fresh spring days. I pedaled my tricycle all around the block. My nose filled with the lemony scent of honeysuckle blossoms. Racing around the block with only one worry—how fast can I go! Later in the summer, I'd occasionally sidetrack to chase butterflies through the waist high grasses. The sun was never hot, the rain never cold. Those were the days when a mother was unafraid to let a child out of sight. I'd never suggest a mother do that today!

Carefree, I skipped across the driveway of concrete ribbons to Mrs. Deem's house on an errand to borrow eggs or sugar. I was always greeted with a smile and begged a cookie; chocolate chip. On the way back I'd pluck a carnation from beside the house to give Mom. It appeased my guilt. I didn't know the treats weren't a secret.

Today, people don't even know the names of their neighbors. Homes are burglarized. I interview neighbors and they don't express concern the crime occurred, only that it happened close by. We used to be neighbors. Now we're individuals living before a frozen tomorrow. Drawn inward...

Dan was brought back to the present when Trouble nipped his big toe. "Ouch! That hurts!" He ran at Dan's shout and hid in the folds of a towel. Dan raised his feet one at a time spraying the socks with Bitter-Apple. "My feet aren't ferrets!"

The ferret ignored his remark.

"Oblivious like the rest of the world," Dan said to Trouble whose head was now buried inside Dan's shoe. "Oblivious, I said. We chase blindly after our treasure chests, and when captured—profitless Pyrite!"

Trouble zig-zagged a random path, banging into everything *en route*, tumbling and jumping in glee. Stuck in a corner, the motionless shoe lost the ferret's interest. Returning to his cage he pawed at the empty food dish through the bars barking with a hollow cough.

"Food, food, food," Dan said on his way to the cabinet which stored the pellets. The rustling sound caught Trouble's ear. He scurried to Dan trying to climb up the back of his trousers leg.

Dan gently shook him off. "Whoa there! Hold your horses!" He filled the dish, placed it in the cage. Returning to the swing, Dan chose a Parson's pipe from the shelf. He began packing the vanilla Cavendish as he watched two neighbors simultaneously pulling out of their driveways. Neither acknowledged the other. He was reminded of Fred Morgan. *People so numerous; yet, help so limited.*

Dan took a long draw on the pipe. Slowly exhaling, he watched the smoke whirling outward as questions swirled inward. *Is my origin and fate an accident? Have I no purpose to fulfill, and my future a bleak death? What a worthless philosophy! There must be more?*

"Get out of your water dish and come here! I have questions for you." The ferret came to Dan's feet, tail wagging high speed, drawn by the clicking of the lighter as Dan refired the pipe.

"What if man is purposely designed? We'd have purpose then? To be true it only requires a Creator." *I have denied it, but it is a possibility.*

Trouble's tail stopped as if to consider, then attacked a wad of towels beside the table.

"Don't be so quick to dismiss. Denying truth does not make it less true. Three years have passed since I pledged to study the scientific facts and carefully observe nature. The evidence favors a surprising verdict: we are NOT cosmic accidents!"

Trouble continued exploring the wad of towels on the floor, pouncing on the folds.

"Do you not care? I found complex intelligent design, and with it an itch I am impelled to scratch," Dan said lifting his head and blowing a bluish donut toward the ceiling. A grinding noise interrupted. Trouble sat in his cage chewing a bottle cap. Dan rose and seized it habitually raking the sandbox smooth before returning to the swing. Trouble pawed the freshened sand. "It's not in there."

The ferret ignored him vigorously digging.

"I didn't hide it. I kept it!" Dan said holding the cap out.

Trouble kicked at the dirt undiscouraged.

"Ignoring the truth will not make it falsehood."

Trouble began in a new spot.

"The truth doesn't matter? You throw dirt because you believe it and act accordingly."

Dan's pipe went out. He knocked the ashes and reached for his keys to scrape the bowl. "I need those keys you thievin' varmint!"

Trouble pawed dirt giving no mind.

"I know your stash holes." Dan scolded going to the far corner and retrieving his keys from a large coffee can. "Busted! Same place every time. Tough luck, it's off to jail with you."

He took Trouble to his cage, set him inside, and closed the door below a sign reading, "JAIL." Leaving the access trap to the play area open he remarked, "You're on probation." Without closing the windows, Dan collected his shoes and went to the bedroom, undressed, and rolled onto the bed. His tired body reached out for sleep, but clasped a fist-full of reflections of his days with Charlotte. They were in their first apartment over the garage.

It didn't work out with me sleeping days, and engines roaring beneath. But cheap--saved money--bought her that washer and dryer for her birthday. She was so happy scratching 'Laundromat' off her calendar. No more rolls of quarters. She read the instruction pamphlet a dozen times, and the special care suggestions. Happy days they...

Scenes of Charlotte in the hospital materialized, the cold loneliness returned Dan to the present. *I gotta force them out of my mind!* Engaging an eight-track in the player, Herb Albert began playing *If I were a Rich Man* and Dan stomped his way to the shower. When he came out he ejected the tape, rolled onto the bed, and closed his eyes. On the doorstep of sleep, thoughts of everyday men and women facing life together emerged.

A woman faces life alone, and all for a measly forty-seven dollars. I would give a hundred fold to erase the images. Who would decline such a bargain? What price a man's life?

Dan tossed and turned, a fog of subdued light drifting behind his eyelids.

What motivates a man to take another's life? What reason could inflict such burden of suffering and grief? This was not the act of an empty stomach, but an empty soul. A depravity nourished from drinking from the dark pits of the damned.

Anger seethed through Dan's torso waking him. Startled up-right and sweating, he wiped his brow and chest with a towel. Laying the towel on the dresser by a Bible, he wondered, *Could it be? Dad called it the 'Instruction Manual.'* He picked the book up. *It must be. There is no other.* All these years Dan knew the truth, but his ego smothered it with counterfeits. Holding the book open in his palms he wondered, *God's 'Handbook for Life?' I will put you to the test. I will see if you are the roadmap to my purpose."* Looking down Dan opened it and read: "Do not rob the poor, because he is poor; or crush the afflicted at the gate; for the Lord will plead their case, and take the life of those who rob them…"[2]

"I hold you to your word," he shouted through the ceiling into the heavens. "I fear last night's killer will never be caught." Sweat dripped across his cheek—or was it a tear*?* Dan whisked it away with the back of his hand and leaned back. His mind raced to make sense of it all, to find a peace, to open the portal of sleep.

Violence makes victims of us all. Greed deceives us to chase recklessly after gain. We're pushovers! In the end, we all return to dust. How profits the slaughtering scoundrel then? No one escapes! Everyone is called to account! The 'Manufacturer's Handbook' declares it. If there is no Hell for such as these, then there can be no justice.

The echoing of his father's favorite quote, *I know in whom I have believed and He is able to keep me until the end,*[3] dissipated the tension. The words comforted Dan. He yawned, his eyes closed and he slept.

Evil would patiently wait for Dan's return to the battlefield. The specifics of the debacle mattered not for the brotherhood of evil delights in variety.

---

[2] Proverbs 22:22

[3] 2 Timothy 1:12 Paraphrased

Chapter Four

Preacher's Nooses

It was one-thirty in the afternoon when Dan's phone rang. Still in his pajamas he lifted the receiver, "Go ahead. You called me."

"Yes, I did Officer Black," said the unwelcome voice of Lieutenant Hess.

Rest of the day's gonna be a flush!

"Officer Black, you're under orders to report to the chief's office at 1600 hours."

"IN TWO HOURS! It's the middle of my day! Can't it wait? I'd rather go in at the end of my shift."

"You don't pick your 'rathers' with the chief," Hess shot back. Dan sensed a glee in the tone.

"So, what's it all about?"

"It's regarding your tie memo."

"Oh—that."

"Chief didn't find it amusing an…"

"Ties in this heat are stupid!"

"I don't care to hear your opinions. Chief Hartwelz doesn't either. Report at 1600 hours. You're officially notified." Hess terminated his call.

He enjoyed that way too much!

A month ago Dan originated the movement for the Fraternal Order of Police [FOP] to petition the chief for elimination of ties. The Chief declined citing a need for a "professional look." The decision frustrated Dan and he submitted a memo of "constructive criticism" to the Chief defining the "professional look." If not valid, a vivid assessment: perspiration spotted creaseless uniforms, sweat blotches painted across the shoulders and underarms, sweat tickling down the crack of one's backside, and a chili stained tie the final complement to a "professional" look.

Dan called Ben at home. Alistia answered. "Hi Alistia, this is Dan. Ben up yet?"

"With these kids? Up over an hour. I'll get him."

"Hello Partner. Give me the bad news slowly."

"What makes you think it's bad news?"

"Called me at home, didn't you?"

"Hess called…"

"That IS bad news."

"Have to report to the chief at 1600 over my tie memo."

"Can't say I'm surprised."

"Yep, how you think I ought t' handle it?"

"Why you askin' me? I ain't goin' with you. Get the FOP to represent you."

"Not askin'. Just a heads up."

"Thanks." Then Ben called a muffled, "Alistia," out to his wife, "If work calls, I'M NOT HEAR. Take a message." Then to Dan, "Can't say I didn't warn you."

"Lookin' back, I guess it was a bit imprudent."

"Bit? I remember you saying—uhh—what were your words? 'I'm prepared to pay the piper'."

"Yeah, what d' you pay a piper? Hail Mary's?"

"Pack your toothbrush. I'll find out tonight how it went."

"Right," Dan hung up. *Doubt he'll try an' fire me. "Days and a 'penalty box' assignment for sure. Wonder which one: impound lot, dispatch center, telephone reporting? Oh well, might as well go down strong.*

Dan searched his closet. Found an undersized shirt, and a tie sporting chili stains to which he added a mustard splotch. Since no directives existed on tie tacks, he selected a one inch Mickey Mouse. Deciding the spray bottle he used to spit shin his shoes perfect to apply sweat stain, he sat it aside.

Slovenly dressed and in the hallway outside the Chief's

Office at 1600, Dan knocked.

"Enter."

Dan stepped briskly to the front of the desk, the door closing behind him. His untidy appearance an overstatement: shirt buttons bulged from a full vest, the tie's knot pushed upward revealing the "clip" nature, and wet armpits. The spray bottle had darkened the arm pits, neckline, and back shoulders. Artificial brow sweat was added from the drinking fountain prior to entering. Hat under arm, he braced, and saluted. "Officer Daniel Black reporting as ordered, Sir!"

"Holy mother of mercy!" Chief Hartwelz stared. In those moments Dan realized there were no witnesses in the room.

OH BLAST! Just went from a butt chewing to serious suspension!

"What DOES THAT represent!" the chief billowed.

Gotta play it out now. "Don't understand the nature of your question, Sir."

"I consider mockery of uniform dress insubordinate."

"Sir, best of my knowledge, my uniform is in full compliance with departmental policies."

"Officer Black, you're fully aware the shirt's too small. And, what's that suppose to be hanging from your neck—a bib? As for those blotches—you haven't begun to sweat. Unprofessional, totally unprofessional, and undoubtedly your objective. I'll not be toyed with!"

The chief left Dan standing rigid and walked out. Minutes later he returned with a Polaroid camera and snapped three shots dropping them on the desktop in front of Dan. Watching the images appear Dan wished he could press 'rewind'.

Chief Hartwelz returned behind his desk, shook his head, and spoke. "Officer Black, upset as I am by this ill-conceived drama, I am far more disappointed. My purpose in calling you here WAS to discuss this imaginative memo."

Hartwelz pulled a memo from an in-basket, waved it, and dropped it on top of the photos. "Your form is insubordinate enough, but I was willing to set it aside. I hoped you'd accept an assignment to an advisory panel on reducing patrol officer heat exertion. It's obviously a matter of personal concern for you. We differ in the role the tie plays, but your imagination, willingness to pursue the unpopular, among other traits showed promise. Now this! You cut my hands off at the elbows. My whole staff's seen this defiant waltz. Puts it out of the question. I left out of here fully intending to fire you. I'm still wondering if a suspension is sufficient. The paperwork will be forwarded to your District Captain immediately. You are dismissed!"

Dan saluted, pivoted an about-face and exited. *Sometimes I wake up stupid and never get over it.* Dan went to his car, removed the shirt and vest, and tossed them in the trunk. He drove home in the T-shirt with the top down. Arriving home Dan changed his pants and went to the porch.

"Well Trouble, shot the bottom out of the boat this time." He opened the cage door and let the ferret run. Smoking his pipe the vanilla aroma settled his nerves but not his regrets. "Well furry friend. The good news is WE may spend some time together. Oh I deserve it. Went off half cocked." His one-sided conversation with the ferret was interrupted by a light knock on the porch's screen door.

"Hi Peggy, come in."

"Can I take Trouble home for awhile," the next door neighbor asked.

Dan chuckled, "You don't know how much I wished you could. Fur ball's all yours. 'Fraid I'll have to keep my troubles."

"Sorry," she said gathering the pet and leaving.

Dan cleaned his golf clubs, ate supper, did some laundry, and then left for the district station. When he walked into the locker room he was greeted by cheers.

"Way to go. Hung yourself on a clip tie!"

"You certified what we've suspected – you're nuts!"

"What kind of jobs you got lined up? Bread truck or elevator jockey?"

Dan shook his head and went to his locker. "Relax guys. Fat lady ain't finished singing."

Ben arrived in the midst of it, "Word's out already?"
"Yep, hung myself."
"How bad?"
"Don't know yet."
"This darn thing' turned into a 'Preacher's Noose'," Ben said tugging at his tie. The name stuck.

They attended to preparing their gear. In ten minutes the duty call sounded. Jansen's hair was cut, and everybody's shoes shined. Sergeant O'Toole took time to comment. They sat at the briefing table listening to the bulletins. A breeze stirred on the mid-August night having no impact on the mugginess. The forecast of a cold front dropping temperatures didn't encourage. Nonetheless, having rotated off Day Relief two weeks ago, they were happy to be on nights. During this briefing, the officer's 'dangled' their clip ties from the button hole of the open collar. O'Toole was in good spirits.

"It says here in the official teletype—so it's gotta be," he laughed reading, "'a green ladies purse was stolen'. I've never seen a green lady."

"Saw one at Saint Paddy's Parade last year," Martin said.

"It also says a blue Chevy Nova is wanted for running over a 'Presbyterian in the crosswalk in front of Saint Paul's Church'."

"That'll teach him to stay out of Catholic neighborhoods," an officer quipped.

The sergeant continued in a more serious light. The large window AC kept the room comfortable with occasionally clatter and spitting steam. When it started shooting out condensation into O'Toole's hair he scooted his chair shoving his papers along. Martin moved over providing space. All done matter-of-fact.

"Okay, teletype's been read. You heard the memos and you have your assignments," O'Toole leaned back lighting his pipe, putting the men at ease to banter.

"Clemons, you get your flashlight back? Last I heard, you let some Iron Horseman steal it," Martin chided.

"Matter of fact, next day. Farnholz spotted it. Stupid enough to tie it to the back of his seat."

"Better 'an Dan, he's still begging Roadhaul drivers."

"Speakin' of braggin'," Dan rebutted. "You bagged that robbery suspect real good. Most of us lock our suspect in a holding room."

"They were full. Everybody thought he was a witness."

"When'd you get your first clue, Martin? When he crawled out the squad room window?"

Sergeant Fleischer entered to oversee late roll call. "Sounds like a slow night?"

O'Toole nodded, "So far." Then addressing the squad, "Okay, men, make room for the late cars. Summer nights and dastardly villains await. No hanging out in the station. Snag a delinquent tag after 0300, and I'll buy coffee for your wrecker wait. Get in, get done, and get out."

"Ah, Serge, have a heart," Harkins replied.

"And, stay in uniform. Put those ties in place."

"We don't want any 'tie time'." Dillon replied.

"These," Reynolds asked holding his tie out, "ain't ties, they's Preacher nooses."

"Be forewarned. Sour spot with the chief right now," the sergeant said. He turned to Dan, "Lieutenant's waiting for you in the Captain's Office."

"Yes, Sir."

"You're entitled to a witness."

Dan looked at Ben. He nodded. They rose and followed O'Toole to the office. O'Toole closed the door behind them. "Have a seat," he offered pointing to the chairs. Hess was behind the desk. Sgt. O'Toole stood in the background.

"You finally tripped over your own arrogance," Hess addressed Dan smiling.

"This? The tie thing, already?"

"Affirmative."

"I kind of expected the captain would preside."

"He signed off this afternoon. Wasn't happy being called by the Chief at 1700 hours. You've put him in the middle this time. Told ME to handle it."

Whu-ee, not getting canned!

"Seems I now have his ear," Hess continued. "You plan on fighting this one?"

"No Sir, I acted hastily, didn't think it out."

Hess paused, seemingly surprised by the response, and then clearing his throat made a show of reading the charges. After another pause he stated, "The Chief's action on this matter is a suspension of five days without pay. To be scheduled by the relief commander."

"Five days!" Dan shouted.

"Not nearly sufficient, but your popularity's waned. It's just a matter of time 'til you get yourself fired."

Glory be! I was expecting five weeks!

"Have him sign off on the order, and assign them sergeant," Hess said leaving.

"Could have been lot worse, Dan," O'Toole bolstered.

"Don't I know. Like to do 'em ASAP, so I can get back to business, Serge."

Dan had to refrain from skipping out of the office. Gary waited in the parking lot and caught Dan at his cruiser.

"Erie trip's all set. Found a charter for Saturday. Booked *The Sandpiper*. Never used it before, but we can't be picky. We're still on our own Friday and Sunday. Let's meet later; work out the details. Your share's eighty-four bucks."

"Meet for coffee around 1400?"

"Where?"

"I'll call you?"

Gary nodded.

"Five days." Dan whispered to him as Gary turned to walk away.

"Someone up there likes you," Gary said pointing skyward.

Upon entering the cruiser, Dan dangled his noose, "Mickey Mouse ties!" Ben drove away without replying. *Wonder what Mickey Mouse episode is lurking on the agenda tonight?*

Chapter Five

A Potpourri of Pleasures

A hundred feet out of District Five's drive they took their first dispatch. "Car 508, 508, fight in the street, 1622 Blue Rock."

"508, copied," Dan replied.

"Natives are restless already."

They turned the corner and approached the 1600 Bar. At the curb of the street two men were attacking a third man. Both about five feet seven and hundred seventy-five pounds, yet the third, stout and capable, was giving "tit for tat." The Duo waded into the ruckus.

"You fellows chat with me," Ben said grabbing the two smaller ones by their collars.

Dan stepped in front of the third man, "I'm ringing the bell. This rounds over." He yielded more to the uniform than the man, allowing Dan to steer him to the sidewalk.

"What do you go by, Hoss?" Dan asked.

"Bart."

"What's this donnybrook over, Bart?"

"That jerk in the green scrubs spilled beer on me!"

"Spilled versus poured? Implies an accident, right?"

"It WAS an accident!" the man in green scrubs shouted.

"Hold on, Dr. Welby, you'll get your say," Ben said pulling him back.

"I'm not Doctor Welby, my name's Jimmy Simpson."

"Sorry, outfit had me fooled."

Dan addressed Bart again, "An accident. Did he apologize?"

"We swapped words. Weren't no apology."

"Tried," said Simpson, "'for I could, he was bashing and shoving."

Ben turned to the unidentified man, "What's your name, and how do you fit in?"

"Mark Wilson. Jimmy's half his size. I was making it fair."

"Gentlemen," Dan said, "I suggest making apologies is simpler than going to jail."

"I'm sorry," Bart said offering his hand.

"Me too," Jimmy responded and shook. Mark did likewise.

"I'm going in and talk with the bar-keep," Dan informed. "You three start up again; I'll split heads with this stick." Dan went to the door. Inside, half-dozen patrons were among overturned chairs and tables and the proprietor was busy mopping beer off the floor. Seeing Dan, he approached.

"How much damage you got, Cecil?"

"Spilt beer and overturned tables. No big deal. Big one took it outside like a snow plow."

Dan rejoined Ben on the sidewalk, "How they doin'?"

"Becomin' best of friends."

"The owner's not pressing charges," Dan said. "You've got a choice. Jail or shake hands and forget it."

"I guess we overreacted," said Bart sticking out his hand again. The other two shook.

"I'll buy drinks all around," Simpson shouted as he headed for the bar.

"Whoa there!" Ben countered. "Ye men of quick wit", yon proprietor of yon pub has lost eagerness for thy patronage."

"It's okay, now, Officer, everything's forgiven," Mark insisted.

"Noble men of the night let us be clear. IT-IS-OVER – fighting and drinking both."

"And, that's the way it's gonna stay," Dan added emphatically. "You two are going your way, and he's going his—different trails. We see either of you again tonight – it's jail."

The new friends separated. As they walked away Dan sang, "Separate trails to you, least we meet again…"

"Car 508, 508, investigate disabled motorist South Seventy-five high speed lane, two hundred yards north of Hopple," sounded the radio.

"508 copy," Ben acknowledged, then asked, "How'd she know we're green?"

"By now you should know they're omnipotent."

Five minutes later they were on the scene, but found nothing. Continuing south toward the next exit Dan spotted a Roadhaul eighteen-wheeler. "Suppose that's Manning with my flashlight?"

"Nope, not him. Don't need to stop it."

"How you know, Ben? Stop him and see."

"You can't be serious!"

"Darn tootin'! I want my flashlight back."

Ben closed the distance pacing the truck at fifty-five miles an hour before flipping on the bar lights. The truck slowed and made its way on to the berm. The driver met them at the rear of the rig. "What's wrong Officer, I was dead on double nickels?"

"Checkin' to see if you're Mister Manning. You know Theodore Manning?"

"No, Sir. He drive for Roadhaul?"

"Sure does," Dan said, "And, he's got my new Mag-light. I called the dispatcher in Mason and got a run around. Said he was out of state and couldn't get in touch with him."

"What's it got to do with me?"

"Glad you asked. Tell everybody I don't care if he's outer space. Look him up. I want my Mag-light. Every night I work without it, somebody gets stopped and checked out real good."

"Now see here! That'll add time to my run!"

"Exactly."

"That ain't fair. I didn't run off with it."

"I understand, but somebody knows Manning. I'm counting on peer pressure."

"This is harassment. My company'll send a formal

complaint to your chief!"

"I'm expecting it. And, since I'm stopping numerous freighters I can't be accused of picking on you. Of course, I'm telling the others it's your guys' fault. The sooner I get my flashlight back; well, you get the drift."

"Okay if I wait in the cab for your so-called inspection?"

"No, better stay here, while my partner finishes checking your rig," Ben answered. "Procedures are procedures."

In fifteen minutes, the trucker was on his way.

Back in the patrol car Ben asked, "You know what my daddy used to do with huntin' dogs that kept barking up empty trees?"

"No, what!"

"Shoot 'em. Said it limited the misery of both."

"So, we aren't on the same page?"

"Not even same book. How long you gonna keep it up?"

"Find my light."

"Bite the bullet. Buy another one!"

"Not yet! I can hear those CBs buzzing. Before long, it'll show up."

"Car 509, 509, Fire Company responding to 1422 Apjones."

"508, U-T-L on the disabled motorist, we'll make it," Dan replied.

Running 'lights no siren', they turned north on Hamilton and fell in behind the fire engine. Soon it slowed at a hydrant and two firemen sprang off the back with a hose. The truck continued rolling toward the smoking house four doors ahead. Ben pulled to the curb fifty feet behind the hydrant. Dan took a traffic post by the car, and Ben walked to the other end of the fire scene to take a post. A news crew arrived, and they pulled in seventy-five feet ahead of the cruiser on the opposite side of the street. From their vantage point they filmed the flames licking the eaves.

Three minutes later additional fire equipment arrived. Soon there were trucks and hoses everywhere. Once the flames were knocked down and only smoke remained, the news crew opened the doors of the van to pack up. Dan went over to them.

"You can't leave now. You're 'hosed' in."

"We don't want to go through that mess," the driver replied. "We're backing out."

"You can't! There's a hose behind you."

"It doesn't matter, it's flat."

"I don't care if it's charged or not! The law's explicit! You cannot drive over a fire hose – period!"

"Why not? There's no water in it?"

"First off, because I said so! But for your information, it weakens the canvas. The hose could rupture next time it's used and kill somebody. Wait until they roll up the hoses!"

"Nonsense! I've got a Press Pass. It allows me to come and go as I please."

"Oh, excuse me, could I see it?"

The driver slipped the Press Card off the visor and handed it to him.

"Indeed, it's in order, Mr. Norton. You're free to go." The driver started the van. "OH, you misunderstand. YOU are free. The van stays put! Am I clear? Drive over a hose and I'll be givin' you bad news."

"This is a bunch of bull! This film has to get to the office!"

"You have a radio. Call someone to pick it up. Driving over hoses IS - NOT - AN – OPTION!"

The driver killed the engine. Cursed, but sat waiting. Dan returned to the center of the street. Ten minutes later the Fire Marshal approached.

"Officer, I think you ought to see what started this fire."

"Arson?"

"No, but I'm sure it'll interest you."

"Okay, but I can't protect your hoses if I leave. News team's getting impatient. I can call another officer?"

"No need, Lieutenant Cotton can stand watch. We're getting ready to roll up." He turned to a nearby fireman, "Don, watch the street while I show the officer the ignition point."

"Sure thing, Captain."

Dan followed the Fire Chief through the main entrance noticing the charred door laying flat on the floor. "Love the way you guys redecorate," Dan quipped. "Smokehouse is so in style."

"If you like what we've done with this one, wait 'til the kitchen."

The fireman led him around a corner and down a short scorched hallway. He stopped at the kitchen door. The corncob textured charcoal panel angled inward on one hinge displaying a gaping splintered hole.

"We knocked," the Fire Marshal said. "He wouldn't open it, so we used our key."

"Axe opens most locks," Dan said.

"We got in the kitchen, the flames were breaking the eaves, and the fool's fighting it with the faucet sprayer! He ate a bunch of smoke. He's with Rescue and lucky to be alive." They stepped over debris into the flame gutted kitchen. Wet suet covered everything. "Here's the point of ignition," the Fire Marshal said opening the oven.

Dan picked up a long cooking spoon with a melted handle and poked around in a charred vegetable mass. There was less charring toward the center of the pile, and pieces of a green-brown leafy substance stuck to the prod.

"Not sure, but the smell's undeniable. My money says he dries his marijuana plants in the oven—or use to!" Dan said with a laugh. "Good thing your men wear masks. They'd be too stoned to drive them pretty red trucks."

"Maybe that explains the sink sprayer."

"I think I'll have a talk with the cook. But first things first," Dan said searching the cabinets for a container.

"If you don't need me, I've got to make sure everything's rolled up." The fireman left chuckling to himself.

Dan found a small box of plastic bags in a cupboard. He cut through the melted layer and eventually peeled way a good one. He filled the bag with the substance, and then emptied a metal waste basket and spooned in the rest. He returned to his cruiser to secure it in his trunk. The fireman who was directing traffic in Dan's absence saw him coming, and rushed over.

"As soon as you left, that news crew backed over the hoses!"

"Calm down. I know where to find him. Can you identify the driver in court?"

"Sure can! He came close to running me over!"

"Trust me. He's going to be real sorry, as soon as I'm done here. You'll be notified when to appear."

Dan locked the evidence in the trunk, and headed for the Rescue. There were two people in the van, a medic and a man wearing an oxygen mask.

"What's your name?" Dan asked the man behind the mask.

"Kevin Kooker," was the muffled reply.

"What kind of cake were you cooking?"

Kooker made no response.

"Old secret family recipe, I bet?"

No response.

"No worry, the lab'll figure it out. I suspect you know you're under..."

Kooker pushed Dan forcibly to the side and jumped off the back of the van. Rebounding Dan gave chase, but Kooker fled with the evasiveness of a field mouse.

"508A, in pursuit; north between the houses, painter jeans, male, white."

Cars started acknowledging and the dispatcher set quadrant positions.

"508A, I've lost him," Dan responded between heavy breaths. "He cut through the back. Male white, early twenties, around five-eight to ten...slender...long brown hair...white painter jeans, tie-dyed shirt...red peace sign on the front. Runs like a gazelle!"

"Copy 508B. What's the subject wanted for?"

"Possession for distribution and resisting. Gave the name Kevin Kooker. Wasn't in the alley when I got here. I'm guessing he's hiding around the garages."

"505, I'm near 1450 Weiglod. I'll see him if he comes this way. Have the other cars check Weipel alley."

"508A, have my partner meet me middle of Weipel Alley. Pretty dark back here."

Ben joined him. "Partner, this is perfect for an ambush."

"Why I wanted your company."

"You're workin' point?"

"Want it?"

"Nope, rather he shot you first."

"Quit worrying. He's a doper not a shooter."

"Does he know that?"

They searched for ten minutes before Officer Follert radioed, "505, got a dog barking at 1454 Pullan. I'm gonna check it out."

"508, we're near there. Hear the dog. We'll try and come through and cover."

"505, copy."

"507, we'll work the alley from Dane Street. E-T-A three minutes."

"505, found the dog. He's friendly enough."

"508, I think we're behind the house."

"505, IN PURSUIT!"

The Duo sprinted toward front of the house.

"South on Chambers."

"Renu Five, he's coming straight at us. Be advised, we're an unmarked car parked on Chambers. He's going to run right by…" The radio clicked static. "…nope, door got in his way."

"505, we've got him at 4288 Chambers."

Dan and Ben met 505 and RENU [Regional Enforcement Narcotics Unit], and briefed them on the arrest. RENU transported Kooker back to Pullan. While the Duo returned, RENU tested the evidence with a field kit.

"Officer Beal greeted the Duo, "It tested valid for cannabis."

"Not surprised. Thanks."

One fire truck remained, hoses were all stowed, and the officers secured. 508 headed for the lockup with Kooker.

"It's been a fun time in the old town tonight," Ben remarked.

“And it’s just begun. After we drop Kooker off, we have an appointment with Brent Norton at Channel Three.” Dan related the details.

“You’re gonna make his day with a citation.”

“Nope, gonna make MY day lockin’ him up. Aggravated case.”

“Make sure your ‘noose’ is in place, likely be on TV.”

They finished processing the arrest of Mr. Kooker and went directly to the television station’s dock. A custodian responded to the service bell.

“Who’s in charge?” Dan asked.

“That’d be Mr. Collins, night editor. I’ll take you to him.”

They walked down a short hallway containing several offices. Voices spilled out the open door of one, “Great fire footage for this time of night.”

Dan turned into the office. Walked up to Norton and announced, “Mr. Norton you are under arrest for unlawful conduct at scene of emergency and driving over a fire hose.”

Norton turned. Seeing the officers, his eyes widened, his jaw dropped, and his face paled. He stood struck numb while the officers handcuffed him.

“Is this necessary?” Collins demanded. “What’s this about?”

“Yes, Sir,” Dan replied.

“You can’t break in here an’ handcuff people without an explanation,” Collins demanded stepping in the doorway.

“This man’s put me in a bad mood. You’d be wise to stay out of it.”

Collins didn’t move, “Norton what’s going on?”

Ben brandished his handcuffs, “This pair’ll fit you.”

Collins stepped aside.

“False arrest! Call the lawyers!” Norton yelled as Dan pushed him through the door.

“He’ll be at county jail in thirty minutes,” Ben said following as Collins dialed his phone. At the exit they heard Collins yelling, “Get down here! Brent’s been arrested! I don’t know!”

On the way to lock-up Ben said, “I’ve had enough fun for one night. Can we slow down?”

“If the conductor’ll stop wavin’ his baton, I’ll quit fiddlin’.”

Arriving at the jail’s check-in the turnkey greeted them, “You guys working on merit badges?”

“My partner’s magnetic personality,” Ben replied. “He doesn’t need a full moon. He is a full moon.”

“I want my lawyer!” Norton yelled. “I got rights! You can’t do this! Free press. I’m suing.”

“Be nice to him, Ternnka. He’s with Channel Three, put you on the news. Film at eleven an’ all,” Dan said facetiously.

“Certainly, look forward to it. However, I’d consider it a personal favor; next one ain’t gonna to ‘sue me for all I got’.”

“We’ll try to be more selective.”

Back in the cruiser Dan said, “I guess he didn’t believe me when I told him driving over the hoses would be bad news.”

“Not sure he believes it now.”

“He will,” Dan chuckled.

“Wouldn’t hold a party just yet. Bet we started a mud slide with this one.”

“What you gettin’ at?”

“High profile, and we made a physical. Could’ve cited.”

“We’re legal, and Captain Kirk’ll back us a hundred percent. They’ve given him bad press more ’an once.”

“I’m not so sure where you stand with the captain right now.”

“Doesn’t matter. I know where he stands with the media hounds. They’ve bashed the ‘police image’ too often.”

Over the next two hours they exploited the street’s sporadic service demands, and the Duo undertook the second step of the OTP Plan. They revisited the street and ticketed twelve vehicles. One was stolen and another had “delinquent” plates [outstanding tickets/unpaid fines].

“Hess, wants parkers? He’s getting parkers,” Dan said.

"He'll be happy. He's seeing numbers on a sheet. When we start towing tomorrow, someone'll clue him in!"

"That's the plan. The complaint will eventually trickle down to Hess."

"Trickle down? More like GUSH!"

They called for tow-trucks, and were in the process of marking when O'Toole arrived with coffee. He found Dan a half block from his cruiser. Dan stepped into the street to greet the sergeant, but O'Toole spoke first, "What are you guys doing?"

Dan shifted the question, "You checkin' on us?"

"Nooo--promised coffee for delinquents," he said handing a bag out the window.

"Thanks, Serge."

"Didn't answer my question."

"You really want one?"

"I wasn't here," O'Toole said pulling away as the first wrecker arrived. In fifteen minutes both tows were headed for impound and the Duo sat sipping coffee.

"Passed the point of no return," Ben said.

"Yep, the hammer's thumbed back on this 'Game of the Blues', Dan agreed. "You ready for an ice cream?"

"You talkin' Dutch's?"

"Is there any other? I'll see if Gary can meet us. He's got an MR-7 and I want to finalize the fishing trip."

The widowed owner, Marvin Sanders, lived three blocks away from Dutch's Custard Shop which he inherited from his wife's father. After his wife died, he developed a passion for wood working and converted the garage into a complete woodworking shop. Since Dutch's didn't open until 1100, it didn't interfere with Marvin working late at his hobby.

Marvin made Dan and Ben's nightsticks which dueled the mighty "Porter" and survived. Porter's signature trait was its two-inch thickness. Although bulky, popular because city issue batons were so thin they fell through the belt's keeper ring and were prone to break. Porter saw a need and filled it. Marvin's sticks, lathed to careful tolerances fit the keeper ring, and ample thickness and fine grain second-growth hickory endowed them with strength of iron.

On the way, Ben drove by Marvin's noting the light in his workshop. When they pulled in beside the Custard Shop, Gary was waiting in the back. He flicked his beacon lights.

They parked and approached Gary on foot. "We're going to trust you with part of a secret," Dan said. "Swear to take it to your grave."

"No problem. What's up?"

"Face your cruiser in on that oak tree, and turn on the radar."

Gary complied and got out of the car. "Now what?"

"Wait," Ben said.

A minute later the radio sounded, "Car 505, 505, alarm drop; Dutch's Custard, West Fork Road. Notifying owner. Car 508, cover."

Both cars acknowledged the dispatch.

"Dip me in chocolate syrup! How'd you know it was gonna drop?" Gary asked.

"That's your part of the secret," Dan said.

"The radar set it off?"

"Yep," Ben admitted. "Now turn it off so it'll reset."

Within minutes, Marvin arrived in a door-less Jeep. "You fellows better check inside," he insisted unlocking the twenty by thirty foot building. "It'll take all three of you to make sure." As soon as they stepped inside Marvin asked, "What can I dish up for metros finest?"

Dan and Ben blurted out, "Sundaes'd be great."

Marvin prepared them while Gary watched silently. Setting them on the counter he turned to Gary depressing the lever and asked, "Your favorite?"

"I'll pass."

"Already half made. Be a waste."

Gary reluctantly watched custard swirl into the cup, "Strawberry."

"Whippy-top and nuts?"

"Plain, thanks."

"Marvin, what's you latest project?" Ben asked.

"I'm working on a burled mahogany smoking table for a

friend."

"This really hits the spot, thanks," Gary said.

"Well, thank you," Marvin said wiping down the stainless counter. "You must be new."

"Marvin, meet Gary Follert, a good man to have sidin' you," Dan said.

"If'n you got Dan's endorsement, you got mine. More strawberries?"

"More than necessary," Gary replied stepping back.

"You fellows?" Marvin offered.

"We're fine."

"So, your hobby's wood working?" Gary spoke while making a show of checking for intruders. "I wish I could make things with my hands."

"Well Gary, okay I call you Gary?"

Gary nodded picking at the ice-cream with the plastic spoon. He no longer ate, but chased a strawberry around the cup.

"Don't much matter what you do, if'n there's pride in it," Marvin said pulling the door tight as they left.

"Appreciate the ice cream," Dan said.

"Least I could do. Side table's near finished. Think I'll be needing some 'iron hickory' for a future project."

"I'm sure it'd be highly appreciated. I'll keep an eye out."

Gary grew noticeably quieter as they talked with the lonely man for several minutes.

"Hey guys, want to see the project?" Marvin offered.

"Some other time. We got bad guys to catch," Ben answered.

"Sticks holdin' up? See they're getting some character."

"Plenty of character. Seems a shame to mar 'em," Dan said.

"Mar? No way! That's personality."

When first presented with the sticks Dan and Ben kept them in their lockers for months to protect the oiled finish. One day Marvin challenged them, "Get those sticks out and give them some character marks or I'll take 'em back."

Marvin slid into his Jeep smiling, "One of these days, I'm getting me a better alarm." He paused then added "Oh, maybe not, so expensive and never had a break in with this one. See you fellows next time." Marvin pulled away waving until out of sight.

"You louses!" Gary exclaimed glancing into the bottom of his empty cup. "You're wrong. That's outright stealing. I had you down for better people."

"You gonna blow us off over a free ice cream?" Dan asked.

"He's such a nice guy, and you're takin' advantage of him!" Gary tossed his empty cup in the trashcan, and turned to walk off.

"Your ice cream go sour?" Ben asked.

Gary stopped at the door of his cruiser. "More 'an my ice cream! You're deceitful; foolin' a lonely man to get it!"

"Hold on! Don't get your panties in a bunch," Dan said walking over to him. "Open your eyes and see the whole picture."

"I got the picture, and it's got an ugly frame around it."

"You want to talk foolishness," Ben said. "Marvin ain't the fool here."

"Ain't anybody foolin' nobody," Dan said. "'Cept maybe you!"

Gary looked at them in silence shaking his head.

"Ghost Rider don't get it, Preacher," Ben chuckled.

"You're telling me he knew all the time?" Gary asked.

"His idea, not ours. We pulled in here on Day Run, way back when, and the alarm dropped. Marvin figured out what happened and set the whole thing up."

"Of course! The rest of the secret."

"Not really. The rest is checking to see he's in his shop and not in bed before we drop in," Dan said. "You pegged him for a lonely man, but you don't understand why. His wife's passed on. His children live out of state. He has no one. Only his woodworking to keep his mind occupied. He's in his workshop because his memories won't let him sleep. Meeting us makes him feel useful—valuable."

"That make your ice cream any sweeter?" Ben asked.

"Never had better. I apologize."

"No need. We set you up," Dan said. "Now let's get this fishing trip settled."

"First off, who's meeting who, where and when?"

"Rick's your man. Suggest you two pick me up soon after work as you can?"

"Works for me."

They continued to coordinate the particulars, and then returned to patrol. In the big city the streets seldom slumber.

"Notice the cab flashing his lights?" Ben asked.

"Uh-huh, I'll call a backup," Dan said.

Ben made a U-turn and followed the taxi, but nothing seemed askew. It pulled to the curb in the bus stop near the Lazy Lion Club. The officers knew the establishment catered to what the media popularly referred to as an "alternate lifestyle."

They approached the cab driver and Dan asked, "Any problems?"

"These queers tryin' to stiff me."

"That's not so, Officer," a tall man defended in a feminine whine. "We was just DISCUSSIN' it."

Verifying it wasn't a robbery, Ben disregarded the backup cars.

"I see. Let's take it one at a time." Dan directed turning to the cabby, "S'pose you go first."

"I'll tell you the way it was! They flagged me down. Told me take 'em to Georgia Court. But, when I get there, they start arguin' over payin'. And then, this one," he pointed, "wants me to haul 'em back here. That's when I seen you. Figured they was up to stiffin' me. The fare's fourteen twenty-six. And …"

"We were just working it out," the tall man interrupted.

"Alright then," Dan said, "let's hear your side of it."

"Well," he began with a puff, "Cindy here, sweet talks me. Makes me promises, and I said I'd go to her place."

"First your name, then your story," Dan said.

"I'm Brenda Bunning, some calls me Bunns," he said,

“and we’ was goin’ to Cindy’s place...”

“What were you going to ‘her-r-r’ place for?” Ben cut in.

“Oh, you’re a ‘b-iig’ one aren’t you, honey?”

“Ain’t your honey. Going to her place? The reason.”

“Lordy, you do get to the point—now don’t you?”

“Aa-nd, the answer?”

“You make me blush,” he cast his eyes to the pavement. “Perrr-son-al business.”

“And that’d be-e-e?”

After a pause he added, “To exchange affections.”

“Got the picture,” Ben said. “So what changed? Little lovers spat on the way?”

“Surely Officer,” the other man began. “You…”

Dan cut him off, “Hang on. We haven’t been properly introduced. You are?”

“Cindy Cameo, those close, call me ‘Cinn-na-monnn’.”

“We’re never going to be that close, Cindy. What you wan’a add?”

Cindy addressed Brenda, “You really didn’t expect me to pay—did you?”

“Sweetie, you said you’d pay the fare!”

“Honey, that was before you changed your mind!”

“I’m not stupid. You’re not gonna to do tha-a-at! Not without…” Brenda stopped short.

“Without what?” Ben pressed, “Spit it all out.”

A short pause punctuated the conversation. Then she snapped a whispered, “Protection!”

Dan had heard enough. “Time out! Ladies, fellows, or whatever. I suggest you split the bill, or you’ll both be making new friends in lock up.”

“I’ll pay half,” Cindy said. “But, I’m telling everybody what kind of whore you are, Brenda Buns.”

“Who needs you, switch bitch?” Brenda yelled stomping toward the club.

“Hold it, where you going?” Dan demanded.

“My clutch is behind the bar.” Then looking at Cindy she whined, “Why I couldn’t pay, drag fag!”

"Go with him, Ben. Don't want he-she-it slippin' out the back."

"Oh, thank you Officer," Cindy said exaggerating the feminine tone. "She's such a cheatin' liar."

"Before we end a wonderful charade," Dan said, "I need to see I D."

Cindy retrieved his wallet and handed Dan a driver's license. It bore the name Horace Billings.

"508, with a query," Dan radioed.

"Switch to Com four, 508."

"508, wants on Horace Billings, male, white, age twenty nine, SS 121-00-4441."

"Stand by."

Ben returned to the sidewalk with Brenda in tow.

"Dig out some ID, then pay the cabbie," Ben said. The man provided a driver's license, and Ben handed it off to Dan.

"508 query," he said into the mike, "also one Walter Gildenstein, male, white, D-O-B 10-1-53, SS 200-00-6665."

"You lying phony!" screamed Horace dropping the feminine overtones, "You've been telling everybody you're Melton Griston!"

"Settle down, Horace," Dan said, "All you switch an' swaps have a dozen names."

"We was closer than that," Horace complained. Then directing his comments to Walter said, "I'm deeply hurt – wounded. You're an insensitive vixen. How'd I ever love you?"

"Tis an uncertain and confusing life chosen, isn't it?" Dan said.

"Are you ladies in the book," Ben asked referring to a free will registry of glamour shots composed of all female dressers they could coerce into posing.

"I am," Horace replied proudly. "Last year, page 109, Line 2, but she's not."

"508, no wants on your subjects," squawked the radio.

"Just between you, me, and this post," Ben said motioning to the streetlight. "If you're going to parade in drag, get in the registry. It's for your own good. Understood?"

"I'll do it tomorrow," Walter promised. "Now can I go? My heart's broken."

"Time you lovers pay the cabbie," Dan said. "One at a time. Billings you first."

He turned slapping a ten in the cabby's hand, "Keep it," he said and stomped away in his high heels.

"Your turn," Ben said to Guildenstein. He sulked over to the cab, handed the cabbie four dollars, and dug in the clutch for a quarter.

Dan cleared his throat. "Math not your best subject? Your half is seven dollars thirteen."

"Oh, what's wrong with me? I'm just so…"

"Cut the act. It's just us guys now. And you probably meant to give him a larger tip than Billings, huh?"

"You're SO right, Officer." He said laying a twenty in the cabby's hand. "Sorry, the witch put us through this. Just no polish in some people."

The cabby smiled and nodded. Brokenhearted Brenda strutted to the door disappearing into the club.

"Thank you," the cabby waved the bills. "You guys got class. Wouldn't pick 'em up, but you know I gotta."

"Yep, no discrimination of fares," Ben said.

"And, nine out of ten, I get stiffed. Glad I saw you."

"Serve and protect, we do our best," Dan said turning to walk back to their cruiser. Bringing his hands to his chest, mimicked in a female voice, "Oh, Lordy, what a fright! I so fretted during your trip inside, sweetie."

"Don't you sweetie me! I got my 'tush' pinched four times 'tween the bar and the door!"

"Next time, stuff your vest down your pants."

"Next time you're step-an-fetch."

"I'm noticing you're worrying a lot about your derriere these days, 'sweet-buns'."

"Cut it out," he said with a feminine lisp.

"Now you ARE scaring me" Dan declared sternly masculine.

"Alternate lifestyle? Why? What's the pay off?"

"Don't ask me. I can't figure what draws people into such opprobrious conventions."

" 'Opprobrious,' that's the 'word for today.' I read the paper too, you know?"

"Then you know what it means?"

"I saw it. Didn't memorize it!"

"Reproachable, confused, outrageous, those words too big?" asked Dan.

"If you're so smart, tell me what's wrong with 'em?"

"Who says it's wrong?"

"I do. Dan, it ain't natural!"

"You mean guys liking guys?"

"Uh-huh."

"Don't think they really do, Ben. Have you noticed in all our encounters with them, they're mismatched? I don't think any are REALLY happy."

"Eech! Not natural!"

"Implying it isn't in line with nature, or just abnormal?"

"Both."

"Ben, you're assuming nature has purpose? And sex is part of it?"

"Everyone knows it's supposed to be a man and a woman thing,"

"That's JUST your opinion."

"It's 'w-a-aay' too weird for me. And whose side you on, anyway?"

"Personally, I think their behavior is fueled by human desperation, just like crime. After all, we've been bombarded by scientific data that the universe is overwhelmingly hostile. We're creatures seeking comforts and delights, in an uninhabitable universe! They've convinced us it can't last long. Thus, self-gratification dawns immediacy, and where and how we find it loses restraint."

"But we've been around for millions of years; adapting, inventing, life's getting better."

"Things are getting better, are they? What a wonderful contradiction to the cry of doom. We've so advanced now we're polluting everything, using up the oxygen, and poisoning the water. The planet's predicted to be spinning out of control, freezing over, burning up, or destined to collide with a giant meteor. If human life is an accident, we're doomed! It struggles in a hostile environment, faces extinction, has no future, and is meaningless."

"Nobody believes that stuff, do they?"

"Hemingway must have. Do I remember him saying, 'a short day's journey from nothingness to nothingness'? A lot of people loved his philosophy."

"Yeah, Dan, but he committed suicide, didn't he?"

"At least you haven't given up! I think the masses are jumping on the 'live for today, tomorrow we die' bandwagon. Feels good, I want it, I deserve it, so I'm doing it, because what difference does it make in the end?"

"Yeah, the 'Me Generation'.

"Uh-huh, and they take pleasure wherever they find it. And, some find it in homosexuality. Must there be honorable pleasures and reprobate ones?" IS there a difference?

"You're getting to deep for me. It's simply against God's church," Ben added unable to cite a better source.

"If there IS a God. BUT, what if, I'm just a chance merger of atoms? My chemical makeup determining what's pleasurable for me. I have no moral laws. There are no 'norms', only individual preferences and differing pleasures."

"Weird people do weird things. That's it, as far as I'm concerned."

"Okay, but another answer might be it is evil. There's a war going on in the supernatural realm. We can't see it, but it's there: A supernatural dark force sparing against goodness. Despair against hope and joy. Given God and Heaven, we are not temporal beings without hope. Remove him from the picture and we are. We live and act in accord with our beliefs."

"You're depressing me. Will earth last long enough for me to play with my grandkids?"

"I don't expect it's going anywhere, until whatever started it stops it."

Ben shook his head and sighed, "Your itch is sure getting deep. Next time I get to church I'll light a candle for you."

"Better make it a bonfire on the altar."

"What time is it?"

They were just coming up on an intersection when a red Cougar sped through. "He's flying," Dan said. "My up. Get a clock on him."

Ben turned the cruiser to pursue. As soon as they 'clocked' the car, Dan activated the beacon lights. The driver of the speeding vehicle pulled to the curb. They made a routine approach. Dan crossed over to the driver, with Ben making the first contact from the curb by flashing his light on the driver. Dan then pecked on the driver's window. It hummed down.

"Sir, I suppose you have a good reason for flying down the road?"

"Well, Officer, I have a reason, but doubt you'll think it a good one."

"Even so, I'd like to hear it."

"I'm late and my wife will be madder than Jesus with the moneychangers."

"Honest, but not good enough."

"Yes, Sir."

"Your registration and pilot's license, please."

Dan cautiously observed the man retrieving the registration from the console. He handed Dan the documents.

"Sit tight. I'll be about ten minutes. I'll try and provide you a good reason."

Dan returned to the cruiser. Ben followed. Seated, Dan read the documents, asked the dispatcher for a records check, and sat quietly. After a short time Ben noticed Dan wasn't writing.

"Finger cramps?"

Dan handed the license to Ben, "Wouldn't you know?"

"Expired," Ben guessed.

"Nope."

"Another smart-aleck. Thinking on lockin' him up?"

Ben asked looking at the license.

"Nope."

"Don't tell me! You asked for his pilot's license?"

"Yep."

Ben laughed uproariously. "Not only a numb-skull, but you've put foot in mouth."

"I deny the first charge. Plead guilty to the second."

"Not a problem. All the info will be on record."

"I know, but …"

"Oh yeah, scruples. 'Chew 'em out' or tag 'em, but both is crass?"

"Yep."

"Your hole. You dug it. For sixty in a thirty-five, I'd tag him anyway."

"You got a point, but you don't have to go back up there."

"He's not in a position to say much."

"Eatin' crow can be a silent meal, but it still tastes bad."

"Car 508, 508, No wants on Ralf Snoopes. One traffic contact; stop sign violation two years ago."

Ben roared again. "You stopped 'Snoopy' and demanded his pilot's license!"

Dan snatched the documents from Ben, "I'm buryin' this nightmare." He slid out and went back to the driver.

"Sir, do you have proof of insurance?"

"Yes, Sir," Snoopes said handing Dan a card.

"Snoopy, you realize the Blue Barron swooped out of the moonlight on you?"

"Just what I was thinking."

"And, at twenty over the posted I can arrest you, impound the car, and your wife will be bailing you out."

"No Sir, I suspect I'd spend the night."

"It's against my better judgment, but I'm not pulling the trigger."

Dan handed the documents toward Snoopes, and as he reached for them Dan pulled them back.

"Ever I get you in my sights again—no mercy; crash and burn. Understand?"

"Yes, Sir, thank you, Officer," he said in a sincere tone, "I was driving foolish."

Dan returned the documents to Snoopes.

"If ever you have an urge to go flying up there," Snoopes said pointing to the sky, "look me up." He slipped a business card from his visor and handed it to Dan.

Dan returned to the cruiser.

"You're right," Ben said. "It won't die a quick death."

The radio crackled another plea for police services. Ben's fun would have to wait. "Car 508, see complainant at the phone booth Mad Anthony and Boyd reference robbery."

The location was minutes away and they responded in silence. As usual, on their beat, they were first to arrive. The streets were empty and they found no complainant.

"508, Signal Thirty-five, U-T-L," Dan reported to the dispatcher.

Within seconds the dispatcher added, "508, updated info, complainant at phone booth Mad Anthony and Spring Grove."

Ben drove the additional block finding a man in his fifties, nervously pacing by the phone booth. Ben pulled behind a four door Oldsmobile next to the phone booth. The man rushed to the cruiser's door before Dan could exit. He addressed them with hurried speech.

"That whore took my wallet! I want her arrested!"

"Whoa! Hold on. We'll get to that, Sir. Take a breath," Dan said opening the door and quickly exiting." First, what's your name?"

"Joe Townsend, they took all my money!"

"Slow down. Someone took your wallet? Okay, where'd this happen?"

"I was at the Step Up Café mixing with ALL the ladies. I had several invites, but this one was 'hot tamale'," he whistled. "We talked. She invited me to her place. I said 'Why not?' So, we left in my car. We get to the room. She goes to make drinks and 'WHAM!' I'm clobbered from behind. Took off with my wallet. Three-hundred dollars in it!"

"Can you give us a description?" Dan asked.

"Yeah, this tall," he motioned to his shoulder. "Wore a black leather mini, and a cream knit blouse. Long blonde pony tail tied with a pink scarf."

"Where's this place of hers?"

"Didn't go there. To avoid her babysitter, she suggested we go to the Low Rates Motel on the parkway."

"She have any tattoos?" Ben asked.

"Yeah," matter of fact, a butterfly tattoo on her inner thigh," he pointed to above his knee.

"Um-Huh. Lime green with yellow hearts?"

"You know her? I want her arrested!"

"Okay Mr. Townsend," Dan continued, "But you'll need to testify."

"Sure, I gotta get my money back."

"Now, Mr. Townsend…"

"Joe, call me Joe."

"Alright, Joe. Gloria and her friend will find a hole for now. We'll find her in a couple days, easy enough. Where you want the court notify sent?"

"Not home—my wife'd find out. Maybe my, uhh…" Joe stopped and fidgeted for a few moments, "Court? What's chance my wife findin' out?"

"No reason to think she would, but court records are public," Ben said. "Usually they don't."

A long silence followed. "I can't risk court! My wife gets wind of it I'm sunk!"

"Sir, we can't make that decision for you. However, you can be sure there'll be more victims until someone does," Dan said.

"Why do you think your wife might hear? She work in the court system?" asked Ben.

"I can't risk my wife hearing. I'm reporting it to you. You're the police! You're supposed to stop her."

"Without your testimony our hands are tied."

"Sorry, officer, gotta do what's best for my marriage. I can't worry about the next guy, that's your job," he said heading back to his car.

"In future choices of recreation, might keep your marriage in mind," Dan recommended. They watched Joe drive away.

"A pick-up, and the 'No-Tell Motel', and it's our fault?" Ben said.

"Certainly. Fault the wall mason, never the cannoneer."

"Car 505, 505, auto accident, auto and pole, no injury, Hamilton Avenue at Glen Parker."

"505, okay, responding."

Ben recognized the dispatch was on their beat, and with Joe driving away, they were free. "We'll take the run," he informed the dispatcher. Disregard 505."

"505, copied disregard."

The accident required little investigation. A northbound truck swung wide in the turn, and the oncoming vehicle swerved to avoid it. The innocent driver hit a telephone pole. He reported no injuries. They cleared the street, and completed the paperwork quickly.

"What time is it?" Ben asked.

"Much too early to secure. Paper's caught up. Want to burn time sitting on a light?"

"Let's gas up first," Ben suggested.

They headed for the garage. After a short drive down the parkway they turned into the maintenance facility. Seeing the mound of trash in the collection bay, Dan was reminded it was sweeper night. The still quiet radio and the clear night presented a perfect opportunity for practicing their night shooting.

"Up to a rat challenge?" Ben asked.

"Certainly. Buck a kill?"

"Right on."

The street sweepers went out nightly throughout the city. On Tuesday's they ran a Clifton route. This temporary dump station in the rear of the maintenance barns saved time over the longer trip to the incinerators. Refuse attracts rodents, and this dump station had its share. The rats made challenging targets for 22 caliber pellet pistols. On sweeper nights, after bar traffic died away, the quiet streets gave an opportunity to hone night shooting skills. Wagers were cast in similar fashion to "Name That Tune." Flipping a coin determined first pick, and started the haggling. A dollar bet froze the challenge. A fully silhouetted target almost immediately brought a dollar challenge, whereas a bobbing head encouraged haggling.

"I can hit that rat for two bits," Dan said.

"Fifty."

"It's yours."

Ben took aim, fired, and made the kill.

"You ever feel like we're fighting the battle of the Alamo against the overwhelming odds of escalating evil?" Dan asked.

"Sure do. Take that one for fifty," Ben said.

"A buck."

"He just climbed out in the open for you? Not fair."

"Always whining," Dan shot. "Now I'm up fifty."

"Yeah, the Alamo. Just how I feel sometimes. Can't win. Hanging on for reinforcements, which ain't comin'."

"Worst part is all the depravity. Floods me every day. Where's fairness? The triumphant good? Ben, are we even making a difference?"

"On top the pickle bucket, for a buck," Ben said taking the shot.

"Easy shot. You're up fifty. We make a difference. It'd be worse without us."

"When are the citizens going to realize crime's their problem too?"

"Probably never. Never worried 'em before, why now?"

"The more I research this evolution stuff, the less logical it is. I reckon I'm rethinking the God angle."

"Interesting, you've declared God dead."

"I know. Not sayin' I was wrong. It's just not coming together like I expected."

"It's been a long haul. As a cop you've developed a legalistic process of evaluating. You're proof oriented."

"Whatever, logic favors a superior intelligence behind it all."

"God always did have my vote."

"I know, but look at the mess it's in!"

"Shhh. Not so loud you're scarin' off targets."

"Life reflects God set it all spinning like a giant top, but He doesn't seem to care if it topples and falls."

"Maybe you don't understand Him," Ben said. "Who understands our job, except another cop?"

"Maybe, but He don't seem involved anymore."

"He still pokes his finger in, but it's through the Church. You gotta go to Mass, do the fasting, try and be good an' all. Then when you mess up, confess, do penance, and be absolved."

"Makes it kind of hard to stay on His good side, don't it?"

"Yeah, it's constant maintenance."

"Who's that turning in?" Dan asked seeing another cruiser approach.

O'Toole pulled alongside them and asked, "Can three play?"

"A buck's top wager," Dan answered, "and we will take your money."

"I can afford it, but I'll need the loan of an air gun."

Dan explained the game, and they waited a few minutes for the targets to reemerge. The first target was no more than a half form against a dark background.

"I can hit that rat for a buck," O'Toole said without hesitation. Smirking and anticipating his first dollar, Dan handed him the air gun. O'Toole took aim, "whap." He hit the target.

"You've played before," Ben said.

"Not at this fine a club, but I generally hit what I aim at. You think sergeants are desk bound, can't shoot?"

"Night shooting practice is hard to come by on a desk," Dan said.

"That's why I don't pass up a chance. Firing at night's too critical."

"Yeah, usually first shot blinds you."

"We gonna shoot or just talk?" Ben asked.

After twenty minutes, O'Toole paid fifty cents to each. Ben looked at the two quarters in his palm. "Wow, and I thought we'd get rich on Pooh-Bear!"

"There you go trying to think again."

They proceeded over to the pumps and gassed the vehicle. Dan twisted the cap tight as the radio sounded. "Car 507, Car 507, 3746 Llewelyn, Apartment 410, investigate medical emergency, premature delivery, no rescue units available."

"That's ours," Ben informed the dispatcher, "We'll make it."

Arriving Ben grunted, "It's four stories."

Crossing the threshold they encountered a circling open centered staircase with landings every five steps. Their narrowness amplified the feeling you were ascending the edge of a cliff overlooking an abyss. On the first step Dan murmured, "Why are all the medicals on the top floor?"

"Murphy's Law. I wouldn't trust that banister either."

Two doors down from the head of the stairs, they found 410. The door, already open a crack, swung wide from Dan's knock. A woman in her early thirties was poised in a Sumo wrestler stance half way to the door. She paused, turned on the balls of her feet, wobbled like a duck to the couch, and collapsed into it. Between pants, she screamed, "I'm havin' a baby…" Three loud groans later she finished "...takes me – oh — takes me to the hospital!"

"What's your name, Ma'am?" Dan asked.

"Ruthanna…Uhhh nooo. Ru-u-thanna Johanson. Everybody just—OHHH, Ohh, Ohhho, there goes one—calls me Sapphire!"

"Sapphire, has your water broken?"

"We gots to go."

"How far apar..."

"Oh Lordy, Gets me..... ohhhhh, oh pleeeease....gets me a goin'!"

"How far apart are your pains, ma'am?"

"Fast!"

"How fast? Ten min..."

"Ten minutes! Shoooo man! Da's fas' enough. We gotta be goin', now."

"Has your water broke?"

"Not yet." she said groaning and panting.

"Where's the father?"

"Heavens oooonlys knows, ain't seen Abraham for six months," she blurted out between groans. "Ain't you goin's t' take me?"

"Is this your first baby?"

"Yeh! Yeh! Can we goes now? I's havin's child!"

"I understand Sapphire, but we're not medically equipped. We're not paramedics and none are available right now. We have no stretcher."

"But, da child, be comin' NOW!"

"Your water hasn't broken, and this is your first. It's best we wait for the paramedics."

"Tells da child. He's da one nots waitin'. Y'us got a polices car, don't y'u?"

"Of course, but, ma'am, its four flights down THOSE stairs!"

"Well, bells of fire," she sputtered rising into a stoop. "Y'u 'ns as worthless as that no 'count Daddy. No more talk!" Waddling toward the door she insisted, "I'm goin' now! Wit' y'us or not?"

"Sapphire," Ben pleaded, "That's a lot of narrow steps!"

"I'll gets down 'em and still give da Devil 'is do. Y'us just drives me to da General." She grabbed her overnight bag and shuffled down the hall to the stairs.

"What we gonna do?" a nervous Dan asked Ben who shruged his shoulders.

Reaching the top step, Ruthanna looked back at the officers. "What y'us waitin' f'r? Sure 'n fire can't be waitin' fir y'us all night! Ohhhhhhh! There's 'nother one!" She dropped to her knees leaning against the shaky banister.

"Let's get her out of here!" Ben exclaimed rushing to her. Taking her right arm, he slowly descended the steps backwards while Dan brought up the rear bracing her left. Ruthanna positioned and supported between them, backs to the wall, they slowly side-stepped down the stairs one at a time. On the first landing Sapphire's knees doubled up as another contraction rippled her. With a loud moan she collapsed on the stairway and Ben felt an unanticipated wetness soaking his left shoe. Looking down, his worst fear loomed before him. Her water had broken!

Dan stood bent at the waist, straddling two steps and holding Ruthanna's arm. His position privileged him to see Ben's facial expression throughout the "foot washing." However, Dan didn't put it together until Ben moved with a 'squish' and announced, "Her water broke!"

Ruthanna regained her squatting stance. Another spasm turned her limbs to Slinkys. Down she went in a sprawl. Ben knelt precariously on the step's edges, "Just keep calm Sapphire, one step at a time."

"LOOORRDEEE, OHHH, LORD-EE!" She trumpeted her knees almost tumbling Ben. The child burst into its new world.

Ben's stance positioned him to intercept the baby which otherwise would have slid down the stairs. Acting instinctively, he supported the newborn in his arms checking for air passage obstructions. The child sucked on Ben's finger. When he withdrew his hand, the baby cried. Mother Ruthanna heard the child and burst forth laughing and crying alternatively. Dan cheered.

The surreal drama had drawn several people out of their apartments. The intensity of what they witnessed froze them in the moment. The laughter broke the tension and they applauded laughing and crying in empathy.

"Outdoor plumbing!" Ben shouted.

Ben regained his composure carefully conveying the child to Ruthanna who cradled him in her arms. He looked up at Dan, and barked, "If you can stop howlin', go find a sturdy chair and some clean towels!"

One of the bystanders responded, "I got one."

"Is it a strait back?"

"Is that important?"

"Yes, it's for a chair lift."

"What do we tie the cord off with?" Ben asked Dan.

"Nothing. It'll wait 'till we get to the hospital."

The neighbors returned. One had a sturdy oak chair. Others offered towels.

Dan squeezed the back of the chair onto the steps between the banister and mother, while Ben helped her wrap the newborn in a blue bath towel. With the officers' help, Ruthanna cradling the child scooted onto the chair. Ben gripped the chair's legs. Dan took a firm hold on the back of the chair by the seat. Tilted, the back laid against his chest and his arms restrained the patient. Tediously they worked mother and child down the remaining stairs. Ben's every step squished as he went. Onlookers followed single file like a bunny-hop train dance.

Painstakingly the patients were transferred to the rear seat of the cruiser, and the owner reclaimed his chair. Closing the rear door Dan said, "I'll drive. You clean up." He wasted no time getting behind the wheel. Dan radioed ahead to the hospital as the car sped off, lights flashing, siren whaling.

Ben was seated, shoe removed, patting at his wet foot with a donated towel. He quickly gave up on his foot and hopelessly tried to clean the blood from his hands, forearms and uniform.

"I thought you said this was your first baby," Dan shouted back to Ruthanna loud enough to overcome the siren. "Came awful fast?"

"Not my FIRST baby. This 'n's number six. It's first one for me an' Abraham. M' other child'ens gots different daddies. M' sister took 'em wit' her, when I called y'us."

"Ohhh!" Dan gulped. *No more questions. These histories just confuse me more. Drive, mind my own business.*

They arrived quickly at the hospital. The staff met them with a gurney, and nurses wheeled Ruthanna away. She stopped them at the door calling back, "What's your names?"

"Black and White."

"No, y'ur first names. Can't be callin' m' child Black

White Johanson!"

"That's Big Ben," Dan said.

"And, this here's Preacher man Dan," Ben added.

She motioned for the nurses to continue. "Benjamin Daniel Johanson," she said to the new born.

On the way to their cruiser, Dan complained, "How come you get first billing? What's wrong with Daniel Benjamin?"

"Cause I did all the work, and she knows it."

"Bet my pay check her opinion differs!"

"Your foot go squishy-squish? Mine does. Get over it!"

Opening the patrol car door, Ben paused holding out his arms. "Look at this mess."

"Yep, you're a bloody mess. Alistia gonna think the cop thing's a cover for a butcher shop job."

"Alistia isn't ever gonna see this shirt."

They rode a few minutes in silence before Ben reflected, "Sure in a hurry to get in this cruel world. Too young to know better, I reckon."

"Well Ben, on the time of our coming we really have no say; and refusing suicide, little on the going out, either." He paused as the newspaper delivery truck flagged him over. He pulled beside it.

"Morning Greg," Ben greeted.

"Peaceful night?" he asked handing a couple papers to Ben.

"A fun one, thanks."

Seeing Ben's arms Greg's eyes widened.

Dan pulled away. "And I might add, if there's a God, we cannot leave one moment sooner than He decides."

"When you get down to the bone, we don't have much choice in anything. Do we?"

"Well, during our allotted time we're left to make choices: good, bad, hard, easy, the indifferent flip of a coin. Problem is the good ones are hardest and scarcest. I, for one, think the world could use some help?"

"But, who you gonna trust? Look at all the people claiming to have the answers; all different."

"Yep, but makes sense to me; whoever put it together left instructions."

"Scrathin' that itch again? Everybody got a theory. With all the different religions, which one's got it right?"

"Not sure it matters. What if I read it for myself? I'm not the smartest bear in the woods, but I managed an engineering degree. Can't be that complicated, can it?"

"Now there's a novel idea. Let me know what you find out."

They fell silent for a few minutes and then Dan said solemnly, "Want to ask you something personal, serious like, if you don't mind."

"What?"

"Well it's real personal. Don't have to answer if you don't want."

"What?"

"Well, I'm kind of wondering…never mind. It's way too personal."

"Out with it! WHAT?

"Well as old as you are and all…I was wonderin'," Dan paused. Ben stared at him in anticipation. The silence itself shouted "WHAT?"

"I was wonderin', Partner,... this your first step-child?"

Ben ignored the remark and Dan parked chuckling. As they came through the door the squad was forming for dismissal.

"Fall In! Let's go home," barked Sergeant Fleischer.

Ben joined the line in his ruined uniform which stopped the proceedings while Dan related an exaggerated account. Ten minutes later the line straightened and the sergeant moved down it collecting paperwork. When he came to the end of the line, he smiled at the Duo. "Ben, I'll write the paper tomorrow for reissue. You two sure do have a picnic out there, don't you?"

"Yes, Sir, every night," Ben answered.

What a proposition. Why shouldn't we have a picnic?" Dan thought.

"Heard Dan had a visit from Snoopy tonight," Fleischer

smirked.

"Yes, Sir, he saved him from the Barron," Jansen laughed.

Dan looked at Ben, "How'd that make the rounds already?"

"Get Snoopy Dog straightened out, did you?" Fleischer asked rhetorically as he side-stepped to Follert, "By the way, war aces didn't have pilot licenses."

The squad inharmoniously broke out singing, "Hang on Snoopy, Snoopy hang on…"

"That'll do! You'll make my ears bleed," Fleischer interrupted. "We do want to go home, don't we?" The question restored order. "You two get Lieutenant Hess any parkers?"

"Parkers?" Ben and Dan asked each other. "Was it our night for parkers?"

"He emphatically instructed me, 'check their parkers'."

"Serge, we got two felonies: one a drugs distribution felony," Dan replied. "Ben took time out for a mid-wife class. Only got eight hours."

"Any parkers?"

"Tell him! We want to go home," yelled a couple other officers.

"Eleven," Ben answered. "Okay?"

Fleischer took the paperwork from them, and snapped, "Dis-missed!"

Dan, Ben, and Gary left together splitting off in the parking lot like a Blue Angels fly by. "I'll be home in bed before either of you," Gary quipped.

The clock at the door stipulated Dan's route home. *Ten after- the longest.* At home he would lay aside his badge and gun. The quest Dan could never lay aside.

Chapter Six

Must It Make Sense?

Dan undressed and slipped into a pair of short, cotton pajamas. He lazily swayed on the "zoo's" swing nursing three ounces of Cabernet. Trouble curled in his lap content as Dan stroked him.

Broke even tonight against the Evil One, Whatever its worth, for He is content to linger in the wings of tomorrow.

Trouble scampered across the end table, jumped on the floor-lamp's post, and tried to climb it. He slid to base, tumbled head over tail, and then ran off chasing a weasel ball erratically around the room.

"A little mishap beset you my fur ball friend? Good thing I screwed it to the floor!" *You don't have to be a frisky ferret to be susceptible to mishap. The ogre of crime is a master at coercing indiscretions into tragedy. Readily energizing bar fights, hooker's hustles, domestics, robberies, desperate addicts. Any and all, turn deadly in a breath.*

Trouble abandoned the ball to climb the outside of his cage and ascend the window screen. "Not the windows!" Dan yelled. Trouble's claws dug in as he froze in place at Dan's hurried rising. He plucked Trouble from the screen. "You know the penalty!" he scolded placing him in the small cage without access to the play area.

The spinning ceiling fan stirred stale musk laden air. So, Dan opened the windows before returning to the swing. As he sipped the wine, fresh morning air seeped inward.

I'm torn between a God in control, and a world falling apart! Affliction lurks in the shadows, pouncing at will on mankind. Is God distracted with other worlds? Where's the hope in that? How can evil be master over the Supreme's creation? So many mysteries, so few answers. Must life make sense?

Dan went to his bedroom and reclined against a wedge pillow. *There must be a balance between depravity and hope.* The light seeped passed the curled blind's edge. *Those useless old shades!* One beam fell across his Dad's Bible on the dresser. *Oh yes, Pop, I still hear you promising, all the answers are in the 'Manual.' I'm reading it. There is much wisdom, but answers of my purpose are not apparent. I have not forgotten YOUR God didn't protect you! Your promises do not erase the scars. They have failed everyone I have dared to love! But, Benjamin Daniel Johanson—now there's promise!*

However, even this feeling of joy was dampened by expectations of a dismal future. *Would Benjamin Daniel Johanson someday be president, win the Nobel Prize, cure tragic diseases, or will darkness draw him into vice? Maybe he'll prevent more suffering than he'll cause. He will—he must grab goodness with the resolve of a clenched fist.*

If every night brought such promise, Dan would feel his time well spent. Benjamin Daniel owned a heart not yet tainted by the world. Dan wanted to believe in him. The ambience found in the innocence of birth took Dan to his childhood. Drawing water from his grandfather's well, he drank from a bent tin dipper. The clear, cool, crisp potion refreshed his weariness on those hot summer days.

I'll see to it! I will give Daniel Johanson the 'Handbook.' He smiled. *Sounds better when I leave Ben off.* Dan sensed a moment's silence, then in emphatic: *Why stop with him? Indeed, the bigger the sample the more valid the test.*

Chapter Seven

Full Moon Nights

When Dan reported to work he went in the station, retrieved the keys for his cruiser, and returned to his Corvette. Opening the trunk he was wrestling a duffel-bag out as his partner pulled in next to him. Once the duffel was clear, Ben asked, "Need a hand, Partner?"

"I got it, NOW!" Dan lugged the bag to the cruiser and stowed it in the trunk.

Ben waited for his partner by the rear stoop snorting at an occasional whiff of the nearby dumpster.

"Evening, Ben." Dan greeted walking past him.

"I wait next to this cesspool and you're not tellin' me what's goin' down?" Ben challenged.

"Overwhelmed by your help," Dan replied entering the building. He passed Castleman at a table sharpening his pocket knife, "Nice knife." Ben trailed him to his locker. "It's my lunch bag," Dan informed.

"Uh-huh, that's it? Lunch bag!"

"Don't worry, brought enough for you."

"Thanks, but I'm still worried."

"Fall In!" The command echoed through the lockers.

The invitation of uncertainty promised nothing as equally as everything. Sergeant O'Toole's "tallyho" snatched the milling officers into a rigid line. What awaited them in the dark streets, cluttered alleys, and dens of iniquity while the city slept—none but God knew? Would it be a pat on the shoulder or a bullet in the back? They didn't waste time thinking about it. Their families did that. "Mommy, will

Daddy come home?" Would only a piece of Daddy erode on this watch? Or would Daddy be lost?

Even Sergeant O'Toole was apathetic resulting in tradition prevailing over purpose in a curt inspection. In short time officers gathered around the briefing tables. Before they were half seated, O'Toole began.

"First up, a Chief's directive; don't leave your cruisers unlocked. Second, too many tickets are kicking back. Get them right the first time. As for the BOLOs, not much here. Wanted for Defrauding a Vehicle for Hire and Robbery, male black or Hispanic, tall thin and dark complexion. Also, for robbery on Calhoun three males, 16-20, medium build, fled in small white vehicle.

"C'mon Serge, you're wasting our coffee time. If they were my brothers, I wouldn't know." Harkins murmured.

"It's the wants. Not my fault crimes have useless descriptions. I give you what's there. It's your job to make something out of it. He then read with unconcerned effort several more vague bulletins, and ended with, "If you corner, 'Some Dude,' haul him in."

"Okay, wake up now!" Sergeant Fleischer snapped responding to O'Toole's nod, "New hot-lists. During slumps, check a few plates." He tossed copies on the table prompting sarcasm as they went around.

"A-TEN-TION!" Came a shout from the front lobby.

Within moments, a black officer in his early fifties, five foot ten, and 175 pounds with a bur cut entered the briefing room. Captain Cornelius Kirk, the District Commander, seldom frowned, yet was known for his no nonsense approach. He was the anti-thesis of Lieutenant Hess and came up through the ranks. Peers and charges alike considered him capable. Unlike most commanders who were rarely seen after sunset, Kirk participated in briefings regularly. He was proud to be part of the Police Division. As the District Commander, he was careful to bolster the police image and thus mindful to praise his officers in public while chastising in private. He majored on getting the job done, keeping it legal, and minored on details. Respected by all,

Kirk had a reputation for backing his men.

"As you were," he barked entering the room.

Kirk took a seat in the corner. The officers put on their "captain's come to meeting manners."

Fleischer, cleared his throat and continued, "Saved this for last. It's not so vague. Wanted for Breaking and Entry, Defrauding a Vehicle for Hire and Robbery is a male, possibly Mexican or Puerto Rican, forty-ish, five foot six, hundred twenty-five, long black hair, cut off jeans, T-shirt, and a Yankee's cap.

"He's believed to have stolen a small safe, from the Dew Drop Inn. He flagged a cab, was transported to 4512 Victor Street, and couldn't pay. The suspect offered the contents of the safe to the driver, but efforts to open it failed. He then brandished a knife, robbed the cabbie, and fled. The cabbie reported the robbery making no mention of the safe until the officers saw it." With the wave of his hand to the lieutenant he ended, "Honesty prevails again!"

"Burglaries are down from last year," Hess began a statistical evaluation of relief goals. "Robberies are equivalent, and misdemeanor arrests are up due to DUI emphasis. Felony crime is up eleven percent yet the arrests are down five. Movers can always use effort."

Then glaring at Dan and Ben, Hess said. "Some parking improvement is noted from last week, but it's inadequate."

OH, you're gonna get parkers all right!

Before Hess could go further, Kirk stood and interrupted, "That's a fine outline of the objectives, Lieutenant. I'm sure the men are motivated to meet them. However, I didn't come to talk stats, so I'm going to pull rank. Have my say."

"Yes, Sir," acknowledged Hess stepping back from the table.

Kirk did not move into the space, but spoke from where he stood making eye contact with each officer. "I know you have heard the complaints Internal's investigating in District Four. I've read the forms. It is a fully justified use of force. We've had some criticism recently from those do-goody-head-up-their-butts self-appointed oversight panels. We have fine street officers and you can be sure I.A. can clear it up.

"My concern is one of you might let it cause you hesitation. Men, hesitations out there," he pointed to the door, "will get you DEAD! Someone gives you good cause to use this," he brought his arm up from behind him thrusting a Porter night stick into the air like a band major. "I said if you have GOOD cause!" Kirk brought the stick down on the table top creating a loud 'WHACK!' The officers recoiled. "Then use it! You be right and I'll be backing you! There won't be any hesitating, right?"

"No, Sir!" the men shouted.

"Some low-life threatens you, what y'u gonna do?"

"STICK HIM!"

"And if you got to stick 'im…" he thrusting the stick upward bringing his left hand's encircling fingers down from the top of the mast stopping at the hilt "...stick 'im up to here!" A hush fell lasting a few seconds, then he calmly said "All right, go crush the crap out of crime, and don't get any on you. It's all yours, Lieutenant," he said briskly retreating. As Kirk passed through the lobby, "Beam me up Scotty," echoed down the hallway with the closing of the station door.

"Now about the parkers," Hess said pausing to look at Dan and Ben.

"Trust us. You're getting parkers," Dan said.

"Yes, your effort has been noted. The Chief's Office called. He had a visit from Father Joseph Gilligan. Seems you two managed to tow the parish station wagon..."

Laughter drowned Hess out. He scowled waiting for a lull. "He's expecting a good explanation. SO AM I. Right after roll call."

"It was an OTP," Dan defended.

Hess moved on to his new crime fighting aid. "Men, technology is making our job easier. I've entered the crime stats in a computer and generated this Robbery Probability Report. There's a copy for everyone," he said laying papers on the end of the table.

Dan didn't consider himself computer literate, but wasn't ignorant either. He listened to Hess but did not hear. *Oh great! Now he's into computers.*

"Computers are the wave of the future."

Yeah, yeah, yeah, street cops are perceived by the paper shufflin' brass-hats as slow and incompetent.

"Robbery Squad compiled the last six month's offenses. The composite trends are shown for our area."

A perfect gadget for you. It depends on man's thinking in order to do man's thinking. It ain't gonna help you!

"This report highlights probable robbery targets."

Garbage in. Garbage out! "Sir," interrupted Dan, "what stats is this report based on?"

"The Robbery Task Force compiled city data according to my parameters."

"Excuse me, but how's city wide trends, going to predict District Five incidents?"

"Officer Black, do you have a programming background?"

"No sir, I'm just trying to determine the value of the conclusions."

"Value? Do you even own a computer?"

"Not yet, I'm waiting for them to prove their worth before I fork out the dough."

Ben poked Dan whispering, "Shut up, fool. We're in deep enough."

"I don't see you as much of an authority then," Hess said. "So please don't waste our time with what you don't know."

"Yes, Sir." *Your hunger for success deludes you to quench your thirst with saltwater.*

"Well sir, I'm anxious to learn," Gary said. "This statement on page two; is saying the most probable location for a robbery is a Dairy Queen at 0-200 hours? Sir - uh - we don't have any Dairy Queens?"

"We have some 'queens' up on the hill at the Lazy 'Loins' Club," Reynolds injected.

"All the DQ's close at 2300 hours," Fleischer said

entering the briefing at the end of the discussion.

Hess glowered at Fleischer. "We have King-Kwiks. They're number three for you flatfoots who can't read. They're open all night, and they've been hit hard!"

Fleischer turned away from the lieutenant and mouthed, "OOPS", then took a chair off to the side.

"I don't need a 'comp-u-tator' to tell me all-night markets are a robbery risk," Dan said.

"Stow it, stupid," Ben whispered again.

Hess ignored Dan. "The R-P-R puts them at high risk between 0-300 and 0-430 hours. That means we're going to give them extra patrol. 507, 515, 508, and 501, note it on your log sheets."

"Lieutenant, considering your report, I'll volunteer to stake one out," Martin said.

"There are four King-Kwiks in our area. We barely have the manpower to sit on one. Choose one, the others get neglected. My way is better. But, I appreciate your initiative, Officer Martin."

A couple officers sneered across the table at Martin, "Appreciate your interest, cherry picker!"

"Run 'r through ag'in, Lieutenant," Willie Clemmons said. "Find out which one they gonna hit."

"Willie!" Reynolds responded in surprise. Clemmons was routinely reserved and mousey. "There's a sign; even Willie 's stirred."

"Yeah, if it's any good," Gary added. "I'll bet my next detail check it kicks out West Fork Stop-N-Go. Be worth sitting on. Quick getaway to I-74."

Hess frowned sensing an insincerity in Gary's voice, although, it could've been the paper airplane sailing past his head. It missed, but the look Hess gave Dan would melt marble.

Dan displayed his best poker face. *This could cost me more days. Naw, he didn't see me.*

"Anything else?" Hess asked without waiting for a reply, "Dismissed! Hit the streets! Black, you and White, in my office!"

Augh! He did see it!

"Yes, Sir," they answered.

On the way Ben griped at Dan, "Enjoy you getting my butt chewed right off the line. Do help motivate me the rest of the shift."

"Anytime. I'm here for you. Besides I thought Lieu's report flew well."

Lieutenant Hess' door was open, and they entered. He stood peering out the window ignoring them for several minutes. "Simple question," he began in a friendlier than usual tone still looking out the window. "Why'd you put the hook to the parish station wagon?"

"It was an O-T-P," Dan responded. "Have to take them where we find them. Can't make 'em up."

Hess turned to face Dan. His expressionless face looked tired.

"I appreciate your efforts to comply with my orders, but towing Father Gilligan's car? That's going too far. Did you know he baptized the captain's whole family?"

"No, Sir," came the joint reply.

"The priest's car, for God's sake!" Hess said banging his fist on the desktop.

"God has nothing to do with it," snorted Dan. "And, no, you didn't order us to tow the priest's car. But then, you didn't tell us not to. We just enforce the violations. Our cruiser isn't equipped with a crystal ball. We can't pick and choose ..."

"Procedures, procedures! You are supposed to query the plate. When it came back registered to 'Saint Bonifice Brotherhood', it ought to have rung bells, if the belfries weren't empty!"

"You telling us to show a bias based on religion?"

"You two knew exactly what you were doing—calculated—very calculated. Now it's come back to haunt you. I want a Form Seventeen right away. You explain it to the Chief. And keep me out of it, or you'll be a foot patrol on the floodwall. You get the drift?"

"Yes, Sir," they replied.

“If common sense were gunpowder you two wouldn’t have enough to pop a cap!”

“Sir, are you ordering us not to enforce a particular section of the traffic code?” Dan baited.

“Of course not! I am telling you to get your parkers like everybody else, and not to enforce, let alone tow, O-T-Ps unless you have a specific complainant. Understand: a specific complainant?”

“Yes, Sir.” With sardonic smiles and a military snap they turned toward the door.

“I have not dismissed you! Get back here!”

They returned to the front of the desk without the snap. Hess waited, looking out the window. At his pleasure, he turned back to them.

“You WILL get your parkers some other way, so the backwash doesn’t come across my desk!”

“Yes, Sir.”

“Have the Form Seventeen on my desk before morning. Now go do some serious police work. Do something worthwhile; like a good felony robbery arrest. Dismissed!”

“We don’t have time for felonies. We’re doing parkers and doors,” Dan said.

“That’s borderline. Watch yourself. You are dismissed.”

They turned to depart. Ben went out ahead of Dan. At the door Dan stopped and faced the lieutenant, “Suppose Widow Tolson would agree on the value of parkers?”

“YOU are dismissed.”

Before the echo fell silent, they retrieved their war bags and were out the back door.

Chapter Eight

Canines, Crazies, and Clowns

"If they left it on empty again, I swear, I'll pick their lockers and fill their hats with cottage cheese," Ben said. "I might have to pick up their slack, but I don't have to like it."

"Sounds like something I'd do," Dan laughed.

Their beat car was near the stoop. Twice this month the previous relief failed to gas it. Dan and Ben stored their gear, and were seated in the car before Dan spoke again. "Did Hess seem a bit friendlier than usual tonight?"

Ben turned the ignition and the engine came to life. The fuel gage read "Three-quarters." Putting it in reverse he asked, "What about Hess?"

"He didn't shout as much. Maybe he's being cagey. You think he knows I tossed the airplane?"

"Based on our last parley, No!"

On the way out of the parking lot Gary Follert waved them over. "You guys up for Box Town after your consultation?"

"Always," Dan replied. "If it gets busy, it may take two cars."

Ben waited behind the wheel. Dan slid out and accepted a square cardboard box. He wrestled it past the prisoner screen onto the back seat, and they were quickly *en route*.

"Partner, did you notice the similarity between Hess' plan and our stake-out request last week?" Dan asked.

"Matter of fact. Milton warned us I-74 would get hit this week."

"Is it a coincidence Hess turned it down 'cause our snitch is 'untested' and tonight comes up with this R-P-R?"

"Was it Shakespeare who said, 'Something smells of fish'?"

"Don't try to be literate. It doesn't work for you."

"Okay, it's fishy!"

Box Town visits began five years ago, after Gary was assigned his beat. The railroad yard under the Hopple Street Viaduct became his responsibility, including the hobos and other homeless camped there. The viaduct overhead spared the cardboard city from most of the rain. Delivery drivers from nearby warehouses discarded large appliance boxes, and the inhabitants appropriated them as needed. The boxes offered protection from wind and kept the dew off. Although dampness destroyed the boxes' rigidity in a week, they procured a new one and discarded the old on the campfire.

They did their best to live off the land and handouts. The citizens of Box Town policed their own closely and evicted the true scoundrels and violent. Whether by nature or preference, they kept to themselves. Occasionally pressed by some privation, some occasionally migrated into the nearby city committing a crime of chance.

After several dealings with the Box Town people, Gary approached Dan asking for advice. "I arrested one of those box campers under the viaduct for stealing food. The mini-market manager wouldn't let me pay for it and demanded prosecution. Then he's a no-show in court. I'm spinning my wheels. You have any ideas how to turn such a handicap into a resource?"

"Not off hand, but the way Ben and I got a handle on the housing area was walkin' and talkin'. Get to know 'em, develop rapport. Not all of 'em are deadbeats, I'll bet."

"You know Mr. Free, the guy I was telling you about, he was grateful. Thought I got him off the hook. He said if he could repay, to let him know. What's a homeless bum gonna do for me?"

"Cooperation and information, maybe?"

"Walkin' and talkin' makes some sense. Since they seem to always need food, what if we could get something together for them ever so often?"

"We could work it a couple nights a month. See what comes of it."

It wasn't rigidly scheduled but a couple times on the Night Run they managed to drop in. Williams and Vaught carried it over from the following relief, but the other relief had no volunteers.

When Dan and Ben arrived at Box Town, Gary stood at the fire talking with Mister Burl. Two dozen men and women were in the camp. It was seldom they encountered anyone under eighteen. Burl, the camp king, officiated with a scepter called the *Dragon's Tooth*: a polished fang shaped root crowned with lion's head carving. He settled all disputes in camp, and his word was law.

"Good evening, Mister Burl, how goes things in camp?" Dan asked.

"'Tis fair to midlin," he replied then turning he waved his scepter in an arching motion and spoke to the inhabitants. "Perk Ye ears Ye 'road-dawgs'. These 'white tops' get glad handed in this camp. They be 'true-dos', and 'overstands' y'ur lot."

"Mister Burl, you're a mystery to me," Dan said. "You have savvy, you have means, and you could easily live a normal life?"

"Oh, but I do."

"Well, it's still a mystery to me."

"It'd be no mystery, if'n you'd chosen to chase rails at nineteen. Back then no-one hassled y'u. A Bo-chaser 'd run y'u, but not wit' anger. Could jump a ballin' jack, top, bottom or inside. Find a 'pay-house' or 'pogey' along the tracks anytime, for a meal. I've been sea to sea chasin' m' giggles, and eyeballed it all with ne'r want for more. I'd not trade f'r y'ur treasures neither."

"Can't argue against what I don't understand, but those days are gone. Aren't they?"

"Indeed, countries changed. Barrel houses be scarce and the 'yeggs' 're many. Violence binds the hearts of the common people, and fear closed their doors to us. It's only been in the last few years my kind've known want and hunger. Your visits are an open boxcar on a cold day."

"It's not much. Maybe it's a start."

"We ain't got time to gab all night, Dan," Gary said. "Burl, there's two boxes of sandwiches and apples in the cruisers."

"Any tiger milk?" asked Burl.

"Ain't never been, don't start expecting."

"Pays t' be careful here," he acknowledged turning to two men standing nearby. "Smokey, you and Plug fetch 'em 'nose-bags' out of the 'bubble cans'."

Two men hustled toward the cruisers. Burl noticed Dan's gaze following the one with a mangled arm. "Midnight creeper got him years ago. He does fine."

The two men pulled the boxes out, carried them over and sat them by the campfire. Dan, Ben and Gary walked through the cardboard dwellings handing out sandwiches and fruit. The sandwiches were peanut butter and jelly. They kept well in the heat. For the first time tonight, each of Dan's handouts contained a small New Testament.

Knowing Burl's custom, they fed everyone else before offering the king a sandwich.

"Thank you, what have we?" he said peeling the bread back. "Peanut butter; one of my favorites. Goes well with stone stew. Would you like some?"

"I appreciate the offer," Dan said picking up a small cup and dipping it in a steaming pot. He blew it cool and drank. Ben and Gary followed. While the empty boxes burned on the fire, they sipped stew and talked individually with the indigent tribe. The inhabitants distrusted outsiders, and had their own culture. With kindness and fair dealings over time the officers earned acceptance with the regulars. The newcomers respected Mister Burl's authority. Within thirty-five minutes the officers returned to their patrol assignment.

"You know, Partner," Ben said, "that stone stew's BLAND! Might as well drink hot water."

"What else have they to offer?"

"If you weren't serious it'd be funny. That's really sad." Ben scanned the interior of an all-night-market as they circled through the parking lot. "Those visits make me uneasy."

"I understand dogs makin' you uneasy, but circlin' an all nighter?"

"No, Box Town."

"I don't get it?"

"It confuses me. A few of them are like Fred, wanting to work, but hard times blindsided them. If they got a break, like Fred's grocery job, things could be different. I can relate to that, but the majority have skills, could work, and some were professionals making more 'an us. They're content livin' in a box! Don't have to, so why do they?"

"It's not the fault of Box Town, but the result. The product of, uh, how can I say it poetically? Uh… lives dashed against the reefs of a daily grind; hopes carried away by raging tides of empty meaning; broken people washed up on a deserted beach."

"That's, just existing!"

"Sometimes I feel stuck on a rudderless ship in a stormy sea. Be honest Ben, ever want to surrender and drift irresponsibly? Just existing?"

"Are you nuts? I'd shoot myself before I'd let my family live like that! You have?"

"Well, not so much Box Town, but the life of no responsibility."

"Kinda enjoy my life the way it is, thank you."

"I yearn for a cabin way back in the woods like Thoreau's. Let the world march into the River Wesser, as long as I have my Walden Pond!"

"You wouldn't be happy livin' alone in the woods?"

"I'm not so sure, Ben. Thoreau speaks to my heart when he says 'for what is the use of a house, if you haven't a tolerable planet to put it on'. In case you haven't noticed; society's growing more and more intolerable."

Is that why you took up policing; to make this planet tolerable? You've been smoking Mary-Jane in your pipe."

"It should be more than tolerable. It should be a joy."

"That's not reality. There's good and bad in everything. You put up with the bad to enjoy the good stuff."

"Ben, what you don't see is Box Town people feel totally insignificant. They see themselves only as a gear in the time machine propelling life toward suffering and death. Their hope for a utopia has evaporated, and they're crushed by lack of purpose. Box Town is built on the ashes of destitute dreams and dehydrated hope."

"I see; you understand them, because your dreams were bashed. Your own pity party? So, why haven't you joined 'em?"

"A valid point."

"And, your reason is?"

"Well, as tantalizing as my Walden Pond is, I rejected it for the same reason as Thoreau. How'd he say it? When he came to die, he'd discover he hadn't lived. I guess I'm too much like him. Afraid I'll miss some great joy. If I surrender, I'll never discover the purpose for which I struggled. To die never having had a purpose is unacceptable to me."

"I got news for you, Preacher. A lot of what you think you're missing is your own fault."

"I won't argue that. Maybe that's why I'm so hung up on my itch: why am I here and where I'm going?"

"Again with the itch!"

"Maybe so, Ben."

They patrolled quietly for several minutes before Ben spoke again. "Something else I didn't get. I saw 'em."

"Saw what?"

"Little black books. Them hobos don't read. What's that about?"

"Never know, but IF the *Handbook* has the answers. Maybe, I shouldn't be the only one reading it."

"Great, you've found your purpose and cured the itch."

"No, not yet, anyways."

"Then, what's with passin' out Bibles? Seems to me a bit hypocritical."

"Not so. There's a big difference. Hypocrites profess as true what they don't believe. I'm up front. I'm not sure, but I think this *Handbook of Life* might have the answers."

"You're one confused puppy dog!"

"I think there's a good chance the *Handbook* can reveal our purpose. What better place than Box Town to test the theory?"

"Test it!"

"Oh come on, the *Handbooks* aren't radioactive."

"You're finally comin' unglued!"

"What's it gonna hurt?"

"Give me a break. Let me see one of them *Handbooks*," Ben said reaching for Dan's pocket.

"Hey, don't get personal!" Dan said batting his hand away.

"Pocket's empty!"

"You really want one?"

"Sure, I got a right to be as fulfilled as them hobos."

"Since you're beggin'."

"I ain't beggin'! Forget it."

Dan extended his hand. A small book flipped up from the palm.

"How DID you do that?"

"Do what? And, it sounds like beggin' to me."

"Never mind," Ben took the book and opened it to the front. "As I thought! It's a New Testament Bible!"

"I know what it is. I've been given 'em out all night."

"That beats all. You, who swore off God, now passing out Testaments!"

"So, we aren't on speaking terms, so what? If the instructions are in there, I wan'a look at 'em."

"Uhhh? I'm not detective grade, but you're either sandbagging' me or gone 'gonzo.' What you expect those books to do? You see any evidence Box Town visits are changing anything?"

"I don't know. How can we know if ANYTHING we do helps?"

"Take it from a guy who's lit a bonfire of candles.

You're just doing personal penance again."

"Okay Ben, I've wrestled with my motives. Do I really care? Tell me, Ben, how much is enough? A greedy nature encourages hoarding, because we never feel it's enough. I fear poverty, and it causes me to be stingy. I have to fight it."

"Sometimes I feel guilty," Ben admitted, "Like I'm playin' them for cooperation. Even so, I have to take care of my family first. Who else is gonna do it?"

"Good question, 'cause you can't count on God, if He don't exist."

"Since I do, I should be more charitable? What a pile of manure you're spreading."

"Not saying you're family shouldn't be first. I'm pointin' out a simple reality: We're all days away from Box Town. My nature tries to deny it, but I know it. Like squirrels in September, I'm bent to stockpile wealth and become materialistic."

"So your charity allows you to overcome guilt for pursuing the American Dream; financial independence?"

"Au de contraire, my biggest fear is climbing too high, because if ever providence knocked me to the bottom, it'd kill me. I'd just lay there in my own little box."

"You'd get back up no matter what knocked you down. Wouldn't be tolerable to be around, but up you'd get."

"Just to show you I've been reading it, the *Handbook* says I'm not in control of much, anyhow."

"Who's it say is?"

"God."

"Then why's it so messed up?"

"Haven't read that far."

"Car 508, 508," barked the radio, "domestic fight, 3910 Turrel Street, first floor."

"Okay on Turrel," Ben acknowledged. As Dan turned the car unhurriedly Ben remarked, "Hilda and Sam at it again. Bet he stayed out too late, came in too drunk."

"You left out her side," Dan added. "Out 'boozin' with a 'floozy'."

"No takers. With them two, it's always too late, too

drunk, and out with a floozy."

Sam Purdy sat on the bottom porch step. Hilda Fickens stood inside the screen door waiting and watching. When the patrol car pulled to the curb, Hilda bolted out the door and began flailing at Sam's head. Too drunk to flee, Sam cowered trying to block her with the eggbeater action of his arms.

Sam appeared in his late forties, but wasn't over thirty-six. His five-feet-eleven frame carried 125 pounds. Thin blond disheveled hair hung below his bony cheeks framing a week's growth of patchy beard. His unkempt hair sharply contrasted with his carefully waxed handlebar mustache. The beard and mustache glowed of auburn highlights. Sam's dirty stained T-shirt hung loosely: Torn neck to navel, one sleeve ripped off, the other stretched. A pair of faded blue jeans with the left knee ripped out, and black work shoes with no socks completed his dress.

Approaching, Dan thought, *He is the love of Hilda's life?*

A couple years younger, Hilda stood five-foot-three and weighed 140. A red sock tied her bleached blond hair in a ponytail. The attempt to match colors with a red tank top and red underwear, which showed pink through the white denim jeans, failed miserably. The unbecomingly tight jeans bore patches in the seat, crotch, and knees. A pair of torn flip-flops miraculously clung to her feet. Her toenails displayed bright red chipped polish.

Nearing, Dan could see Hilda was attacking Sam with a large plastic fly swatter. *And she is the love of Sam's life. What a package!* It took both officers to intervene and separate an irate Hilda without doing or receiving harm. Once they settled her down on the far side of the porch, Dan went back to check on Sam. "You okay, Pall? What's got Hilda riled?"

"I schwear Offisher, I ain't done noshin. I wussh down to Murphy's and hads me two – countsh 'em," he held up three fingers. "Jush two beerssh. I schwears."

Hilda's hearing was never an issue. Sam's statement

rekindled her anger. She raced halfway across the porch shouting. “Out wit’ some fluzzy, Thinks I don’t knows?”

Ben managed to keep her at a distance, but he couldn’t stop her raging.

“You two timin’ two faced tail tuckin’ egg suckin’ belly crawlin’ c’yote,” Hilda yelled, unconcerned about neighbors. “Y’u run off and left me here in dis hot‘r’n Hades house to go flam dang some floozy! I slaves for y’u! I washes y’ur clothes! I cooks y’ur food! I lives like a slave, and what ’s I get f’r it? He runs off, stays out all night, and get soused with some floozy!”

“I dids no such a things, t’ere ain’t no osher womas I tells you,” he replied somewhat sobered by the excitement.

“Then how’s come y’u don’t n’er spend time wit’ me likes y’u used ta? If’n y’u ain’t got no floozy? Y’u ain’t ne’r here. Might as well not be married.”

“Hilda, we aints never gots married—no hows,”

“Same if, Officer. Common wed, whats we is. Same ’s married, taint it, officer?”

“No church ceremony?” Dan scolded Sam. “How long you been together?”

“Ne’r on sheven years,” Sam admitted holding up three fingers.

“Should be long enough to know. Why not have a church hitch you for real?”

“Church!” Hilda shouted across the porch. “Don’t go t’ no church! And, I’ll tells y’u why. He don’t keep no job, ne’r can he keep ’is word, and I ain’t makin’ no oaths to no God that ain’t gonna be kept. Common law’s good ’nough for ’im.”

“Welsh I don’t wansh be common laawsh no mor’,”

“Me ne’thers,”

Dan, seeing a chance to settle things for the short term, cut their argument off. “Enough’s enough. Both of you!”

“Enough of ’is trash, be right,” Hilda agreed.

Ben ignoring Hilda, turned his attention to Sam. “If you aren’t married to Hilda, you can’t stay here. You have some place else you can go for a few days?”

“Shure. I cans go live wisch my brosher over on Vicsher Shreet.”

“In that case,” Dan said, “I can divorce you two, but you, Sam, will have to go over to your brother’s and stay. You understand?”

“Fine witsh me.”

Dan turned back to Hilda, “You want a divorce too? You’ll have to pay your own bills?”

“I pay the bills anyhow. He don’t have no real job. ‘Sides, he drinks up ’is money. Yeah, what I got t’ do?”

Ben looked questioningly at Dan who winked.

“Hilda—Sam,” Dan began solemnly, “you both know I’m ‘ordinated’ by the state—right?”

They had no idea, but nodded.

“Very well, then. Hilda, put your left hand palm down on Ben’s badge; and yours, Sam, on my badge – left hand Sam – left hand – easy – don’t fall over. Now raise the right one—the other right one Sam—left on badge, right in the air. Very good, Sam. Now hold it.”

There they stood on opposite ends of the porch, positioned side by side, yet separated by fifteen feet. Hilda’s one hand spread on Ben’s chest the other in the air like some frail Statute of Liberty. Sam stood similarly, swaying and waving as if bidding friends a bon-voyage. Dan craned his neck to face away to avoid the stench of Sam’s alcoholic breath. There they posed in view of numerous curious neighbors attracted by the commotion.

Dan couldn’t resist the theatrical nature of the circumstance. Taking hat in hand, he began in a loud voice, “Dearly beloved we are gathered in the presence of these witnesses,” waving his arm across the crowd, “for a most ‘unsolemn’ occasion. If any have reason these two should not be ‘disunioned’, speak or forever hold your peace.”

“Huh?” Ben asked.

“You have reason?”

“No, not me.”

Speaking to them in turn, Dan instructed, “I, say your name...”

Dan waited while they answered in unison.

"Having lived in common law marriage with, say the other person's name…"

Again Dan waited for them.

"Having given true and earnest effort to compliance of that common law..."

They repeated the phrase.

"And here-to-with, having failed for reasons other than my own..."

Again they repeated the phrase as best they could glaring at each other and becoming noticeably louder when saying "other than my own."

"Declare I, to disavow, decease, and descend my love for thee."

Each stammered their version of the last phrase, and Dan sidestepped having them face each other across the porch. That made Hilda nervous.

"I ain't a gonna kiss no dog face varmint!"

"No, no, no kissin'," Dan assured.

"Oh, alright then," she said resuming her Statute of Liberty pose.

"By the power vested in me by the governor of this state; this common law marriage is 'dis-unioned'."

Dan immediately looked Sam in the face, "Get your clothes, we'll take you over to Victor Street."

Sam, scurried, as best he could in his condition, gathered some clothes, and shoved them in a large paper bag.

"I'm ready."

After they dropped Sam off at his brother's and called back in service Ben asked, "Common law divorce? That's not in the Procedure Manual. Where do you come up with this stuff? What in God's green acres is 'Declare I disavow, decrease, and dispend my love?"

"Not sure that's exactly what I said."

"Close enough."

"You fussin'? Next time, you face to face it with the lizard breath drunk. Gag a maggot I tell you!"

They both chuckled then fell silent for a few minutes

reflecting on the absurdity of it all. But, Ben couldn't let it go. "Where'd you get that 'disavow' phrase?"

"Not from any book you've read."

"What does it mean? I hope the onlookers couldn't hear you."

"Had to 'dis-unionize' them somehow. It sounded pretty authoritative to me."

Another pause ensued before Ben broke in chuckling.

"I heard it with my own ears. Tell me the crowd couldn't. Tell me it's okay for me to show my face around there again."

"Honestly," Dan said, "their relationship reminds me of what my granddaddy called 'two ticks and no dog'. No wonder it don't work."

"Partner, what scares me the most is you don't even have to think stuff up. It just happens, doesn't it? Comes natural to you. I know you've got more marbles than most, but they're floatin' loose."

"Oh, shucks, Ben. You're jealous 'cause the voices only talk to me."

"Surreal thoughts just hover around waiting on your summons. And what'd we gain with all the theatrics?"

"How often do we get dispatched to the Hilda-Sam fights?" Dan asked.

"Once a week or more."

"Well, they're happy now. No more fighting. We don't have to go back."

"Fixed their unhappiness did you?"

"Maybe not, but they aren't any more miserable."

"We'll see."

"Okay, would you get over your embarrassment faster, if I used my gift to be more productive for you," Dan suggested. Ben saw a familiar twinkle in Dan's eyes, but only grunted in recognition.

"Your indigestions sounds bad tonight?

"Oh no! You're thinking get me fired thoughts! Leave me out of it! We haven't heard the end of the last caper, and still have a form to the captain due!"

"I did the form, waiting on the wreckers."

"Already? What'd you say?"

"Kissed it off. I said Hess brought to our attention our parking enforcement did not meet reasonable expectations. We did our best to remedy the deficiency, but inadvertently towed a priest's car. And, we were instructed by Lieutenant Hess on better methods of meeting our goals, and will comply. Captain Kirk can read between the lines. It's over, 'Pard-ner'."

"Suppose you did put that fire out. Why light another one so soon?"

"Okay with me if you're not interested in catching a robbery suspect."

The traffic light turned green and Dan drove in silence knowing the seed was planted. Five minutes passed.

"How?"

"How, what?" Dan asked realizing the seed sprouted.

"What you was about to say?"

"About what?"

"Come on, how we gonna do it?"

"You mean, keep King Kwick from getting hit?"

"How we gonna do it?"

"We? The plan you don't want any part of?"

"Yeah, you gonna babble all night or let me hear it?" Ben asked. "Starting with Plan 'A'; how to keep Hess off our case. Then Plan 'B'; explaining why we disregarded a written denial for stake out. And, oh yes, Plan 'C'; how I keep my pension when Plans 'A' and 'B' go sour. Then, I listen to how we nab the bad guy."

"You finished?"

"Yeah, that covers it."

"We nab the bad guy," Dan began, "by being at the right…"

"Stop! That's Plan D! Didn't hear A, B, or C, yet."

"Alright, follow this. Plan A; Hess won't be on our case 'cause he'll look good at the Captain's Staff Meeting tomorrow. Plan B; the lieutenant told everybody at roll call only manpower for one stake-out existed. We can infer permission, a misunderstanding at worst. Everyone heard him call us into his office. Hess reconsidered our request. At least, I understood it that way. Wasn't his last directive to do some serious police work like 'a felony robbery arrest'? Door was open. Deskman heard it. Since we're pursuing the felony arrest as directed, your pension's secure. That leaves us with Plan D; being at the right place at the right time."

"Could've been what he meant, but it's a stretch."

"It's settled then. We have a plan, and we'll swear by it."

"I'm swearing already," Ben said.

"And, die professing it," Dan added.

"Still sounds a lot like a stake-out."

"There's a big difference. Our action is a response to a directive, and an example of our impeccable timing."

"Impeachable timing?" Ben said with raised eyebrows.

"Impeccable," corrected Dan, "having no flaws; incapable of going wrong"

"Like I believe that! I prefer impeachable."

"Either way we're off the hook.

"What time is it?"

"Why don't you get a watch?"

"I've got a watch. What time is it," Ben reiterated.

"Look at your watch for once!"

"Not THE time, the impeachable event's time."

"Oh that. We can probably stay out of service an hour between 0300 and 0600."

"Let's go with 0330 to 0430. Give the bar traffic time to clear out."

"Done!"

Minutes ticked into hours of routine dispatches, and door shaking. Cancelling the OTP plan freed them considerably. They responded to several domestic altercations, a couple street fights, a report of gun shots, two prowler runs, an auto accident, and wrote three parkers.

"We haven't checked the expressway yet," Dan said as he turned down the ramp.

"We're looking for hazards and disabled motorists, and

not a flashlight, right?" Ben said.

"Of course."

Coming off the end of the ramp they were several hundred feet behind a Roadhaul Truck.

"Curses!" Ben sighed.

This driver, Alfred Green, was emphatic, "I've been driving Roadhaul fifteen years. Been to every terminal within three hundred miles and I don't recall any Manning. No idea where he's out of. You guys can't keep stopping us on account of him."

"You're stopped aren't you?" Dan pointed out. "And 'Mickey' here says it's cost you eighteen minutes. Now wouldn't you rather spend your time on the road?"

"You're not making any friends."

"Got enough friends. Need my flashlight."

Ben returned from a trip around the rig and handed the driver a piece of paper.

"Inspection's over. Here's a warning. Two running lights are out. You're free to go."

They stayed back slowing traffic so the big rig could pull out safely.

"I did your dirty work. Now, if I buy you a Mag-light, will you quit this?" Ben asked.

"No. It's a matter of principle," Dan answered.

"Yeah, principle spelt H-E-D-S-T-R-O-N-G."

"You left out the 'A'."

"No, you're the 'A'."

"Oh, good one. Smarts a bit."

The truck pulled away, and they called themselves back in service. Swung up the next ramp and into the Northside area.

"Ready for a picnic?" Dan asked.

"Riding with you I need a picnic."

"I've been pondering our meal time. Routinely at this hour few restaurants are open. What's our choices? Greasy spoons and junk food, which we gulp down between radio dispatches—if we eat at all! I'm tired of eating this way and tonight's gonna be different. Tonight, we picnic! Pull in the gas station over there."

Dan chose a location between two of six converging streets. One of them, a viaduct, housed the precinct on the other end. It stood at the southern point of their beat, and the busiest.

"Ready for lunch?" Dan asked.

"Here, at Knowlton Corner? More to this 'an lunch."

"Yep, we're going to have a picnic."

"A real picnic? It's the middle of the night?"

"It's my turn to deal a hand in Lieut's Game of the Blues."

"You forgetting you're walkin' a tight rope? Chief, captain, all are in Lieut's corner right now."

"You notice Hess has been riding us hard. The 'noose caper' bolstered his ego, and he thinks I'm a lame duck. We gotta level the playing field or we aren't gonna have any peace."

"We're liable to be what gets leveled!"

"Naw, did my homework. Checked with the F.O.P. attorney. As long as nothing is directed at him or command, and we don't violate written procedure, we're good."

"He thought it a good idea?"

"Didn't say that. Legally he thought it could be justified. Personally he called it 'most imprudent'."

"He gonna defend us if we need him?

"Didn't ask.'

"Didn't ask?"

"Didn't see the need."

"Got anything to do with the bag in the trunk?"

"Of course, it's lunch. You gonna eat with me, or sit this out?"

"My better judgment is fighting with my rogue desire to mess with Hess."

Ben was parked conspicuously at the corner. Dan pulled the duffle from the trunk and removed a checkered table cloth spreading it across the hood. Magnets held it in place. "Being Snaggles thinks it's a picnic out here and all we have to do is pad his numbers, we'll picnic," Dan said tucking the corners of a matching napkin into his collar. He handed one to Ben, "Must protect the tie." Dan then leaned over the hood to place a candelabrum and discovered it uncomfortably hot. Undaunted, he opted for the trunk and quickly reset the stage. "Well, light 'em, Ben."

Ben lit the candles which flickered in the light breeze. Then like a magician pulling a rabbit from a hat, Dan produced a set of wineglasses and a bottle of ginger-ale. "The plates are in the bag." Ben reluctantly retrieved two Melmac plates, placing them on the temporary table and stepped back to admire their handiwork. Dan stacked milk cartons into make shift stools.

"Here's to crime and job security' Dan said raising a cup of ginger-ale. "Pass me some chips, Partner."

"And here's to a long career," toasted Ben. "This sandwich is superb. You make these?"

"Cannot tell a lie. Picked them up at Red Squirrel on the way in. Wait 'til you see what else we have."

Dan removed a jar of gherkins and a container of deviled eggs. "All the delicacies of home."

Motorist beeped in recognition as they passed by, and the Duo waved back. Savoring the moment, they fed body and psyche beneath the streetlights. Within ten minutes an unmarked police car approached over the viaduct.

"'Spect that'll be Snaggles," Dan said putting his tie in order beneath the napkin.

"Okay, I'll get my butt ready."

They watched the unmarked car swing into the gas station and stop. The driver's door flew open and a fuming Hess leapt out. His eyebrows were raised and his lip twitched. Dan imagined steam shooting from his nostrils. As Hess approached, Sergeant O'Toole followed unable to conceal a smile.

"What in blue blazes do you two think you're doing?" Hess demanded.

"Lunch," Dan replied.

"Makin' buffoons out of my relief!"

"No, Sir. Not a buffet, a brown bag lunch."

"Lunch? It's a sham! Turning us into a laughing stock! In the middle of town like this!"

"No ham, Sir, Ben's got turkey and mine's roast beef. It's a picnic lunch. We've extra chips. Want some?" Dan extended a paper plate toward Hess who swatted it away.

"Umm, wind must've caught it. Don't bother yourself chasin' it. I'll get it."

While Dan picked up the plate Ben joined in, "I'll split my pickles with you. They're sweet gherkins." He held one up to the lieutenant on the end of a plastic fork. Hess ignored the offer.

O'Toole reached out and took it, "Thank you?"

Hess scowled at him.

"Dan returned with the errant plate. "If you two care to join us, you'd be welcome. We'll make the lemon meringue pie in the cooler go four ways."

"I won't have your insubordination! You won't listen here; you will in my office!"

"Sorry Sir, but I have been listening to you all along. And, you've inspired me to meditate on the projected relief goals and envision new parameters of implementation."

"Don't get smart with me. You two clean this up. Be in my office in ten minutes! And, that's an order!"

Once the lieutenant's car vanished over the viaduct, Dan turned to Ben and asked, "Did he say I was smart? That's a pretty big compliment coming from him."

"I'm convinced. You're suffering from insanity!"

"On the contrary, I don't suffer from my insanity. I enjoy every minute of it."

"You're right! I'm the one's suffering! Playing along."

"Yeah, good touch offering him a pickle."

"How'd I let you get me caught up in this? You're going to get me fired."

"Did you see Pooh Bear? Holding it in? Thought he'd bust a gut."

"No wonder. He's got his own grudges when it comes to Hess. It was his name died on top the promotion list when Hess' 'affirmative action' jumped him. Pooh-Bear ain't thrilled Hess is in his slot."

"Bet his soul bubbled with joy when he took the pickle. Glad we could give him a break. And, since 'what will be-will be', we might as well finish our picnic and then play the hand out."

Dan and Ben finished their lunch and discussed the impending meeting. Twenty minutes ticked away before they arrived at Lieutenant Hess' office. They knocked formally.

"Come in," a disgusted Hess responded.

They stepped to the front of the lieutenant's desk, saluted and barked, "Officer Black - and White - reporting as ordered, Sir."

Hess gave a salute, but no courtesy to stand easy, "Suppose you jokers tell me what you were doing?"

"Just having lunch," Dan replied.

"That's not the way police officers eat lunch and you darn well know it! Your display was total disregard for the profession; demeaned the uniform!"

They did not respond.

"Well, speak up; what do you have to say for yourselves before I write this up?"

"Sir, I would like to be informed of what regulations we have violated," Dan said. "In the first place, we are permitted to take our lunch after 0200, although not off our beat. We are permitted to do so outside our vehicles, although not more than two patrols at one place. It is night run and few restaurants are available. We are permitted to bring our meal, and we should not be denied common convenience of table and chairs. Further, we were available for dispatches and within our beat boundaries. That is, until you took us out of service."

"You want a table? Come in the district and eat."

"We prefer to remain vigilant on our beat, Sir."

"You two are one ring short of a full circus."

"Sorry, Sir, we've tried so hard to be worthy of three rings," Dan quipped.

"A disgrace to the uniform!"

"As for disgracing the uniform; the table cloths, napkins,

and dinner wear are the sign of a gentleman's table. All were chosen to avoid spillage and protect our professional appearance. The importance of which has recently been impressed upon me."

After a lengthy pause Dan added, "You might want to check with the city solicitor's office before making a charge, because you know we'll fight it all the way. The publicity you receive from this will really advance your career. I'm sure command will back you, even if they are laughing in private. Don't you think? I bet this could even make the newspaper."

Another pause ensued as Hess apparently considered Dan's comments. Then as if someone threw a switch electrifying his chair, he sprang up. His mouth open and he stood motionless pointing a waving finger saying nothing. After a few seconds he sneered, "You two are going to get yours. I promise!"

Dan and Ben stood silently at attention.

Hess paced behind his desk staring at the floor and murmuring to himself. His nature drove him to worry over the impact of things on his career, and would command back him or think he over-reacted. Finally, waving a thumb like an umpire at Dan he shouted, "Out!" The finger went immediately to Ben, "You too, out!"

"Yes, Sir," they responded executing an abrupt about-face. As soon as they were outside the office door they exchanged glances and smiles with the desk officer. The door had been open, and the desk officer sitting nearby heard all. In passing they shared restrained spastic snickering. Sgt. O'Toole witnessed it, and turned loose a bellowing laugh.

"O'Toole, what's so blasted funny?" barked Hess from his office, "You better not be laughing at those clowns!"

"No Sir, not at them. Oh, noooo Sir, not them."

Once in their cruiser they did not restrain their glee as they headed across the viaduct toward the scene of the picnic. Dan keyed the mike.

"508, we're two-six from meeting 520."

The radio crackled with static from officers clicking

their mikes; an anonymous cheer.

"Boy, word travels fast," Ben said.

Coming down the other side, they were greeted from the 'picnic area' by four squad cars' and a flickering of beacon lights.

"Yup," Dan said, "especially when it's razzle-dazzle."

"Preacher, one of these times I'm going to lose my pension sidin' you. When that happens, swear to God, my whole screaming family's moving in with you."

"Never happen."

"Straight up, I wished I could be as cavalier as you playing the Blues Games," Ben chuckled. "They give a unique thrill, but I've got family."

"They work out, Partner."

"So far."

"We've sided each other straight on since we met. You never once let me walk down a dark alley alone, and when your gut says 'back off' you speak your piece. It's the same whether playing the Game or facing some degenerate thug in an alley. The day you don't, you'll become the first six-foot midget in the world. 'Cause, I swear, I'll kick your butt clean up between your shoulder blades."

"If I got any left. No call for gettin' contrary, Dan. You know how we stand; side-by-side should we die. We both go down together. As for the Game, yeah, it worries me, but shucks alive, no Game? What'd be left? Job wouldn't be any fun without it."

Minutes later the radio interrupted their reflections. "Car 508, 508, at 4267 Badgeley Street. See the complainant, possible prowlers."

Ben accepted and logged the run, as Dan turned the car in the direction of the call. *Ghost Rider's available. We can expect him to show. So, I'll make a direct approach, slow, and lights out.*

The building contained four apartments, two on each floor separated by a center hallway.

"508, do you have an apartment?"

"Card says prowler in second floor hallway," the dispatcher said. “No apartment given.”

They went to the second floor, but found no prowler. There was nothing more they could do. They exited through the laundry area to double check. Halfway back to the car, the dispatcher updated them. “508, we have a return call. Complainant says the prowler’s there now, Apartment Three.”

“The complainant must have heard us,” Ben suggested. “We’ll have to go back in and set him at ease. What’s one more flight of stairs in a night’s work?”

“Looking at your tummy, you might want to run up them.”

“Me!”

They arrived back on the second floor. Again they found no disturbance. At the door with a brass “3”, Dan tapped gently with the nightstick. He didn’t want to wake anyone else, so he spoke softly, “It’s the police. Did you call?”

The response was a rustling from behind the door drawing their attention to a sheet of aluminum foil sliding out under it. “Sign in with your badge,” whispered a voice behind the door.

Gary joined them at the top of the stairs in time to see the foil flapping under the door. They exchanged questioning glances. “What’s up? I’ve checked a radius of two blocks. Didn’t see anybody.”

Dan pointed to the sheet of aluminum. Gary shrugged his shoulders with raised eyebrows. It disappeared back through the crack.

“Car 508,” beckoned the radio.

“508,” Ben answered.

“Complainant on the phone again. Says they’re trying to break the door down.”

“Tell him it’s us!”

They waited in silence.

“Says, he doesn’t believe it’s the police, because they won’t sign in?”

Now hearing a hissing they looked down to see mist coming through the bottom door crack.

"What's he doing now?" Dan asked.

"Smells like bug spray to me," Ben answered.

Dan keyed his mike, "508,You still have him on the phone?"

"Affirmative."

"Tell him to put his bug spray away and open the door."

The hissing stopped, and the foil reappeared as the radio broke in, "He says he wants proof you're the police."

Dan unpinned his badge, bent down and made an impression of it in the foil. "There," he said disgustedly, "I signed in. Now open your door." The foil retracted and seconds later the bolt turned.

The door opened a crack as the man peeked out, then he quickly open it half way guarding the opening. "Come in, quick. They'll sneak in behind you."

As the officers stepped in, the occupant waved a yard's length of foil behind them in the hallway as if shooing flies. Closing the door, he shoved it in the threshold crack. They were greeted with windows and doors covered with aluminum foil. Foil hung in narrow strips from the ceiling, on furniture, and covered baseboards. The occupant, a gaunt elderly six-foot man, wore plain white linen pajamas. His chest was wrapped in foil, as were his upper arms and thighs banded. The aluminum foil turban made it hard to keep a professional front.

"Sir, what's your name?" Dan began.

"I can't tell you. They might hear it."

"What name do I put on the official log sheet?" Dan whispered.

Putting his fingers to his lips, he took the pen and wrote "Craig Birdman," on Dan's pad.

"Tell us about the prowler."

"It's the Gamensoots," he said seriously speaking slowly and distinctly. "They want to take me back. I told them I like it here. I don't want to go."

"And where is it they want to take you?"

"Back to Zormetts, It's the fillings in my teeth." Birdman opened his mouth to point to the fillings. "Down here we use gold. Back there they trade amalgamates."

"How long have you had this problem?"

"They started coming last year."

Ben slipped into the bath, bedroom, and kitchen to check for medications, while Dan carried on the conversation. When Ben came out he indicated nothing unusual. Dan, being senior on the run, would have to make the call. Did the man pose a danger to himself or others? If so the law provided for a hospital evaluation. However, no sign of violent behavior existed, only irrational hallucinations.

"Seems you have everything under control. I think they're scared off for the night." Dan said stepping toward the door.

"No, NO! You can't go! They'll come back out."

"You're doin' a fine job keepin' them away. Just keep up the good work."

"This only irritates them," Birdman said holding up the roach spray. "It's like your tear-gas. Once they're in, they're hard to see. Got to catch their reflection in the foil."

"I know," Gary chimed in. "They chased me around last year, but I outsmarted 'em."

"How'd you do it?" Birdman asked attentively.

"Yeah," Dan said, "Tell us, we're anxious to learn."

"Well, uh, uh…"

"We're all ears," Ben coached. "Tell us, so we can help Mr. Birdman."

Finally Gary said, "I snuck over to the professor's when they weren't around. He knows all about Gamensoots, and Zelenboots, and the Gorbbucons. Had to stay with him a couple days but he fixed it so none of 'em want anything to do with me."

"I can understand that," Ben quipped.

"What'd he do?" Birdman asked excitedly.

"Don't know. He's the scientist. But, I know it only works on people who are good and don't want to hurt anybody. If that's you? Possibly we could go see him."

"Will you take me, Officer?" the man asked like a child begging parents to go to Disneyland.

"Well it's late." Gary pointed at his watch. "But if we hurry, I think we can catch him. Grab your robe."

You sly Devil. I need to remember you can be clever, Dan thought.

The man hurried into the bedroom, and returned one arm in the robe's sleeve, the other searching. Gary opened the door and stepped into the hall with Birdman. Dan and Ben followed. Ben turned to lock the door, and the owner yelled, "Wait!" He disappeared into the room returning with a large streamer of foil trailing behind him. "Just in case."

Finally, Ben secured the door and gave the keys to Gary to hold. Birdman hurried outside. At the cruiser, Gary patted him down. "Makin' sure no Gamensoots are hanging on you."

"Oh, thank you. Sneaky aren't they?"

After Mr. Birdman was seated in the rear, Gary turned to Ben. "You guys follow me up to State. Don't expect any trouble, but you never know."

"Got you covered, and we'll radio ahead for you."

Gary arrived without incident, and Mr. Birdman hurried into the hospital Receiving Room. His flapping robe exposed the bands, and his head still bore the turban. The nurse looked up and Gary spoke first. "This is Mr. Birdman, he's having trouble with those pesky Gamensoots. Thought maybe the professor could help him out."

"I believe you are in luck. He's still here."

The patient voluntarily checked himself in for observation without difficulty. Outside Dan patted Gary on the back. "That may not be the most kosher Medical Hold, but it beats having to fight them."

Gary opened his cruiser's door and as soon as he sat, Ben yelled, "Gary, watch out! Behind you!"

Gary rolled out of the seat. His reflexes sent his hand to his holster. However, not seeing a threat he asked, "What?"

"One of them Canonspots," was about to get you," Ben laughed.

"They're Gamensoots! And I told you, I'm immune to 'em. But you better watch out. They're real." He laughed diabolically sliding into his cruiser.

The Duo cut through the Clifton neighborhood *en route* from the hospital to their beat. “This area is such a smorgasbord of eccentric people, Birdman would blend right in,” Dan quipped.

“Except, his actions aren’t eccentric. They’re irrational,” Ben said.

“That’s relative to your point of view.”

“Oh yeah? He’s the only one with that point of view.”

“But, if there really are Gamensoots, his actions are rational.”

“Rational? I don’t believe so.”

“But, he does. And, then there’s Gary’s confirmation. See? It’s point of view.”

“Right, and your point?”

“The point is; he’s acting logically based on what he believes true. The fact he’s wrong is irrelevant to his behavior. All our actions are based on our beliefs.”

Crossing the viaduct the radio summoned, “Car 508, 508, in the vicinity 2874 Henshaw Ave, noisy dog complaint, anonymous, neighbor wants to get some sleep.”

“508, copied.”

Ben leaned his head back as if he could see beyond the roof, “I believe I see a solar storm from Venus and Mars aligning.”

Dan chuckled. “If you’re right there’s no hope, but I believe it’s just the full moon.”

“Too crazy a night for a just a full moon.”

“Then it’d be rational for you to go ahead and shoot yourself.”

“But what if I’m wrong?”

“Oh, well, — Hey, where’s Gary?” Dan asked knowing the run was on Follert’s beat. “We’ll give him a minute to disregard.”

“Don’t expect he will. Caught a dispatch leavin’ the hospital.”

“I didn’t hear one.”

“You were in the car. He’s got government business?”

"So, what's so important?"

"He's on a dumpin' complaint, if you must know."

"Don't matter anymore. We're here."

With the cruiser's windows down, they honed in on the howling. Dan pulled to the curb in a middle class neighborhood. "Close as we're gonna get."

"What time is it?" Ben asked logging the arrival.

"Time for all the doggies to be asleep."

They walked toward the howls and came to a fence at the rear of a brick four-square house. An Alaskan Malamute stood on top of a shed doghouse arguing with the moon.

"Why doesn't this ever bother the owner?" Dan asked.

Ben shrugged his shoulders and they went around to the front door. The doorbell brought no response. "Must be broken."

"Broke? I can hear it ring." Dan rapped loudly with his nightstick. The lone response was renewed efforts of the dog.

"Stick must be broke too," Ben chuckled.

Additional attempts to raise the resident only excited the dog.

"You want to tackle him while I cuff him, or do I wrestle him while you cuff him?" Dan asked.

"Sorry, I don't do dogs! 'Sides the cuffs won't fit."

"Suppose, if we ask nice, he'd 'paws' for awhile?"

"Silly talk isn't solving anything. What's more, it's close to our stake-out time. We better get the Dog Warden up here."

"You get a hold of some secondhand weed? No Dog Warden's gonna get out of bed without a court order."

"If we don't get this mutt shut up, there won't be a stake-out. Neighbors 'll be calling all night."

"Well then, we might as well camp out."

"Maybe not, you see what I see?" Ben said referring to a patrol car approaching.

"Bet it's the Ghost Rider."

"Shame on him 'cause he'll inherit the howlin' hound."

They walked back to meet the car at the sidewalk. The vehicle pulled to the curb, and Gary stepped out. "I heard the run. Stayed off the air to see what you had."

"Well Gary," Dan said, "Thanks to you, we don't have anything. You do. It's your beat."

"Is that it?" Gary asked, hearing the howling.

"He's mean, with big nasty fangs," Ben said. "Good luck on shutting him up. We'll be goin'."

"Nooo problem. Got just the thing." Using his flashlight Gary searched through his war bag perking Dan and Ben's curiosity. "I know it's in here. Know I got some." Dan and Ben waited patiently for his secret weapon. After several minutes Gary set the hook. "Found it!" He closed the door and started toward the dog carrying nothing but a flashlight.

"What?" Dan exclaimed, "That's your big secret? You gonna hypnotize it with a flashlight?"

"I gotta see this," Ben said. "Change your name to dog charmer."

"Oh no," Gary replied, "I got these." He turned opening his hand revealing a small pill canister. "Dog-gone-doggie-downers. You mean THE DUO doesn't have any in their war bag?"

"How you planning on stuffing them down his throat?" Dan scoffed.

Ben laughed. "He'll take your hand off!"

"No problem. I have PBJs leftovers from Box Town," Gary said.

"That'll do. Pooches love peanut butter," Dan noted.

"Take notes, Dan," Ben suggested. "Gary's writing a new page in the Procedure Manual."

Taking a sandwich and peeling back the top layer, Gary laid three capsules on the peanut butter. "That'll do it. Maybe, one more."

"You still got to feed it to him!" Ben reminded.

Ordinarily, they'd let the dog howl, and have Day Shift contact the owner. However, Gary saw a chance to get one up on his companions. The sandwich assembled, they all walked back to the fence.

Dan called the animal, "Here doggie, doggie, here boy."

He stopped barking and glared. Gary launched the

Mickey. The dog charged off his house to investigate, and was snapped back at the end of a chain.

"Just great! We're short." Gary said.

"What you mean, WE, Kemo-Sobie? You made the pitch," Dan said.

"My toss ain't short! The chain's not regulation length."

"Regulation length, doggie-poo!"

"Should have known. White boys can't shoot," Ben said. "Here, I'll give you a boost over the fence."

All this activity renewed the frenzied howling.

"I'm not getting that close! 'Sides, the chain doesn't look very strong. You go. You have longer arms."

"What's longer arms got to do with it?"

"You don't have to get as close."

"I don't do dogs!"

Gary looked at Dan hoping he'd have a better suggestion.

"Let's review, uh, your beat, your idea, your Mickey Finn, your pitiful pitch," Dan said raising a finger with each 'your'. "Use your stick. Shove it over to him."

"Yeah, remember your training. It's an extension of your arm," Ben chuckled. "Let me give you a boost." Ben again made a stirrup with his hands.

"Come on! GO! Or, forget it. We got a stake-out to get to," Dan urged.

Gary conceded reluctantly. Half way to the bait, the dog realized his domain was invaded. He became furious and strained against the chain. Howls became fierce snarls and growls. Stalactite fangs caused Gary to hesitate.

"It's further back to the fence than the bait," Dan encouraged. "A couple more steps!"

Gary's nightstick nudged the bait into range. Jaws clamped around the stick and a fierce tug of war ensued.

"Let go of the stick you demon dog!" Gary screamed yanking with both hands. "Nooo! Release beast!—Release!"

The dog snapped at the stick for a better bite and it jerked loose. The sudden lack of resistance sent Gary sprawling backwards into the fence. The hound dispatched the sandwich in gulps. While he licked peanut butter, Gary clambered over the fence.

As they retreated, Dan noticed a robed man standing on the porch next door. *Just walk away. Don't even look at him. But, he saw the circus! Ignoring him might make it worse.* The man motioned for them to come closer. *Swell, no escape.*

Gary also saw the man and went to the porch, "Are you the one who called?"

"Officer, this goes on every night. Is there nothing more you can do?"

"No sir, not unless you're willing to go to court and testify."

"But, officers, can't you testify to its viciousness? Why do you need me?"

"In the wisdom of our Justice System I cannot testify to your sleep being disturbed. It's hearsay, not firsthand knowledge. I can only testify to my own sleep being disturbed, but it hasn't been because I'm working."

"That's asinine!"

"No argument here. We don't make the laws; just try to figure out how to enforce them. Sometimes, a citizen has to take a stand."

"Maybe, you're right," the man replied scratching his chin. "When I complain about crap in my yard, that neighbor tells me I'm over-reacting. When the dog barks all night, every night, I'm exaggerating. His retaining wall is collapsing taking my hillside with it, but it's my problem. If my son's ball goes in his bushes, the boy's unruly. And, the icing on the cake; if I poison that howling hound, I'd be the one arrested!"

"You've got it figured. Some people get the idea the world turns around their birthday. Sometimes the courts can educate 'em, but more often, not. Unfortunately, the courts are crowded. A little common sense would make life easier and keep us out of court. You want to sign the complaint go to the clerk's office. List us as witnesses: Officers Follert with a T, Black, and White."

"You'll win," Dan said.

"Not sure what," added Gary. "He'll get a fine. Dog'll still be there."

The complainant slapped his arms against his sides in disgust, turned and went inside his house. The officers returned to their cruisers, and the dog continued to howl.

Reaching the sidewalk Dan remarked, "All that hullabal-loo, and what did we accomplish?"

"Not much, but Gary's 'show-n-tell' was fun to watch," Ben said.

"What's wrong with you two? Listen. It's already quieter, isn't it?"

Dan ignored the question with his own, "You get the downers from Doc. Pherson?"

"I'll answer yours after you answer mine," Gary said. "What 'stake-out' you going to?"

"It's a shot in the dark we worked up. We'd bring you in, but it's shaky. If it goes bad, a third man kills our alibi. But, our next caper that won't get you fired, you're first in."

"Fair," Gary said. "Doc. Bowser on the parkway. Tell him I sent you. We can split the take. Let me know how it goes. Good luck."

In route to the stake out Ben casually remarked, "Isn't it great to live in America where everyone can have a lovin' pet?"

"You're a big fearless cop. You have to get over this thing with dogs."

They patrolled for a half-hour before feeling comfort-able with laying off the air for the stake-out.

"All's quiet. Want to check on YOUR bow-wow buddy?" Dan asked.

"Nope, Gary's problem. Let sleeping dogs lie."

Dan accelerated heading for the Stop-N-Go Market. He parked the cruiser a block away behind Dutch's Custard shop, and walked over. The short clerk, Lehra Oama Armadondase, had adopted the name Larry. Their many coffee stops and patrol checks gave Dan and Ben good rapport with him.

"Good friends, officers, you come in," Larry greeted.

Ben walked to the counter, and Dan phoned the dispatchers to take them out of service.

"Larry, we have some news. We have solid information someone might try to rob you tonight," Ben said.

"I close store!" he responded grabbing the keys from the counter drawer. "I no stay!"

Ben grabbed his shoulder to stop him. "We'll stay with you."

"What? Okay, I stay."

"Yes, you stay. We stay too."

"You stay. I stay," Larry said courageously.

"I will hide outside," Ben explained. "Dan will take a post inside."

Dan looked around, "I'll hide in the cooler box. I can see and watch your counter."

"Cooler cold, not good you stay."

"Got a jacket; it'll be perfect. When the robber comes in, you cooperate, and when he turns to leave duck below the counter."

"I go home. You duck counter," Larry suggested.

"If the robber sees a stranger at the counter he'll get scared off. Then he might come back some night we aren't here."

"You give me gun?"

"A gun would put you in danger. You'd never have a chance to use it. We need you to act the same as every night. We'll be here. You'll be safe. Stay calm and duck under the counter when he leaves."

"I do same as last night? Robber not come last night."

This guy's too nervous. I can't get through to him. "Ben, don't think he's getting it. See if you can explain it."

"Until the man takes money, or shows a gun, no crime," Ben said. "You no argue. Do what robber say. When robber goes to door," Ben pointed, "duck under counter."

The clerk seemed to identify better with Ben. He had Larry walk through the scenario for practice. "I think he's got it, Dan."

“What are you going to do when the robber comes in?” Dan asked.

“I do last night. He go, I duck like this,” Larry disappeared behind the counter.

“Right!”

“I top rate. Robber go. Larry duck,” he said disappearing under the counter once more”

“It’s doable. Should work,” Ben said to Dan.

“Should, but Burns echoes in my mind.”

“Burns?”

“Burns’ infamous warning, ‘The best laid plans of mice and men, go oft awry, an' leave us naught…’”

“Oh that.” Turning, Ben continued, “Larry stay calm. It’s a waiting game.”

Ben and Dan took their posts. Larry went to his counter. Each customer increased Larry’s nervousness. After twenty minutes he resembled a spectator at a ping-pong match; glancing door to cooler. Thirty-five minutes later, Larry left the counter going into the cooler, “Robber come. You shoot robber man?”

Great! He’s losing his nerve again. Best we scrap it. “Looks like we were worrying about nothing,” Dan said. “It’s past time for the robber. We get lots of bad tips. Happens all the time.”

Larry relaxed and returned to his counter. Dan picked up his clipboard and mug shots, and turned for the cooler door as the next customer walked in. The customer was dressed casual with his shirt tail hanging out. He selected items without consideration. It caught Dan’s attention, and he alerted Ben by radio, “Something’s not right with this last guy.”

The man came to the back of the store. At the end of the center aisle he pulled a stocking mask over his head, drew a revolver from under the shirt tail, and started for the counter. Dan was out of position.

Blast it! Can’t step out, might force hostage crossfire! Dan thought as he keyed the radio whispering. “Ben, it’s a go. Male, five ten, 165, blue T-shirt, jeans, red bandana.”

Larry saw the mask and dove under the counter. "Robber! Robber!"

Dan had to wait. Stepping out would position the clerk in his line of fire. Larry's cries did not alarm the perpetrator. The robber walked to the counter, peered over, but saw no one. Larry had doubled up at the waist and crawled into the cabinet. The robber jumped over the counter, grabbing Larry and yanking him to his feet.

"Open it. Give me the money. Drop-box too!" he demanded shoving a paper bag at Larry.

Larry hurriedly stuffed the money from the register into the bag shouting with a breaking voice, "No key! Box no open! No key!"

"Open it!" demanded the thief pointing his gun at the night safe.

"No key! Take wallet! No key!"

The bandit grabbed Larry's wallet, and shoved the billfold into the bag ripping the paper. Bills fluttered to the floor like maple seedpods. Throwing Larry aside, the bandit scooped them up and headed for the door. Seeing opportunity, Larry dove back under the counter shouting. "Cops shoot now! Shoot! Shoot now!"

The hostage problem alleviated, Dan stepped out. "Halt! Police! Drop the gun!"

Rotating, the bandit raised his weapon. Dan put tension on the trigger. The hammer started to rise.

"Drop the gun. I WILL SHOOT!"

The crook paused, and then raised the weapon. Dan fired twice. The impact spun the bandit into a display of detergent boxes. Both boxes and bandit went sprawling across the floor. The gun hit the floor and slid to Dan's feet. Broken boxes released detergent on the floor. The thief kicked in a futile attempt to right himself in the slippery spill.

"Thanks Bucco," Dan said stooping to retrieved the weapon.

The perpetrator regained his senses rolled halfway down the aisle onto clean floor. He sprang to his feet to flee. In three strides he encountered Big Ben's huge form in the doorway; weapon in one hand, night stick in the other. "You're kiddin' yourself."

The thief tried to stop abruptly and the soap powder, on the soles of his shoes, sent him sliding into a wire cage of rubber balls. Grabbing the cage for support, it pulled over on him collapsing backwards onto the floor. The bandit pushed himself into a sitting position facing Ben, looked at the blood on his shirt, and started whimpering.

"You gun wielding bullies are all cry babies," Ben scoffed.

Dan checked the perpetrator's wounds in preparation of taking him into custody. "Come on, Bucco, too late for teary eyed remorse." When Dan touched the man's injured arm, he collapsed backwards. His head fell against one of the large balls and then bounced from one to the next. Two bounces later, he lay unconscious on the floor. Dan radioed for paramedics. While waiting, he dressed the wound with bandages from the store shelves.

They also notified the dispatcher and their supervisors. The rescue team arrived within minutes, and shortly later two backup cars. The medics revived the culprit with an ammonia capsule. He coughed and sneezed.

Dan's search found no identification. After reading the Miranda warning he asked, "You want to tell us who you are?"

"I got nothin' to say, Copper."

"Where'd you get the 'roscoe' – it stolen?"

"Talk to my lawyer."

"What's his name and number?"

The man did not reply and remained uncooperative.

Sergeant Fleischer arrived and Dan briefed him. "We need to tie the loose ends up and do the paper."

"Sure, Watkins can transport and Harkins can secure the scene until Robbery Squad shows."

The Duo returned to their cruiser and headed into the station. It took the rest of the shift for Fleischer to finish the "shots fired" paper work. Their part complete, they sat in the briefing room, "Pretty slick work," Dan commented.

"SLICK! Slick you say? I never saw such a bungled mess."

Gary walked by on his way to stow his gear and remarked, "Heard you guys had some excitement. Appreciate you looking after my interests."

"You're welcome. But how'd we do that?" Ben asked.

"Keeping me out of it!" Gary walked on snickering.

"Well, tonight was serendipitous. Wouldn't you say?" Dan remarked.

Ben looked at Dan's blood stained shirt sleeve, shook his head, rolled his eyes, "'Serendipitous', sweet surrender, where do you get these words?"

"Well, it was."

"Yeah, that Burns guy had it pegged."

"Better'n most plans. Think it was the timing."

"TIMING! What timing?"

"Well, one thing I can't figure," Dan said. "I had the draw on him, and he tries me anyway?"

"Maybe he's suicidal."

"Or unbelievably desperate. What's wrong with people? Look at what we dealt with tonight. First we visited Box Town, Sam and Hilda at each other's throats, a foil fanatic, unreasonable neighbors, and Bucco Bandit."

"I'm telling you the Yen and Yang are out of balance in the universe."

"Simpler than that, Ben. A rebellious people deny the true identity of good and evil."

Ben winced, "Not that again."

"Yep, gotta be."

"All societies have laws, Dan. Need them to maintain order."

"There's the issue. Society makes laws, but they keep changing. Look at the speed limit. Expressways were seventy, then with the gas crisis fifty-five. Same road. So is it wrong to go sixty, everybody does?"

"That's kinda a gray area, Dan."

"That's what I mean. No absolutes. People assume everything's a gray area. Toeing the line would be easier if we could find it! I tiptoe down a thin blue line which separates evil from good. Lean as far as I dare—just don't fall! The world's paintbrush is gray. Where does black end and white begin?"

"Okay, there must be a line for the sake of order, if not justice. But we don't make the rules, just enforce them."

"That's the point, Ben. Who can draw the line? Who defines right and wrong?"

"Not us, that's for sure."

"And rightfully so, it takes a God to decree absolutes. All else is social politics, which people feel free to violate. And, if we arrest them, who they mad at?"

"Us."

"What upset them?"

"Getting caught, of course."

"If they step in a ditch, fall and break a leg, do they get mad at the doctor?"

"Of course not."

"What's the difference?"

"Beats me."

"The difference is gravity, Ben. Gravity is a natural law. It's accepted as absolute, but moral law isn't."

"Now wait a minute. It's different. Step off a cliff and you incur immediate consequence. Ignore a moral law and nothing happens."

"I think not. Consider your guy-girls from the taxi. Would you agree it's against moral law?"

"I'll give you that, but other than themselves, who's it hurt?"

"I suspect everybody. No disease can be confined in a segment of culture. AIDS is a perfect example. As for other moral laws, there's unwanted pregnancy, hardship of single parent homes, and mental problems incurred from rape, incest, abortion. I could go on. Are these not consequences? Less immediately identifiable, but society as well as individuals incur consequences?"

"Okay, preacher, I give. I haven't had this much fun since parochial school debating 'Can God make a rock He can't pick up?"

"Well, sorry, funs over. Here comes Serge."

As Fleischer came down the hall he sang out, "Fall in!" The men sauntered into place. "Come on. Get with it. You want to stay here all day too?" The men assembled into a winding line.

"Harkins, paperwork on your DOA is messed up," Fleischer began. "Check with the coroner and get it straight. Henderson, neat, complete report, on a messy accident. Martin, you kept the canine boys busy with four PFOs—good work." The sergeant paused for a moment and then said, "Oh yeah, Officers Black and White went to the circus tonight."

"Yes, Sir," Dan replied, "Front seat tickets for Bucco Bandit's soft-shoe clown act."

"Hess hasn't heard. He went home early. I'll put a copy of the paper on his desk. He'll have it first thing before the Captain's Meeting—if I ever get finished. He won't be happy with the shots fired, but the arrest will sure put him in a good mood."

"It ought to. It's the felony robbery he wanted. 'Sides it's a righteous shooting."

"And we stapled our parkers to it," Ben added.

"Did we have parkers tonight? Dan, not on a serious police work night."

"Shucks man, never will get this job down."

"Enough," ordered the sergeant. "You fell into another pile of your own manure and once more came up smelling roses. For your benefit I'll leave a note with the report telling how Lieutenant Hess' personal guidance has helped ..."

He stopped short as Gary's gnarled nightstick caught his attention. "How'd you… Naw, don't even want to know. You're spending too much time with them." Before anyone spoke he shouted, "Dismissed!"

Dan passed Fleischer on the way out. "Thanks, but please, do us no favors!"

Fleischer chuckled. "You two whine like puppies pulled from the litter, but I know you really love the streets." He walked away smiling.

Ben was parked next to Dan. “Well Partner, if nothing else we earned a couple days off until the hearing.”

“Yeah, now the news media hype starts. I’m a heartless racist despot killer,” Dan groaned.

“Ignore ’em. Their heads are up their butts. Keeps ’em blind, deaf, and ‘ig-nor-ant’.”

“I know, but it grates on me: The activists ignore truth and paint it racial. It’s intentional divisiveness.”

“You got plenty of hang-ups,” Ben said. “But, racism isn’t on the list. Wait ‘till it comes out I was there. They’ll label me worse: a lying hypocritical betraying Uncle Tom.”

“Wouldn’t matter which of us shot him. Him being black is the catalyst.”

“I can deal with the activists, but city council never sticks up for us.”

“Ought to expect that, too. Politicians chasing votes never serve truth. It’s all conniving for a vote. I’ll give you a real worry. Present trend is the affluent are moving to the suburbs in herds turning the city core predominately uneducated, poor, and minority. One day city council is going to have to cater to a core of activists and discontents to stay in the gravy.”

“Can’t do anything, but get worse, can it?”

“Worse! I predict at some point a good policeman’s going to pay the price. The truth will be buried, a scapegoat provided, a cop indicted and his life ruined for trying to serve society.”

“Try to put it out of your mind. We have two days, let’s take advantage of it.”

“I’ll concentrate on how few years I have before retirement. Maybe I can beat the hangman.”

“Good advice, expect you to take it.”

The car doors shut and they departed for their respective homes. Dan drove north and Ben south. The clock sent Dan home the long route. *Murphy’s law.*

No matter. I’ve got two days to recover. The hearing will be routine. They’ll have read the reports, looked at the security video, and interviewed Larry. On and on with redundant questions about how we happened to be there. A hunch --a tip --we decided to sit on it while we drank our coffee or just fate? Asking over and over why we HAD to shoot the poor misguided, but good, man. The second guessers offering their unqualified opinions!

Then, they'll dismiss us. Order us to report to the 'shrink.' That'll waste another couple hours. Maybe I'll let him tiptoe inside my brain instead of the cat and mouse go-around. Let him tour the whole wax museum of horrors. Scare the 'heebie-jeebies' out of him! That might be fun. Teach him right, too!

Chapter Nine

Broken Ambition and Hope

Dan pulled into his garage feeling like an old man coming home from a geriatrics clinic. He pried himself out of the Corvette. With a careless toss, his gun belt caught a peg near the door, teetered but stayed. Entering the kitchen, he stepped in a small box on the floor. A "foot in the pail" routine ensued.

Sloppy bachelor. He shook his foot lose. A good kick sent the box flying into the sitting room. He popped open a Dr. Pepper from the refrigerator, and slurped at the foam. "Uh-no! Rat droppings!" *Too late. Oh well, listen to 'THEM' and everything kills.*

He picked up a second box, and kicking the first soccer style sent it onto the porch, "Goal!" Dan sat the drink on the side table turning the rambunctious ferret loose. Trouble darted out pouncing on the crumpled box.

Dan sat, legs extending down the swing, kicked off his shoes, and laid his head back on a rolled towel. He gazed out the window. Dark stringy clouds spanned the vista and a blend of rose and scarlet cut the canopy of heaven. *Even dawn struggles; darkness will not surrender to the light.*

Dan offered Trouble an arm up, and the ferret accepted. He raced across Dan's lap, springing at the can knocking it to the floor. Trouble jumped after it lapping the sweet spill.

"Trouble, you're quicker 'n thunder after lightning to make a mess."

The ferret dragged the can toward his cage by the tab.

"Stop! You're making it worse!" Dan jumped to reclaim the can. "I hope it makes you sick!" Grabbing a towel, Dan soaked up the spill, took the towel inside to the hamper and returned. Trouble was occupied with the boxes. Having dragged both boxes into his sandbox, he attempted to stack the smaller on top.

"So, you too, prefer empty boxes to soft beds?"

The ferret answered with a bark.

"Why do I care?"

The ferret scurried from the cage. Finding no additional building blocks it looked up at Dan and "hee-hawed."

"Because, I visited the walking dead tonight; people who fled the playing field to sit under the bleachers. I will stack your boxes," Dan rose from his swing, "But, I warn you sandcastle thrones soon collapse." Dan stacked the boxes against the side of the cage. Trouble rushed in. Dan closed the door. "It's time to call it a night, furry friend."

In the bedroom Dan pulled his shirt off, hung his pants on the bedpost, made the hamper shot with both socks, and flopped on the bed in his shorts. He fluffed the pillow. Soon he dreamt.

He was shooting from a basketball foul line. Shot after shot missed. Each rebounded off the backboard as two balls, then three, and then four. Shooting and missing, the balls piled up. He waded, knee deep through the balls, ever closer. Under the basket. Too close to miss! The ball circled the basket, stopped on the rim. It laughed at him! It bounced away. Now shoulder high in balls, he found it hard to raise his arms! His voice echoed in his mind, "It's useless I can't make a difference!" The balls were over his head.

"AIR! I can't Breathe!" His cry woke him feeling ice cold, but, sweat beaded on his brow. *Where am I! What's happening? Oh, just a dream. What a feeling of desperation! I had no will to continue! I just stood waiting for the end!*

Dan took a warm shower, toweled off, and stepped into cotton pajama bottoms. The shower had not soothed or relaxed him. Returning to the bed, he sat on the edge contemplating.

Man can have no self-esteem without achievement, and there can be no achievement without hope of accomplishment; a secure reward. Is hope then nurtured in self-esteem or security of reward? He watched the second hand race around the clock. *Security, hope is linked to security. But where does it come from?* Dan checked the alarm setting and laid back. *I'm too tired to care.*

Rolling on his side he tucked the pillow under his head and fell asleep again. Once more, Dan was carried away.

He looked out over a golf course. The fairway of gems sparkled beneath cotton-puff clouds. As a slight breeze massaged his hair, he watched the first player in a green shirt step to the tee and drive his ball. Turning, the golfer walked past Dan.

"Eee-gads! He's faceless!" Dan thought.

The second man in a red shirt and third in a yellow teed off. The third ball, struck poorly, fell short.

"They have no faces either!" Dan realized. "They're just shirts!"

Dan took his turn and hit well, his ball sailed. No one spoke as they walked toward the balls. Dan followed proudly.

The yellow shirt passed his ball going to Dan's.

"I believe that's my ball," Dan said.

Yellow shirt hit it.

"You hit my ball!"

"It was no longer yours, as mine dropped shortest, I may claim any other ball. Here it's in the rules!" Yellow-shirt held a small book open for Dan.

"Very well," Dan said accepting the other ball and playing on.

At the next tee, Dan's drive landed shortest, so he walked to the farthest hit ball. However before he could strike it, Red-shirt complained. "I say! You're on my ball, good man."

"Not according to the rule Yellow-shirt showed me."

"Don't be daft. That rule applies to the prior hole.

Don't you know? Rules change every hole. Buck up, and use a wedge."

"A wedge from here!"

"Too bad. Ball's a bit mucked, too." Red-shirt chirped.

"It's the rules!" the others chimed.

"Who makes these rules? Who decides when they change?"

"We do," said the three shirts.

"But it contradicts the rules set forth by the PGA."

"What right do they have to make our rules?"

"What gives you the right to override the PGA?"

"We claim the right, because you aren't wearing a shirt."

Dan stood in the middle of the fairway. "It's no fun! I won't play!" For the first time he heard a gallery of people laughing. "What are you pointing at?"

Dan was wearing only his Jockeys!

An overwhelming wave of embarrassment hit Dan knocking him down. The laughing ridicule faded as he awoke.

Feeling flushed, he went back to the porch swing, packed a pipe, and smoked it watching the sky. It no longer seemed angry, its crimson cry gone.

Could it be true hope comes only from the promise of achievement? Yet, there is no guarantee of achievement without absolutes? A caring Creator, having anticipated the problems, established absolute rules to prosper mankind. It has been accepted for thousands of years, and only recently questioned. The absolutes never limited creative freedom, but gave us guidance and protection. No if, ands, or buts! If we'd set aside our pride and arrogance long enough to adhere to the rules of the 'Manufacturer's Handbook,' the world of policing would change. Would there even be a need?

He finished the pipe, knocked the ash out, and returned to the bedroom. Entering he pulled the ceiling fan's chain, shoved an eight-track tape in the player, and impulsively picked up the Bible laying next to it. He doubled the pillows and lay back leafing through the *Handbook* reading randomly; "…just as they did not see fit to acknowledge God any longer. God gave them over to a depraved mind, to do those things which are not proper…"[4]

Truly, this is the key! It is our choice. But the world has chosen to race away from "shall nots" like a robber's getaway car. Such being, all the police in the world, cannot protect us from ourselves! Has it come to that?

"…although they know the ordinance of God, that those who practice such things are worthy of death, they not only do the same, but also give hearty approval to those who practice them.[5] *This writing is ancient. Has it always been this way?* He reflected on his childhood. Days lost to this society. How the world was different, less violent:

Dan heard his mother call. She was in the kitchen standing by the bakers cabinet digging money from a coffee can. Carefully counting the coins, she told him what to buy. He was off to fetch cheese and cold cuts from Marland's Grocery. It was longer than the five blocks when on a chore, and shorter when he had fifteen cents for a kite.

Dan bent low on the meat case looking through it watching the slices fall as Mr. Marland worked. Dan chuckled to himself remembering how he bought pickle loaf instead of baloney, because it was his favorite. He could taste the Longhorn cheese, yummy. Nibbling away and kicking rocks ahead of him on the gravel road he meandered home. Nobody bothered him. He'd come in the back door, his mother yelling, "Don't let it slam! WHACK – too late. Then she'd opened the package, "Danny, its half gone!"

Dan also remembered his Grandmother walking to the grocery store. If anyone looked at her funny, bystanders

---

[4] Romans 1:28

[5] Romans 1:32

rushed to help. Dan felt sadness because today's people watch muggings unconcerned or flee in fear. Police go door to door searching for a witness, but no one wants to get involved.

Reclining on the bed, the chords of *What Are You Doing the Rest of Your Life* played in the background. Dan thought, *so different then; a fearless time when man respected God.* He started to close the *Handbook* but noticed a ruffled page. While smoothing the page he read:

"Unless the Lord guards the city, the watchman keeps awake in vain."[6]

He closed the book setting it aside. It had comforted him. *At least my failures at fighting crime aren't my fault. I like that verse! I'll put it on my calling card!* Several minutes later the player ejected the tape, but Dan didn't hear it. He slept as exhausted men do, and dreamed no more. He would need his rest. Dan was destined to encounter his antagonist – face to face!

---

[6] Psalms 127:1

Chapter Ten

A Sergeant's Challenge

Going to his locker, Dan prepared his war bag and joined other officers in the squad room. *Thundershowers? The weatherman's always wrong.* Half the relief milled around and Dan sensed a mixed buzz of joviality and foreboding. The ambience of Damocles sword permeated; all was well, yet a certainty something would spoil it.

The two sergeants at the table tonight were Hallister and Fleischer. Thirty-one years old Hallister received his stripes ninety days prior at Vice Squad. His curly brown hair and unpredictable behavior earned him the name "Squirrely Curly." Now, as a sergeant, higher command objected to "Squirrely" as disrespectful. The men changed it to S.C. The only complaint voiced by the beat officers was his passion for arresting criminals made his favorite words, "Lock him up." Openness offset his occasional pretentiousness. The men gave him a cautious respect.

"Listen up gentlemen and meatheads alike, important stuff first. Here's the paper that needs corrected," Hallister announced handing a few parking tickets and reports back. Clearing his throat, he began again. "Wanted for attempt robbery at Miller's Pharmacy yesterday is a male, white, five foot six, hundred twenty, squinty eyes, and oval face. He wore a dirty white dress shirt, brown slacks, hemp rope for a belt. Dan, you guys might check Box Town for him.

"Anyway, he went into the drug store, approached the pharmacist, pulled a gun, and demanded morphine and money. Then realizing he hadn't concealed his face, pulled a black trash bag over his head which he forgot to cut holes in.

The pharmacist jumped the counter and knocked the gun away. An altercation ensued, the bag came off, but he managed to escape. Last seen on foot south on Colerain. He left his fingerprints on the bag recovered at the scene, no match on file.

"Competing for the bungling bandit award is a male, black, medium height, and weight. He walked through the doors of a Central Trust Bank on Fifth Street downtown yesterday afternoon at closing time. However, that's the sole thing he did right, because he caught his foot under the doormat 'tripping him up'. He stumbled into the service table, and knocked his Lone Ranger mask off. Staggering to his feet a bit confused, he waved what the teller described as a dark green water pistol and yelled, 'This hold is a stiff-up!' The tellers laughed so hard they had trouble setting off the alarm. He fled on foot westbound Fifth Street.

"I know you think it's unnecessary, but from now on you need to turn in your tag jacket logs fully filled out. I know for years we tossed them. No more. Fill them out. The DA wants better accountability." He paused to allow the men to vent.

"Ours is not to question why." He said to regain their attention and waited for quiet. "And that's it, except for one minor thing. My probation period ends at noon tomorrow. I'll thank you now for not embarrassing me with initiation tomfoolery, because I'm off tomorrow. So, hit the streets a running, and lock someone up before the sun comes up." With a gesture of his hand he asked, "Sergeant Fleischer anything?"

Fleischer shook his head.

"Lieutenant Hess?"

"The captain has noticed our burglaries are down compared to last night run. He sends his compliments. But, don't let it go to your heads…"

"A-TEN-TION!" The "clack–clack–clack" of heels down the hallway announced Captain Kirk's approach which brought him in view before all the ties were buttoned up. "At ease, men. Let them nooses dangle, 'til you hit the street. Do continue, Lieutenant."

Hess resumed, "I was just informing them of your compliments on the Burglary patrol."

"Yes, Sir, excellent effort indeed! Stays that good to the end, I'll buy a keg for the relief party."

"On the other hand," Hess said, "I've noticed the PFOs weren't very numerous last week. The scarcity of cars when I make my rounds after 0300 gives me concern. Being past the halfway mark doesn't mean we let up. We have some impressive stats, and we can end this run on top of every other district. Low burglaries ..."

"More than a start, I'd say!" Kirk replied, "They're cruising in warp speed."

The lieutenant realized the futility of pressing his point with the captain interrupting every sentence, so he yielded, "Anything else, Captain?"

"No, just came in to put the Channel Three thing to bed."

"Very well then, men, clean those ties up and hit the street. That's all, dismissed." As the officers stood Hess added, "Don't pass up any movers or parkers. Make it a balanced sheet."

"Go crush the crap out of crime, and don't get any on you," Captain Kirk remarked in a strong voice watching their departure.

On the way to their patrol cars, Gary buttonholed the Duo, "Okay, I'm in. What are we gonna do about it?"

"Do about what?" Ben asked.

"Squirrely Curly's challenge."

"Means nothing to me?" Dan said.

"Nothing! If he respects us enough to toss the gauntlet, we should respect him enough to pick it up."

"Don't think it's a matter or respect. Hallister a bit cocky over new stripes, that's all.

"A rooster's got to crow once in awhile," Ben said.

"Give 'im time. He'll be alright," Dan agreed. "It means nothing. Fresh rank always spreads their feathers. 'Sides that, Snaggles is working."

"Dan's right," Ben agreed. "For once I'm proud he's staying out of it. It'll snap back on us."

"I figured you'd lead the charge," Gary said disappointed.

"Figured wrong. I'm on thin ice with Hess, and Hallister didn't make it personal. Best I just let it pass."

"Amen, amen," Ben sang.

Chapter Eleven

Serge Make It Go Away

Ben and Dan stowed their gear in the vehicle. Ben took the wheel. “Did you hear Kirk mention Channel Three?”

“Sure did, been expecting it. Don’t go far. Swing in Whitie’s and get us some starter fluid.”

“Coffee already, I can’t drink and drive, ’less you’re promising a quiet night.”

“Rainy nights are slow, ’cept for accidents and sneak thieves.”

“Sure, after my butt chewing, everything will seem quiet.”

“Relax! Kirk wouldn’t have mentioned it at roll call if we were in line for a chewing.”

“You’re buying,” Ben said turning into the restaurant lot. “Might be right on Captain Kirk?”

“Yeah, to coffee; and on Kirk, I’ll bet you coffee for a week.”

“You’re too sure. No takers.”

Ten minutes later the Signal-Two came, and they drove back to the District. As soon as the desk officer saw them he pointed to the Captain’s Office. The door was open, but they knocked anyway. Captain Kirk waved them in, “Take a seat, men.”

Hess sat to the far side of the desk. Dan and Ben were provided chairs in front.

“I’m not going to waste time pussy-footing around,” the captain began. “Chief’s office forwarded a complaint from the General Manager of Channel Three, initiated by a night editor. According to it, you two stormed into his office, interrupted their meeting, slapped their newsman in cuffs, refused to discuss the arrest, told him it was none of his business, and hauled their man to the caboose. Over all, cost them some bucks." He glanced at the lieutenant, "That cover all the bases as you read it?"

"They're also complaining of 'Gestapo rudeness'."

"Add 'Gestapo rudeness.' Furthermore, they are contesting the charges in court and threatening to sue the city." He again turned to the lieutenant, "Does that cover all their points of contention?"

"Yes, Sir."

"I see," Kirk said then paused to light a cigar and give it a few good puffs, "If we satisfy those, then we can put this thing to bed?"

"I would think so," the lieutenant smiled.

Kirk turned his attention back to the officers.

"Before you say anything, Dan, I remind you, being cops we get few rights. You have the right to know Lieutenant Hess thinks disciplinary action is in order based on all the news people complaints and your recent stupidity attack alienating myself and the chief. He favors we draw and quarter. As far as I'm concerned, a penalty has been assessed on the tie thing and it's spent brass on the range floor. I can't speak for the chief. So, care to tell me what went down, or you feel you need representation?"

"Sure, I have nothing to hide," Dan said confidently. "I did my job, and Ben had nothing in it but backing his partner."

"You agree with that, Ben?"

"Yes, Sir, I pretty much went along for the ride, and it turned out a good one."

"That being the case, you're excused."

"I'll stick with my partner, unless he objects."

Kirk paused, hearing no objection he said, "All right, Dan, what would you like to say?"

Dan laid the complete story out in detail. When he finished, he looked captain in the eye and said, "Cap'in, fair to tell you, I'd do it again without a minute's hesitation."

"You say, the fireman witnessed it?"

"Yes, Sir, name is Don. He's a lieutenant with the Company on Cherry Street."

"Officer Daley!" Kirk yelled out to the desk officer, "Get me the number for the Fire Company on Cherry." After a short pause, the desk officer yelled a number back and the captain dialed it.

"You're calling him now?" Hess asked. "It's close to midnight."

"So, they're getting paid aren't they? I'm working, no reason the smoke eaters shouldn't… Hello, this is Captain Kirk at the Fifth Police District. You have a Don on duty, lieutenant I believe, on a fire a while back on Chambers. Sure, I'll wait. Thank You."

Placing his hand over the receiver he turned back to Hess, "See how simple. 'Fabbo', he's in the Rec Room."

When Don came to the phone Kirk explained his inquiry, and asked several questions, thanked him, and hung up.

"Pretty well settles it. Fireman Don backs up Officer Black's account. Says another fireman saw the whole thing. They'll definitely testify in court. Seems Channel Three doesn't have enough 'macro coil to fire a laser stun'. Their 'force shields' are gone and they're noise is nothing but a smoke screen."

"Sir, that's the fire hose part of the complaint. The unprofessional conduct hasn't been addressed."

Kirk leaned back in his chair taking a slow draw on the cigar. The blue smoke rippled across the ceiling tiles before he spoke. "One phone call verified this officer truthful. Something the news media has never demonstrated. If they win the case in court, I'll revisit this. Until then, it's a dead issue."

"Yes, Sir," Hess replied disconcertedly.

Kirk looked back over his desk at Dan. "You're dismissed."

They stood to leave. The captain waved a scrap of paper at Dan. He stepped back and took it.

"The other witness," Kirk said. "Be sure those two fire eaters appear and report the outcome to me. Lieutenant and I are expecting a conviction. Right, Lieutenant?"

"Yes, Sir."

"Yes, Sir," Dan acknowledged and they turned to leave.

"Watch your backs out there, men," Kirk cautioned. "It's no picnic you know."

"Yes, Sir," they replied leaving. In the parking lot Ben sighed. "Beam me up Scottie! Was that a fun time or what?"

"I told you he hates the news media."

"Who's this Fabbo guy in the Rec Room?"

"Not a guy! That's Star Trek slang. Probably short for fabulous or something."

"Think Hess went into it with his 'macro coil busted shield evaporated' or whatever he said."

"I told you; do your work and he'll back you," Dan said.

"Yeah, but what was that picnic comment?"

"I'm thinking he's letting us know he heard, and won't be put in the middle."

"What can I say, Partner? These dogfights stress me out. My family's counting on a paycheck."

"Ben, Ben, Ben—lieutenant just loves brushin' lint off navy blue flannel."

"Sometimes you give him more than lint. But, I loved that ending; 'expecting a conviction, right lieutenant.' How sweet was that?"

Dan retrieved his coffee from the dash and took a sip, "Luke warm." He poured it out.

The radio interrupted. "Car 508, 508, Denton Ford on West Mitchell, alarm on the showroom and sales offices."

Ben pressed the lid down on the coffee clamping it between his thighs.

Dan keyed the mike, "508, request a cover, canine if available. The 'perps' usually run across Mill Creek to the expressway."

"Car 508, closest canine is District Three."

"506, I'll swing down and cover the expressway."

Ben handed Dan his coffee, "Cold anyway." Dan poured

it out shoving the empty cup under the seat.

Denton Ford's front driveways were blocked when closed. Ben swung through an abandoned warehouse alongside the car lot. They came in from the rear with lights out giving the perpetrators less notice of their arrival. The parking lot's high intensity fixtures cast a glow upon the surroundings. Parking in the rear they proceeded on foot toward the front. Dan peeked around the front corner surveying the large bowing showroom window.

He immediately saw what activated the alarm. The rear fender of a new Ford Fairlane stuck through the showcase window. Two men were trying to push another vehicle away from the door. Dan whispered, "Watch these clowns." Stepping back pointing to his radio, he signaled he would circle the building. Dan updated the dispatcher as he made his way to the other side.

"Car 506 is in place southbound on the expressway," she informed. "507 is exiting northbound to approach the front of the dealership. K-three reports a ten minute ETA."

From his corner Dan observed 507's approaching from under the overpass. He keyed his mike, "Go Ben."

Ben stepped out and confronted the thieves. "Police! Hands up!"

They bolted toward the Mill Creek. Dan waited, and pounced on the last to pass him. Ben joined him.

Castleman and Jansen, of Car 507, slid to a stop at the first drive, and bailed out on the run after the fleeing men. Caslteman's long legs closed the distance quickly leaving Jansen behind.

Dan and Ben subdued their man and placed him in their cruiser. Ben keyed his mike, "508, does 507 need any help?"

"507, we're good, second suspect apprehended. 506 is with us. We'll bring him back down shortly.

Ten minutes passed before 506 and 507 arrived at the dealership. "I expected to see him in your cruiser, B.C. Last I saw, you were crashing through the bushes on his heels. How'd Daley end up with the arrest?"

"Actually, Daley sprung a stiff arm tackle on him. Best I

let him tell it."

"I found the 'get-a-way' parked on the side of the expressway just as 507 arrived at the dealership. I parked off the shoulder out of sight, and walked to some bushes alongside it. The radio alerted me. BC chased him right to me. Heard him coming up the slope and just waited. When he grabbed the door, I grabbed and yanked him backwards. He hit the pavement fightin' mad. B.C showed up and jumped in."

"Looked like two cats, tails tied, and tossed over a clothes line, 'cept it was on the ground," added Jansen.

"A real twerp of a perp," Dailey continued. No ID, but a set of keys in his pocket fit the ignition. No registration on the temporary plate taped in the back window or the VIN. But, BC did a fine job of interrogating the creep."

"Ask him, 'Pretty please', did you." Ben said.

"Grabbed the front of his shirt, got in his face and said, 'Listen buster, you made me chase you through a stinkin' cesspool of a creek.' Told him I ruined a pair of shoes on his account, and dared him to play 'Cool Hand Luke'."

"Dared him, alright," Daley snickered. "Dragged him by the belt back down to the creek, kickin' and yellin."

"Told him I'd drown him in the sewage.' BC said. "When his nose got close enough, he turned cooperative."

"Just didn't understand how bad he wanted to talk to us," Jansen added.

"So he gave up and laid it out for you," Dan said. "How nice."

"Yep, couldn't talk fast enough," BC stated. "They duped the keys on test drives. Showed up to drive the cars off and found them blocked in. Trying to push the car out of the way it got away and crashed into the showroom."

"Why'd the fools stick around?"

"Oh, get this," Dailey said, "They believed there was plenty of time. Not hearing an alarm, they didn't realize they'd set it off."

"Acting on a false assumption always disappoints," Ben said as the group chuckled.

"Tell you what BC," Dan said. "You want to haul our prisoner while we wait on the owner?"

"Two assists are better 'an one?"

"You'd think, but if you don't have parkers you'll be on Hess' hit list."

"I'll get the parkers later," he chuckled as he helped Dan transfer the prisoner. "Its 'one in hand..'," he said pulling away.

It took another twenty minutes to notify the owner of the dealership, secure the building, and process the paperwork. Leaving the dealership, Dan quipped, "I'd say that's a good start for a quiet night."

"Except, we haven't had our coffee yet."

"We'll stop at the Daily D on the way in."

"Thanks, mighty big of you to offer."

"I'll go one better. I'll even drive for awhile."

Dan pulled away from the Daily D with fresh coffee. In the background the radio chattered as cars conducted business with the dispatcher. One call caught Ben's attention.

"505, traffic stop, Henshaw near Hopple, green 61 Valiant, Ohio plate COL 116."

"508, we're on the parkway, we'll swing by," Ben informed by radio. Then releasing the key he said to Dan, "Ten to one Gary's got a hit on the 'no turn' sign."

"Car 505, copied Henshaw, COL 116, Car 508 in route," relayed the dispatcher.

"505, we're a hundred yards south of Hopple."

Turning onto Henshaw, Car 508 saw the cruiser ahead in a dimly lit area. The violator's vehicle door opened. Immediately the driver swung out and Gary's hands went up as the man pushed him toward the sidewalk.

"Gary's stop's gone bad!" Ben blurted.

Dan accelerated watching the figures. The unknown man led Gary toward some bushes.

"505, ALL CARS BACK OFF—RIGHT NOW!" Gary's urgent voice sounded on the radio.

Hearing the call Dan stopped fifty yards short of the

vehicles staring at the scene.

"We have a hostage situation with 505," Ben radioed. "Have a supervisor meet us behind the Shell station, Hopple and Colerain, with alternate 'coms' and no sirens."

"Attention cars 505, 508, cars responding on Henshaw. Plymouth Valiant registered to Bruce Moore. Signal M, warrant."

"508 copied."

"I'm going to walk up there and see what's up," Dan told Ben.

"You nuts! We have a hostage situation!"

"He's just panicked. Don't believe he wants to kill anybody, or he'd have done it."

"You can't know for sure."

"Gary's been taken somehow, but he's got a family. I don't. I'm gonna swap places."

"That's rookie thinking! You could get killed."

"It's now or never, Ben. I know how you work. I can count on you to crawl close and be there when the opening comes. It gives me an edge Gary doesn't have."

"You're assuming there will be an opening! You could escalate the situation. Even worse, end up with two hostages."

"I believe he's panicked, and I believe I can make an opening, and I don't believe he wants to shot a cop. As for two hostages, there's no room in the cover for three."

"519, I'm Thirty-five at the station where's 508?"

"You can't be sure. Time's on our side."

"Gotta go sometime. If I've believed a lie, yellow roses will be just fine," Dan said as he began walking down the middle of the street.

"Car 508, 508 forty-four your location for 519," the radio barked.

"It's against procedures!" Ben shouted after Dan.

"So, what's new? My conviction trumps their procedure," Dan yelled back. "I'm counting on my partner." A chill went through him. *You're acting on pure supposition, what if you're wrong?*

"Car 508, 508, Signal Forty-Four!"

"508B, I'm here!" Ben vented his frustration in the radio. "Tell 519, I'll meet him shortly."

Dan sauntering toward possible death whistling as if he had not a care in the world.

"It's pure insanity!" Ben shouted at him.

As Dan approached the bushes he called out, "Bruce Moore, I'm unarmed. I'm coming to negotiate."

"Stop where you are or this Copper gets it," responded a voice from within the shrubs.

Dan stopped. "You can see I AM UNARMED. I would like to approach close enough to talk. Five more feet?"

"Go ahead, but I'm watching you."

Dan stepped a half dozen paces to the sidewalk. "Far enough!" Moore demanded. "Say what you come for and get."

"I want you to swap your officer for me."

"Why would I wanna do that? I have both of you now."

"Where you gonna put me? You don't have room for two hostages."

"I could just shoot you!"

"You could, but that'd make your problem worse, and you're back to one hostage. If you wanted to shoot cops you'd have done it. Officer Follert is married. He has family. I do not. If you have to shoot somebody, wouldn't you prefer me? Besides I'm the hostage negotiator, and a bigger chip to bargain with."

After a brief pause Moore agreed, "Okay, I'll swap, but I want a car out of here."

"I can make it happen. First, you have to swap."

"Alright come on in."

"No. That's not the way it works. It's an exchange. You have your gun on me. I'm not going anywhere. Officer Follert comes out first."

A short period of silence followed.

"Hurry up and decide. Once SWAT snipers get here, neither of us is any good to you."

Dan heard rustling, "Okay, I'll send him out." Within a

minute Gary appeared.

"Officer Follert, leave your vehicle as is. Walk straight to the middle of the street then up to the Shell Station."

"Yes, Sir, Mister Negotiator," Gary said emphatically as he walked away.

"Okay, Mister Negotiator, come over here real slow."

"As soon as Officer Follert is out of range."

After Gary walked halfway down the street Dan approached the cover. At seven feet Moore became visible. He sat Dan in a trampled area and tossed Gary's handcuffs at his feet. "Put 'em on! Hurry up! No! Around the tree! I want to hear clicks."

Dan complied. Moore checked them. They sat close in the clump of trees facing each other three feet apart. *He's going to see backup coming. I need to get him ready for it, or things could go bad in a hurry.* "Look Bruce, all you're wanted for is a misdemeanor. What makes you think you'll do time on it?"

"I ain't for findin' out. 'Sides don't much matter now?"

"Hey, so you panicked. Big deal. You haven't hurt anybody. Keep your head, stay calm, and we can work this out."

"If anybody gets hurt," he said shaking the gun threateningly at Dan. "You'll be on top of the stack."

"519, exactly where is 508?" the radio barked.

"508B, I'm behind the station. 508A has exchanged places with 505. We'll meet 519 in front of the station."

Hearing the broadcast encouraged Dan. *Ben and Gary joined up.* Gary would give critical information to command and Ben would be working his way to him. "You have any idea what's going on out there?" Dan asked Moore.

"Don't see nothing!"

Whooa, that made him nervous. But, I've gotta risk it. He's has to be scared enough to think surrender's a way out. "You aren't supposed to see it. Listen to the radio."

"507, Thirty-five, Colerain post."

"Notice the silence and spacing of the calls, Bruce."

"503, at Rachel and Henshaw."

"It's started," Dan said, "and you're smart enough to know neither of us can stop it."

"501, Thirty-five on Sidney post."

"The net's closing. Bruce, we're boxed."

"Don't matter. I put this gun in your ear," he said sticking the barrel against the side of Dan's head. "They'll let me walk out."

His stress is focusing on the gun. That feeling of desperate power growing! But if I don't build his stress, he won't surrender!

The radio continued to cut in, "519, request 514 to close Henshaw at Hopple, and the SWAT Team's ETA is ten minutes. Have all other cars remain out of the area."

"You heard that didn't you?" Dan asked. "Now they wait, but not for you to negotiate. They're waiting for the snipers."

"520, I'm pulling in the Shell station. Where is 519?"

"I'd like us to settle this before they get here. They'll set up with a green light. First opportunity they'll fire."

"Maybe I just end it," Moore's voice quivered.

He's edgy...Gun equals big power. Dan experienced this before at a market robbery gone bad. That abductor fed off the gun's power growing bolder and bolder. He became reckless and a hostage died. *Maintain balance. Keep an out visible.*

"Bruce, we still have time to work this out. But it's ticking away."

His eyes narrowed. Moore shoved the revolver in Dan's face again. His voice fluttered. "Yeah there's time. You and me right now."

Okay, he's as nervous as I dare let him get. Sure hope Ben's close enough to see what's going on.

"519, I'm in the rear. I'll come around." the radio crackled.

"What's he doin'?" Moore shouted daring to crawl out a few feet to look.

"Get back in here! You'll get yourself shot! I got an idea might keep us both alive. Want to hear it?"

Moore crawled back and sat pressing closer into the bushes than before.

He knows he's trapped. Ben, I'm counting on you to be close.

"I ain't gonna wait around no more! Get up…"

"Look Bruce, I've known you a couple years. You've been in stuff, but nothing bad. Why all this over a misdemeanor? Go in with me, it gets you out of here alive."

"As long as I got you, I'm alive."

"Okay, you don't want to surrender. Your call, but you have to get out of here. Take my hat and shirt. Make a dash for the car. They'll think you're me. By the time they figure it out, you'll be gone. Ditch the car, and disappear. *"Hope Ben's close enough to hear. Grab him when he makes his move.*

"It could work. If'n you don't try something."

"Try something?" Dan forced a chuckle, "Bruce, I'm cuffed to a tree! What can I do? You've got Gary's gun, plus the radio. What am I gonna do? Who am I gonna tell? Sure it'll work. It'll take time before they give chase, and look—the cruiser's still running. You've got emergency lights. The switch is on the clipboard console."

"Where's the siren? How you turn it on?"

"Blue box, center, bottom of dash. It's your best out. *C'mon, you're desperate enough. Bite!* "Real soon now, snipers will be sighting in on us. You'll lose your chance to escape."

"They best not, or you're dead!" Moore cocked the pistol.

"*Oops, too much pressure. Focus him on the getaway.* "I'm not trying to scare you. I'm the one scared. Ease that hammer down. An accidental discharge and they'll rush us. We'll both be dead."

He took a moment to think it over, and then carefully lowered the hammer.

"Okay, we both know they're closing in. It's procedure. You need to make your move NOW, or you'll lose the opportunity. Bruce, your hostage is a cop. They'll set up under a green light. That's procedure. First open shot – bang! They take you out. This is not enough cover. Take the car."

"I think I'll take you with me."

"Up to you, but I'm handcuffed. Be clumsy. Slow you down. You need speed. Besides, they see both of us and they'll chase, just a white shirt they won't."

Moore did not reply immediately. His fidgeting increased as time crept by. "Okay, give me the shirt."

"I'm handcuffed around a tree."

"Hold your palm up." Moore dropped the key in it. "Slow and easy. Try anything I'll shoot you dead. Got nothin' to lose."

Dan followed the instructions. Carefully removed his shirt, exchanged with Moore, and re-locked the cuffs around the tree. Moore kept peeking around the bushes.

"I don't see no cops, but there's cars at the Shell station," he said nervously.

"Then go for it while it's open. Now or never. Go. GO! Good luck!"

Moore bolted into the cruiser. As it accelerated away Ben crashed through the brush.

"You in love with that tree," he quipped pulling his cuff key out.

"Hurry up!"

"You okay?" Ben asked grabbing the mike, "Suspect stole cruiser. West on Derby! He has Follert's gun-belt and radio."

"Get these off!"

One cuff freed, they ran to the sidewalk.

Dan watched the stolen cruiser approach Car 503's roadblock. Officer Watkins took cover behind his vehicle with a shotgun.

"503, is Dan in the cruiser!" Watkins asked by radio.

"No," Ben radioed as they watched Moore crash into the rear of 503's cruiser spinning it away and forcing Officer Watkins to the side. Watkins rebounded uninjured, but the car sped beyond range by the time he brought the shotgun on target.

Gary pulled up in 508's vehicle. Dan jumped in the front seat while Ben piled in the back. The car squealed off in pursuit.

"He wrecked my car! I'm going to beat him senseless," Gary complained.

"You expected Watkins to move the roadblock? He didn't ask 'pretty please' you know," Dan said.

"Gotta catch him first," Ben said.

"507, in pursuit of stolen cruiser north on Colerain," the radio blared.

At the corner, Watkins waved them on. The engine's quad carburetors roared. The distance shrank.

"508, we're north on Spring Grove parallel with Colerain chase cars. We'll attempt to intercept."

The fox had scrambled from its cover, but the speed and number of hounds on his tail was unexpected. Moore no longer had opportunity to dump the car and slip into the night.

"Its escape, or crash and burn for him," Dan said finally buckling up. "Don't get too close."

Moore sped toward the dead-end turning left just prior to it. Cars 504 and 514 waited a block away. Because the suspect rammed the roadblock car earlier, the officers were parked to the side shotguns ready. Moore hit the intersection at such speed it didn't provide a safe backstop to shoot. Speed carried the suspect vehicle wide. It sideswiped the corner of a brick building and careened through the parking area of the railroad yard. Moore slowed slightly before exiting back onto Spring Grove dragging a section of chain link fence.

At Hess' directive, Fleischer joined in the pursuit and chase vehicles were limited to Cars 508 and 514. Moore activated the stolen cruiser's bar lights and the traffic yielded. Recklessly, he twisted through the streets onto Interstate 74. The chase proceeded at times over a hundred miles per hour. The vehicle fled toward the Indiana State Line and jurisdictional limitations. However, county deputies already waited at the city-county line where they joined the chase.

"519, advise city cars to back off. County has the pursuit," Fleischer ordered by radio."

Moore sped down the interstate unable to lose the county officers. After a few miles he took an off ramp, and accelerated down a curvy country road.

"Ta-woo-Beep, Ta-woo-Beep," the radio sounded with an all county broadcast. "Attention all cars all departments, David Seven and Charley Four in pursuit on Dry Fork Road. All units, Henry Five alerts the BRIDGE IS OUT north of Short Road. Barricade reported stolen by juveniles. Attention all cars, Henry Five's on the side, beacons activated, at 'BRIDGE OUT' sign."

The storm, which took the bridge, left a wide fissure. A creek meandered through boulders below. Moore saw the officer's signal to stop, but whizzed past him at fifty miles an hour. The cruiser catapulted into the air. The sound of crashing and tearing of metal accompanied the vehicle bouncing off the boulders like a ball in a pinball machine. The chase ended. The seat belt saved Moore's life, but he incurred some broken ribs, a minor concussion, and a broken arm.

By the time the city officers converged on the scene, the county had called an ambulance. As the medics carried Moore to the conveyance Dan stopped them. He pulled the sheet back and removed his badge from the shirt.

"Real stupid, Bruce, my man, you didn't steal the General Lee. It was a city police car." Walking off he shouted back, "Oh, keep the shirt. It's ripped and bloody anyway."

The rescue transported Moore under guard back to the city's General Hospital where the felony charges kept him off the streets for some time. Gary doubled up with Ben, while Dan attended to the required paper work. After an hour Dan's part was complete. Fleischer would be banging out the incident report on a typewriter for most of the night. Dan slid into the cruiser and radioed, "508A, have my Partner rejoin me at White Castles, Knowlton's Corner."

"505, copy. We're Thirty-five."

They're drinking coffee, while I'm wadded through paperwork!

Dan pulled side by side to Gary's cruiser parked in the back row. Gary was alone and Dan just scowled at him. "What, Preacher?"

"I got stuck with all your paperwork! That's what."

"Hold on, Mister Negotiator, it was your cockamamie idea. Which, I don't think anybody was too fond of."

"Ghost Rider, you started it all!

"And to show how I appreciate your help, I bought you coffee. Ben went for it."

"That's the price you put on my sacrifice—a coffee?"

"Here comes Big Ben now and he's not smiling."

Ben opened the door, "You dumber 'an dirt rookie brain!"

"I'll let you two get reacquainted," Gary said pulling away.

"Seemed like a good idea at the time?" Dan said, "Guess, I mostly reacted."

"I guess? How do I hold my head up? My partner's a dumb as dirt rookie. You got a death wish? Do something like that again and I'll shoot you myself. Would right now if I weren't too old to train another partner."

"For cryin' out loud. You like me."

"No way, I'm just use to your ugly face. Don't read nothin' into it."

"Worked didn't it?"

"Do your braggin' to your undertaker. You call that greased pig chase working?

"Boils down to professional risk, and I was comfortable with it."

"Stupid people are comfortable with stupid fool tricks!"

Dan and Ben returned to routine duties. They stopped several suspicious vehicles, wrote three FIRs and two red light violations. In time the radio summoned them again.

"Car 508, 508, loud party, 1612 South Argyle."

They arrived in a neighborhood of assorted Cape Cod and Bungalow style homes. At 1612 several cars parked on the front lawn. Walking to the door, they heard a penetrating drum beat. Dan tapped on the door. He saw a person shrouded in a black robe standing inside with his back to the door. Without turning to look, the shroud stepped backward to open the door. "You're late, Brandon, he'll be furious," the robed form whispered quickly retreating into the main room.

"Shall we take it as an invite?" Ben suggested.

"We will, but watch out," Dan replied.

They entered the empty unlit foyer. Flickering light dimly illuminated the main room of the house. They stepped in cautiously. A lone drummer pounded out the slow beat from the rear corner. Numerous candles provided light. Eleven additional figures formed a semicircle around a small table draped in a dark cloth. All present wore long black hooded robes tied with red sashes. The participants swayed and chanted to the cueing of a bearded man standing behind the table. His robe opened over a red frock. Coal black hair shrouded his head under the cape. An elongated head accentuated the high cheekbones and pointed goatee.

Dan immediately keyed his mike and whispered, "508, send me a couple backup cars." The radio clicks caught the attention of the leader.

"Who dares trespass in this sacred chamber?" he demanded approaching from behind the table. The robe obscured his feet making it seem he floated. "Depart or be cursed!"

"Been there, had that done already," Ben replied firming his grip on his nightstick.

"You're trespassing. You will depart!"

"You're good at intimidating talk," Dan said, "but we can't go 'till we've finished our business."

"You will go! There are enough of us to put you out!"

Normally six to one odds encouraged Dan to retreat and wait for backup, but this costumed aficionado's attitude provoked Dan's stubbornness. He stepped back and flipped the light switch. Nothing happened. *Why'd I think that was gonna work? Okay make a show of standing your ground.*

Dan stepped forward and faced the leader.

"Before you do something stupid, consider we have six bullets apiece. I think the odds are on our side."

Dan flipped his stick to the left hand and unsnapped his holster. Ben followed suit. The man did not retreat, but stood glaring at them. To Dan's relief he heard 505 and 509 signal their arrival. Soon Gary Follert and Gene Martin joined them, and the atmosphere changed. Dan and Ben secured the holster straps.

"What right do you have to barge in here and interrupt our religious service?"

"It's pinned to my shirt," Dan replied. "Now if you want to stop playing games, we'll do what we need to do and you can get back to your séance or whatever. We have a neighbor complaint regarding a loud party, so first I need to know who the owner of the house is."

"It's joint ownership."

"Okay, seems you don't want to play nice. Keep in mind, if I lock you up, all the toys are mine. Now, your ID, please. And, I'll tell you up front, if you don't have one I'll haul you downtown to the Bureau of Identification to find out who you are."

The man gathered in his robe until he reached his pants pocket, retrieved his wallet, and provided a driver's license.

"Everybody, see that? Time to play 'follow the leader'," Ben announced to the crowd.

Reluctantly they all provided IDs. The leader's license identified him as Douglas Willis, with an address in a different neighborhood.

Gary stepped to the front window where some additional light came in from the streetlight and queried the information for wants. While they waited, Martin meandered around the room. He noticed an absence of furniture, and spotted a hash pipe. Close inspection revealed the bowl contained a residue. He confiscated the pipe. Martin joined Dan and raised the pipe up conspicuously. "Gentlemen, whose pipe?"

No one responded.

"Come on now. I have a lost pipe. Will the real owner

please step forward?"

Again, no response.

"How come there's no furniture in the house?" he addressed Willis.

No response.

"Humor him, Willis," Dan derided. "Where's the furniture? Haven't you moved in yet?"

"It's an investment purchase. Like I said; a joint ownership venture. Nobody lives here. There's no need for furniture. We're going to turn it over for a profit."

"Can't help notice you found a need for the table under the black sheet. Just exactly what is it you all do here?" Martin asked.

"Right now it's an in-house religious study."

"You emphasize religion, and it's hard to miss the star and goat logo draped over the table. Is this an altar?"

Willis did not respond.

"What religion are you participating in?"

"Natural holistic worship."

"For future reference, Mr. Willis," Dan interrupted, "in order to meet the residential code for an in-house gathering there must first be someone permanently living in-house."

"Car 505, your queries are ready," the dispatcher informed.

Martin abandoned the questioning. Gary stepped into the foyer out of earshot and received the results. He pulled Dan aside. "We have a misdemeanor on Kellogg, a Domestic Violence Restraint violation on Puggs, and our main man's wanted for felonious assault. I called for two more cars."

"Wait here for them, and we'll play twenty questions 'til they arrive." Dan returned to the main room and approached Willis.

"Okay, before I left, you were explaining your religious status. Are you recognized as a religion by the Federal Government?"

"Would be if we applied for it."

"So, you're implying this structure is a church rather than a residence?"

"No, I keep telling you we're having an in-house meeting."

"Yes you do, but you keep dancing around whose house it is. Who is having the meeting?"

"I'm having the meeting."

"Are you the owner?"

"No, it's jointly owned."

"See, once more round the merry-go-round. There appears to be some contradiction. If this is a function of a corporate party it's business and requires business zoning, but this house is in a residential zone."

"You're full of double talk. People meet in houses everywhere to discuss their religion, pray, or whatever. We're no different. We are free to pursue our life as we choose!"

"Joint ownership sounds corporate owned. Business or residence? This may seem foolish to you, but Residence Zoning requires an intent to reside. Gets technical doesn't it, but that's how lawyers make a living."

"It's a free country. We're free to perfect our lives as we see fit."

"Cars 507, Signal Thirty-five." The radio sounded, followed shortly by, "Car 514 Thirty-five.

"Excuse me a minute," Dan said. "I have a couple things to take care of." He left to meet Officers Kirby and Castleman in 507 and Officer Daley in 514.

"Here's what we have. We responded to a loud party. We get here and the door's opened. We slip in to find a cult thing going on; black robes, drumbeat, weird chanting. There's a dozen in all and the holy man's pushy. We called backup, queried everybody, and three hits. Martin snags a hash pipe, and a sixteen year old whose mommy doesn't know what the Devil he's doing. When we go in, Gary will take the Juvee, and one of you take the misdemeanor. The head spook's got a felony and we'll see how he takes to the news after we cuff the others and kick the clan out."

"Sounds like a plan," said BC Castleman.

"Better, we back your felony, and Daley grabs the

misdemeanor, Jansen suggested.

"Okay with me," Dan said. They all nodded and went into the main room. Dan gave his traffic whistle a couple short bursts. "Listen up folks. There's a couple misdemeanor warrants in the crowd, and a juvenile with no parental accompaniment."

While Dan spoke, Gary stepped alongside the juvenile as Kirby took custody of another man, and Dan pointed out the third for Daley. The leader relaxed since no one approached him.

"The rest of you need to call it a night," Dan announced.

The participants pulled off the robes and packed them in purses, nap sacks, and bags. Soon all but three departed.

"Gentlemen," Dan addressed them, "I can provide you a blue cab, but they're all express to the county jail."

They hesitated.

"Fares paid, but doubt you'll like the accommodations."

"We're waiting for Councilor Ischyres. We'll leave together."

"Is-ki –res?" Dan sounded the name out. "According to his license he's Douglas Willis. But whoever, I need to confer with him privately. You've been directed to disperse."

Escorted by BC they reluctantly left, and BC closed the door. Dan turned his attention to Willis. "Sir, the reason I called this private meeting is to inform you of the felony warra ..." Willis swung at Dan. Anticipating it, He blocked the blow with his nightstick. As they struggled, Dan yelled, "No mace! Closed area!"

The four remaining officers struggled to subdue the five feet nine hundred sixty pound assailant. Willis' veiled strength took them off guard. He fought like the Devil he looked like, and the four officers were tossed about like a loose tarp in a strong wind. They held their own, but made no headway. BC managed to grab someone's radio mike and yell, "507, we need a Taser..." The transmission broke off as he fell backwards from the impact of Willis' backhand. BC shook it off and grabbed Willis' arm.

The dispatcher, unable to raise any of the struggling

policemen, broadcast, "Officer needs assistance." The morning quiet erupted with screaming sirens from every direction. The closest cars were occupied with arrests, and couldn't respond. Cars responding from the south end and adjoining districts were going to take a few minutes.

The struggle continued. The officers wearied, but the combatant grew stronger as if energized by the excitement. Dan finally managed to apply a restraint headlock. He held it with all his might, but with little effect. Willis threw his shoulders forcefully, twisting frantically and Dan's grip weakened. The officers engaged in one of the fiercest struggles of their careers.

Dan's restraint hold did not last. When it slipped his hand caught under the amulet the man wore around his neck. As Dan fell back, he broke the chain and landed on his backside with a thud. Stunned, Dan sat looking at a glass eyeball encased in a three inch round black oval disk. The pupil starred and flickered in the candlelight.

With the loss of the pendant, Willis' energy waned. They easily handcuffed him, and Dan immediately called off the assistance response. Shortly thereafter, Officer Becker rushed in. He observed a less than average size man being easily handcuffed without resistance, and yet four large hefty officers, uniforms in disarray, out of breath, and perspiring.

"Give it back," Willis shouted at Dan. "It's my property. Return it!"

Dan then connected the amulet with his will, and strength to fight.

"Do I look stupid?"

"Its personal property, you can't take it away!"

"You don't like to share at all, do you?"

"I demand my property! You've no right to take it!"

"Prisoners are not allowed jewelry," Dan advised. I warned you. You go to jail. I get the toys."

"I'm holding you responsible for it!"

"And, I'm holding it for you. You play nice, and you'll get it back when you get out of jail."

The three pulled him up off the floor and double handcuffed him. Martin blew out the candles, and locked the door behind them with the key found in the prisoner's pocket. Outside they discovered his counterparts did not wait on the grand Ischyres. Dan was grateful; *a Devil a day is plenty.*

Dan and Ben took the opportunity of Willis' calmness to secure his feet with another set of cuffs and strapped him into the back seat. Since he took to spitting at them, a cotton pillowcase was pulled over his head. Before he closed the door, Dan warned him, "You start up again, and I'm just going to shoot you."

Dan and Ben transported him to the lock up. Deputy Ternnka saw them coming, and yelled back to the other guards, "Got a spitter!"

The search and paperwork was completed and Willis passed through to the inner chamber, two receiving deputies took him aside and instructed him quietly. His head nodded, and they slowly removed the pillowcase.

Dan held up the amulet and swung it back and forth singing. "I got your power. I got your power."

"Give my property back!" Willis shouted, "When I get out of here I'll put a dark curse on you. You won't be so flippant then!"

"Hey, don't be getin' him all wound up," Ternnka complained.

"Nighty-night Willie boy," Dan baited still holding the amulet. "Don't forget to say your prayers."

"We have the right to pursue our destined purpose without interference," Willis shouted back as the jailer walked him out of sight."

"Come on guys! Leave him alone, unless you want him back," Ternnka demanded.

"Sorry, got carried away."

"We have to put up with him the rest of the night, you don't."

"Sorry Bert, just demonstrating this eyeball's effect. He fought like a grizzly protecting her den until I yanked it off, then he lost his ferocity. Whether it's real or not, he associates this with some special power."

"You don't buy that hocus pocus, do you?"

"It only matters that he does, and five of us couldn't restrain him until I yanked it. You return it at your own risk."

"I'll mark the arrest sheet."

"You'd be smart to do that," Dan said. The Duo turned to exit and they could hear Willis arguing with the deputies, "It's a free country. I was in my own house…violated my civil…"

They were back patrolling their beat when Dan remarked, "Willie just wants to be free. That's all. But, none of us are free. Without rules life's a hodgepodge and freedom is absorbed in the demands of fighting the chaos."

"He was crying about fulfilling his purpose. You should have asked him what it was, Dan."

"Gee, wasn't it nice of us to funnel him into city government whose purpose is to provide every citizen life fulfillment."

"Thought that was 'pursuit of happiness'."

"Either way, best government's mud pond of regulations can do is pursue order and security."

"Dan, I think he'd make a good politician."

"Probably fit right in, but no one who relies on majority popularity for his welfare can pursue the good of the whole. Trust government to champion the people! Ha, there's a pirates pledge! And they're the ones making the laws."

"Don't be so down on government, Dan. We need it. It tries to do what's right. Some matters have lots of concerns to consider, before they can sort out solutions."

"Interesting, absolute freedom requires an adherence to unchanging boundaries, and government is the process of changing boundaries."

"So government can't save us," Ben sighed. "Tell me, have you been watching that white Volvo we're following?"

"A bit erratic, but it's staying in its lane."

"You imply we aren't really free to pursue happiness?"

"I don't know, but the *Handbook* seems to imply it can't be found outside the guidelines our Creator established.

Those boundaries are the outer membrane of true peace and..."

"Your itch again," Ben broke in. "Where we came from, and where we are going dictates..."

"Purpose!" Dan added as he pulled alongside the Volvo at the light. "And for now, Willis will pursue his brand of fulfillment, as we do ours. Both hampered by self-interests."

"Let me guess; therein, is the mystery of rising crime?" Ben said glancing out the side window. "And, there's the answer to another mystery! The dog's helping grandma drive her Volvo."

The light changed green and the car pulled away. With one hand on the wheel, the driver attempted to control the dog with the other. She accomplished neither effectively. Dan followed to a straight section. He activated the bar lights, but the distracted driver did not acknowledge the flashing lights. Ben "bleeped" her, and the siren excited the dog. The driver stopped the vehicle in the middle of the road. Her attention focused on the dog.

"Pull to the curb," Dan commanded over the PA. It took several minutes for her to comply.

They approached the vehicle. Ben crossed over and distracted the yelping dog as Dan confronted the woman in her late sixties. "Your license and registration, please."

"Why was I pulled over?"

"Because you were weaving in traffic. License and registration."

The distracted woman gave her best impression of Jack Benny; with hands to her cheeks she muttered "Well!" Stirring through her purse she eventually producing a wallet.

"Ma'am," instructed Dan, "You must restrain your dog so it does not interfere with your driving."

"Ma'am! Do I look like your grandmother!"

"Mrs. Benton-Whitmore..."

"MS," She corrected.

"Ms. Benton-Whitmore, You must restrain your dog so it does not interfere with your driving."

"Woofy's no problem. He rides in my lap."

"Not anymore."

"Woofy doesn't like the back seat. He can't see out the windows."

"It's after midnight! Where does Woofy need to go or see at this hour?"

"Well! I don't know it's any of your business. He's not driving."

"Had us fooled. Either tie Woofy in the backseat, or I'll have to issue a ticket."

"You'd give a defenseless little dog a ticket," she demanded angrily.

"No, you'll get the ticket."

"What on Earth for?"

"Weaving, load interfering with driver."

"Well, I never!" she huffed opening the door forcefully. The woman struggled to keep the terrier in her arms as it yapped and lunged at the strangers. "I can't obey your demands if you're standing in the way."

Dan checked to make sure traffic was clear, backed up, and opened the rear door for her. She placed the dog on the back seat, and tied the leash to the seat belt. Ms. Benton-Whitmore slammed the back door shut, and Woofy jumped clear. She whirled around with indignation and slid back behind the wheel with another slam. "The Humane Society will hear of this! It's dog cruelty. What's your badge number?"

"Two-nine-six," Dan answered drawing out each number.

"And what's 'thaa-at' suppose to mean?"

"Mean? I have no idea. It's the badge number you requested."

"Are you done harassing us? Can we go, now?"

"Yes, and do drive careful."

She pulled from the curb making an unlawful U-turn. Dan shook his head in disbelief.

"We could tag her for the U-turn," Ben suggested.

"No way, that little lady will tie us up longer on one traffic tag than any two felony arrests. I'm cutting my losses and going the other way."

"I can see why she's still a Ms," Ben said.

The radio quieted down as was customary for midweek. Taking advantage of the lull Dan suggested, "Best we check our doors before the bars let out. Keep some scoundrel from sneaking in on us."

"Your turn to yank awhile."

"Who says?"

Lightning streaked the sky followed by a tumult of thunder.

"Okay, I'll get wet. I ain't arguing with HIM! How come he's on your side?" Ben asked.

"Not sure He is. We can sit it out for a few minutes see if the rain slacks."

Again the sky lit up like a Fourth of July finale.

"The lightning gods are messing with us."

"Lightening gods," Dan responded. "I thought you Catholics had saints."

"I'm speaking mythological fable."

The cloudburst lasted ten minutes before it subsided.

"Oh, myth-master," Dan said. "We can get back to work now."

The dispatches and priorities weren't demanding their time so they continued shaking doors. Dan turned in beside Max's Vending Supplies and drove down the side parking area studying the windows. Two-thirds of the way back, he noticed light didn't reflect off a pane and stopped. "Check the bottom of that one."

Ben found the glass missing, and keyed the radio. "508, put us on a PFO [Place Found Open], 1224 Ellis St."

Dan parked and joined Ben to investigate. They found no broken glass in or outside. Nevertheless, several crates stacked under it allowed anyone to reach in and unlatch the window.

"Looks old to me," Dan said.

"Why chance it?" Ben asked keying his radio, "508, is there a canine available?"

"K-Five, available," Officer Young answered. He

arrived in minutes and Dan briefed him.

"How bad you want it searched?" asked Young with the glee of a bear finding a honey tree.

"No problem. I played hide and seek last time," Dan said.

"No way! That was a lost coin toss. It's still your turn!"

"Sorry, toss or no, counts as a turn."

"Ohhh, no! I'm allergic. I don't do dogs!"

"Shall we toss again, then?"

"Hold on, guys," Young interrupted, "Maybe we get lucky and get a bad guy. You want it searched? If not, I got places to go."

Dan looked at Ben, "I say we search it. What say you?"

Ben buried his face in his hands. A muffled answer came through.

"Couldn't hear you," Young said.

"Search it."

"You two decide on the short straw while we search," Young said. With that he climbed the crates with Sentry and they entered the warehouse.

"K-Five, canine in the building on Ellis Street," he informed the dispatcher, and then added, "Number three." It alerted others of a possible 'empty third'.

Canines hunt for reward. When the rewards stop, the conditioned response stops. Therefore, after every third unsuccessful search the beat officer would hide. The dog searched again guaranteeing a find and reward. Thus, the dog remained focused. Officer Young was aware of Ben's aversion to dogs having worked with them many times.

Young and his dog made a thorough search. A few minutes later, he notified the dispatcher they were leaving the building. By the end of the search, Cars 505 and 507 arrived with Officers Follert, BC, and Jansen.

"It's clean. Sentry perked up in the office area on the first pass, but it wasn't strong. Second pass he ignored it. Could've been someone in there earlier, or lingering perfume. Anyway, I'm sure it's clean now," Young paused then added, "So, who's playing burglar?"

“Not our beat,” the newcomers cheered, “We just came for the show.”

“Come on guys,” pressed Young. “Need a bad guy. Ain’t got all night.”

Hearing “bad guy” Sentry’s ears perked, he let out a shrill bark. Ben retreated toward his cruiser.

“Okay, okay,” Dan said turning to Ben, “It’s fair we flip for it.” The others joined in agreement.

“My coin, and I flip,” Ben demanded.

“Fine! My call. Heads.”

Ben eyed the dog. Reluctantly he fished a quarter from his pocket, flipped, but dropped it. The coin rolled in front of Sentry who sniffed it.

“Tails,” Yong announced.

“Dropped don’t count,” Ben said digging for another. This time he caught it.

Ben revealed it. “CURSES!”

“Put the bad guy suit on and let’s get on with it,” Dan said smiling.

“He doesn’t have my size.”

“Oh, yes I do,” Young remarked handing him a pair of folded overalls.

Ben stripped his gun belt. “A partner who cared would step in for me,” he said sliding in a leg.

“It’s tough love; making you all you can be.”

The overalls on, Ben disappeared through the door with a flashlight in his hand and a radio in his pocket. Ten minutes later he radio, “508B, I’m ready.”

The handler entered the building this time keeping the dog on leash.

“Never thought he’d do it,” Gary said.

“Me either,” BC agreed. “The way he shies off dogs? Wow! Doin’ a hide-and-seek.”

“Peer pressure in action,” Dan said.

“Listen to the fit the dog’s having,” BC noted.

“Bet he’s locked himself in a closet,” Dan chuckled.

They were belly-laughing when the radio called, “K-Five, need help in here!”

Running for the door, someone yelled, "They've found a burglar—it's gone bad!"

Flashlights in one hand, weapons in the other, they worked their way to the rear truck bays. Dan was first to clear the door. Ben lay on the floor, his torso encircled with large tires, and the dog stirred to frenzy. Ben was unsuccessfully trying to kick off the tires. Young worked to calm the dog. The arriving officers had no idea what had transpired, but they joined the dog's howling with their laughter.

Dan and Gary helped clear the tires, and Ben rose to his feet yelling. "Don't do dogs! No more! NEVER!" Giving the canine ample clearance, he stomped out of the building.

"You are going to let us in on the whole story," Dan asked Young.

"Certainly, but he's really agitated. Let's give him time to calm down.

"He's not barking anymore," Gary pointed out.

"Not Sentry, Ben. After I get Sentry secured, we'll have story time." Young returned the dog to the car while the others locked the building. Then he joined the group. Ben handed him the overalls and went back to lean on the rear of his cruiser.

"I can't tell it anyway near as good as it was, but I'll do my best," Young said. "But, it's Ben's story. Sure you don't want to tell it?"

Ben shook his head while adjusting his gun-belt.

"Okay then. Sentry immediately picked up Ben's scent and pulled me to the truck bays. He went straight for the tire storage loft's ladder with such excitement I thought he was gonna climb the thing. Took all I had to settle him down, praised his find, and hollered for Ben to show himself. I'm not sure what happened, but that's when it went crazy. Ben, you sure you don't want to take it from here?"

"You're doin' fine," he said unemotionally.

"Well, I saw Ben stand up and Sentry went crazy again. I called him off, rewarded him, and pulled him to the back of the bays. Then I told Ben to go ahead and leave. Like I said, not sure what happened, and doubt Ben's going to say," Young stopped to look at Ben who shook his head.

"Come on, tell us firsthand what happened?" the group begged.

Ben shook his head emphatically.

"I'm guessing nerves, too big a hurry or something," Young said. "'Cause he was standing, then all of a sudden disappeared. Reckon he tripped. Fell over. The next I see are all these tires rolling all over the loft."

The group was chuckling as Young laid out the picture.

"They banged off the brick wall and careened down the loading ramp with Ben inside screaming. I could hardly hold Sentry off, and called for you guys. You should have seen it," He laughed. "Four tires coming at me, kicking legs out one end, flailing arms the other. Rolling down the ramp like the Michelin Man."

The group broke out in laughter.

"Bet he's ready to re-tire now," Gary quipped.

"Go ahead, laugh! NO MORE DOGS!" Ben turned and entered the cruiser and closed the door forcefully.

The story group disembarked chuckling. Dan slid in behind the wheel of the cruiser. They sat quietly while Dan completed the PFO-317 report.

"Hey, what's with the silent treatment? Big Ben mad at Danny Boy?"

"I'm not doing any more hide-and-seeks! Not part of the job."

"I'm proud of you. You put a full effort into this one. Bet you're tired."

"That supposed t' be funny?"

"It IS funny. You just aren't in the mood."

Ben did not reply, and Dan gave him a minute before saying, "You were never in any danger, except breaking your fool neck with the roly-poly trick."

"You aren't standing even with me. I side with you on all your stupid dogfights. Stuff could get me fired. Least you could do is one lousy hide-and-seek in return!"

"Didn't know it meant so much to you."

"Cocky-poo-doo-doo! You really are dumber 'n dirt!"

"Cocky-poo-doo-doo? Are we havin' a lover's spat, Sweetheart?"

"Curses, to you, and your bunch! Go ahead laugh, I'm payin' the bill."

"Go ahead an' cuss. Know you want to. Get it out."

"You deserve it more 'an anybody. But, I start cussin' you, and next I do it at home in front of the kids. You ain't gonna suck me into that!"

"Okay, I'll admit, maybe, I'm a heartless knave."

"MAYBE! You're a bum! You know I hate dogs."

"My word! Tell you what. The next two are on me."

"How BIG of you. Next two? Watch my lips. NO—MORE—DOGGIE HIDES!"

"Okay, you tell me what happened in the loft, and I'll do the hide-and-seeks from now on. Fair enough?"

"It's not negotiable, and you wouldn't keep it to yourself if I did."

"Probably not. It's good isn't it?"

Ben did not reply.

"Doesn't matter. Young gave us plenty." Dan pulled away and drove quietly.

It was fifteen minutes before Ben spoke, "I really believed I had a good spot."

"Getting up high was smart. I give you credit on that."

"On top of that, figured the rubber smell would cover my scent."

"Makes sense. But, sometimes our logical lets us down?"

Neither spoke for awhile and again Ben broke the silence, "I don't think I'm going to live long enough for this one to die."

"No sir. Not even your grandchildren 'll live that long."

"That wasn't fun for me."

"It was for us! That's why I keep you around. You're full of surprises. Unfortunately, they're usually far less memorable. And, that's as close to an apology you're gonna get, except I'll buy coffee."

"I accept both."

On the way they passed Morgan's Irish Pub. 'Last call' past, the bar was closing, and out straggled the patrons. One of the subjects staggered around the parking area. Dan and Ben pulled to the side to watch. He wobbled his way through the lot fumbling unsuccessfully to unlock a Chevy, and then a Ford. After trying several vehicles, the man unlocked a Plymouth.

The other patrons demonstrated no affect from the night's imbibing and quickly dispersed, while the officers' attention focused on the obvious drunk. The door not fully closed the dome light flickered as he fidgeted within the vehicle looking for something.

"Go on start the car already. Can't make a case just sitting there," Ben mused.

"You want to take him for 'public intox'?"

"No, it's citable, and he'll be back in his car drunk before tomorrow. Let's wait."

"Might go to sleep on us in this drizzle."

"If so, won't kill nobody, and we can impound his keys 'til morning."

They watched him for five minutes. Then the windshield wipers and headlights intermittingly alternated off-on-off-on. Shortly the vehicle moved forward in the empty lot toward the sidewalk, but stopped at the walk and backed up. Finally, it pulled out onto the roadway. Dan tailed the vehicle for several blocks without noticing an infraction.

"Partner, he's driving pretty good," Ben observed.

"His driving doesn't seem affected, does it?"

At the next intersection the vehicle rolled through a stop sign.

"That's enough to stop him. It's borderline, but I'd like to know how a guy who can't stand up ten minutes ago, drives so well."

"Me too,"

They activated the bar lights and the vehicle pulled to the curb.

"License and registration," Dan requested.

The driver fumbled in his wallet and produced the documents.

"James Corbin? Knew an actor by that name."

"Yes, Sir."

"Still livin' on Cherry?"

"Yes, Sir."

"Smells like alcohol. You been drinking?"

"No, Sir."

"Not even two beers?"

"Earlier today, maybe."

"I'm going to ask you to step to the sidewalk for a few minutes, Mr. Corbin." On the sidewalk, Dan patted him down and conducted sobriety tests. Ben stepped to the side and queried the plate, "508, Wants on Ohio plate EPH 518.

"Mr. Corbin, you're coordination seems a bit wobbly," Dan announced. "Can you account for that?"

"No, Sir."

"Are you on any medications? Have any physical impairment?"

"Don't think so."

"Mr. Corbin, any idea why your coordination is so jerky?"

"Don't know. Maybe I'm just tired."

"You came from Morgan's. Have any alcoholic beverages?"

"Had a couple drinks. Ginger ale mostly."

"We're going to take you in and run a breath test."

"Whatever you say, Officer."

"We'll have to call a wrecker, unless you choose to allow us to drive your car into the station."

"It's okay with me, go ahead, drive it in."

Dan took Corbin, and Ben followed in his vehicle. Ben parked in the abandoned gas station across from the district, as Dan turned into the district and escorted Corbin to the test room where he sat staring at the floor while Dan prepared the machine.

Ben joined Dan as he was instructing Corbin, "Take a deep breath and blow in this mouthpiece until I say stop."

Corbin blew hard and long.

"That's good."

Dan verified the results and looked at Ben quizzically, then reached over and checked the calibration log. "It was calibrated three hours ago, but look at the print out."

"Try a vial with a different batch number."

Dan reset the machine. Corbin blew again and the reading of ".000" repeated.

"Sit tight for a minute," Dan said to Corbin nodding to Ben.

"Okay," Corbin said with a slight smirk."

Dan and Ben stepped out in the hall.

"Triple ought! This guy's not drunk and the pat down found no drugs."

"That's a record," Tony chuckled from the station desk.

"We'll have to take a urine sample or turn him loose," Ben said.

"Considering probable cause is weak. I'm not foolin' with no bottle. Think we ought to cite him for the roll through?"

"No, he cooperated and we put him through enough."

"I love it! The Duo does zeros," Tony chuckled. "Get back out there. The streets aren't safe without you."

"You have his keys?" Dan asked Ben ignoring Tony's chiding.

Ben produced the keys, as they reentered the test room.

"Mr. Corbin," Dan said. "The test shows no alcohol in your system. We're sorry to have troubled you. You may want to see a doctor. Find out why your coordination is off. Could be medical."

"I'll think on it."

"Here's your keys with our apologies. We aren't citing you for the stop sign you rolled through, so you're free to go."

"No problem," Corbin said standing.

"We're sorry to have inconvenienced you," Dan said as they escorted him to the front counter and released the gate.

"Think nothing of it.

The door closed behind him. Tony was laughing as Gary came in the back with some recovered property. "What's so funny? Can hear you in the parking lot."

"Our Dedicated Duo just ran the drunk of drunks. Set a new record with triple zeros." Tony said amongst chuckles.

"That's interesting," Gary said. "I just heard from one of my snitches Morgan's has a decoy club."

"Gotta be!" Ben cried as the Duo sprang through the gate to the window. They watched Corbin walking away laughing. He unwrapped a piece of chewing gum and dropped the wrapper.

"Gotcha back!" they both exclaimed.

He crossed the street and entered his vehicle failing to use the nearby crosswalk.

"Gothcha again." They dashed out the back door to give chase.

They were at the end of the driveway in time to see Corbin's car pass. Dan pulled him over again at the bottom of the viaduct. It was no longer raining when Dan approached the driver's window. "Your license, please."

"I don't understand. You just told me to go home."

"Indeed, and with an apology. Now you're getting a couple tickets based on aggravated stupidity. Your premeditated decoy pool might eventually kill somebody by keeping us from stopping an intoxicated driver."

Corbin did not reply. Dan wrote the prior stop sign violation and the littering while Ben completed the jaywalking. Dan returned to the violator.

"Are you married?"

"Yes, Sir."

"Have any kids?"

"Yes, Sir, two. What's that got to do with the tickets?"

"They'll help remind you of your foolishness. The decoy was imaginative, so imagine your wife and kids at home and a burglar breaking in. They call the police, but the officers assigned your area aren't available because they're tied up on decoy drunks. Closest car is now twenty or thirty minutes away instead of five. Make a difference to you then?"

Corbin sank into his seat, but did not answer.

Dan handed him the license and copies of the citations, "Listen up. There's a payout for the stop sign you rolled through earlier, and a fine schedule. The littering and jaywalking are warnings. Take 'em home an' tape 'em to your mirror, and think about it. Three fines would be as tacky as your decoy game. I suspect your buddies still believe they can get away with it. You believed you could. You were wrong and it cost you. Tell your buddies, we're wise to 'em. Next one gets hit with the book and jailed. Drive careful now."

Dan returned to his cruiser. "Hope there's no more surprises tonight," Ben commented.

However, back on patrol, the Devil kept spinning disks and the Duo were obliged to dance.

"Rain quit, and here comes the fog," Ben noticed.

"I hate fog almost as much as you hate dogs!"

"Impossible! And for the record, it's them don't like me. I've learned to be indulgent."

The half-open window of the cruiser drew the moist air in revealing a distinct odor. "Smells like smoke," Ben remarked sniffing the air. The smoke crawled toward them with the foreboding of a corpse from a grave. "It's pretty strong." He keyed the mike, "508, we've got smoke in the area Langland and Pullan. Notify a Fire Company."

"Car 508, do you have an address?"

"508, negative, just smell smoke."

"Fire Company responding to the area," the dispatcher radioed setting a quadrant search. When the cruiser turned onto the next street, both officers saw flames licking up the sides of a house.

"508, we have a working fire at 1545 Donaldson Place. Frame house small patch of flames on the side. Hasn't been burning long."

Ejecting from the rolling cruiser, Ben shouted, "Clear the occupants!" He grabbed a garden hose hoping to slow the fire's spread. Its spray hit the charred siding and sizzled morphing into white smoke. The billows tasted of old paint and quickly engulfed Ben. He was forced back to breathe cleaner air.

Dan, fast on Ben's heels, went to the door and banged with his nightstick, but raised no one. Realizing his partner's attempts to alert the occupants were failing, and his small spray was proving ineffective, Ben joined Dan.

"Time to go in!" Dan said, knocking the glass out of the kitchen door. Reaching through and unlocking it, they rushed in. Immediately the heat burned their throats, smoke stole their breaths, cotton and creosote tastes gagged them. They fell to their knees.

"Upstairs! You take the front! I'll check the back!" Ben choked.

They took the steps on hands and knees. Yelling "POLICE, FIRE GET OUT. POLICE" At the top they went in opposite directions shouting, "Fire! Fire! Get out!"

A door opened and a woman emerged holding a towel to her mouth coughing and gasping for breath. She cried hoarsely, "My kids! Save them!" Dan pulled her to the floor, "This way!" Instead, she turned toward the front bedroom. Ben was crawling back with a three-year-old cradled to his chest with a sling made from a sheet. Seeing the mother he shouted, "How many others?"

"Two —older—other room!" she coughed out.

"Go with Ben. I'll get them!" She hesitated. "NOW! Dan ordered. He heard sirens, *It's about time.*

She still hesitated and Ben asked, "Husband?"

"No, works nights."

Ben grabbed her arm and pulled the terrified woman away. She crawled away looking over her shoulder.

Dan bumped his way down the hall squinting through tears. The chilling stillness broken by crackling timbers feed a feeling of abandon. Ash coated his skin, and tongue. Looking back, his flashlight beam was eaten by the smoke. *Getting too thick. Can't go back!*

He moved on placing his hand against the bedroom door, *Not hot!* He checked the knob and entered. Two boys of about ten slept in separate beds unaware of the danger. *My ears are getting hot. 'Bout out of time.* Dan tried the light switch. *Hallelujah, still works*. Smoke was entering the room through a transom over the door, but it wasn't thick. Dan swiftly crawled to the window looking out over the front porch. Outside firemen pulled hoses and ladders off the trucks like darting humming birds.

Rushing to the farthest bed, Dan shook the child. The boy woke seeing a stranger's puffy ash smeared face hovering over him in a cloud. Petrified, he swung his arms and kicked at his rescuer. His screams woke the second lad who went to his brother's defense. Dan found himself pelted by little fists and feet from both sides. They only hurt when they found his shins. As the smoke thickened, so did the boy's efforts to fend off their attacker.

Losing precious time! Dan thought stepping back. Each breath burned like whiskey on a raw throat. Holding his breath, he grabbed the boys pulling them toward the window. "FIRE! FIRE! GET OUT!"

Now on their feet, the yells alerted the lads to the smoke. They ran for the door. Dan blocked them. "Go out the window!"

"Momma and Sissy!" the bigger boy yelled pushing for the door.

"ALREADY OUT. GO OUT THE WINDOW!"

The boys ran to the window. In their panic, they failed to unlatch the sash. Dan rushed to their side and forced the latch. The window was stuck. "Get back!" he said shoving them aside. Grabbing the desk chair, he smashed the glass. The noise alerted the firemen below and they scurried to raise a ladder. By the time the first boy ventured onto the porch roof a fireman was there to help.

A gleeful mother below shouted, "My boys! My boys are safe!"

Soon both boys were at their mother's side and Dan descended the ladder. The fireman extinguished the flames and doused hot spots. The medics washed Dan and Ben's eyes, irrigated their mouths, and dressed minor wounds. They relaxed breathing an oxygen supplement. After a few minutes the Fire Marshal arrived and asked the medic, “How you ‘Blue Warriors’ doing?”

“Nothin’ major. Just, swallowed some smoke. We’ve been suckin’ oxygen for twenty minutes.”

He asked them a few more questions then turned to Dan, “Feelin’ better?”

“Yep,” Dan said, “Only a nasty cotton mouth.”

“I like it better when you pull ’em out and I do traffic,” Ben added.

“We’ve got the burn under control,” the Fire Marshall advised. “If the alarm had come any later it’d been a total loss.”

“Any idea what started it?” Dan asked.

“It started in the first floor outer wall. Old timber spreads fast. My report says ‘suspected tube and knob wiring defect.’ You guys were lucky. A few more gulps of smoke and you could’ve passed out.”

“You tellin’ us we shouldn’t have gone in?”

“No, the risk comes with the job. I’m saying you must have someone praying for you.”

“I keep tellin’ people to light them candles,” Ben said.

The Fire Marshal nodded and returned to his duties. Having knocked the fire down, the firemen began rolling up hoses. The medics reexamined the officers and released them. No longer needed, Ben slid behind the wheel, and they drove away. Turning the corner, Dan broke out in song. “Whoa-oa-oa! I feel good, I knew that I…”

“Whoaaa! That’s pitful!”

“Hurts some to, I need a drink. Then with less gusto he continued, “Yeaaaa, I knew that I would, so good, so good, cause …”

“Who originally sang that?” Ben cut in.

“James Brown, I do believe.”

“Well, I DO BELIEVE, you should let HIM sing it.”

“Whoa-oa-oa! I feel good…”

“While I was doing oxygen, you must’ve been suckin’ on laughing gas,” Ben cut in. “Will some food in your mouth stop the noise? ‘Belly Bombers’ or chili?”

"You offer delicacies too difficult to choose," Dan mumbled.

"Won't matter. Our tongues won't taste it."

They visited White Castle's and ordered several cheeseburgers and drinks. Ben drove behind the Shamrock Pub for a well-earned break.

"Take advantage of the roof overhang," Dan suggested.

Ben backed into the dock. "I sure hope it's late enough the accidents don't start."

"You kiddin? With bars closed and the rain, it's a ghost town."

"Did you get fries? There's just one order."

"Yours."

"Right," Ben said as he watched a fourth of Dan's small burger disappear in one bite.

Conversation lulled as they ate, discarding wrappers in the sack. Finished, Ben wadded the bag tight and slid out to toss it in the nearby dumpster. As he did, he noticed the rear door of the Pub was ajar. "We've got a PFO, Partner."

Dan jumped out calling it in. "508, PFO, Shamrock Pub, 4126 Hamilton."

"509, I'll cover," Martin offered by radio.

Flashlights in hand they cautiously entered noting a box of assorted whiskeys at the door

"On your toes," Dan said. "Looks like they're still in here."

Quietly continuing to the small office they found the switch panel and flipped on the lights. The room was ransacked, but no culprit. They moved with deliberation into the dimly lit main bar area. Their flashlights revealed coin boxes pried from the pinball and cigarette machines, but they found no culprit.

"Car 509, Signal Thirty-five. Where do they want me?" asked Martin by radio.

"508, we'll meet him at the rear door," Dan radioed. They backtracked to meet him, "Think the culprits are still here, but we haven't found 'em."

"There's an old trap to the cellar under the rubber drain

mat behind the bar."

They checked it. The mat was still in place and the trap locked. Dan felt two empty beer bottles on the bar. *One's still cool and moist*. "Not open long."

"You're arrival could have scared 'em off," Martin suggested.

"Doubt it. We were sittin' on it for several minutes before we found it. The only place unsearched is the pool room on the south side."

Entering the room, Ben flipped the light switch. The single fixture over the table bathed the table in subdued light. The thief, a sack of coins for a pillow, lay on his side in a sleeping stupor. In the dim light, his green work clothes blended with the table felt. Ben motioned to Dan, and then carefully handcuffed the man without waking him. "On three," he whispered.

They stepped back. Ben counted with his fingers. When the third finger flipped up they screamed.

"COPS! Run for it—COPS!"

The inebriated thief jumped off the table, staggered into the bar, bouncing off into a table, and collapsed on the floor. Ben helped him up and into a chair.

"I had two drinksh, offisher. Honesh."

"Yes, I can see that. But, the problem is you're still here, and the place is closed."

"I knowsh itsh raining."

Dan patted him down finding a raggedy wallet containing the social security card of Terry Tommich and seven dollars. There were no outstanding warrants. However, he had a record of several "Breaking and Entering" charges.

"Tell me if I'm wrong, Mr. Tommich," Ben asked. "You broke in, busted open the coin boxes, and set aside a take home order of whiskey. Leaving, you see it's raining, and while waiting for it to stop you killed off those soldiers on the bar, got sleepy, and took a nap on the pool table."

Terry sat quiet trying to digest it all and finally shrugged his shoulders, "I didn't knows y'ush was here."

"Do tell, Terry," Dan said. "How'd you break in?"

"I din't breaksh in. I hidsh in the closhets."

"Okay, we'll write it up so your public defender can make sense of it, being you won't remember."

"I'll handle the evidence collection, and secure the building," Martin offered. "I yield another arrest to the Duo who can't even hide and eat!"

They transported the arrested. The rain stopped and the streets dried before they returned to their District. Dan keyed his mike, "508, request 518 on Tac 4."

"518, copied."

Dan switched, "508 to 518, what's your location?"

"Clifton"

"You still have a full crew if we decide to use some comp time and cut out early?"

"One or both? Either way it's no problem. No-one's bailed yet and it's a real quiet night."

"Thanks, we haven't decided yet. We'll get back with you."

"518, clear, returning to Tac 2"

"Car 508," came the dispatcher's voice.

"508, go ahead."

"All's quiet over the city. I've made your requested inquiries. They're positive. Do you wish me to make notifies?"

Dan looked at Ben, and he nodded. "508, affirmative. Clear, back to Tac 2."

Returning to their district operation channel, Dan advised, "508, available for service."

"Coffee?" Ben suggested.

"If you think we have time."

In five minutes they were backing into the donut shop. As they sat bantering who would buy, the radio interrupted, "Cars 508 and 505, 508 and 505, burglar alarm 1379 Sassafras Avenue, Windermere Distributors."

"508, copied," Dan replied without logging the run. The game is a foot, Officer White. When duty calls, coffee waits."

They arrived in the front of five hundred foot warehouse

when they heard Gary's arrival, "Car 505, Signal Thirty-five.

Even with his short tenure, Hallister was established as an active hand on field supervisor who often covered runs. With Fleischer tied up on the chase's paperwork, and the assumption 508 would be relieved early, his arrival surprised no one. Ben and Dan were checking the west side railroad doors when the sergeant arrived at the northwest corner and worked toward them. When they met in the middle, Dan keyed his mike. "Advise the other cars at Windermere's we are with Car 518 at the railroad loading doors. All secure."

Within a couple minutes, a loud slamming sound of metal against metal and shouting erupted at the rear of the building. As they ran toward the rear, the shouts became clearer.

"Halt! HALT!" Followed by the echoing sound, "BLAMM, BLAMM-AM."

"GUNFIRE!" Ben shouted.

They all ran around the end of the building with their guns drawn. The large parking lot was empty. Hallister keyed his radio. "Check 505 and 503. See if they're okay?"

"505, okay on the south-east corner."

"Car 503, Car 503, you okay?"

There was a long silence, and Dan saw worry creep into the sergeant's face.

The radio buzzed, "Car 501, in route. 507 responding. 514, I'm in the area."

"Serge, you want all them rushing in before we know what we have?" Dan immediately asked Hallister.

"518, use the cars for a quadrant, not needed here," Hallister radioed.

The dispatcher began setting the quadrant.

"He's probably chasing someone. Likely fled down toward Brashers Street, behind Keebler," Ben suggested.

The sergeant looked in the direction indicated. "No way, that's two hundred feet in line with us. We'd have seen him. They had to go around the far side." Hallister hurried toward the opposite corner.

"508, advise the cars we're approaching the northwest

corner with 518, and will check the east side."

The dispatcher verified the information, "Car 503, Car 503 respond."

"503, I'm all right. No additional cars needed," he blurted over the radio.

Hallister, in the forefront, they proceeded cautiously around the corner. Twenty feet ahead a rustling was heard in the bushes alongside the building.

"503, 503, have 518 meet me to the rear on the east side of the warehouse."

"518, we're already there," Hallister said as Tom Watkins emerged from the overgrown slope.

Tom was extremely excited and spoke rapidly, "I yelled, Halt. He just kept running. I couldn't tell. Too dark."

"Take a minute, get your breath," Hallister said, "then give it to me slowly."

Tom took a couple minutes to regain composure, and Gary joined them.

"It's bad, Serge. It went down real bad," Watkins explained. "He ran. Didn't stop for me. I didn't know. It just went bad."

"I still don't understand. WHAT went bad?"

"Serge, everything happened so fast. The guard! I—I shot the guard! I don't know why he didn't stop—unless, he was chasing a burglar."

Hallister then aimed his flashlight down a thirty foot slope into a gulley. A man in a Pinkerton uniform lay prone with a large glimmering spot on his shirt. Dan rushed to the guard's side, and Hallister began to follow, but Tom grabbed his arm. "It wasn't my fault, Serge! You got to help make this right!"

Dan reached the man, checked him over, and came back up the slope. "He's dead, Serge. Hit in the center of the kill circle."

"That's a cold report, Officer Black," Hallister scolded.

"What are we gonna do?" Watkins asked.

"We'll have to call homicide. I'll call for the lieutenant."

"Hold on, Serge!" Gary shouted. "Tom's a good cop.

Wasn't his fault. It could've happened to any of us."

"Yeah," Ben admitted.

"Serge," Dan said, "You just go get a coffee. We'll fix this. Make it go away."

"Sure, Serge," Gary and Ben agreed. "Dan'll know how to fix it. You don't want to ruin a good cop's career and family over something like this. Go get a coffee. You were never here."

"Never here, right?" Dan agreed.

"I-a- I can't do that," a brokenhearted Hallister replied. "I wish we could, but it just won't fly. In addition to violating everything we stand for, there are dispatch tapes, and family. He'll be missed. I'm going to have to call Hess in. He's going to have to handle this."

"Not Hess," Dan said, "You know he'll make a mess of it and fry Tom.

"There's no way out," Hallister replied, "It's just not going away. We'll deal with it honestly. With this many witnesses, it'll come out okay."

The sergeant walked a short distance down the building. Dan kicked at some empty beer cans sending them rattling across the corrugated metal siding. Startled, Hallister turned and shouted, "Get hold of yourself! All of you!" Then he keyed his radio, "518, have 520 meet me." After the lieutenant acknowledged the request, Hallister returned to the group.

"We probably should bring our cars around, Serge," Dan suggested. "It'll save time when Hess gets here."

"Good idea," Hallister confirmed, "but someone needs to remain on the scene. Dan you and Ben go first, I'll go get mine and some crime scene tape, and then Gary."

Dan and Ben hurried to their cruiser. Dan drove around to the front. Stopping, he opened his door, "I gotta see how this plays out. Wait here."

"I'm not gonna miss this. My butt's on the line too."

"Alright, turn your radio down and get the lead out."

Stooping, they worked down the brushy east side of the building to within twenty feet. Hallister was just returning.

The lack of light limited the view to occasional flashlight reflections, but the voices were distinct.

It was five minutes before anyone spoke. It was Gary's voice, "It's taped off, Serge. Do you mind if I wait in my car? My stomach's a little - uh - you know."

"Sure, go ahead. The Duo will be back soon. I'll wait here."

It took Hess another ten minutes to arrive. "520, in the rear of the distributers. 518's car's here, but I don't see him."

"505 can bring him around," Hallister advised.

"I don't see 505, only car in the lot is 518's."

"Car 520," the dispatcher responded, "He's on the east side of the building."

Hess walked around and met Hallister who snapped a salute and said, "We've got a real bad situation here. The officers responded to a burglar alarm several minutes ago, and in the excitement a guard was shot."

"SHOT! Where is he?"

Hallister led the lieutenant along the warehouse to the taped off area. Shining his flashlight down the slope Hallister said, "There…" he broke off not seeing the body, and almost stumbled rushing down the slope. There were trampled weeds, but no body. "They snuck back and got him!"

"Who did?"

"Black-White-Follert—and…"

"Stop this nonsense and get up here!"

"It's obvious to me now. The bad news is I wasted your time. The good news is nobody got shot."

"Make sense. I've got important things to do!"

Hallister climbed up the slope, "We're done here. I've been bamboozled."

"I don't know what's going on, Sergeant. But, I'm warning you. If you want to stay a sergeant you'll give that 508 bunch close scrutiny. I ever catch you cutting them slack, you'll regret it the rest of your short career!"

"Yes, Sir, I'll remember. My apologies. It won't happen again, no sir. I appreciate your warning. If I have your leave, Sir, I need to go read them the riot act."

Dan signaled Ben to retreat. Back in the cruiser they headed for the donut shop to meet Gary and the security guard. Dan pulled up next to Gary's car. Hendricks, having changed out of the guard shirt, handed their order to them.

"That went down pretty slick," Hendricks laughed.

"Except for one minor detail," Gary agreed. "Dan, I thought you said Hess would be gone."

"Hess always takes off early the night before a Captain's Briefing," Dan explained.

Dan was not surprised to see Hallister pull in near them. There were two major routes out of the warehouse district. One went to the district and the other passed the coffee shop.

"Officers, seems I need to report a missing person," Hallister greeted them.

Dan took the lead, "Sergeant Hallister, have you met Officer Jerry Hendricks, formerly of Pinkerton Security?"

"I believe so, although not face to face. Also the subject of a discussion I just had with Lieutenant Hess which—did not—end well."

"Sorry, Hess always takes off before staff meets. But, you insisted on calling him."

"What did you expect me to do?"

"Good point."

"This'll spread fast and chase me forever. I admit I taunted you all at roll call, and as a result, my mettle's been tested."

"If it were me, I'd carry it with pride -- a badge of courage," Dan said. "Turns out, you weren't stung so much as legitimized."

"Was it planned that way? What if I'd walked away? It'd ruined my life, and your consciences would've carried it all of yours."

"Some things you can't plan, but we really didn't think you'd do that. I reckon there's risk in any initiation. In reflection, I think we got carried away."

"I was cocky. I thought I was home free. Believing in a misconception is a big mistake. It won't happen again, and such antics won't either. When on the street, we're going to be professional. My butt's in a sling with Hess. I can't afford anything less now."

"Wouldn't have it any other way," Dan said. "What about you guys?"

"It's understood, Serge," they replied.

"Are we dismissed, Sergeant?" Dan asked.

"You're dismissed."

They braced and saluted. The sergeant returned it with gusto. Hallister went in the restaurant to order coffee. He tried to pay, but found his arrival anticipated and the bill paid. When Hallister turned to leave they were gone.

En route to their beat Ben remarked, "You know, I've done enough police work for one night."

"No argument, it's remained quiet. What do you have in mind?"

"It's still pretty dark. I'll put a 'fiver' on Winton Road Hill."

They proceeded to a long four-lane road, containing photo sensor streetlights every two hundred feet. One section of lights was oriented to the slope's direction allowing the sensor to be deactivated by the cruiser's floodlight. At thirty-five miles an hour it wasn't an easy target. Each took a turn driving while the other spotted. The one turning off the most lights in a set of passes won. A pass took a couple minutes. Ben was first immobilizing twenty-six lamps. They pulled into a warehouse lot in view of the stretch of lights to switch drivers, chat, and wait five minutes for the lights to reset.

On the second run, Dan hit twenty straight targets before missing and totaled twenty-five. "I demand a re-run. It's too light. Half didn't come back on. We'll finish this tonight."

"Day is breaking, but there were plenty of targets. You're aim's off."

"If my aim's off, it's from that blasted curse the eyeball jockey put on me."

"Oh, gracious me, now you have a readymade excuse for everything. There'll be no end to it!"

"Speaking of curses, we better check and see if all our

doors are on their hinges, one more time, before we swing in to quit."

They quickly fell into a relaxed although vigilant exercise. Finishing in time to drive by the fuel pumps, top the tank off, and pull into the station in time to stand dismissal.

"Okay, at ease," Sgt. Hallister said once they fell in line. "It's been a long hard night for all of us, so let's just get this done and get out of here."

"Say the word and we'll disappear quicker than a Pinkerton Guard," BC remarked. The comment caused a room full of laughter.

"Settle down, we can do this at attention if you want," Hallister said.

An immediate hush fell on the room.

"Here's the way we're going to deal with the Pinkerton caper. I'm admitting I challenged you, you responded, and I fell for it. I'd call that fair and square. You have five minutes to get it out of your system, starting now. So have a good laugh on me, but then it's over, forgotten, and we move on to new business."

He looked at his watch and the seconds ticked by. Hallister took the fun out of it, and laughter was short lived. "Apparently, that's enough time. We're turning the page on it, and hereafter we're serious. If you're not sure what I mean, see me after head count and I'll spell it out. End of story. Everybody have their paper in? Everybody accounted for?"

Hallister counted heads verifying all officers present. "BC, you get a new Ford out of that deal last night?"

"No sir."

"Shame, but, more important neither did the bad guys. Good team work."

"Dan, you kept your head on tonight and it came out okay; more great teamwork. I don't want to hear any bad mouth on this, Follert made a good stop. It wasn't his fault it went bad. There's risk in this job. The verdict's out on Black's swap maneuver. Downtown will likely weigh in on that soon enough. Everybody needs to remember, what works once don't necessarily work twice."

"I'll say," Ben said.

"Gotta say, 508's run the gauntlet tonight," the sergeant said. "They started out in conference with the captain…"

"One of their favorite coffee spots," Watkins chimed in.

"Nabbed a drunk leaving Morgan's who blew a triple aught."

"The new district record," Lewis kidded.

"Yep, we need to post that one," another remarked.

"Took time to show their respect to me…," holding up his hand palm outstretched. "Laugh time's over!" interrupted Hallister. "They didn't just favor me. They got most the relief half beat to death and a hex put on 'em by a voodoo vicar. And Ben rolled through it all showing when the rubber meets the ramp, he can handle it."

He paused shortly for the squad's banter.

"It's nights like these which keep us coming back for more. Anything important?" Hearing no response Hallister said, "Get some sleep. Same time, same place, same insanity tomorrow. Dismissed!"

Quickly they stored their gear and headed for home. As always, Dan checked the clock and rounded the minutes to pick one of the five routes home.

Shortest route of course, when I'm in no hurry. I'll grab breakfast, swing by the drycleaners, and run a couple errands.

Chapter Twelve

Who Plays By The Rules, Anyway?

The clackety-clack of the garage door announced Dan was home. Entering through the kitchen he noticed it was passed nine o'clock. He hung the gun belt across the pantry doorknob and headed for the bedroom. He hung the dry-cleaning on the back of the door, and slipped out to check on Trouble. *Curled in a ball, you're good.*

Turning back he went to the turntable. I'll unwind awhile. *Can't ever get to sleep right off, anyway.* Selecting three instrumental records, he loaded the turntable, adjusted the volume low, and slumped into the easy chair. The ceiling fan beat the air above him and the sax stirred him inward. Outside he heard children playing in the empty lot. *They're at it early today.* Happy cries blended with the lazy waves of the orchestra. His tired body relaxed and his chin dropped. "Oh blast it!" he fussed spying a jelly blob from breakfast on his shirt pocket. *It'll stain.* Instinctively he jumped up to go to the laundry room, but reconsidered: *To heck with it! Demon man's ripped the pocket half off!*

He stepped out onto the rear porch. Dan positioned the Adirondack chair to watch the children. *No cushion! I won't stay long.* Next door, four youngsters were taking on three in a game of kickball. It summoned back the days he played children's games.

Oh yes, in the days worries belonged to another world. But, how did life become a game of survival where the trophy is a faded glory? Society has slipped its restraints! Life's tournament is not played in a stadium where spectators are safe. Everybody lives on this playing field. There are penalty boxes, but no safe zones. Scarce is the contender who plays nice. Rarer yet, one who plays by the rules.

Dan heard the record changer resetting for the third time, *enough of that*. He went in to change the albums and heard Trouble banged at the porch door. *How did he get out?* Hoping to prevent the ferret sneaking past, he carefully opened the door to the front porch. However, Trouble is impossible to forestall. Flashing by, the ferret nosedived into a laundry basket of old towels.

"That'll keep you busy while I find how you escaped." It didn't take long to find the cage roof pulled away in the back. "How you managed it I'll never figure!"

Dan repaired the cage and returned to the sitting room. Picking up the basket he carried it to the porch. Closing the door, Dan plunked the basket down. Responding to the bump, the ferret peered over the edge.

"You're not playing by the rules. Look at the mess out here. You've been into everything from the magazines to the flower pots."

Dan kicked a Nerf ball and Trouble gave chase. He tried to drag it back to Dan, but it bounced erratically against the porch planks. While the ferret worked untiringly to retrieve the oversize ball, Dan picked up his corncob pipe from the side table, grabbed his pouch from the shelf behind, and settled in the swing. While he packed the pipe, Dan watched the ferret struggle with the ball; pulling and tugging determinedly. Finally it broke free with an erratic bounce tumbling the ferret.

"Trouble, you love playing ball. Listen to the games I played today: pick Ford; hostage, hostage who's the hostage; serious pursuit, drunk or not drunk, burglar billiards, doggie hide and seek, and the vanishing guard. Some were fun, but most are serious. Yet, regardless of risks, men unrelentingly devise game plans to avoid the opposition and score their goal." Dan puffed then packed more tobacco. "And, for what: some temporal gain, a fleeting thrill, a confirmation of worth?"

"Even this night, showroom thieves rationalized their crime as a move in a game of cops and robbers. I can hear their alibi: 'It harmed no one, after all the cars were insured.' Like a football game, it's one play of many to cross their goal. Ah, but this linebacker stopped them."

The ferret abandoned the ball and ran to Dan for treats. A beach towel hung through the arm of the swing dragging to the floor. Trouble climbed it nestling in Dan's lap. Dan packed tobacco in the pipe one pinch after another, but the strands spilled out into his lap. He continued while storytelling to deaf ears.

"Yet, the game goes on, my furry friend. Bruce Moore found himself fourth down and goal to go. He had no intent to harm. He made a good run for it, but ran out of bounds short of the goalpost."

Curled up in Dan's lap, the ferret nibbled tobacco. Dan flipped the lighter to the pipe. There was too little tobacco to hold a flame. Puffing the fireless pipe he dropped a treat to the ferret. Trouble paid it no mind. *What are you eating?*

"Tobacco! Varmint, you've chewed through my pipe! Seeking thrills, huh? What did you gain? Hah! A mouthful of corncob? Humanity suffers like delusions. Seeking thrills of gain, they believe they've scored even when they've been sacked and lost."

Dan dropped the corncob into his lap, "Here! Take the spoils of your exploits."

Trouble sniffed the pipe and nosed it off Dan's lap.

"Your prize does not satisfy? I'll tell you why. But, first, a new pipe." Dan rose slowly as Trouble slid down his legs to the floor. Dan went to the sitting room, put a new records on, and chose another pipe. Returning he slid back into the swing. Trouble crawled back into Dan's lap in seconds. "No treats, you exasperating varmint. But, I promised an explanation."

"Some crime is personal, but the lion's share is a calculated risk. Trouble my friend, the criminal mind has no focus outside of itself. His victim is neutral; seen as a means to an acquisition, be it material or power. Here's the rub: greed, is never satisfied. Even our seducer fails to acquire all. His misery he vents on us, deceives, and then laughs in our face.

"I've felt the urges of his dark nature. It whispers, 'Go ahead! Snatch the profit. Nobody will know.' It's personal for that instigator. Although a few openly embrace his lies, most set their feet to resist. Nevertheless, some are knocked off balance by anger, jealousy, or greed. The result is many innocent are hurt."

"Even Hess' mission to suspend me is not malicious. He's cursed to prove himself. His ego competes against his ghost for approval. Our greatest enemies come at us from within?"

The briar was drawing hard. Dan inattentively over packed it. He reached for his pipe-nail. It was missing. "Ferret, you thief! You've made off with it!" *Where did you hide it? The porch isn't that big?* Dan surveyed the porch.

"The dirt on the floor betrays you, as greed betrays mankind." *The planter, you love to bury things* Dan found the pipe-nail in the loose soil. "Did you think you would not be discovered? Never!"

Returning to his swing and began cleaning and repacked the pipe. The ferret wrestled with the throw the swing was dragging on the floor. Dan propped his feet on a crate, smoked the pipe, and reminisced of carefree days.

Dan remembered stealing a friend's baseball glove at age ten. He worried at first, but time passed. His concern gone, he thought he'd gotten away with it. Then, one afternoon, the glove showed up on his father's desk! "Boy, did I get a whippin' over that one! "Dan mussed aloud. *Worst part was returning it to Jamie.*

Dan treasured the memories of his father, even this one. He also recalled how his father seemed immune to troubles. *Always deferring to the 'will of God. 'All things for the good'...dah dah dah!*

"He must have been sheltered from the miseries I wade through. Trouble, unlike your mischief, the duped mind of crime is energized by greed. It comes in various degrees, but its source is the full-strength evil."

His pipe out Dan put the pet in his play cage and retired to the bedroom. Pulling his shirt off, he inspected the torn pocket and sleeve.

"Who is this Ischyres with empty eyes?" he shouted tossing the shirt in the trash. *He who wears an eyeball necklace is up to no good.*

Sitting on the bed he pulled off his socks and cleaned the 'toe-jam.' Both socks missed the hamper. *Society has declared war on poverty,* Dan thought, *but it worsens. Massive attempts to make schools equal, and reinventing of social programs over and over in the pursuit of human dignity have made no progress. Their philosophies miss the target as bad as my socks!*

Dan lay back on the bed. Light flooded in past the crooked blind. He went over and adjusted it. Picking up the four darts on the dresser he sized up the target on the opposite wall.

Am I not wise as most? Then why is my understanding scoffed? WHAP, sounded the first dart sticking in the third ring.

Is it because, I work the city's dark passageways hauling societies refuse beyond sight? I too have spent time in society's sacred halls of education. But, no Master's! No Doctorate! No credentials recognized by the influential upper crust? WHAP. The second dart hit within the first circle.

I don't know how man's heart is corrupted, but I've rubbed against the repugnant, waded through depravity's mire. Crime is an outcropping of rotten hearts! "Reality declares a dissipating common goodness! There's my credentials—REALITY!"

"WHAP," a dart hit within the first circle.

'*Everyone is fundamentally good,' HOGWASH! If so,*

how do we lose it? Poverty, environment, unemployment, racism, nor ignorance has stolen goodness. These are by-products of abuse and misuse; of greed and disregard. Councilor Ischyres, a misunderstood good person? Foolish proposition. Ha!

"Here's one for you Is-ky-ress!"—WHAP. "Right in the evil eye!"

"Here's to society's good men misunderstood!" WHAP. "Another bull's-eye!" *Far more to that encounter than I will ever understand!* Shivers went through Dan, and he shook them off. *I need something to settle my nerves.*

He went to the refrigerator. Found a bottle of Napa Valley Cabernet Sauvignon. *Louis Martini will you, too, let me down?* Along with the bottle he grabbed a wedge of Colby cheese, and inspected a glass on the table. *Clean enough. Wine sanitizes.* Dan poured three ounces, re-corked the bottle, and returned it to the fridge. Nibbling and sipping, he concentrated on the fruity flavor. Dan waltzed his way to the bedroom, a half empty glass his partner. He sat on the small cedar chest at the foot of the bed, sipped from the glass pondering.

Ben's right, I need a female companion! Maybe he'd settle for a dog? Dan's laughter shook the bed. *Surely Ben would approve of a dog,* he thought cackling aloud. *And Hallister! Oh, to have seen your face, when first you understood. These games divert the tension, but temporary is the relief. It's more comforting to know I'm on a good team and still in the game. Hallister's solid. It gives me hope. Yet in it all, I am saddened. Should I have let the challenge pass?*

The reminiscence tempered the tears of Dan's heart, and the wine quieted his subconscious. *It's fun chasin' bad guys, sometimes. As for Ischyres, power of darkness, I'm studying your ploys. The 'Handbook' warns me: "Be of sober spirit, be on the alert. Your adversary, the Devil, prowls around like a roaring lion, seeking someone to devour."*[7]

---

[7] 1 Peter 5:8

Dan raised the glass eye level, *Be of sober spirit?* Looking at the fluid, Dan declared, "Ischyres, to you this pledge." He went into the bathroom and poured the wine in the sink. "And, this I vow: abstinence to strong drink. I shall remain vigilant, sober minded; your games shall not prevail."

Setting the glass aside, he returned and reclined on the bed. *Would the One who created this world, this life, stand by and let such 'games' of injustice prevail? NO!*

Dan drifted, slumbered and dreamed. *He was in a stadium. He saw a banner blown in the wind overhead. It read, "The game of life." The referees escorted contestant after contestant into the winner's circle beaming with arrogance and pride. All eyes turned upon the Judge. In His hands was the record of offenses. 'Disqualified! Step aside to account!' he demands. It has to be! If good does not win, it's no better than evil.* As the men were lead out the vision gave way to restful sleep.

Soon the fishing trip would be upon him. Dan needed to get away from the city and his turmoil, but was it possible? His anticipation grew as he imagined the serene waters, the boat's rocking, and the absence of agenda. Dan's outing was poised with a surprise catch, and an unpredictable release.

Chapter Thirteen

Rousting Out Counterfeits

Dan counted himself fortunate because it was a slow night. He'd be home by eight. Looking forward to the three-day weekend, fishing occupied Dan's mind on the drive home. A crisp sunrise promised good weather. *What's this "Professor" guy all about? Gary is so sure we'll click. Am I that predictable?*

The charter supplied all the equipment. Dan only needed the fishing clothes which he packed yesterday. The two next door teenage William's girls were eager to look after Trouble. *Shoot, Trouble will have more fun with them than I will on some barge float!*

Gary said Rick'd be here by nine, Dan thought arriving home. He changed into jeans and a safari shirt, grabbed the straw Panama Jack, and carried his duffle to the porch to wait. After working all night, he was tired. Dan customarily switched back to the 'land of the living' by staying up and taking an afternoon nap. He leaned back against the duffle and yawned. *This really could be fun. How long are they going to take?* Twenty minutes later, Dan slept sprawled across the porch snoring.

The horn launched Dan upright. Instinctively, he rolled left tumbling down the three steps. He lay on the sidewalk fully awake. "I'm coming!"

Dan stowed his duffel, in the back of the four door Mercury wagon and slid into the back seat. "What's with the horn? In this neighborhood we use doorbells."

"Couldn't get to it," Gary replied.

"There appeared a Grizzly in the way, and Mr. G here

was fearful to go on the porch," the Professor added.

"Bear?" Dan asked.

"Indeed," the Professor said, "he wanted to load you in the backseat without waking you."

"Really?"

"I told him I'd rather fight a Grizzly," Gary said.

"AND, 'Mr. G', I assume?" Dan said. "Refers to this pile of shark bait, known as the Ghost Rider, which rumor has it ain't scared of nothin'?"

"Exercising caution and being scared are different. Dan, make the acquaintance of Richard Lumaspas, professor of Physical Sciences and Anthropology at the University. Lumaspas speaks for itself and he doesn't like to be called 'Lumpy' or anything similar. 'Professor' works best. And, Professor, this red-eyed questionable human mass is Dan Black. Although he denies ever being one, he's known as the 'Preacher'."

"Glad to finally meet you, Dan," Professor Lumaspas acknowledged, "The term 'Professor' is my colleagues' choice, but 'Rick' fits casual affairs better. I have heard plenty about you."

"You can believe ten percent of it, if you hear it from him. Thanks for allowing me to join the greatest fishing expedition of all times." They shook hands. *Firm grip*

"Enough frivolities," Gary said. "Here's the agenda. Professor will drive up to Lake Erie. Since you're half gone, I'll join you napping until we arrive in Port Clinton. We'll check in, eat, and go find a headboat. How's that sound?"

"You expecting an argument from a sleepin' man?" Dan mumbled sliding down in the seat. The sound of wind and passing cars faded. Four hours later he was jarred awake. *What – where am I, oh yeah – gone fishing – the banging – must be there.* Dan raised a stiff skeleton to see his two companions, bags in hand, headed for a cabin door. He got out, lifted his duffle through the rear hatch and closed it. By the time he entered the cabin, the unclaimed bunks were top decks.

"G.I. bunks. Economy class, eh. You guys know how to

make a man feel welcome; grabbin' the bottoms."

"Sorry," Gary responded. "Snooze you lose."

Dan dropped his duffle in the corner. "What do they call this place?"

"Angler's Cabin Camp," Gary said. "They cater to the no frills fishermen."

"That's definitely me," he said going to the nearest bunk. He pulled the mattress from the top and spread it on the floor near the window. Then he took the mattress from the other and laid it alongside. "I'm a down to earth guy. Top bunk gives me nosebleeds."

"Two mattresses?" Gary asked.

"I'm used to a man sized bed, unless either of you…?"

"Not me," Rich said. "I came to fish."

"Then let's eat and find us a headboat," Gary suggested. "It's going on 1300 hours."

A short walk from Angler's Camp they came upon a wharf offering them three places to eat. The first was Harbor Grille and Pub. Its sign pictured a seaman in storm gear blowing suds from his beer.

"What do you think?" Dan asked.

"Looks more pub than grille. Not on a liquid diet," Gary said.

A block away they stood before Bligh's Wharf Restaurant. Checking a posted menu Rick commented, "Kind of upscale. Too much money for lunch." Around the corner was Ginger's. Its weathered faded blue clapboard and venetian blind facade did not encourage them. The rust stained metal roof displayed three large repairs, and the warped waiting benches seemed to shout 'Don't sit here'!"

"Its unpretentiousness," Rick noted.

"It's all we got," Dan said, "unless, we go back."

Ginger's interior was plain. At the entrance stood a full sized puffy faced plywood chef nailed to a column. "First Come, First Served. Seat Yourself Mate," was written on its apron. The late forties décor remained; booths of splotchy dark green vinyl, Formica tops worn thin, and black and white linoleum tiles scuffed through by traffic. For what the exterior lacked, the folksy clean interior compensated. There was no grease buildup, nor dust on the windowsills. The aroma of mother's kitchen captured them.

To their left were a dozen booths along the windows. Across from them, a counter with ten stools partitioned off the service aisle and kitchen porthole. A jukebox stood at the far end blinking red, orange and green. A double swung door opened to the kitchen across from the entrance. The section to the right housed an overflow area. Nautical implements appeared everywhere; captain wheels, anchors, stuffed fish, and a carved mermaid ship figurehead on the wall behind the cashier.

They selected a table. A thirty-something waitress approached quickly. Her hair, blends of black and brown, was pulled back and obscured by a net. A pea green apron hung over a loose fitting cream princess dress. At around five-seven, and over 200, her attire camouflaged her build. She listed backwards and glided toward them like a geisha girl with a slight limp. All three travelers were mesmerized.

"Might as well close 'em mouths 'til you got y'ur food, fellars," she said with a raspy voice.

"We'd like some lunch," Gary said.

"What a coincidence. We be servin' lunch. What'll it be?"

"We haven't been given menus yet."

"Honey, y'u didn't need help findin' them seats did y'u?" the waitress asked rhetorically. "Menu's in the napkin rack. Be back." She turned to attend other tables.

They found cards titled "LUNCH" listing burgers, sandwiches, and fish. As soon as they laid the cards on the table the unusual waitress reappeared, "Figur' it out boys?"

"Flo," Dan began, reading her plastic nametag," I think I'll have a ham and beef double-decker, heavy mayo."

Not hearing an acknowledgement, Dan looked up. When he made eye contact with her expressionless face, she shook her head slightly, "Y'u sure on that?"

"It's between that and the fish sandwich?"

"Fair pick, fish," she replied hoarsely, unemotionally

jotting on a pad.

"With fries and a Coke."

Flo nodded and turned to the others, "and y'uns…"

"I'd like the barbecue, and…" Gary stopping short noticing her turned up nose and squinching expression. "On second thought, I'll do the fish sandwich and a Coke?" Gary said timidly. Noticing her slight agreeing nod he added, "Light tartar sauce?"

"Honey, y'us bein' new here, I'll tell y'us. Words like small, little, light, and rare ain't in Larr's cookin' book. I'll fetch y'u a dab on the side."

Flo turned her attention to Rick.

"I'll have a cheeseburger with everything on it, and iced tea."

"You allergic to fish?"

"No ma'am', I just have a hunger for a burger, well done, thank you."

"Y'u'd, likely prefer med'um. Cooks it wit' real fire."

"No, I believe I'll be happy with well done."

Flo didn't reply. She simply pivoted and made a beeline for the kitchen door, which seemed to open by her aura. "Two Fish special. One chee-burger, well, in a tux."

The doors slapped closed as she vanished.

"What kind of fish you think it is?" Dan asked.

"I don't know." Gary replied.

"Probably ocean perch," Rick suggested.

Speaking of fish, look at this Fishing Report," Gary pointed to an insert on the napkin holder.

WALLEYE:

LAST WEEK BOATS HAVE FOLLOWED LARGE SCHOOLS OF WALLEYE FROM WEST OF GREEN ISLAND INTO THE SOUTH PASSAGE. LIMITED SUCCESS FOR WALLEYE NOTED IN SHALLOW WATERS OF THE SHORELINE AND ROCK PILES AT LESS THAN 30 FEET. WATER IS STAINED BUT GOOD NEAR REEFS. TROLLERS AND

DRIFTERS ARE TAKING LIMITS OF MIXED CLASS WALLEYE. LAST WEEK TROLLERS WITH COPPER AND GOLD STINGERS WITH LONG SOLID BAITS WORKED WELL. DRIFTERS AVERAGED FAIR CATCHES WITH SILVER/BLU/GOLD BLADED BOTTOM BOUNCERS AND 1 OZ LONG LINED GOLD BLADE HARNESSES.

"I can't wait to get at 'em," Rich said.

"Sounds like they're still runnin' hot and heavy," Gary agreed.

After awhile Flo floated toward them again. She carried a tray of drinks in her right hand, and plates of food balanced on her left arm. Flo sat the tray on the front of the table and handed the food orders to each without spilling a crumb.

Rick inspected his order. "Excuse me, but my burger's plain, and I didn't order a side salad."

"Salad? Where y'u from? Ain't no sal-ad. That's y'ur fixin's. Sauce 's on the table."

"Oh, sorry," Rick lifted the lettuce to find onion, tomato, cheese, bean sprouts, pickles, and a dab of mayo.

The half-pound mounded hamburger hung off the bun and with all the trimmings was two inches high. The cornbread dusted fish fillets dwarfed hoagie buns.

"This fish is thicker 'an your wallet," Gary mumbled through a mouthful, "This is the place."

"I'll second it," Dan agreed. "How's the burger, Rick?"

Rick's face showed regret. "It's rather dry. The chef's definition of well done is cremation."

"Y'u likely me'nt med'um," Gary mimicked with a chuckle.

Flo showed up, as if 'med'um' was her cue, "That burger done enough, sweetie?"

"Yes ma'am, perfect." Rick answered.

She wiggled her nose, left the refills, and sailed away.

The threesome finished eating, and hurried for the dock. The last headboats shoved off at two o'clock. Two boats,

Reel-M-In and *Yank-M-Up,* operated by the same company were loading as they approached the peer.

"Which one?" Gary asked.

"I'm seeing gold thing-a-ma-bobs on 'Yank-M,' and blue doodads on 'Reel-M.' If the fishing report means anything," Dan said.

"Well, Rick, you're the scientist. Which one?"

"Five pennies to a nickel. I suspect both captains have an assortment of baits."

"All-a-board!" sounded a hearty voice as a bell clanged.

"Yank, has fewer heads," Gary noted.

The threesome crossed the gangplank handing the deck hand twenty dollars. A thin but muscular young man, very tan, cleared the gangplank, and pulled in the mooring rope. The barge churned away from the dock.

Not too impressive," Dan considered. *Basic barge with a cabin. Maybe twenty-five foot across and twice as long. Big row of coolers behind these benches, must expect to catch something. Whatever, it's not crowded with eighteen people. A colorful looking bunch. Wonder if I look as ridiculous to them?*

Gunwales rose two feet high off the deck with a baluster extending another foot. Every six feet, tubing supported the canvas overhead. Rolled side-curtains were tied at the top. Two-thirds forward was a small cabin with more electronic equipment than a destroyer.

There's the heart of this floating surrey. If there's fish in this pond, he ought to be able to find it.

"Might as well settle in," Gary suggested. "It'll be awhile 'fore we wet a line."

"Settle in? My cheeks are tingling already," Dan commented rubbing his buttocks.

"Be numb soon."

Things were quiet, outside of the engine.

What am I gonna do with all this fish I catch?

Soon the captain throttled back and the deckhand's shrill whistle caught their attention.

"Your attention please, everybody calls me 'Squish'.

The Coast Guard requires…"

He then recited numerous safety requirements showing life vest locations ending with, "Should the boat sink." Most gave it less mindfulness than scratching an itch.

"As for the fishing," Squish continued regaining their attention. "The limit on Walleye is six and keepers must be over eighteen inches. Yellow Perch it's nine, and White Bass seven. When you land one, me or Billy-Bob will help you remove, measure, tag, and store the keepers in the coolers.

"We'll start on blue and red willospoons with minnows. They were hittin' 'em heavy this mornin'. If they're runnin' deeper, you can choose 'tween, lime green, or a pink and gold Slo-pokes. Your choice of minnow or worm trailers. We'll help chang the lures, but this is a headboat not a nursery and you bait your own hooks." He walked to an equipment rack and sorted fishing rods, handing them to those who needed them. Most had their own.

Then the quivering deck stilled, as the engines faded sounding more like Dan's Harley idling. The anglers sprang to the gunwales like horses loosed by the Preakness gate. Dan was nudged forward where Rick claimed a portion of the starboard railing alongside the cabin.

"Cap says there's Walleye at twenty-three feet," yelled Squish, "and we're driftin' with 'em. Billy-Bob's goin' forward, I'll stay aft."

Twenty-three feet don't help. There's no marking on this line.

Dan lowered the bait to the water line he estimated at ten feet, and tied a knot in it. He lowered the knot to the water to tie another, but a deep rough voice stopped him.

"Hey mate, you knottin' up my rig. Just let 'er fall. Slow count to fifteen. Light jerk, three times, and pull 'im in."

Dan turned and saw the captain leaning out the cabin door staring through him. "Yes, Sir." *Count of fifteen.right! But, I'll play along. He'll go about his business.* Dan played the line out as the captain watched. *One--two–three-----fifteen—jerk--jerk – jerk. I don't feel any fish!* Dan peeked over his shoulder. *Still watching. Okay, I'll reel it in. You go play with your gadgets.* Halfway in, the pole flexed and at the surface a big fish broke the water.

"I can't lift it in!"

"Net coming!" Billy-Bob called out.

"Still doubting, mate?" The captain said retreating into his cabin grinning.

Billy-Bob bounced over the coolers like an Olympic hurdle runner. Leaning over the rail he scooped the fish into a net and brought it on board. "Fine catch." He placed the measure to its tail. "Twenty nine and three quarters, this is the catch to beat!"

They maneuvered between spots and switched baits for another two hours before the wind picked up, and the clouds darkened. The headboat took the waves well, but tossing waves made the fishing difficult, and few were caught. Nevertheless, the captain respected paying anglers and stayed at it to the last feasible minute.

When the sprinkles began, the captain turned the vessel for port. The storm came like a cattle stampede. Within minutes, the full force of the gale buffeted them. The deck hands lowered the side curtains limiting the drenching spray.

Gary and Rick sat on Dan's left. Unconcerned they watched the pelting wind ripple patterns in the side curtains. A white haired woman in her late fifties clenching her teeth hung to the bench with white knuckles and fearful eyes.

"These storms seem worse than they are," Dan encouraged her.

She did not reply.

"Captain's, a good man, and this barge is well built for rugged water. Waves can wet us down, but they won't sink us."

Dan's assurance wasn't authoritative enough. She stood and clamping onto anything along the way, the woman slowly inched her way forward to the cabin.

"Hey Lady! SIT DOWN!" Squish's cries were muffled by the storm.

A death grip on the door rail, her body braced in the frame, she screamed at the captain, "We going to make it!"

"Won't be long to shore. You need to take your seat."

She hung in the doorframe with the tenacity of a snapping turtle, bouncing back and forth with the waves. The captain slid the back window open and yelled, "Squish! Get her in a seat!"

Bobbing and swaying, Squish navigated to the cabin, "You have to sit. You'll be safe there."

Again the woman addressed the busy captain, "The boat's going to sink, isn't it?"

The captain's patience thinned by the storm was emptied. "Lady, how' should I know! Never been in such a blow."

"OH, God save us!"

"Squish! Sit her down 'fore she falls overboard!"

Squish pried the gasping woman free and returned her to the seat next to Dan.

"You can see the shore! Look! There's the Marblehead's beacon on the canvas," Dan pointed. "We're almost in!"

She nodded with a trace of a smile, but remained rigid until they docked. It was slow crossing the gangplank and bucking peer with the catch. Their feet on land, they stood gathering their bearings.

"Let's run this catch to the cleaners," Gary suggested. "It's worth twenty-two cents a pound to have them do it."

Standing waterlogged in a downpour, cleaning fish was the last thing any wanted to consider. They crossed the street to the warehouse. A sign on the door read:

Sandusky Fish Co.
You catchum - We cleanum.
Enter door on bay side.

They went in. The fish were weighed and set aside for processing. They would pick them up later filleted, packaged and frozen. They agreed and paid for the order. When they exited, the rain had stopped, but not the wind. Seeing Ginger's Galley open, Dan headed for it. The others followed him. The door didn't close before they were greeted by a familiar voice. "Hold on thar mates. Ye be floodin' the bilges. Ain't you got no slickers?"

"Sorry," Dan apologized, "we got caught in…"

"N'ery y'u mind dem tales less'n dey fatal, we heard 'em a'fore. Just stand to!"

She hurried into the kitchen storage. Her short legged heavy frame rocked like their boat ride. None of them knew what she expected. Hoping they'd be welcomed, they stood dripping.

Shortly she reappeared pushing a wheeled bucket by the inserted mop handle. Slung over her shoulders were a dozen terry cloth towels which she distributed among them.

"Sop da spate out of y'ur duds." Then pointing to the section on the right said, "We serve drown'd sea dogs in there."

Regardless of her sandpaper voice and abrupt manor, her smile and eyes welcomed. They squeezed as much water out of their clothes as they could and slid into the first booth. Flo danced the mop over the puddles.

"I was thinking of take out," Rick whispered.

"Tell Flo you're doing take out?" Gary snorted. "Your brain wash overboard?"

"I'm with you," Dan agreed, "I don't want the mop used on me."

"I'll leave a healthy tip," Rick reconsidered.

They found the evening menus in the napkin rack, and Dan reviewed the choices. "What you suppose is good here?"

"Everythin' comin' out of m' galley's good, mate," Flo's hoarseness announced.

Oh great, no telling what'll happen to my order now! He looked up. "Indeed, we ate lunch here. The fish sandwiches were delicious. I wondered what could be better."

"So y'u wanna fish sandwich?"

"No, no, I'm wondering what your specialty might be?"

"There it is," she said pointing to the card. "Sea water stingin' y'ur eyes, eh? Friday's 'Cunt-er-y' Steak, and comes wit' mashed 'tators, an' mixed veggies."

"What do you recommend?"

"I recon 'u pick sometin' y'u got a hankerin' fer."

"I know, but, what's your favorite on the menu?"

"Larry do a real fine rib-eye, wit' a baked 'tattor, and greens," she replied with a motherly smile as her tongue raced across her lips.

"I'll have it—'me-de-um'."

Since Flo made no sign of disapproval, Gary figured it was the most reasonable response, "I'll have the same—'me-de-um'."

"Good idea," Rich said, "medium, please medium."

"Larr' only cooks 'em one way. Unless some fool says otherwise."

They exchanged quick glances and replied, "Sounds perfect."

Flo turned and scurried off to the kitchen.

"Rick, I think you're getting on her good side," Dan chuckled.

"Better hope Larr's 'one way' isn't well done," Rick laughed.

While they waited for their orders, they talked casually of the day's adventures. The time passed quickly and a lanky fellow delivered the food efficiently.

Cooked to "good" turned out to be medium, juicy, slight trace of pink, and flavorful. The potato came loaded and double baked. It left their palettes begging more. The spinach was splashed with acerbic vinegar sweetened by a hint of honey and mustard.

"The food here is such an adventure," Gary remarked. "You never know what you've ordered, and it comes out anything but plain."

They left behind the eatery, their hunger, and the rain. Soon they were dry, changed, and settled in the cottage. They split a box of stove matches, and played Texas Hold 'em. In twenty minutes Rick had all the matches.

"Glad I wasn't playing for money," Gary said flipping on the television. Adjusting the rabbit ears, he discovered the programming limited and the reception worse. "I'm worn out, anyway."

"I haven't managed much sleep, either," Dan agreed. "I'm with you."

"To each his own," Rich said. "It's only nine and I've some research papers I need work on."

Two hours later they were all asleep.

Rick was first to rise, and had coffee perking, and bacon frying by six. Dan lingered between sleep and wakefulness visualizing every villain of his career walking out of jail. Some judge ordered the prisons opened. Wham! Bang! Clang! Rick's drumming of a metal spoon on a pan dragged Dan down the corridors of his dream frantically slamming doors shut before inmates escaped.

Gary woke in time to join Rick watch Dan fight the imaginary villains. Dan lay in the crack of the doubled mattresses fighting the sheet as if it were an octopus. Gary grabbed the corner of the sheet yanking it clear.

"Wake up, Dan! Fish are biting! Let's go!"

The familiar voice cut through Dan's delusion. He sat up between the two mattresses wearing his Fruit of the Looms. A look of embarrassment paraded across his face. He didn't speak, and neither did they. He sat for a few seconds.

"What chamber of horrors were you lost in?" Rick asked.

"Trust me, you don't want to know," Gary answered.

Rick dropped the matter. "Eggs and bacon in ten!"

They ate with little talk. Gary showered while Dan did "KP" and Rick played maid. Ready, they headed out to find their charter, *The Sandpiper*, but all were unaware they would find much more.

Chapter Fourteen

Fishing for Truth

"Unlike headboats, with a charter we can be fashionably late," Gary noted.

'*The Sandpiper*' was lettered in gold script on the stern board of the Owens Express twin cabin cruiser. A long aft deck led into the galley cabin, which supported the higher pilot's cabin leaving ample foredeck. She rode proudly on the water displaying twin exhaust ports, white plank sides, and short gunnels extended with brass stanchions and white ropes into a bow rail. On the starboard aft deck was a tall, yet stout, man loading gear.

"We're the Follert bunch," Gary informed him.

"Eye, welcome aboard mates, I'm Fletch. Most call me 'Fletch' 'cause it's m' name."

"Right captain."

"I'm not ye captain. He's below. I'm the stores mate. Do most the fetchin' for the charters along this pier."

"Permission to board," Gary asked.

"Go ahead, he's expectin' ye."

Gary stepped aboard. As Dan followed, as a passing boat's wake caught him straddling deck to pier. He clumsily seesawed aboard. They heard a slam as Rick swung his leg on board and a head appeared in the lower cabin. The captain emerged from the galley. His round nose seemed to bounce over blond highlights of an uneven auburn walrus mustache like a sing-a-long ball. He was six feet, around two hundred, lean and muscular with skin of holster leather. His short blond hair was combed with a washcloth. His wrinkled cotton safari shirt and cargo pants were clean, with the exception of two fresh grease smudges. "You'll be the Follert booking, I suspect. I'm Captain Skepich."

They introduced themselves.

"Can't catch fish on the dock. Ready to shove off?"

"Let's do it!"

Captain Skepich climbed to the upper bridge. The engine's rhythmic gurgle preceded his command, "Cast those moorings, mate!" Fletch debarked, released the mooring lines, tossed them aboard and waved as the boat drifted away.

"You fellows just settle in and relax!" Skepich shouted down from the bridge as he maneuvered toward the open bay. "Feel free to raid the red cooler any time. I suggest we go for Walleye first. Open water's thirty minutes out." He turned his attention to piloting. The passengers relaxed on cushioned recliners.

"Night and day compared to yesterday," Dan said. "I could get used to this."

"I'll bet we pull in bigger ones today, with just us on board," Gary boasted.

"This can't help being a good time," Rick chirped.

Dan leaned back in the deck chair, *Wow, this is peaceful! I'll just sit here and let the fish jump in the boat.*

The motors cadence, an occasional gull's cry and the slapping of waves silenced all conversation. Dan fed on the serenity. Time passed quickly and he didn't notice the motor quit. It was the anchor's splash which interrupted his mood.

"Time to wet a line," Skepich roared. "Sonar says the big ones are at twenty feet."

Skepich busied himself passing out gear, selecting fishing lures, and opening bait. They pursued the task of pulling in the big one. Rick landed the first Walleye. At twelve inches it was no prize catch.

Dropping it overboard Captain Skepich casually remarked, "Back into the sea from which we all came."

"The sea from which we came?" Dan asked. "What makes you so certain, Captain?"

"Everybody knows life began in the seas."

"So you're reflecting a predominant opinion?"

"Seems pretty well decided. It's right there in my daughter's fifth grade science books."

"Decided?" Rick asked. "Who was there to watch it?"

"Nobody. But, science says so."

"GOT ONE!" Gary screeched. "This one's gonna break the rod!" They rallied to his side. His pole flexed as Gary worked the line like a bullfighter flourishing his cape.

"What'd you hook? A whale?" Dan asked.

Captain Skepich had the net waiting and the fish captured as soon as it broke surface. "Twenty-one inches, first keeper of the day and the mark to beat."

Dan and Gary took the challenge. After forty-five minutes and two more catches, they had settled in again.

"What scientist were you referring to earlier, Captain?" Rick asked.

"Was what?"

"What scientists proved life came from the seas?"

"Just a comment. Meant nothin' by it. Don't talk religion with my charters."

"I see. I used to think science possessed an ironclad integrity, but I've changed my mind."

"Well now Professor Rick," Dan interjected. "I'd like to know. Tell you the truth, I'm confused. Darwin's suppose to have proved it, but I've studied it some. I only find evidence of natural selection. It's like selectively breeding horses for speed, or draft, or other traits. In all the time it's been under the microscopes, organisms have remained within their species."

"If apes evolved into humans, how come there are still apes around?" Gary chided.

"That's one of the common misunderstandings applied to Darwin," the Professor instructed. "He only proposed a common ancestor between apes and humans; the infamous 'missing link'."

"Hold that thought. I got a 'Wallee'!" Gary shouted as he began frantically working the reel.

The captain's net captured it. The fish measured eighteen inches. “Record holds!” He said placing it in the wet well. Rising up he addressed Gary, “Telling humans they’re cousin to apes isn’t popular. Most don’t like the inference. People are mighty stuck on being special regardless how they act. We feel better thinking there’s a god taking care of us, but out here there’s only one god, Mother Nature; and one law, Survival of the Fittest.” He walked back to the cabin murmuring, “I don’t talk religion on charters.”

“Getting back to your question, Dan,” Rick said. “Darwin just proposed a theory. Latter a philosopher named Spencer labeled it ‘Survival of the Fittest.’ Darwin pursued it observing white moths were easier for their predators to see than black ones. Thus, more black survived to breed, and the color trait was passed on. More white moths were eaten, thus fewer offspring. He observed a natural selection process for survival. However, it was within the specific genetic structures. No evolving to a higher organism.”

“Is that all there was to it?”

“Oh, it’s more complex than we have time to discus. For instance, later mutations were observed but not fully understood. Nevertheless, it was concluded as part of the adaptive process and applied to species evolution. It was supposed to account for progressive forms of life originating from a single cell. The theory was soon discovered to have big holes. The first plug used was limitless time.”

“He just suggests millions of years, and since it fits, everybody accepts it?” Dan asked.

“It wasn’t just Darwin’s doing. The scientific community of the 1800s trusted influentials like Spencer, Huxley, and Russel. What they suggested carried weight.”

“But what proof did they have?” Dan asked.

“It seemed to fit!” Rick said. “Darwin, being an agnostic, discounted creation on the basis there was no-one to create it. He and his bunch proposed the observable universe exhibited the properties expected if there was no design, no purpose, nothing but pitiless indifference as found in random events. Common people found it hard to argue. But, his observations did not exclude other possible causes.”

"If nothing is proven, why's it in all the text books?" Dan asked.

"People looking for answers expected science to provide them. Darwin and his contemporaries formulated a theory which seemed apropos. Enough people believed it. Religion compromised, formal education took up the banner, and the theoretic nature was overlooked."

"I remember some university lab creating life in a test tube; some kind of ameba thing. That's not so theoretical!" Dan said. "It's confusing! "So what's with this ameba?"

"You're probably thinking of Stanley Miller or Sidney Fox from the early fifties. Miller formed amino acids by combining simple chemicals. But, and a big but, even though amino acids are the building blocks of life, the experiment had major failings! His amino bonded in random structures. Neither experiment produced specific peptide-bonds required for a living cell."

"See there!" Skepich interjected. "That's scientific evidence; them one cell am-e-ba things. Created 'em didn't they. Give 'em time they'll find the peptos."

"Peptide, Captain. But keep in mind, they hedged. Fox started with existing amino acids and forced a bonding, and Miller used pure chemicals,"

"Suits me. Given time they'll do it to suit you."

"Does seem significant," Dan agreed. *I'll bring this line in and change baits while we chat.* "Why don't you buy it, Rick?"

"It's tainted, because they manipulated the outcome. They assured a non-hostile environment and used pure elements. Nature is extremely hostile, and pure elements do not exist outside the lab. Agreed, it's an interesting experiment, but flawed proving nothing."

Reeling his line in Dan was surprised to discover a catch, "Get the net Cap'in!" Dan shouted, "It's a keeper!" Dan's catch met little resistance and broke the water limp.

"It's just your bait dragging," Gary taunted.

"Don't lose that minnow, mate." Skepich chuckled.

Dan dropped the fish on board and it lay motionless. "I

snagged a dead one."

It was a notable catch, however. Not from its size, failing "keeper" length, but for dual dorsal fins. "What kind of fish is it?" Rick asked Skepich.

"Looks like a Wallee."

"None of the others have double fins," Dan noted.

"I've seen extra fins here an' there. Could be a sign it's evolving. You might have something. When we get back we'll get pictures for the record keepers."

"Hey, it's half way to sproutin' wings? Dan you'll be as famous as Darwin!" Gary kidded.

"I think it more likely a genetic mutation," Rick responded. "Either way it was created Walleye and Cap'in says it's still a 'Walleye'."

"Don't talk religion," Skepish insisted. "I'm a charter captain not a priest."

"Sir, the creation-evolution debate is not about religion, but pursuing unbiased scientific evidence to an understanding of the universe's origin."

"People come out here expecting God to take care of 'em. I've had 'em, pair shaped blowfish, gold dangling from their necks beseeching God, 'give us our limit'. What do they need of it, their wallets full, their bellies bloated!" He walked away, then paused, "But, bein' its science," he said turning back. "You saying them fins have nothing to do with evolution?"

"Look for yourself. You think that half dead creature is a good specimen to champion a case for genetic advancement?"

"Reckon not, scientific speakin', that is."

"Granted that's the way it's supposed to happen," Rick agreed. "But, if you look close, it's definitely a fin and not structured anything like a wing. Mutations in species are common, but they don't create new species. They're degenerating. Mutated dogs remain dogs and cats never become birds."

"Well now, it's possible though, speakin' scientific."

"There's big differences in possible, plausible, and

probable. Besides, a slow process of change would result in extinction. Consider it, Captain, how would it breathe halfway between lungs and gills? It couldn't breathe in or out of water. Add to that, fins half turned to wings, couldn't fly nor swim. You know the lake better 'an me, what'd happen to it?"

"Ummm, must happ'n some other way."

"Must, if at all, but science has never been able to observe the process."

"They've got enough fossils in museums to know it's happenin'."

"That puzzle's not too clear, since more than half their pieces are still missing. And remember, unless we're talking religion, only unbiased scientific evidence counts."

"Ummph! Sure 'nough a puzzlin'?"

"Anyway you stack it, neither view can be proven, the two theories compete. Few people take time to research the truth for themselves. Thus, considerable misinformation is propagated. We pick what seems to fit us, cite its authorities, and beat their drums."

"Incoming! Flying fish!" Gary shouted yanking his pole firmly. The force sent the fish high in the air before thudding to the deck.

"Seven inches. Record smallest catch!" Rick laughed.

"I'll throw this one back 'til it grows," Gary said tossing it overboard.

"Professor, what's your take on this DNA stuff. There's a lot of excitement over it," Dan asked. "Does it support evolution?"

"It's not doing evolution any favors. The more we learn of it, the less probable evolution appears. Cambridge College, in '58, constructed a DNA model demonstrating our genetic structure is extremely complex."

"Are we still talkin' scientific?" Skepish asked.

"It's an observable fact, so it couldn't be religious, right?"

"Okay, what are you getting at?"

"Say you're walking the shoreline and see scribbled in

the sand an arrow and heart with John and Sue written inside. How'd you figure it got there?"

"Reckon, I'd assume lovers drew it?"

"If you come across some irregular line patterns in the sand what might you expect caused them?"

"That's not hard, either. Waves rippling in or a wake wash."

"Why didn't you think the heart was wave action?"

"Everybody knows waves don't draw hearts and write words." Skepich chided.

"How is it you're so sure?" Rick continued.

Skepich slid his hat to the side as he scratched. "It just don't happen that a way."

"Right, it's too complex to be the result of a random act of nature. Isn't it? And human DNA is the most complex thing known. It's more precisely ordered than words in the *Encyclopedia Britannica*!"

"So much for Darwin's universe without design," Dan said. "SO, if we didn't evolve, were did we come from?"

"The sixty-five thousand dollar…," Rick stopped short because he hooked a fish. Skepich quickly stowed the White Fish. Closed the well, and sat on the lid.

"Back to Dan's question," Rick said. "Where did we come from? Only God knows!" He turned to Skepich, "Figure of speech, Captain. No offense intended."

"None taken. What's it matter? We're here. Let's make the best of it and fish."

"It matters to me—a lot," Dan said. "I'd like to know why I'm here. And, that starts with where I came from. Why I am here matters! Everything I do is based on it." Rick's telling me it's impossible to know scientifically. Big help you are, Rick!

"It don't matter!" Skepish injected. "Our purpose is to enjoy life. Eat drink and be merry, for tomorrow cannot be known. We live for a time and die. Look around you, the whole world thinks life evolved. Can the whole world be wrong?"

"That's just my point," Dan declared. "Maybe it is? It

would definitely account for why it's such a mess. Aside from that, I want to know what if anything is beyond death."

"Like I said, mate, it can't be known. You got a better answer?"

"Sure do and it makes more sense to me because it answers all the problematic questions."

"And now you want to talk religion? I told you fellows, I don't talk religion!"

"It's a pursuit of the unknowable," Rick responded. "The dilemma of how it all began-simply cannot be proved. It's a choice of faith."

"But, that choice is significant..." Dan's shifted his attention to reeling in a twenty-six inch Walleye.

After stowing the catch, the captain busied himself with the equipment in the cabin, and the threesome attended to their fishing. An hour passed before the captain stuck his head out of the cabin to address them, "The *Julie May* is weighing anchor and offering us her place on the reef. They've had good luck last hour. What d' you say? Shall we have a go at some Yellow Perch? They're good eating."

"You're the captain," Gary said. "Go for it."

The engines purred and the boat swayed as the captain changed the heading. "Ain't none of ye a-feared of ghosts are ye? 'Cause if'n so, best we pass. It's deemed the likely sinking spot of the *General Anthony Wayne*. Set out from Sandusky one night in 1850, ne'er to be seen a'more. Many a ghost guard the gold coins she took to Davey."

"Ne'ry yea find a mor' fearless three," Dan imitated. "As f'r any treasure—it'd be even splits."

"The crappie rigs and perch spreaders are in the aft locker. I'd go for the three hook rigs. Drop the 'Wallee' leaders in the yellow bucket," Skepich instructed. Within fifteen minutes *The Sandpiper* anchored.

"As you drag 'em in keep count. The daily limit's twenty-five per man. Use the shiners. Chubs is good too. Fish a few cranks up from the bottom; thirty feet."

There was a large school of perch directly under them, and they pulled in two or three at a time. At the count of fifty-three Dan made an unusual catch. "Captain, I've hooked an eel. What d' I do with it!"

"No eels in this lake. Likely a water snake," he said stepping to the rail to look. "My-my, she's a big 'n; don't get much longer 'an three feet."

"I tried to shake it off, but can't. Now what?"

"Bring it aboard and release it."

"Rather cut the line. Not gonna chance it sinkin' its fangs into me!"

"Ain't poison, 'sides don't have fangs. Law of the lake: you catch it; you take it off the hook."

"Toothless snakes? You sure?"

"Said, no fangs. They gotta nasty set of teeth; painful bite. Usually gotta cut their heads off!"

It looked sinister enough slithering through the water, but the idea of reeling in a 'nasty set of teeth' spooked Dan. He dropped it as far away as possible. It lay motionless.

Skepich handed him a paddle, "Club it good on the head, first."

Inching toward it, Dan stalked the head. Raising the club to strike he exclaimed, "That ain't no snake."

The others rushed over to peer at the remains of an old belt.

"I've found the General's treasure!" Dan exclaimed. He examined the corroded buckle and slimy leather.

"Dan scraped away encrustations and muck on the oval buckle with a pocketknife. The roughness tore at his fingers, as wings took form. Skepich provided a magnifying glass. In time Dan read the inscription: "USA 1949."

"Not off the *General*, you can toss 'er back," Skepich said.

"Wait, there's more." Dan scrutinized the buckle, "Can't make it out. I think it's Sterling."

Gary tossed his line in, "Maybe there's more where it came from."

"Tourists," Skepich muttered shaking his head.

Interests returned to fishing, and in time their limit on Yellow Perch was reached. *The Sandpiper* again trolled in search of elusive Walleye. The wind picked up bringing choppiness to the lake. Dan noticed darkness in the distant clouds reminding him of yesterday.

"Captain, do we have a storm moving in?"

"Nothing coming our way, what y'ur seein' is a far piece off. Blowin' around us. This be as rough as it'll get."

"How's this boat handle in big waves?"

"She holds firm. Has the finest yare of any I've piloted. She came thru the gale last year that sank the *Glenda May* and the *Laughing Yank, and* Both hearty vessels. It were a blow of all blows. Turned me into a prayin' man."

"That bad? Bet it takes a fearful blow, before an experienced seaman of your stature turns to prayin'?"

"Indeed it do, but I'll 'fess I was sayin' m' Hail Marys that night. Waves breakin' the fore deck 'til you couldn't see the bow riggin'."

"That's a double comfort to me. First to know this vessel's seaworthy; and second, to hear you believe in God."

"I said no such thing! I'm not claiming God exists or don't. I don't talk religion on my charters!"

"Well, if not, I'm wonderin' who you was praying to during the storm."

"Didn't mean nothin' by it! And even if I did believe in God, not sayin' I do mind y'u, I don't talk religion. And, He could've put it all together using evolution."

"Captain, I don't believe you're the agnostic you profess."

"If'n I had a religion, wouldn't be agnostic, be Catholic."

"The truth is; what we really believe affects how we live. For instance, praying in a storm."

Skepich ignored the subject. He throttled the engine back and dropped anchor. "Lunch will be served in the galley in ten," he said disappearing into the lower cabin. The anglers followed. Skepich supplied sandwiches from an ice chest. "Make yourself at home while you're chowin' down. Drinks are in the cooler. I'll see where the 'Wallee's are having lunch." Grabbing a sandwich and apple, he retreated to the pilot's cabin. Moments later the motors rumbled.

Gary sat on the bench and handed Dan a Coke, "You run him off?"

"Reckon so; think I hit a nerve."

"You get him riled, and he'll park us on an empty hole."

"Guess I better be more tolerant of the old sea dog." While Dan chewed so did his mind. Eventually, he asked, "Gary, doesn't it bother you not knowing?

"Not anymore," Gary answered. "If a Supreme Being created us, He did so for a purpose. If I just happen to be here, then my reason is simply survival. That means I eat dessert first 'cause I might choke on dinner." He bit into a piece of apple pie.

"Well it does me."

"I tell you this, Dan, maybe I can't prove it scientifically, but I know there is a God and my purpose is to honor Him. But, I also think something's bad broke. We're far more mindful of survival than purpose."

"Consider this, Gary," Rick responded. "The world is affected less by what is true, than by what we accept as true. For instance; if God exists, but the world doesn't believe it, how will we act?"

Gary considered the question, "As if there were no God?"

"Precisely!"

"That makes sense," Dan remarked, "If I believe a chair won't hold me, I don't sit in it. On the other hand, if I believe a weak chair will, I sit, and it collapses with me. Its strength is not the issue! I acted on what I believed."

"How consistent," Gary said. "The world behaves with disregard for an ultimate accountability. Increasing crime and violence is equally in accord with a world having no God, as well as one having a God and denying it."

Rick nodded, "Consider the area of ethics, if I may dissertate with you."

"Dissertate?" Gary chuckled. "Sure we'd love to have you 'dissertate' with us, whatever it means."

"Oh, indeed Professor, do 'dissertate' on the cause of

escalating crime," Dan kidded."

"I'm afraid my experience is with education," Rick said. "Yet, I'm sure it's corrupted by the same influences which bring crime. However, before we can understand, we must realize the importance of the existence of God question."

"I thought we'd put that to bed," Gary said. "We want to talk crime and violence." The motors growled as if in agreement, and the boat began moving again. No one seemed to care.

"If God created us, He did so for a purpose He alone knew. It's impossible for us to accomplish what only God knows, unless He tells us what it is," Rick proposed. "Therefore, it's rational to assume He left instructions, and irrational to ignore those instructions. On the other hand, if we evolved, it's rational to dismiss all forms of religion and base morality on scientific knowledge. Further, without a God, ethics have no absolute authority. Thus, evolution provides no objective basis for human behavior, and we are left with ethical relativism. How's that for dissertating?"

"You mean, everybody's doing what they feel like, and social disorder follows?" Dan asked.

"That's a real possibility."

"I see it on the streets, already. I can break THEIR laws all I want, because I'm doing what's right for ME!"

"Wow!" Gary exclaimed, "Without God, I can act crazy without my conscience bothering me."

"Exactly," Rick agreed. "Without a God, no law has final authority. Hence, social order becomes political policies judged by the elite as advantageous. Plus, societal goals of engineering utopia are inherently sabotaged by self-interest. What's more, the self-serving 'me only matters' attitude is prevalent in the criminal mind.

"Rick, you refer to the criminal mind as if it is a separate entity. Why?" Dan asked.

"Recent research in criminal personality suggests repeat offenders think different from responsible citizens."

"How so?"

It's complex, but in a nut shell: a criminal's super-ego

rejects any outside principles or abstract concepts. He sees himself the absolute authority of what is right or wrong for him at any given moment. His singular social consideration is whether he can avoid society's interference in his life: getting caught and punished. No God, no absolute authority prohibits his self enhancing behaviors and use of violence to avoid those social interferences.

"As a teacher, I believe we should focus on absolute truth, and not social policy. It's a very difficult task, if not impossible, to accomplish without an absolute source of truth. More importantly, by who, and how is the betterment of society best defined?"

"Aren't laws based on political agenda inconsistent?" Dan asked.

"If the politicians were setting the absolutes," Gary said, "I'd expect government to end up a bit wishy-washy."

"And how do YOU find it?" Rick asked.

"It's a mess!" they all cheered.

"Why?" Rick prodded.

"Because they're always arguing," Gary answered. "Politicians fight among themselves, blaming each other and getting nowhere."

"I think we're there," Dan added." A self seeking government and a society abandoned to ignorance, chaos and crime."

The boat slowed and the familiar splash of the anchor sounded. They ignored it.

"Blah-blah-blah,blah," Skepich interrupted from the deck. "You philosophers want to catch fish or did y'u come for a boat ride?"

"We've had more luck with fishing than solving world affairs," Dan replied.

"Can't say I'm bored, but I'll have another go at it," Rick agreed.

"Whilst you were solving world's problems, I radioed other charters. I think we've found the Wallees. They're deeper, forty-five feet, near bottom. They ain't movin' much, and less likely to bite.

Rick stayed aft while Gary ushered Dan to the fore deck. "There's a good spot for you," Gary pointed.

Trying to keep me away from the captain.

They refreshed their baits and dropped their lines. While the waves slapped the hull they waited and hoped—waited and hoped—as the sun neared the horizon. Losing interest, Dan leaned back against the lower cabin, his line limp. Seduced by *The Sandpiper*, his troubles danced into the lake. The magic rhythm from below and the breeze above, cast a spell soothing as a feather duster massage. *I don't want to catch any more slimy fish.*

"Hey-hey-hey-what-a-you-say?" Gary's cry broke Dan's spell. Dan sauntered unhurriedly over to witness the measuring.

"Twenty-eight and a half inches," Skepich declared, "The new boat record."

Did he just hoodwink me? He knew I had the record at twenty-eight. "I demand a second opinion."

"Okay," Gary said. "Rick, what's your opinion?"

"Rick walked to the well, lifted the lid, looked in and said, "Twenty eight and three-quarters!"

"New record," Skepich resounded. "Best get at 'em. Plenty of thirty inchers down under. More gear aft, if'n y'u care to run two lines. Time's a wastin,' mates."

I'll double my chances with two, drift one play the other.

"Catch in the aft!" Rick shouted. It measured thirty inches.

"New record. Now we're fishin'!" Skepich yelled. "Watch that drifter mate," Dan's second pole skidded down the rope between the stanchions. Dan grabbed it and felt resistance. He reeled in the fish and stood over it proudly while Skepich measured.

"Twenty-nine and a half, good catch."

He's short stickin' me! Gotta be. Dan baited the hook and returned to his spot to find his second pole's clicker squealing. Again he reeled it in and stood close over the measure.

"Twenty-nine inches, good catch."

That really was short!

Dan moved aft to crowd Rick's luck. "How come Skepich's favoring you?"

"You're jealous. Happens to all first timers."

There were three more fish caught before the captain ended it. "Seven o'clock mates, and wind's pickin' up fast. Stow your gear. Time to head in."

At the pier they bid Captain Skepich a farewell, and compliments on a rewarding day.

"I'll see the catch is cleaned and frozen." He volunteered.

Steadying their sea legs they headed for their favorite restaurant, oblivious to the adventure which would be served up to them.

Chapter Fifteen

Confronting the Counterfeiters

"You think Flo will be on?" Dan asked.

"I'm starting to like her earthiness, Rick commented.

"Earthiness?" Gary asked. "She does grows on you."

"Grows or grates? Either way, she's likely gone," Dan replied.

Few patrons remained at Ginger's. Orange traffic cones and a bucket blocked the right side where a "Section Closed" sign hung from a mop. Two men in work clothes occupied stools at the counter, and a couple in their late twenties sat close on the same bench in the farthest booth. The Jute Box played, *Chick-A-Boom,* and when it clicked on *Good Morning Sunshine* the couple danced.

Flo was mid-way wiping tables. They interpreted her wave as an invitation to sit anywhere and decided on the second booth. It distanced them from the door and provided separation from the couple.

"You Limeys want fed?" Flo asked from across the room.

"If it's not too much trouble," Rick answered. "Didn't expect you'd be on."

"Split shift." She took three steps, sailed utensils wrapped in heavy napkins onto the table, and turned back to wiping the counter in one motion. The bundles landed in the center of the table.

"That takes skill," Gary said.

"Or something," Dan agreed. "It's worth coming for the show. Think she puts it on?"

"Likely as eggs from roosters," Rick replied. "She has

enough spunk to moonlight as a knife thrower at Cedar Point carnival."

"That a scientific observation…"

"Y'us ready yet?"

"I'll try the meat loaf," Rick requested.

"If'm y'u must," she answered with a hint of a chuckle.

"Second thought; how's the clam chowder?"

"Hot."

"It any good?"

"Some thinks so."

"You ever ate it?"

"Yep."

"You like it?"

"Yep."

"I'll have it. With the clam cakes, coleslaw …"

"Y'u say toss salad; house dressing?"

"I did and whatever else you think's best. Don't wait to bring the chowder."

"Weren't gonna," she said turning to Dan. "An yu's?"

"I'll try the open face turkey sandwich with green beans,"

"Worth a try."

"Make mine the same, but fries," Gary said.

"Y'ur' learnin' mate. Want dem mugs filled, wit y'ur wat'r?"

"Sure."

Once Flo passed through the kitchen door Dan asked, "What do you think we just ordered?"

"Only Flo knows," Gary said."

While waiting, the two men at the counter left. Gary went to the counter and brought back a ketchup bottle. Returning he saw some folded papers under their booth and picked them up.

"Ketchup on an open face?" Dan asked.

"Got fries, Gary said unfolding the papers. One was a map, the other sketchy notes.

"Here she comes," Rick announced.

Gary slid the papers to his side.

Flo sat the soup bowl down and slid it toward Rick. "Chow" Then she raised a pot to hold it at Dan's cup.

"Oh, its coffee."

Wha' y'u spectin'? Bilge? It's a coffee mug ain't it?"

"Great! Coffee's perfect. Caught me off guard."

"Sure y'u was, and I'm a mermaid."

"We'd all love some, you recommending it," Rick said.

"Been sweet talked 'efore, but yu' keeps on."

"Shucks Flo, you're a romantic," Dan added.

"Comes natch f'r mermaids. Help y'ur selfs to refills," Flo said leaving.

They sipped the strong coffee and were soon eating. Two bites into his sandwich Dan remarked, "Whatever else this place is – the food's great."

"Once you learn how to order," Rick said.

"Yeah! Let Flo do it for you," Gary said retrieving the papers and examined them between bites.

"You find a treasure map?" Dan asked.

"Not sure, but doubt it's kosher," he handed the papers to Dan.

. Dan studied the first one, "I think this is a map to Ginger's Galley," he said handing it back. Opening the other sheets he studied them murmuring, "Interesting—real interesting." Water stains partially obscured the handwriting smudges:

"Drop se- --r 8:0- ----- exchan-- --from barn ---- - dest--- ---ss

"They --- --pposed to --- --front ---- --fix——--ble cross. – Care—l

Buyer will arr--- --cadilack.

Has ot--- half bill.

Check ser—numb-- --- make match.

Off load at ------------- stay with tug."

The other was a scrap of smooth paper with greenish smudges. Although the paper felt familiar to Dan, he didn't know why. He returned them, "What do you make of it?"

"Off the wall—smugglers."

Just then four men clad in a blend of motorcycle and pirate's attire entered the restaurant. One had a full beard, the other three unshaven. They were in their late twenties to mid thirties, and physically fit. A red scarf wrapped the head of the biggest man. He went to Flo, "We left some papers behind. Did anybody find them."

"Didn't tell me if'n they did."

"We were in that booth," he pointed at Dan's booth revealing a tattoo of a skull and cross bones holding a dagger in its teeth on his wrist.

"I remember y'us. Don't know not'in' about y'ur papers. She turned to the kitchen cut out, "Anybody give y'u papers?" Larry shook his head and kept on cooking.

"They got to be here," the man said stepping toward Flo. Dan slipped a blackjack into his palm, slid from the booth and stepped over to Flo's side.

"Tolds y'us, dog breath, ain't seen 'em. Look f'r y'urselves," Flo snarled.

The man starred at Dan and barked, "You seen any papers round here."

"Since you're askin' nice, no I ain't seen your love letters. Like the lady said; check for yourself," Dan said taking a defensive stance facing him over his left shoulder.

Gary and Rick stepped out of the booth and stood aside.

Glaring at Dan, he shouted at a companion, "Well, crawl under there and find 'em."

The man stooped and looked. "They ain't there, Skull."

Skull slapped the man on the back of the head, "Get out of my sight, idiot!"

The bearded man left.

His eyes swept the floor and once more locked with Dan's, "We're gonna meet again." He turned to leave.

"Please hurry. I won't be able to sleep 'til then."

The door slammed behind them. Rick slumped into the booth. Gary slid in beside him noticing his pallor and remarked, "Weak knees are often a problem around Dan."

"I thought there was going to be an AWFUL fight,"

Rick said.

As Dan sat back down, Flo appeared at the table. "Honey, y'us got a death wish. But, I be luvin' y'u f'r it."

"Don't recall you backin' off any."

"Y'a, lost m' senses. Them bottom feeders only been in a few times last couple weeks."

Dan and Gary returned to their food, but Rick's appetite was gone.

"What you think now?" Dan asked sopping the last bite of bread in gravy.

"Dope smuggling, Turkish, comin' in through Canada?"

"Hey-uh, Dan, Rick interrupted. "They are waitin' outside."

"Humm," Dan mumbled quietly. Gary and Dan finished their food but lingered sipping coffee. "They gone yet?"

"No, they're still back tracking their route," Gary noted.

Why those scraps so important?

Pulling several bills out, Dan waved Flo over. "Is there a back way out?"

"Ain't no check at y'ur table. Scoot out through the galley."

"Leaving the money he departed. The others followed him round the side of the building. They concealed themselves in bushes and watched Flo's 'bottom feeders.'

"What now, Dan," Gary whispered.

"After meetin' Skull, I'm sure it's not on the level. Not our jurisdiction, either. Smart move is notify the locals and move on."

"Is that what you want to do?"

"Not more 'an you."

"Hey-hey-hey," Rick interrupted, "Am I invisible? What are we talking about?"

Dan shrugged his shoulders. "He's YOUR friend."

"We're trying to decide what to do," Gary replied. "Tell the locals and forget it or find out what it's about."

"You mean a crime in progress?"

"Our guess, drugs or smuggling," Dan said.

"What're we waitin' on?" Rick urged, "Let's get 'em.

Nothing like this ever happens at the university."

"Hold on, Rick," Gary cautioned. "Smugglers and dopers are dangerous. You saw but a sample of mean. People get killed getting in their way."

"Ahh, you're just trying to scare me."

"Yeah! He is!" Dan admitted, "with good reason. How about you going back to the cabin and call the locals. We'll keep tabs on them."

"Not in your lifetime. I came fishing because it's the most excitement my life ever sees. Not shoving me in a closet. One for all and all for one."

"You watch too much television," Gary retorted.

"Yeah, and they're likely to take off any minute," Dan warned. "So decide. Kick this ball or run it?"

"Run it," they responded together.

"Alright then, they probably have a vehicle. So, we're gonna need wheels," Dan looked around the vacant lot, "from somewhere."

"There's a taxi barn around the corner. Two blocks down Perry Street," Rick said. "Saw one there this morning."

"Could be a good undercover car."

"It's all we got," Gary said.

"Alright," Dan sighed. "You two stake this place out. I'll fetch the car."

"How?" Rick asked.

"Don't worry about it."

Dan headed out on foot, as dusk brought shadows. He ran the block and a half and found the Plymouth taxi. *OH BOY! Yellow fenders on a bright blue body! It's ugly as sin, but no choice?* The office door bore a sign "Port Clinton Livery" with hours of operation and a phone number. *Whatever happened to plain ol' 'Taxi?'.* It was past closing time, but Dan heard a television. *Guy must live here.* He knocked on the door. The weathered grain skinned his knuckles. He looked for a pay phone, but saw none. His eyes caught a large marlin spike by the door. He picked it up and rapped. The loud sharp sound provoked response, "Go away! Closed!"

He banged three more times and yelled, "Open up! Police!"

He heard movement. The blind slats parted revealing a face which reminded Dan of the logo on a box of fish. "Don't know you," he said. "And, I knows all the law 'round abouts."

"I'm not from 'round abouts!' And I don't have time to play twenty questions! Open the door or I'll take the window out with this marlin!"

"I'm callin' the real law!"

"Fine, but it'll be after I'm through the door. I have an emergency and I need the car!"

"Let me see your badge!"

Dan pressed it against the window pain.

"Don't look like a real badge."

"I told you. I'm not local!" Dan shouted pulling his revolver from his leg holster and tapping it on the window. "This badge any better?"

The man inside dropped to the floor and crawled away.

Great! Fool thinks I'm gonna shoot him! Worse—if I bust in he's likely to shoot me. As Dan considered his next move he heard a scraping noise at the foot of the door. Dan looked to see a long leather strap poking out the threshold crack.

"Take the car!"

Dan didn't waste time. Explanations were for later. He started the car. *Don't have to notifying the locals, anymore.*

The gaudy Plymouth pulled into the restaurant parking lot. It's door advertised "Por Clint Liver." Dan bumped across the rough apron. *Needs shocks too.* On the third jolt the gas gauge dropped to "E." *Great! Butt ugly car, broken gas gauge, and I'm out of jurisdiction!*

At Ginger's, he whistled out the window, with no response. *They were in those bushes. Where'd they go?*

Dan parked and searched for a trampled spot. *Probably following 'em. Which way? In what? Must be on foot. I'll start a search. Better leave word in the restaurant.* He rushed in the Galley as Flo charged out. They collided in their haste. Flo staggered back a couple steps. Dan went to the floor like a defeated Sumo. *Wha'd I run into?* He looked up. Flo's over-towering form met his gaze. Hands on hips, she squawked, "Y'u only bumped y'ur ego! Get y'ur carcus up! Gary needs y'u!"

"What do you know about Gary?"

"I know you all's the law, and him an' the other feller's doggin' 'em vagabond ruffians. Went down the dock road fifteen minutes ago."

Dan made it to his feet just as the cook came slapping through the kitchen door, waving money and shouting, "Hold on Flo! Where'd you get this fifty?"

"From 'em four bottom feeders in seven, Larr'."

"It's bogus, and if you hadn't been in such dad-blame hurry to light out, you'd 've noticed! It's out of your wages!"

"Not if'n you e'r wanna see m' carcass a-g'in!"

"That's it!" Dan exclaimed. "They're running counterfeit." He grabbed the fifty from Larry, "I'll explain later," and ran out. *I still don't have a clue where my partners are—OH, and, worse—two sheriff deputies are 'running' the cab!*

They noticed his abrupt reaction "Hold it!"

Should I make a run for it? Oh that's ridiculous! I'm only guilty of aggravated stupidity. Dan joined them.

"Is this your car?"

"No. But, I did commandeer it."

They threw him spread-eagled against the taxi patting him down. *This is gonna get uglier!* They found his off duty revolver and the slap-jack.

"You're under arrest for vehicle theft, possession of concealed weapons and aggravated assault," one deputy informed while handcuffing Dan.

Who'd I assault?

Before Dan could respond, Flo converged on them. "Arty, turn 'im loose! Y'u outs of y'ur fool head? We's gots hornswagglers to nab."

"Flo, this is police business, you …"

"Stops jackin' me around, Arthur Justin Hamilton! I know'd y'u from when y'us grasshopper high. I'll gets Frank down here an makes da fools of y'u."

"Flooo..."

"Chester, best y'u reign Arty in," she addressed the second deputy. "Them argonuts hornswaggled me f'r fifty bucks. Look!" Flo took the fifty out of Dan's front pocket and shoved it at Arthur. "Dis ain't comin' out my wages. He's on to 'em good. We's got to get after 'em, NOW!"

The deputy took the bill to examine.

"Deputy," Dan said, "I'm a police officer. Shield's in my wallet there. I realize I'm out of jurisdiction, but I stumbled into a counterfeit buy. It's going down somewhere close soon. If you'll take the bracelets off, I'll lay it out."

"Y'u goin' to listen, now! Or, does I call Frank!"

Arty examined the badge. "Okay, we'll go in and verify you're authentic and..."

"We don't have time! Play it by the book, and you'll miss the biggest bust of your career."

"What do you think, Rog?"

"Looks good, sounds real, and Flo's vouching. I'll play along, for now. But mister, if you're scamin' me you won't ever see daylight."

"You worryin' 'bout scamin'?" Flo shouted red-faced. "You keeps treatin' me likes I ain't here I'll kick y'ur shins blue! Y'u's holding fifty clams of scam an' ain't got sense t' know!"

The deputy removed the handcuffs, and Dan turned to Flo.

"Cool your jets, Flo. I stepped across the line. They're just doing their job." Flo relaxed, and Dan briefed the deputies.

"Okay, hop in, we'll see if we can find your friends," Arty offered opening the back door.

"Leave it to y'u to find a whacki-taxi," Flo said, stiff-arming Dan and plowing in the cruiser. She pulled herself to the far side of the seat. Sensing their surprise added, "My fifty ain't it?"

"The problem I'm seeing," Dan said, "is sneaking up on them in a squad car?"

"We could split up and take both," Chester suggested. "Hold marked car back until the other scouts the situation."

"Arty, let's you and me take the whacky tax?" Dan offered. "Chester and Flo can follow."

"Sounds like a plan, what do you think, Rog?"

"Let's do it."

"One minor detail," Dan added. "I don't have a clue where my partners went."

"He's markin' trail," Flo answered, but no one paid her any attention as they discussed a search.

Flo raised her voice, "SAID! He be markin' trail!"

"What are you fussing about?" Arthur challenged.

"Watch m' lips Arty! Dey's - markin' - the – trraaail! Best y'o clean da wax out."

"You mean Gary? How?" Dan asked.

"Don't y'u know? Could be wettin' hydrants f'r all I know. He grabbed cray'ns from da kiddie pail--if dat helps."

They were off looking for the crayon marks. The cruiser remained behind, much to Flo's dismay. Dan found the first yellow mark along the curb where Flo last saw them. They found others guiding them to the pier where yesterday's headboats docked.

"Arty, pull over," Dan directed. "Your uniform shows up like the lighthouse beacon. You're going to have to trust me to go ahead on foot."

Dan left the taxi and a reluctant deputy behind. The markings guided Dan though the docks several hundred feet until he came to an "X" inside a circle. *Blast him, what's with the wait here? There has to be something more*, but further searching convinced him there were none. *At least he wasn't captured, or he would have left a slashed circle - if he had time?* Dan rubbed out the center of the "X" with the heel of his shoe. *Wish I had a crayon.* Then he returned and updated the deputies.

"If they're that far down the pier," Arty suggested, "we might as well bring the cruiser closer."

"Be a good time. There's plenty of places around the buildings to hide it. Meantime, I'll go back to the mark and wait. If I'm not back in forty-five minutes, best, you hunt me up."

Dan returned to the mark he had found on the pier. Quickly he checked for new markings, but found none. He slid down amongst a grouping of pier posts nearby to wait. Slapping waves, intermittent boat horns, and the odor of fish oil and seaweed were his companions. No matter where Dan went, or what he did, Dan couldn't shake the impression he was on his own. Half the allotted time passed before Dan heard a dragging sound. *A rope pulled by a mooring?* Then he saw someone slowly approach using the boats, freight boxes, and fishing gear along the pier for cover. *Gary – Rick-- no it don't fit them. The way he moves is somehow familiar.* The newcomer stood over the mark. *It's Flo!*

"What are you doing here?" He whispered forcefully without moving.

"Same as y'u. Huntin' 'em sea dogs. Here's y'u sumpin' to clubs 'em wit'." She held out the marlin he left in the taxi.

"No need, Arty gave my off-duty back. You get back to the cruiser."

"Naw, they're at the foot of the pier. Waitin' f'r me to blow this," she held up a large brass whistle. "'Sides, I knows these docks."

"Find you a spot, then. All we can do is wait."

She settled in against a post draped with netting, the dark haul of a tug behind her. Five minutes later Gary walked down the pier. Dan waited to be sure he was alone before speaking, "Over here. Where's Rick?"

"He's posted keeping an eye on 'em."

"What's the deal?"

"They met a tug here. Talked with a man, but I couldn't hear. Then cut back up toward Perry Street. There's a warehouse a hundred yards south, smells like burning algae…"

"That'd be the ol' Brannigan Smok'ry. Been closed f'r two years," Flo offered.

"They're holed up in…What IS she doing here?"

"Long story. No time," Dan apologized.

"They're holed up in a livery barn with wide double doors on each end and bays along the sides. I could see a bunch of fishing gear, nets, and boat rigging. The front left bay is packed with food provisions, and there's an a big press in one bay alongside several reams of paper. Five minutes ago they started loading a pickup with banded boxes. I'm guessing uncut bills. I haven't been able to drum up any probable cause, but Rick's behind some barrels on the lakeside watching through a window."

"Let me at 'em. I'll give 'em probabilities. Fifty bills is cause 'nough."

Gary had a concerned expression.

"Cool your jets, Flo. We've done this before, you know," Dan said. She remained quiet while Gary finished.

"It fits. But, we still don't have enough to move in."

"What if I drove the taxi up looking for a fare?" Dan asked. "Might get close enough to see something incriminating. At least scope the place out."

"Don't think it'll help, and they'd recognize you. Best wait. There's going to be a pow-wow soon. They didn't meet that boat, or load the truck for exercise."

"Let's go back and brief the deputies, and then meet up with Rick," Dan suggested. "Flo you… Where'd she go?"

"Is it my night to watch her?"

"Hope she didn't light out for the warehouse. She'll blow the whole setup."

"Whose brainstorm was it to bring her along?"

"Nobody's, 'cept hers. Somehow it was trump! This whole caper's a bad dream. She's just part of it."

"She can hold her own. Flo's got street savvy. Let's get back. She'll show up."

"That's what worries me."

They walked back to the deputies and quickly briefed them ending with Flo's disappearance.

"Flo came back," Arty informed them. "Said you sent her for the taxi, and drove off right before you got here."

"Where'd she go?" Gary asked.

The deputies shrugged their shoulders.

"Let's get over to the warehouse – quick!" Dan cried. All four jumped in the cruiser. Arty assigned posts; he and Dan to the front, and Gary with Chester to the back. This gave them radio contact and a plan could be coordinated after reconnoitering. Dan would fetch Rick into their team. They parked behind a plumbing warehouse adjoining the south side of the smokehouse concealing the vehicles between bathtub and shower crates. The teams split and headed for their posts.

Dan and Arty hid behind a stack of old plastic barrels and discarded pallets fifteen feet from the doors. They were out of view. As he tried to become accustomed to the sickening sweet musky odor, Dan whispered, "What's that stench?"

"The barrels. Sour molasses, Worchester or both used to season smoked fish."

"As long as it ain't toxic."

"It's harmless. Could make you toss your cookies though."

"I'll fetch Rick."

Arty nodded, but a loud scraping "WHAMP" from the street stopped Dan. Both heads turned. A car bottomed out on the uneven driveway. *Oh no! It's Flo!*

She approached the doors blowing the taxi's horn like a fire truck siren. Slowly the left door slid half opened and two men exited. Bathed in the taxi's headlights, Dan recognized the men from the diner.

"Taxi's here!"

"We didn't call a taxi! Get out of here!" Skull shouted.

Flo opened her door and stepped halfway out, "Looks h're I can't be wastin' gas at today's prices! "Y'us change y'ur mind—fine wit' me—but fair's fair. Yy'us ows me a fiver f'r showin up."

"We don't owe you a plug nickel," the second man replied starting to slide the door back. "Now get that hunk of junk out of here!"

"I ain't goin' wit'outs m' gas money!"

"Hey, I know you!" Skull said suspiciously. "You're the

waitress from that Galley place."

"So's what? Taxi's m' moonlight. Don't specs me t' raise m' young'ns on tips like y'us leaves me. Does y'u?"

"You ain't moonlightin' here!" Skull bent over and picked up a broken slat.

Dan started to move to Flo's defense, but Arty grasped his elbow whispering, "Play this close. Let her run her line out."

With the threat, she fell back into the driver's seat, slammed the taxi in gear, floored the accelerator and roared through the doors. Fragments flew and the men jumped.

The taxi struck the rear of the pickup truck inside. Flo slammed the car in reverse. It jerked back and stalled. Skull dropped the board in the melee and headed for her. Flo jumped from the car darting through the barn like a butterfly in a meadow.

With the doors splintered and knocked off the tracks, Dan and Arty watched the show. The argument grew louder, but remained a stalemate. Flo was standing her ground.

"I'll keep an eye on her," Arty whispered. "Get Rick while they're distracted."

"You know the situation better 'an me."

"She's such a handful. They don't know what to do with her. She'll be okay."

"It's your ballgame." Dan took the opportunity to find Rick who was peeking through a side window.

"What's SHE doin' in there?" Rick whispered.

"Long story. No time." Dan could see Flo was now scurrying like a mouse chased by cats, but eventually the villains corralled her in the bay with the offset press. Cornered but not lassoed, she grabbed a sheet of paper. "Okay! Here's my insurance agent!" Flo dipped a brush by the press into some green ink and wrote, "Will Getzu Allstate 555-1919," and thrust it at them. "Forget the blasted gas money!"

Her response caught them off guard, and she calmly walked to the rear of the truck and knelt. "How bad I get y'r fool bumper," she asked. Rising up she declared, "I ain't payin' for none of that rust neither. Just m' own damage." Turning in a huff, she walked to the taxi. Without a backwards glance Flo plopped in, backed down the drive, and drove away.

Crook and cop were dumbfounded. The counterfeiters attempted to pull the broken doors unsuccessfully. Rick and Dan shook their heads in unbelief. Gary and Chester heard the commotion, but having no vantage point and lacking radio communication had no choice but to wait.

"Follow me," Dan directed and they joined Arty.

"How much of that spectacle did you see?" Arty asked Dan.

"Most of it, what'd you catch?"

"Not much of the inside stuff, but I covered her retreat. I've known her all my life. Saw it with my own eyes. Still can't believe it."

"Want me to sneak out and try to corral that wild mustang?" Dan asked.

"I'll go. You two wait. When clear, I'll brief the back-door, and try and get some backup." Arty left on the run.

"Here's what we have so…"

"Oh something's rank?" Rick interrupted.

"It's the barrels." Dan said.

"Rick reached over to touch the coating of an open barrel. "It's sticky as fly paper."

"Yeah, toxic too."

Rick's eyes bulged.

"Not really, it's sour molasses or something, but don't eat it. Wipe it off on the ground." As Rick worked to remove the residue Dan finished updating him.

They were no longer aware of the odor when a black Cadillac pulled up to the entrance and beeped. Dan noted the plates from habit, *MAT 245.* Faces peered around the sides of the broken door's slats. The Cadillac pulled inside. Four men in suits emerged with automatic weapons.

Come on God give us a break here. Arty isn't back, no radio, and we're out numbered two to one, including armament. This nightmare just keeps getting worse!"

“Can’t walk away now, can we?” Rick whispered.

“Nope, we’re on this merry-go-round ‘till the music stops.” They waited. *Never again out of jurisdiction. Just walk away!*

The men conferred, but Dan couldn’t hear the conversation. Eventually, one of the suited men retrieved a duffel from the trunk. Returning he tried to pull the remains of the doors shut, but they were snagged. He gave up and returned setting the duffel on the tailgate. *Finally a break.* Skull opened it, examined the contents. In the dim warehouse light, he appeared to flip through a bundle of bills.

Good bills for bogus, probably a dollar on a hundred.

The suits accompanied by Skull entered the Cadillac and it backed out of the barn stopping parallel to Dan’s hide. The other three boarded the pickup. Dan heard the truck’s starter grinding and grinding, but it didn’t start. The passenger door opened and one of them raised the hood and toyed with the motor. Another continued the futile cranking.

Skull shouted from the Caddy impatiently, “What’s wrong with it!”

“Won’t start.”

“I see that you nit wit. Didn’t you gas it?”

“Yeah, we gassed it!”

The cranking slowed.

“Don’t have all night.”

“Battery’s dead now.”

“Useless as screens on submarines! We’ll get the van. Be ready!”

Shortly after, Arty returned from his errand.

“Did you find her?” Dan asked.

“Yep, she’s headed back to the docks. And, get this. She grabbed some samples of bogus! That’s one courageous tiger in a dress!”

“Where’s she now? She okay?”

“In the cruiser, and she’s fine. Had enough excitement for one day. You won’t believe how she put it.”

“I think I might. She has a way of getting her message across.”

“Yeah, I asked her if she was coming with me. She said, ‘Naw, I limits m’self to wetin’ m’ pants t’ once a day.’ ”

Dan chuckled as Arty asked, “What do we have here?”

“Apparently some good luck for a change. They’d be gone, but their truck didn’t start.”

“Weren’t luck, Flo stuffed the tail pipe with a potato when she checked the bumper.”

“I’m glad she’s on our side,” Rick whispered.

Dan finished briefing Arty.

“Okay, you take this shotgun,” Arty said handing the Remington he brought back to Dan, “I’ve got my side arm. I radioed Chester and he has the other shotgun.” He turned to Rick and asked, “You have your off duty?”

“I’m not a cop. I’m a college anthropologist.”

“Where am I? A costume ball?” Arty asked turning to address Dan. “You a real cop?”

“I am,” Dan assured Arty while offering Rick his off duty. “Here, point it, look mean, just don’t pull the trigger unless it’s life and death.”

“Is it loaded?”

“Yeah. Why, you want me to take the bullets out?”

“No-o-o!”

“The way I figure it, Dan, when they come back they’ll load the bogus,” Arty said. “We’ll have two options; move in and make the arrest, or follow the parade hoping to uncover the next rung on the ladder. If we want the head honcho, we’ll have to tail ’em.”

“True, but the tailing option chances losing it all,” Dan said.

“They’d have to be blind for it to succeed. Face it; we’ve got a cruiser and a tawdry taxi. I’m drawing to an inside strait. I’ve requested an undercover team, but it’s a big county on a busy weekend. If it doesn’t happen we’ll have to move on what we have and let the Feds clean it up.”

Fifteen minutes passed and no truck. The radio alerted Arty two undercover vehicles were *en route,* and he left to coordinate their arrival. Twenty minutes later a cargo van arrived and backed up to the disabled truck. Dan noted the license, HEB 139, *Probably a rental.*

"Rick, sneak over and tell Arty it's going down," Dan whispered.

Rick slipped away as the counterfeiters transferred the bundles. Arty and Rick had not returned as the last bundle was transferred.

I can't spring the trap. I got no trap! This whole caper's melting away like ice on a summer beach.

Skull entered the Caddie with the suits, and it backed down to the street and waited. The others boarded the van.

I could unload on the tires as the van rolls past. The blasts will alert everybody else. They'll converge and we'll take them down. Not good. Too risky! They've got automatic weapons. Be skydiving without a chute. Gotta let it go.

The van backed down the driveway. Instinctively the shotgun came to Dan's shoulder. He steadied the sight bead on the rear tire. Dan's finger brought pressure to the trigger. *Oh well! Let the chips fly! I can't let it go!*

Dan felt the nudge on his shoulder before he heard Arty's whisper, "Let 'em go."

Dan watched the van pull away with the Cadillac following. "Please, tell me someone's tailing them."

"A fellow we call Deputy Dawg, with Chester and Gary. Come on. Rick's waiting in the second car."

They hurried to the staging area. A nondescript brown Chevy Nova sat alongside the cruiser. Rick stood beside it with another man.

"Meet Deputy Victor Morgan. We call him "Morgue-man", Arty said.

Morgan briefed them as they piled into the vehicle, "Flo took the taxi back. She's had enough. The Coast Guard is on standby in case our bogus bandits head for the lake."

"Ocean-Charlie-23," the radio whined, "Lake don't appear to be their destination. They're headed down Perry Street toward the main interchange for State-53."

"Ocean-Charlie-31," Arty spoke in the radio, "We'll be up with you in a couple minutes."

"Ocean-Charlie-23, we're passing the exchange and

going north on Sand Road."

"Ocean-Charlie 31, I can't figure this. Catawba Peninsula extends only six miles."

"Ocean-Charlie-23, we're sure they haven't made us."

"This road's a dead end at the ferry to South Bass Island," Arty spoke openly. "I suppose they could have a boat around Put-in Bay, but why not load off sooner. Plenty of better places."

"Hey, you're the tour guide," Dan said, "I don't know the lay of the land."

They silently weighed the event. Five minutes later the radio reported again. "Ocean-Charlie-23, the suspect vehicle is approaching the ferry."

"The ferry," Arty said, "That's it!" He called the lead car. "Ocean-Charlie-31, can you hold back? They're using the ferry to watch for a tail? We can catch up and take the lead. You follow on the next one." He slapped the driver on the shoulder, "Hit it Morgue-man! To the ferry, double time."

The car sped up and closed the gap.

"Okay Dawg," Arty radioed, "we're on your six. Break off left on Cliff Street. It'll look like you're local."

Morgan trailed behind watching the lead car turn left and then seconds later the villains went right toward the ferry. Morgan made a quick diversionary right and picked up the county road. As Morgan negotiated the route, Arty removed his uniform shirt exposing a white T-shirt. Timing brought them back in behind the target at the ferry.

Five cars were loaded on the ferry behind the target vehicle. The suspects were in the front row of two wide and three deep. It placed Dan behind the suspect vehicles with another van between them. The ferry ride took thirty minutes to loop around to the back of Bass Island and unload.

"Ocean-Charlie-31, we just off loaded, and are following them up the ramp."

"Ocean-Charlie-23, we've half way to Bass. A Coast Guard defender class ship is standing by at Rattlesnake Island, but the proximity of Canadian waters concerns them.

They're notifying the Canadian Navy."

"It just can't get any crazier," Dan said.

The radio clicked again. "The Coast Guard is now advising of an auxiliary crew of two at Miller's Marina at Put-In-Bay with a six man rigid hull inflatable, but there's no mounted armament."

"It just did," Arty said.

The van moved out of the main harbor area. Dan and his companions followed as it wound around and took the county highway south.

"Round and round we go," Dan murmured aloud.

Soon they left the county road onto a State Park dirt service road. It led through a grove of pines.

"This wild goose chase is ending," Arty said. "After these trees, it runs dead at lakeside. That means they can't escape by land without coming through us."

Arty informed the tail car and requested his dispatcher to notify the Coast Guard. They approached slowly without headlights. Their eyes adjusted quickly, and the full moon and clear night provided ample light. Dan went ahead on foot to be sure the road was clear. Within ten minutes, he walked into view of the van backed up to the water's edge a hundred yards ahead. He wouldn't have seen them if the tug hadn't been using flood lamps to load. Dan signaled Arty who joined him. A couple minutes later the second car arrived, and Arty briefed Morgan and Gary.

"Ocean-Charlie-31," the dispatcher alerted, "The Coast Guard's inflatable is in route from Miller's with an ETA of twelve minutes. The Defender's moving between the islands so it can intercept on either side of the island."

Twenty minutes ticked by as the tug loaded; the men in suits guarding while the workmen ferried boxes. The forty-foot tug had a black hull with a pilot's cabin mid shift. Arty examined her through his binoculars. "She's under an American flag, and my guess is drafting a couple feet. Means she's pretty empty." He lowered the glasses.

"In another ten minutes they'll be loaded. I figure the limeys will stay on the tug, but expect the suits to drive back this way. We're stuck. The Coast Guard will have to intercept the tug, and we'll take down the Caddie full of suits. Let's get a limb shoved behind our front wheels. Maybe they'll think a couple lovers got hung up. At least put them off guard enough to give us an advantage."

As the others worked at the diversion, Arty put his uniform shirt back on. The six officers would be ready with four service revolvers, three shotguns, and Rick with Dan's off duty. With a tree limb under the front right tire, and a rear wheel buried in the sand, the car appeared abandoned. Cardboard from the trunk placed on the windshield read "gone for tow." The second chase car backed up around the bend. They also briefed the dispatcher and requested her to alert the Coast Guard.

"Okay men," Arty directed. "This isn't going to be an ice cream social. In order to contain them, we must cover both sides of the road. That creates a potential dangerous crossfire. Be careful! Three on the driver's side, four on the other."

Arty spaced the men at staggered intervals, and marked the positions by tying strips of a sheet from the car's trunk on the trees. "Pay attention to these. I don't want anyone shot in a crossfire. Wait 'till they get out. I'll yell 'Ottawa County Sheriff Department, you're under arrest,' then we'll see what happens. I emphasize, BE PATIENT, don't jump the gun. Wait for my order. But, if they try to back up take the rear wheels out with the shotguns. If they start shooting—and you have a clear shot—take it. Be mindful of the strips and watch the crossfire. We're all elevated on these roadside berms so be sure to shoot down. Take your places, and God protect us."

The workmen finished loading a short time later and stayed aboard as the tug chugged away. The men in suits boarded the Caddie. The ominous sedan crept toward the snare leaving the van behind. When it encountered the roadblock, it came to a complete stop.

Minutes passed. Both rear doors opened and two men stepped out with weapons. Slowly they approached the abandoned vehicle. Illuminated by the Cadillac's headlights they worked on clearing the limb. Then they tried to push the car by joining bumpers. One man steered the car through an open door, but the car slid sideways. "Willie, get your lazy behind out here and help!" he yelled.

A passenger emerged from the Caddie slamming the door. When he reached the front of the vehicle Arty yelled, "Ottawa County Sheriff! Hands up! You're under arrest!"

The command startled them. The Cadillac attempted to retreat and a shotgun flashed reverberating from the trees; "CABOOM! CABOOM! CABOOM!" The tires flattened. The car stopped. The man between the vehicles swung a short-barreled automatic weapon from under his coat spraying Rick's cover. Immediately, return fire came from Morgan's position striking the man twice in the upper chest. He sank to his knees and fell forwards.

The other two culprits dove into the abandoned Chevy through open doors. Momentarily, the officers accepted it as a sign of surrender. The Caddie driver, not yet persuaded, lay across the front seat, lowered the passenger window, and fired randomly.

Dan felt a hot poker jab his shoulder. *Pain didn't last. Arm still works. Flesh wound, but close enough, scumbag. Time I teach you manners.* Dan fired the remaining shells into the door. *Not enough to get through the door? Okay, I have time to reload.* However, the rattle and impact impressed the driver. As Dan thumbed more rounds in the tube, a white handkerchief appeared in the window waving frantically.

"Guns out first!" Arty ordered. "One at a time! Caddie driver first! Any hint of a gun, and it's all over!"

A hand dropped a gun out the window. The door opened activating the dome light revealing the driver. There were red specks on the gunman's forehead, and right cheek. He exited in slow motion as if stepping out on eggs.

"Turn around. Face the car!" ordered Arty. "Dan, cuff him."

His ears ringing, Dan stepped into the sulfuric air and

secured the man. Arty took the other two prisoners through the same routine, and then everyone left their cover. Everyone except Rick.

Dan went into the cover with dread. "Rick! It's over! Rick! This is Dan coming your way! You okay!"

There was no reply.

"The music's over! Time to get off the merry-go-round!" Dan came to Rick's post. The strip of sheet fluttered in the breeze, but no Rick. *Get hit, panic? Disorient and run off?"*

Heavy cover made searching difficult even with the flashlight. *These pine boughs hang so low, lying under a tree he'd be easy to miss.* After searching another ten feet he saw Rick prone on the ground. "RICK, you okay?"

Rick groaned, "Is it over?"

"Yeah, it's all over."

"Good, it hurts my ears."

"Come on, follow me out."

"That was loud! Not what I expected! Here, take this thing 'fore it goes off." He gingerly handed Dan his gun. Dan checked the hammer position. *Safe.* He opened the cylinder. *No spent rounds*. Dan closed it. It was a short trip back to the road. As soon as Rick saw the criminals were secured, his composure changed. "We sure shut this gang of cutthroats down, didn't we?"

"We certainly did," Dan said smiling.

Two additional uniform cars arrived, and transported the three prisoners. The fourth man was dead. The driver incurred minor cuts from fragments of glass shrapnel. The bleeding stopped, he'd be treated later.

The county Crime Scene Unit took another fifteen minutes to arrive. Dan, Gary and Rick gave statements to the investigators. An hour into processing the scene the investigators removed the body.

While Gary was giving his statement, the dispatcher advised Artie the Coast Guard had followed the tug to a small freighter. According to the Canadian Navy, it had drifted into U.S. waters. The USCG invited the Canadian

Navy to join the boarding party. Ten million dollars counterfeit was confiscated along with the tug. The freighter of Greek registry would be detained. Thirty-eight crewmen were pending official charges.

The trio sat on the roadside taking turns relaying their specific part in the adventure to the investigators. Gary was last. Returning to Arty's cruiser he commented, "That about raps it up. They said our stories meshed."

"Meshed?" Dan chuckled as Arty walked up. "Arty, your boys give you any advice on handling us loose cannons."

"There's no problem, guys. You know how it is with a fatal shooting; by the numbers, no loose ends." He walked to the driver's door. "Let's get out of here. Where're you staying?"

"Angler's Camp," Gary replied pulling a door closed.

"Somebody will be out to take you to the Sherrif's office for formal statements in a few hours. Get some sleep," Arty advised on the way back.

By the time they reached the cabin, Rick's anxiety attack was over. He reveled in reliving the event in every detail. "From the beginning, I knew it'd be exciting," Rick said walking through the cabin door. "Never dreamed it so exhilarating!"

"When I get back to work Monday, I'm going to score those thirty-eight felonies on my sheet," Dan boasted. "It has to be a record."

"You can't score 'em. You're out of jurisdiction," Gary laughed.

"Well, I can take assists, can't I?"

"Okay with me, anything to mess Hess' stats up!"

"You guys have this much fun every day?" Rick asked.

"No, just on vacation," Dan answered.

"As late as it is, morning's gonna come fast," Gary warned from the bunk's edge. He flipped his shoes off, heel-to-toe. Still dressed, Gary flopped on the mattress as the second shoe hit the floor.

"I hear that," Dan said following suit.

"You guys aren't gonna undress?" Rick asked.

"Hey, it's the way stakeouts work. Down time's short. You don't waste it."

Rick pulled his shoes off and lay back on the bunk. "Boy, that was something else!"

No one answered they were already asleep.

It was a short nap, and not even Rick wanted to respond to the alarm. Nevertheless, they rousted, packed, and were on the stoop when a sheriff's car arrived.

"You guys Black, Follert, and..." the driver hesitated trying to read a paper.

"That's us," said Gary.

I'm Allen Tremont. Call me Alibi, everyone does. Short for Alibi Al. Great bust! Secret Service already showed up."

"They tell you we're buying breakfast?" Dan asked.

"Nope, my orders are to fetch you straight to the Sherriff's Office," Alibi replied.

"Deputy, are we under arrest?" Dan asked.

"Of course not! This is a courtesy."

"Then we're going to breakfast first. Like I said we're buying."

"Sorry, Sherriff Labide'll have kittens I take that long!"

"Well, we aren't going peaceful until after breakfast. You joining us?" Dan said walking away.

"Hold on! I have to bring you in. If you won't go and I can't arrest you, I have to deal. If I let you all take me to breakfast will you come in peaceable?"

"Got our word."

"Don't see I have a choice. I have to complete my mission."

"Alibi Al fits you, Com'on."

"So, where we eatin'?"

"Ginger's!" they responded in unison.

"Think she'll be there?" asked Rick.

"No doubt," said Gary.

They were barely seated, when a rough voice trumpeted from the kitchen, "Y'e ol' sea dogs! Best not b' dragg'n no more sinkin' sewage scows in t' m'y gall'y!"

They all looked, but saw no one. Alibi Al's face showed confusion. "Was that meant for us?"

Before they could answer the kitchen doors burst open propelling Flo toward them. Her hint of a limp was gone. She skipped like a flat rock across a pound. "Sees da law's ridin' y'u close. Suits me fine, it do. F'r one, I's still not ov'r the nerv'us twitches. Ye dang ne'r gots me kil'ded, ya did!"

"Flo, meet Deputy Alibi Al," Dan said.

"Y'u fits 'em, 'Ale-bi'. Watch 'em closer 'an hawk her 'yungins."

"We're kinda in a hurry," Gary said. "Thought we'd do breakfast before we take on all the reports you got us into."

"Y'us was at the helm, sailin'into dat storm. As for breakfast, ain't holdin' this pad for not."

"Sorry, we haven't checked the menu yet."

A bell sounded from the service window and Larry yelled, "Number seven!"

"Y'us jus' ain't n'er gonna learn," she said turning away to deliver the order for another table.

"Who's the character?" Alibi asked.

"Talk later. Order now," Gary said shoving a menu card at him.

"You see that 'cat got a mouse' grin?" Dan asked. "As she'd say it, 'h'r main sail's, still bittin' in t' a full wind'."

"Who is she?" Alibi asked.

They didn't answer, because Flo was back, "Y'us ready yet?"

"Coffee all around," Dan said. "We'll order when you get back."

Y'us d' ones got da scurry on," she said heading for the coffee urns. Flo picked up the coffee pot and returned without stopping. Everyone flipped their mugs over and she filled them. "Ready yet?"

"Two eggs sunny side, crispy bacon, hash browns, and toast," Dan rattled off.

Flo nodded, "Ex-press num'er three."

"Bowl of oatmeal and a grapefruit," Rick said.

"Y'u puttin' m' on, mate? And we's done rode d' riggin' together?"

"I don't like fried eggs, too runny."

"Num'er six, for da ol' salt!" she yelled back.

Rick didn't reply, but Gary did, "Right on Flo. That's what he's tryin' to say."

"And, I'll have a six also," Gary said.

Flo nodded and looked at the deputy, "Y'us eatin' or just comp'ny?"

"Give me what he got."

"Uh-uh," she grunted and left. "Two m're sixes!"

"Ocean Charlie 21," the deputy's radio broke in. "Your ETA for the Sherriff.

"Ought-O, Sherriff's tracking me," Alibi muttered before keying his mike, "Ocean Charlie 21, ran into a snag. Be thirty to forty minutes." Then turning back to the threesome commented, "I'm gonna half to dance all around this. It better be worth it."

"It will," Dan promised, "Even though I'm not sure what you ordered."

"Same as you."

"Maybe, but when you said 'what he got', you didn't specify which, 'he'."

They all laughed at the consternation of Alibi.

"Don't worry Alibi. We've never had bad food here," Gary assured.

Flo floated to the table with newfound energy and orders stacked up both arms. Rick's number six was poached eggs. The whites were solid, the yoke firm. Alibi's order was the same as Dan's.

"Flo, you're psychic, and you're kitchen's magic," Gary said.

"Take a coffee break. Pull up a chair and join us," Dan offered. "Wanna discus your adventure."

"Y'u alls got d'em bottom feedin' scallywags, didn't y'us?"

"Sure enough and we couldn't have done it without you," Dan said. "Wanted to stop in and thank you."

"Shucks," she said bowing her head, "twern't not'in' much. Then raising her chin added, "When I gonna get m' fifty back?"

"Right now," Dan said, pulling fifty dollars from his wallet. "I'll put a voucher in for it."

"Plugging the tail pipe was a smart trick. Key to the whole shootin' match," Gary said. "It stalled them long enough for the calvary to get there."

"Fixed der wag'n good, did I?"

"You're a courageous, fast thinking lady," Dan said. "We're all proud to know you." The others chimed agreement. "Tell me, how you're holdin' up, now it's over. Sometimes the aftershock's worse than the real thing?"

"I'm good, long as 'em Argonauts is chained in da hold."

"Argonauts?" Alibi asked.

"Don't ask," Rick said.

"Yeah, 'em vag'bo'nd bottom dredgers. Ought t' be drown'd in da bilges?"

"You put them out of circulation for some time, Flo," Dan encouraged.

"Good 'nough. Gots m' tables t' get backs t'. Remember, when y'u're in this port, it's Tex-Rex; d' grubs on me."

They ate quickly. Gary, Rick, and Dan each left ten bucks on the table. The Sherriff's office was nearby.

The depositions and paperwork took most of Sunday morning. The "commandeering" was forgotten at the urging of the deputies. They learned Arty submitted Flo for a Citizen's Bravery award, which was accompanied by a certificate and a hundred dollars.

Sheriff Abel Labide personally bid them farewell, "You boys put us on the biggest bust in years. Have to give credit. Well done. Sharing it with us was the smart move. Can't help feeling you'd have preferred dropping it on my doorstep all wrap up in a pretty bow. So, if you cowboys ever play rodeo in my county again I'll lock you up in a dungeon so deep the fires of Hades will warm your toes, and feed you bread and water till your beards drag the floor."

Dan chuckled as they left Labide's office.

Gary asked, "What you so happy about? Other than not getting locked up?"

"Sheriff Labide really makes you feel right at home."

Chester chauffeured them back to their fishing camp. He wasn't as talkative as Arty on the short trip back, but after they debarked he rolled the window down. "You know, me and Arty got called on the carpet by the Sheriff, but considering the results he couldn't make it stick."

"Sorry about that," Dan apologized. "The brass hats are the same everywhere."

"Wanted to tell you, we both think it was worth it. I had the best day of my career! Don't expect to ever top it."

"I appreciate you telling us, Chester," Dan replied.

"You headed back right away?"

"Soon as we can get packed," Gary replied.

"You come back any time. Look us up. We'll ride any trail you pick. And, don't worry about Labide. He doesn't have a dungeon."

The cruiser slowly pulled away, flashed its beacon lights and disappeared around the corner.

"Well," Gary said, "time to head for the peace and quiet of home."

Dan was looking forward to returning home, but chuckled at the thought of 'peace and quiet'. *There's no escaping. Crime is everywhere! Peace is just a word in the dictionary."*

Chapter Sixteen

Convictions Come Home

The trip home seemed longer than going. Dan attributed it to sleeping going and war stories returning. When the Professor pulled into Dan's driveway, Dan was slow to exit. "How much is my part of the gas, Rick?"

"We're good, forget it."

"You guys want to catch some grub before we split up?"

"Better not. Need to get caught up and ready for classes tomorrow," Rick replied.

"Well, guess that pretty much puts the lid on it," Dan said stepping out of the car and opening the tailgate. "Gary, want to help me drag this grip and cooler in?"

"Sure." He jumped out and they carried it to the garage.

"I'll drag it in later, thanks. All things considered—a great time," Dan admitted slapping Gary on the back. "Let's do it again soon."

"The fishing part, okay!"

Dan returned to the car and went to the driver's side. "Appreciate you driving. I enjoyed adventuring with you," he said pumping Rick's hand through the open window.

Dan watched the car disappear before dragging the heavy cooler into the kitchen. He crammed the fish in his freezer by removing half a quart of ice cream, several packages of freezer burned hamburgers, and microwavable pot pies past expiration. *I'm hungry. What I wouldn't give for one of Flo's fish hoagies! Oh well, I'll get a pizza, but first, better check on Trouble.*

He went to the porch and found Trouble asleep in his cage. *Great! They've worn the fur-ball out.* He clicked the television remote, and the screen brightened with an advertisement for LaRosa's. Going to the phone he decided he wasn't in the mood for pizza, and went to the kitchen.

Nothing here, and I don't feel like cooking.

A short time later, Dan parked his Harley at the Sunbright Diner. He found an open booth at the front and slid in. A plump middle-aged woman with bleached, flax-colored hair waddled over on bowed legs. A long curled lock bounced as she approached.

"Evening Anita," Dan said. She reflected his smile and offered a menu. "Don't need it. Fish hoagie with double fillets, lettuce, pickles and heavy mayo, onion rings, and a Dr. Pepper. Tell Delaney one slice of cheese."

At the service window, Anita slipped the ticket under a clip, "Danny B's got wild hair tonight," she said then returned with the drink.

As Dan sipped the cola, he noticed a well-groomed middle-aged man nearby watching. *Somebody with a grudge?* He was nondescript except for a primitive jaw, cold eyes, and weathered complexion. *Maybe I locked him up once, but can't recall.* Dan avoided eye contact to no avail. The stranger rose and approached.

Standing at the table he spoke softly, "Officer Black, you probably don't remember me."

Dan's defensive nature had brought him to his feet. "No I do not. Can I help you?"

"You already have." He reached into his back pocket, and Dan instinctively dropped his hand to his off-duty. The man withdrew a small black book from his pocket. "You gave me this in Box Town. It helped me get my life together."

Dan stared at a small New Testament. "Join me. I'm curious to hear how that got you out of Box Town."

"Thanks Officer…"

"Call me Dan, I'm off duty."

"I'm Theodore Roerink. Ted, works fine.

"So, tell me, Ted, how'd you up and leave Box Town?""

"Most of us sat around laughing about your *Handbooks.*

Some went in the fire, but three days later I was sitting on the sidewalk with my hat at my feet. I was sick of people looking at me sideways. I started reading it. Can't say why, but the words captured me and I read for days; several times through it. I got up and went back to my old firm, and asked them for a position—any position. I'm not a C.E.O. anymore, but I'm getting my life back, and reestablishing ties with my family."

"What did you read that changed your mindset?"

"It wasn't anything specific. No one thing I could put my finger on. It was the whole thing. It gave me my purpose back."

"How? Where in there does it reveal our purpose?"

"It made me see the big picture."

"The big picture? I don't understand my place here, let alone the 'big picture'. Sure would like to."

"You gave me this book, and you don't know? What do you believe?"

"I believe the world didn't just happen. Further, I believe we have a purpose."

"That's where I started."

"I don't have all the answers," Dan admitted. "Doubt I ever will, but I believe they're in that *Handbook*."

"Me either, but Dan, I found this out. Here isn't about here, it's about the hereafter."

"How can I understand that?"

"When you understand the hereafter, you'll find your answers about here," Ted said standing to leave.

"Ted, you've only given me another riddle!"

"Read the Book. It reveals what was, what is, and what will be. In that, you'll find the wisdom you seek and no man can give." The man turned and walked out of the diner. Dan rushed out behind him, but he was gone. Returning to the booth, Dan found his food on the table. He ate, left a good tip and went home.

All the way home the words echoed in his mind, *Here isn't about here, it's about the hereafter.* The garage door closed behind him and he went through the kitchen grabbing a Coke. The telephone surprised Dan. It seldom rang after supper. *Let 'em talk to the machine.*

"Dan, it's Rick. I'm missing my research papers. They're in a manila envelope. By chance find it in your gear, call me." Dan returned to the garage, checked his duffel, found the envelope, and returned the call.

"Hey Rick, I've got it. Don't know why it's in my stuff. What you want me to do with it?"

"I gave it to Gary to put in my duffle. He probably put it in yours by mistake. I need it tomorrow. Mind if I come get it?"

"No, just sitting around."

The 'lived in look' didn't embarrass Dan. His domestic service cleaned on Thursdays so there was little time to make a mess before he went fishing. When the doorbell rang, things were in order. Dan opened the door, "Come on in, and sit awhile. I can offer Coke and cookies."

"Why not? I'm curious about your ferret anyway. Can we visit with him?"

"You'll have a hard time keeping him away from your cookies."

"Just the Coke, then."

"Sure," Dan went to the kitchen, "Wanna glass?"

"Can's fine."

Dan returned and motioned to the front porch. Rick followed choosing the Adirondack chair. Dan released Trouble then took the swing. The ferret scurried off to pounce on the Wiffle Ball cradled in a pile of old towels.

Rick laughed, "Looks like a washing machine agitator escaped its housing."

"He's perpetual motion," Dan said."

"Something bothering me, Dan," Rick admitted. "I can't seem to settle my mind."

"What's on it?"

"I feel bad killing that man, even if he was a criminal."

"Oh—I see."

"I've seen people die, but never that way. It was… Well, I contributed."

"Rick, who is really responsible for the man dying?" Who initiated the event?

"I know. I didn't pull the trigger. But, I was still part of it. I participated in killing a man."

"Well, first off, we acted in self-defense. We offered surrender. He started shooting knowing the risk. What else could we do? We responded in SELF-DEFENSE."

"I know. However, I can't help feeling we backed him in a corner where the only option he saw was to shoot. What happened was to be expected. That doesn't bother you?"

"Absolutely not. He wasn't acting instinctively. HE CHOSE the crime that put him there, HE CHOSE not to surrender, and HE CHOSE to start shooting. I lose sleep over a lot of things, but not defending myself."

"I felt good, until I got home and it hit me. What right did I have to do that?"

"Let me show you something," Dan said leaving to return with a Bible. "I call this the *Handbook of Life*. He gave it to Rick, "read what I marked." Rick read it aloud:

> "Every person is to be in subjection to the governing authorities. For there is no authority except from God, and those which exist are established by God. Therefore whoever resists authority has opposed the ordinance of God; and they who have opposed will receive condemnation upon themselves. For rulers are not causes of fear for good behavior, but for evil. Do you want to have no fear of authority? Do what is good and you will have praise from the same; for it is a minister of God to you for good. But if you do what is evil, be afraid; for it does not bear the sword for nothing; for it is a minister of God, an avenger who brings wrath on the one who practices evil."[8]

---

[8] Romans 13:1-4

“Rick if you believed you evolved, then survival and self defense would be justification enough, but I know you don’t. You’re struggling with life being sacred because God created it, owns it, and He alone has the right to take it.”

“I suspect that’s so,” Rick agreed.

“In that case, this reading should settle your conscience. Governments, or police, are the agents of God acting in His behalf. The counterfeiters got their just deserve. According to the *Handbook*, God had a lot more to do with it than we did.”

“I can see why they call you ‘Preacher.’ But I still feel lousy inside—sad—keep wishing we’d stopped it without killing him.”

“We were all wishing for a peaceful surrender. It was out of our hands. Trust me, it’s normal, but you’ll get over it. Give it time”

Trouble was at Rick’s feet pulling on his shoelaces. “I think he wants my shoe.”

“Fetch will occupy him.” Dan handed Rick an old police saucer hat. Rick tossed it like a Frisbee, and the ferret scampered after it. He nosed it back to Rick’s feet. “Trouble never quits coming to you,” Rick said playing tug with the ferret to free the hat.

“Give it a toss and we’ll sneak out,” Dan said.

He accompanied Rick to the door. After Rick left, Dan fed Trouble, secured him in the cage, and retreated to the back porch to ponder Rick’s visit. As he backed into the hammock, Dan noticed yesterday’s paper lying on the floor. A woman’s picture caught his eye. “Marathon Runner.” *I know this woman.* He picked up the society page, and read:

> “Nancy Caudill completed the Chicago Marathon in 6 hours and 46 minutes. Her dedication was apparent in her willpower, adherence to strict training; and most admirably, her ability to resist happy hour. Congratulations Nancy Caudill on your achievement!”

I know you from library last Wednesday! Presumptuous! Brash! Barging into my space! Alarmingly bewitching you were. Those white shorts and teasing neckline knit top, Oh—and those green as grass eyes, auburn hair, and glowing cheeks! Indeed, how could I forget!

Dan had gone to research the structure of atoms, and chose a far table to study without interruption. Dan paid Nancy no mind until she pulled the chair out to sit. She opened her book, *Spanish Phrase by Phrase*. Dan kept glancing her way. *Odd, she doesn't look Spanish. Why study Spanish? Unless planning to travel.*

Unable to concentrate, he kept sneaking peaks, and it wasn't long before she caught him. To hide embarrassment Dan whispered, "You planning to travel?"

"No," she said retuning to the book.

"Why the Spanish if you're not going to use it?"

"Oh, I expect to use it. In ten years it'll be America's second language." She answered in a low voice and continued reading."

"America's second language! Why would the great 'melting pot' need another language?"

"Since you ask…" Nancy replied, her voice irritated.

You're annoyed? You *butted into MY table!*

"…I'm from Arizona. And as for why, I'll give you three reasons. First, eighty percent of America's immigrants speak Spanish. Second, their size encourages entrepreneurs to court their purchasing power. And third, the unlawful nature of migration, will force government agencies to deal with them."

"Interesting; people entering our country illegally and your solution; learn their language!"

"Shhh," the librarian interrupted. "The library is for reading. There are discussion rooms over there," she said pointing.

"Certainly," Dan apologized. Then turning to his debater asked, "Shall we?"

She picked up her books.

Dan followed her to the reading room. The *flopity-kaalumph'* of her sandals across the hardwood floor would have annoyed Dan, but he never heard it. *Double barreled trouble: Voice of Dietrich—body of Monroe! Why must beautiful women be offish?*

The small room contained a table with four chairs. They sat across from one another.

"By the way, I'm Nancy, and I'm working on a degree in holistic medicine."

"I'm Dan, and I'm pleased to meet you. I work for the city. Nothing so dignified; I take large pieces of garbage off the streets."

Nancy leaned forward extended her hand and remarked, "Someone's got to do it. Never forget, all work is honorable, even a tail-gunner on a garbage truck."

Cute! And with a sense of humor. Dan gave her hand a gentle squeeze, noticing a strawberry clean scent. "I'll try, but it's difficult at times. Now, where were we? Oh yes, patronizing criminals by learning their language instead of dealing with crime."

"Don't assume a woman can't think logically!" Her light freckled checks blushed as she replied. "I've earned a Bachelor's in Health Sciences and…"

"Whoa there! Formal credentials aren't important. Your awareness of the topic intrigues me. I'm interested in what you think and why."

"Thank you," she smiled. "I don't condone their actions, but I'm realistic. Government reacts to crime. It cannot stop it, particularly this one. I accept this fact, and prepare to deal with it."

She's so full of herself! But blast it, she's right! Maybe I should learn Spanish. "Why do you assume so many immigrants will be involved in crime?"

"You're kidding, right? We are talking ILLEGAL immigrants?" she said. "Their goals differ from ours and they don't accept our laws. Crime, as you call it, is not the problem. It is only a symptom of the problem."

"So, you don't believe there's a solution to crime? In

fact, you are alleging it isn't controllable." *Careful girl, you're intruding in my field.*

"Not as long as we deny the human bent toward evil. People are survival driven not humanity oriented. 2000 years of history records us trying and failing to build a moral society."

"So, if we can't eliminate crime, I must accept its reality, prepare for it, and deal with it? Unacceptable! Too much compromise for me! If we discover the cause, we can eliminate crime."

"Aren't you the optimist? We've discovered cigarettes cause lung cancer and death. Can we cure it? No. Why not? Because—people will not stop smoking!"

Just that simple, is it? "If smokers know the risk and smoke anyway, why do we care? It's not a crime. I enjoy my pipe. Smoke it in private. Why should I give it up?"

"Because, it isn't healthy! But you miss my point. You KNOW it isn't healthy. It's not a matter of 'belief.' You believe the risk and do it anyway. Why?"

"OH, I see, Crime can't be solved because it's an addiction? Sorry Nancy, I don't buy it."

"Crime's not an addicting, it is a human condition; our response to our inborn self-centeredness. A baby wants to be satisfied. 'I'm wet, change me. I'm hungry, feed me.' From birth we have an 'everything centers on me' focus. Learning to regard others is about controlling ourselves. The baby naturally cries, the child cheats, and the adult commits crimes. It's in our DNA. People break laws for many reasons. All of them selfish. Crime can be restrained somewhat, but never eliminated."

"It is the nature of criminal violence to escalate," Dan pointed out. "When it reaches the point, police officers cannot protect themselves, how then will they protect society? If there is a cause there is a cure. If crime can be restrained, it can be reduced. If it can be reduced, why not eliminated?"

"Society has the power, but not the will."

"And why not?"

"Basically, because we're self-centered greedy people. Some more than others, but we all go after what we want."

"You miss my point. People accept societal restraints for their own good. So, why do we violate what is in our best interest? Are we without reason?"

Nancy stared blankly at Dan, "I don't know. Do you?"

"I believe it's our world views on origin."

"What do you mean, 'world views'?"

"Where did I come from? What is my purpose? Where am I going?"

Nancy peered past Dan in contemplation, "This is most interesting. What did you say you did for a living?"

"I didn't. You offered, 'tail gunner on a garbage truck.' It's accurate enough."

"So, how's a tail gunner answer those questions?"

"I believe I was created by God. The purpose is disclosed in a manual of instructions for fulfilling it, which is my eternal destiny."

"I see," she said with a kittenish smile. "There's an opposing view called evolution, and the scientific community has very convincing arguments,"

"Indeed, yet neither theory is provable. The reason they are 'views'." For my money, life demonstrates Creation more plausible. More important to our discussion are the consequences of denying our true origin. Where I came from determines my purpose, where I'm going and how I get there. Thus, view dictates behavior to achieve the goal."

"I can see they're linked, but, cause of crime? Seems a stretch, Don."

"It's Dan," *Purposely annoying, but intriguing.* "Okay, say you deny a Creator. Then, to find purpose, you dull your consciences with a promise of a utopian society. But, in a short time see it unobtainable. What do you do then? Pursue your own goals, your own way? That's consistent with crime and escalating violence."

Nancy raised her knees against the table pushing her chair back on two legs. "I can see how denial of hope would cause serious stress." She paused for a moment, her chair rocking.

Miss 'confidence' is going to dump herself on the floor.

Nancy brought the chair forward and continued, "Actually, I can see myself rebelling."

I like her honesty.

A glimmer of respect passed across Nancy's face. "Crime and violence are conceivable by-products of a hopeless view."

More open minded than I expected!

"Well, THANK YOU," Dan acknowledged. "With evolution, there is no solution for crime because its life purpose is hopeless! This is why you sense society has the power to eliminate crime, but not the will. Do not athletes contend within the rules for the hope of the trophy? And, who, but a fool, goes to war for a known worthless cause?"

"I think you may have something. I will think on it," she said.

"Does that mean I have gained an ally?"

"No," she said with a flip of her head. "You're not all bad, though—for a tail gunner."

"Any chance I could get your phone number? In case I get a sudden urge to debate."

"I don't think so."

"Two rides on the tailgate."

"You don't work in waste collection. Your hands are to clean. And, I don't know enough about you."

"You never will, unless you meet me at Scarborough's for dinner next Friday—say seven?"

"Say, not. You're too secretive."

"It's public. It's a free meal. And, what better way to learn my secrets?"

Nancy did not respond. She stood to leave.

"Seven o'clock, Friday the tenth?"

"Over a week away. You need that much time to get your story together?" she smirked turning away.

"Nope, prior commitment."

"Another lady?" She said looking back her long hair whipping.

"Yep, named the *Sandpiper*, I'm goin' fishing."

Nancy paused at the door and Dan noticed her sleek athletic legs. She swiveled around and said, "Don't bring your pipe and don't be late." Her full lips smiled.

Dan watched her turn with the grace of a ballerina and walk away. *You're perkier than Trouble.*

An annoying bitter dryness in Dan's mouth nudged him back to reality. *Interesting woman!* Staring at the picture he said, "So, crime is the result of our inborn self-centeredness!"

Nancy, you may be a scarce commodity; good-looking woman with brains. I anticipate Friday. The unanswered question is can you be tamed?

Dan went to the kitchen, poured a glass of milk and grabbed two cookies from the Donald Duck Jar. He washed down a bite of cookie.

Nancy stumbled on the cause of crime, and what the 'Handbook' calls 'sin.' She is aware nothing can be done about it as long as we rebel against the dictates of the Creator.

The assumed absence of sin provides denial of accountability. How often have I heard it, "Not my fault!' However, there's the rub! To deny sin we must deny God. Crime then is our free will 'kicking against the goads' of God's restraints!

Unsettled by the thought, Dan went back to the porch, picked up the *Handbook of Life*, and retired to the bedroom. He lay on his side flipping through the pages. *I know it's here. Somewhere it says there is hope!*

"Yes here it is," he brayed as if expecting the walls to cheer. "... *(should)My people who are called by My name humble themselves and pray and seek My face and turn from their wicked ways, then I will hear from heaven, will forgive their sin and will heal their land."*[9] He closed the Bible stood and shouted, "We do have a choice!"

---

[9] 2 Chronicles 7:14

We do not comprehend our purpose! We aren't sufficiently connected to understand it. Is it any wonder we are blind to the consequences of our ignorance? Intoxicated by self-indulgence, we violate our Creator's laws. Then faced with the consequences, we curse the jailor in anger and beat our heads against the bars.

Dan left an itch behind, but brought more than fish home. Aware mankind is a created thing which has neglected its purpose and forfeited its destiny, he had a new itch; Has God turned His back on us, as we have ours on Him?

Nancy, I'll deal with it, and the struggles within the cement jungle, in all the tomorrows. Things are not as destitute as I once believed. Dan went to his desk; there he opened his new friend, the *Handbook of Life,* and read:

> In the beginning was the Word, and the Word was with God, and the Word was God. He was in the beginning with God. All things came into being through Him, and apart from Him nothing came into being that has come into being. In Him was life, and the life was the Light of men. The Light shines in the darkness, and the darkness did not comprehend it.[10]

Dan remembered a similar passage from when he began to investigate this book anew. He turned back to the first page:

> In the beginning God created the heavens and the earth. The earth was formless and void, and darkness was over the surface of the deep, and the Spirit of God was moving over the surface of the waters.[11]

---

[10] John 1:1-5

[11] Genesis 1:1

Such an interesting statement, 'In the beginning God...' There is no dissertation of doubt. No need to debate. The scribe assumes it fact. It seems to be, we contemporaries have grown arrogant to think we possess greater abilities to know and verify the existence of God! When has man, how has man, climbed into the abode of God to question Him and prove He is or is not? I am now convinced God created this world. I am His wondrous handiwork.

Dan's heart was doubly encouraged; God's 'Handbook' would reveal purpose, and he would see Nancy soon. Yes, Dan would be back to the grind, but it'd be Day Run. He'd continue his vigilance, because depravity would continue its assault. Dan would find time to laugh at every opportunity when the crying ended.

Dan reclined in the hammock a smile on his face. *Crime is not my fault. Its cure is far beyond me. We had the answer two thousand years ago and blew it. I'll find my true purpose and chase it as sure as Trouble does a Frisbee. As for that ridiculously winsome woman, we have a date.*

The exploits of Dan's pursuit continue in
The Darkness in Daylight, Day Run.
Volume Two of the *In A Pig's Eye* Trilogy

APPENDIX of TRIBUTE

Ultimate tribute is given to the brave men of the shield of justice slain in the days of my watch. ***Greater love hath no man than this; he lay down his life for another***. [John 15:13 - paraphrased]

1972 -Detective Howard F Smith
Killed by a shotgun in a bank robbery.

1974 - Officer David L Cole
Shot by two robbery suspects at a street stop.

1974 Sergeant Charles F. Handorf
Shot and killed while negotiating with a barricaded man.

1975 Officer William J. Loftin
Shot and killed by a drunk disorderly person in a public street

1975 Sergeant Robert A. Lally
Shot while conducting burglary prevention door checks.

1978 Officer Charles Burdsall
Killed by gunfire after stopping a suspect robbery vehicle.
Working exchange day so another officer could be off with family

1979 Officer Robert Seiffert & Officer Dennis Bennington
Killed by gunfire while attempting to arrest a robbery suspect.

1979 Officer Melvin Henze
Shot and killed by a suspect of felonious assault.

1982 Officer J. Gary Weber
Struck by a vehicle driven by an intoxicated driver
Charles Klug also run down retired with serious disability

1987 Officer Clifford George
Shot trying to defuse a domestic dispute by a man with mental illness.
Officer Norton, also wounded and police canine, Bandit, .killed.

---------------------------- // ----------------------------

Unless the LORD guards the city,
The watchman keeps awake in vain - Psalms 127:1

How Quick We Forget

Police officers are real people, with real emotions, hopes, and aspirations. Their vision is entwined with a quest to improve the life of all. A commitment to a humanly impossible calling: a bankrupt oath.

Our present society defaults to complacency and self-indulgence, while harboring a demand of perfection from its civil servants. Unyielding to any hint of weakness in the humanity of a police officer, it demands a cogent compliance to unrealistic expectations. Better to be a bond slave in Rome.

This trilogy calls common people to consider the officer's full commitment: not perfect, yet pledged to our well being; not a "super hero", how be it preferred, but a human hero; and yet still in the making. Would giving benefit of doubt be too high a price for the peace of mind this fragile, but still holding "Blue Line" gives our heads upon the pillow?

While society lives among many shades of gray, its expectations are black and white. Therein conflict inadvertently lies. Nonetheless, it need not lessen our security, peace, or well being. Although the threat is real, the target is sure, the aim precise; and evil and injustice should not prevail. The system has its weaknesses and its victories. It can be no other way. The masses cry, "If, I wore the badge, justice would prevail!" Pin it on–if you dare. In a crumbling society you too shall fail. Perfection upon this earth comes not on the shoulders of the police, but on the wings of the Messiah.

It is inherent upon the understanding heart to express thankfulness for its blessings. Portrayed in these pages are the mundane, routine, and deadliness of police work. Not pausing to count cost, police officers rush into the unknown in our behalf, per chance to aid, to buffer tragedy, to save a life--to oft to die.

How small the single rose seems, first laid upon a coffin. How grand it becomes. Count your blessing this night before a loving Holy God. Join others in prayerful appreciation for the officers' safety on the streets of your city. In the briskness of the day, boldly take an officer a yellow rose and a smile, "Thank you for being someone I can call upon." The efficacy of a lifted spirit cannot be measured.

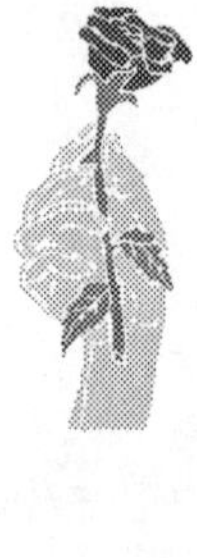

GLOSSARY OF TERMS
and
Professional Acronyms

----- / -----

A.K.A - Also Known As

A.O. - Arresting Officer, usually gets credit for the "collar"

ASAP - Alcohol Safety Analysis Program

Atta-Boy - A slang term for a commendation

B&E[B and Es] - Breaking and Entering: The unlawful entry or trespass into a structure of another with the intent of committing a crime; such as theft.

Capias - A bench warrant for arrest issued

Clocked - Pacing a car at the same rate, then locking in a calibrated speedometer at the speed.

Closures - A formal disposition of an offense; **closed inactive** meant no leads were available and in thirty days it would be filed; **closed unable** meant the probable suspect was known but lacking evidence or for other reason no prosecution or arrest could be affected; **closed arrest** indicated the case was solved by an arrest.

Collar - Credit for the arrest; usually the most instrumental in effecting the arrest; or the beat officer.

Colerain Hilton - city workhouse and jail

Dangling noose - a clip tie worn with the collar open and clipped through the button hole

Dicks - Detectives; stems from Dick Tracy

D.U.I.	- Driving Under the Influence of alcohol or drugs
Drop the hammer	- to shoot at someone
ETA	- Estimated Time of Arrival
Fender Benders	- Minor traffic accidents.
FIR	- Field Interrogation Report; a 3x5 card filled out on who, where, when, what and why a suspicious person was stopped and questioned on the street.
FIRed/FIRing	- To execute a FIR [Field Interrogation Report]on a subject
four to six/4 to 6	- parking violation; areas where parking is prohibited from 4pm to 6 pm.
HK	- "Who cares" phrase of unknown origin
HMVs	- Hazardous Moving Violations
Hot-List	- List of stolen or wanted vehicles
Hummer	- A citation written in a questionable circumstance related to accuracy
I.A.	- Internal Affairs; a team of officers who investigates improprieties, and crimes of other officers
LKA	- Last Known Address
I.O.D.	- Injured On Duty pay status
Mover	- A moving violation
OIC	- Officer In Charge
OTP	- Over Time Parking (violations or complaints)
O.R.	- Court released without bond, on "Own Recognizance"
Parkers	- Citations for parking violations

Pop a cap - to shoot a bullet

Porter stick - larger than issued night stick rumored to have been made by a man named Porter. Popular for their resistance to breaking.

Rap Sheet - Arrest record

Roll Call - an informal time of briefing and beat information exchange before officers respond to patrol the streets.

Scrambled eggs - gold squiggle braiding on the visor cap of command officers.

Skipper - Officer who skipped from one beat to another when assigned man was off.

Spares - a reference to police cars used as loaner while the regular equipment is in repair.

Signals
- **1**- Call your station
- **2**- Go to your station
- **3**- auto accident
- **26**- Signal announcing the availability of a unit for service
- **27**- Signal announcing the unavailability of a unit for radio service
- **30F**- Felony Wants Indicated
- **30M**- Misdemeanor Wants Indicated
- **35**- Arrived at scene
- **44**- Answer radio with location

"Siding" a partner - reference to covering him, standing by him, being on his side.

Thin Blue Line - a reference to a police squad or department. Such as; "Crime would be rampant if it were not for the Thin Blue Line."

UTL - Unable To Locate

Walk-away - Someone under an institution's care, not arrested, but usually restricted because of their inability to care for themselves, and their safety, who manages to leave the grounds unaccompanied.